The Seer's Sacrifice

LEGACY OF THE TIME STONES TRILOGY
BOOK THREE

BRITTANY FICHTER

Want more from your stories?

Sign up for free short stories, sneak peeks at books before they're published, and exclusive secret chapters as they're released in my no-spam newsletter.

Details at the end of this book.

Iilaedin
The Northern Mountains
Blood Fire Fjord
Mhira
Spear Garoth
Lady Seren's Fortress
Solva Breghda
The Sphinx Fields
Port Nehmanid
Richlien Mountains
The Walled City
Korach
The Garden
Mhaedin
Rangvald's Fortress

Chapter One

Drystan's feet hurt as he ran. But then again, everyone else's feet must hurt as well. They'd been running for two weeks, stopping only to eat and hunt when they could and for the barest stints of sleep. Drystan's wings ached to take to the skies, and he wondered if he'd have to relearn some of his flying techniques after this endless stretch of running.

Even if he'd wanted to ask Callispa to help him practice, however, he could not, nor could she answer him. They had all been silent for two weeks now, and there was no end in sight.

The only person who spoke at all these days was the Wizard, who whispered incantations over Eirin and then their camp every morning before she slept. It was dangerous, yes, but Eirin wouldn't survive this deep into Solevar without it.

Thane, who was leading the group through the dense forest, put an arm up, and everyone came to a halt. He looked up into the sky through the towering trees above them. Drystan made a slight jerking motion when he stopped. Hopefully, Eirin was awake and didn't fall off. She was sleeping more and more often these days, even as he ran.

An answering pat made him give a slight sigh of relief. If he needed to take off into the sky, he needed her to be ready.

Fortunately, or unfortunately, depending on how one looked at it, the night was clear, and the moon and stars made the world nearly as visible as day. Callispa, who stayed on Drystan's left side, had an arrow nocked, and Isayas, who stayed on Drystan's right, held his staff several inches off the ground. Qeb, who brought up the rear, searched the sky with glowing eyes, his war hammer and axe clenched tightly in his large hands and his Griffin wings outstretched.

A moment later, they all felt what Thane had first sensed. A winged figure shot out of the sky and landed in front of them. Drystan's muscles uncoiled as the Sphinx straightened and stretched her shoulders and wings.

Thane threw up his arms in annoyance. When they'd realized the Goblins were following them, the night they'd decided to move as silently as possible, they'd all agreed to make certain signs and signals to ensure that none of their party accidentally attacked one another. Nuru had not bothered with the signs or the signals.

"Don't get your trousers in a knot," Nuru said, her voice sounding like a roar after the nearly overwhelming silence of the last two weeks. "The Goblins are gone."

"How do you know?" Callispa whispered. She glanced around with large eyes as she did.

Nuru rolled her eyes and held up a paw on which every claw was extended. Even from where he stood, Drystan could smell blood. The Dragon within him writhed with pleasure.

"Because I killed the last one," Nuru purred.

"Not to echo Callispa," Qeb said softly, "but how do you know?"

"Smell," came a weak voice. Drystan's relief immediately turned to worry. In the two weeks since he'd heard it last, when they'd realized the Goblins were tracking them, Eirin's voice had grown significantly weaker.

"What?" Thane asked.

"Sphinxes have an excellent sense of smell." Eirin yawned. "And Goblins have an exceptional scent."

"More like an exceptional stench," Nuru scoffed. "I could smell the last one a mile away."

"Were you able to tell if they were from Rangvald?" Isayas asked.

Nuru tossed down several severed ribbons of purple. Rangvald's color. "I'd say they were."

"Drystan," Eirin said, her voice strained. "I need to get down."

Drystan immediately knelt so she could climb off, but she must have struggled because Nuru flew up to her and gently carried her down. As soon as her feet hit the ground, Eirin turned and began to retch into a bush. Drystan shared a long look with Isayas.

"Let's make camp here," Callispa said. "The sun will be rising soon. And with the Goblins gone, it's a good time to catch up on some rest."

Everyone agreed and set about making camp. No one said it, of course, but they knew Callispa's words were for Eirin. Each night of travel seemed to get shorter as Eirin grew weaker.

Their journey had barely begun, but at this rate, they would never make it to Iilaedin.

After escaping from Rangvald, Drystan's desperate uncle, their party had been traveling only three days when they realized Rangvald had sent Goblins to track them. There had been so many. Each night as they traveled, nearly every member of the party had taken turns, all but Drystan and the Wizard, trying to pick off the Goblins, one-by-one, and staying silent to make it more difficult for the Goblins, who had keen hearing, to find them.

And now the Goblins were gone. But Drystan was sure it was only a matter of time before his uncle sent yet another batch of undesirables to track them down. This wasn't the first time Rangvald had sent deadly trackers after them in an attempt to bring them to him. Back when they'd still lived in the underground city of Torbaine–as city within the mountain–he'd sent an army of mixed races, and when that failed, Griffins. Who knew what kind of seeker he might come up with next?

Soon their two tents were unpacked, and a small fire was lit, just long enough for the Wizard to prepare his materials to speak his usual incantations of protection over Eirin. As soon as the first tent was erected, Nuru helped Eirin inside. Drystan shifted back into his Human form and waited for Nuru to emerge.

At the end of every night, water had to be found and then purged of its toxins by Isayas. Then Eirin had to be bathed from head to foot to try to rid her of the poison of the curse that floated through the air and stuck to the trees and flora and fauna. Nuru usually helped with that, though Callispa had aided from time to time as well. In the meantime, Isayas would take Eirin's clothing and do his best to remove the poison from the fabric. Once she was clean and dressed again, the Wizard would join Nuru in the tent, lay out his powders, rocks, and other tools, then he would begin to recite the incantations of protection against the curse.

And at first, it had seemed to work. Eirin had stayed strong and healthy during their first week. But after that, she had begun to collapse. She struggled to keep her food down after eating, and for the last three days, she was always tired.

To say Drystan was worried was an understatement. And it didn't help that the Wizard showed signs of unease on his ancient face whenever he left the tent.

The others ate and chatted with great animation, eager to

converse again, as the Wizard and Nuru tended to Eirin, but Drystan's plate went untouched until Nuru and the Wizard emerged from Eirin's tent. Well, really, it was the girls' tent. But only Eirin and Nuru slept in there. Callispa slept outside by the fire, where she said she felt safest. Drystan would have thought this simply an excuse, given her history with Eirin. But he reminded himself that she was, however, a Phoenix after all.

Drystan exchanged a concerned glance with the Wizard as Isayas went to sit by the fire, but they said nothing as they passed. Instead, Drystan turned his attention to Eirin as he knelt to enter the small tent.

"How are you feeling?" he asked, sitting beside the pallet on which she lay.

Eirin gave him a poor attempt at a smile. "Well enough." Then she immediately closed her eyes.

She wasn't getting off that easily.

"I can tell you have a headache," he said with a wry smile. "And you barely ate anything when we broke fast."

She shrugged and rolled over to face the tent wall. "We knew what we were facing," she said quietly. "There's no reason to be surprised." Then she closed her eyes.

Drystan wanted to press further. He'd known she would decline once they made their way into the valley forests, but with the Wizard's help, he'd hoped her fall from health wouldn't be so fast.

He also knew why she was being so distant with him. But that lay solely at his feet. He had hurt her. Granted, it had been with all the best intentions. But he had pushed her away, and even though she knew why, he knew it would take time for her to heal. That was the least of his worries now, though. If they couldn't get Eirin in better health, none of their lesser worries would matter by the end of the year.

Because no one would be alive for much longer if their mission failed.

He sighed as he stepped out of the tent. Everyone but Qeb, who was on watch, was gathered around the small fire the Wizard had built. Supposedly, according to Isayas, it couldn't be seen from above by any except those who were included in the spell. Drystan could only suppose that it worked because no one had succeeded in sneaking up on them thus far. Thane held out a stick with a small animal speared on the end, and Drystan took it. The Dragon inside wanted him to eat the thing whole, but for the sake of his friends, he contented himself with eating in a...more Human style.

"So now that we can talk," Thane said, "is Eirin..." His eyes were void of their usual humorous gleam as he glanced back at the tent. The group was quiet for a moment as Drystan tried to find the right words. No, Eirin wasn't well. Far from it. But if he spoke it aloud, it would seem far too real.

"I'll say it if no one else will," Nuru said, putting her stick down. "Eirin's dying."

Drystan's blood ran cold as he and everyone else looked at Nuru, who was glowering at the fire.

"We don't know that–" Callispa began, but Nuru scoffed.

"All you have to do is spend five minutes with her to know that." Nuru looked at the Wizard, challenge glinting in her eyes. "Am I wrong?"

Isayas met Drystan's gaze and held it for a long moment. Drystan silently pleaded with him to say it was otherwise. It had to be otherwise. They couldn't have come all this way...from Torbaine, through the mountain and back, to Mhaedin, and now down into the valley for Eirin to...

Isayas looked down at the ground, and Drystan swallowed hard, trying to force what little he'd eaten back down.

Isayas let out a long, gusty sigh. That sigh was like the echo of a nail in a coffin. "I'm afraid Nuru's right," he said in a tired voice. "I'm doing what I can." He looked up at the trees surrounding them. "But this is a far more difficult path than I've ever tried to escort a Human through. That she's made it this far is a testament to her tenacity, but..." He stood suddenly and grabbed his staff before stomping off into the woods.

Drystan felt his friends' eyes on him, but he didn't look up. He knew why Isayas was so upset. The Wizard had watched his own wife–his beloved Human–fade away after the curse fell. And to watch Eirin was like seeing it happen all over again. An old wound, open and festering. It was exactly what he'd feared when agreeing to take one last Human to Iilaedin.

But it wasn't an old wound for Drystan. More like the knife was still inside him, cutting slowly each time he looked at her and saw her fade a little more.

The sound of wings broke the silence, and everyone looked up to see Qeb, his massive wings lowering him into the center of their circle.

"Is everything all right?" Drystan asked, jumping to his feet. Qeb never returned early.

"There's nothing amiss, exactly," Qeb said, shifting back into his Human form. "But Eirin was right."

"About what?" Thane asked.

"Rangvald is trying to push his way through the forest by clearing a road and building a tunnel over it."

"Which means," Nuru said grimly, "that he either has Mannish, or–"

"Or he's planning on using Eirin as soon as he finds her," Drystan finished for her.

"That's quite bold, don't you think?" Thane snorted.

"Unfortunately," Callispa said, "he can probably afford to be as bold as he wants."

"What do you mean?" Qeb asked.

"Mhaedin fought to free Eirin," Callispa said, her fair cheeks looking paler than usual in the moonlight. "Which means that if Rangvald's forces are already this deep into the forest, Mhaedin's forces most likely damaged themselves too much to keep him in check. And he's free to do as he wishes." She looked at Drystan, her green eyes wide. "So now, it's a race."

"A race we've barely started," Thane said softly, looking back at Eirin's tent once again.

To everyone's surprise, the tent flap opened, and Eirin stepped out. Drystan hurried to her side to support her, but she waved him off and made her way over to one of the empty boulders someone had dragged into the circle. Her legs shook, but Drystan knew better than to try to tell her that. She'd made it very clear over the last few weeks that she wanted as little help as possible. Especially from him.

"Stop looking at me like I'm half-buried already," she said, taking one of the small rodents Thane had skewered and cooked. "We're going to get to Iilaedin. I'll be fine."

Everyone sat down again and began to speak quietly amongst themselves, and Qeb took off once more into the night. But Drystan just watched Eirin.

She said she was fine.

Drystan, however, knew she was not.

Chapter Two

Eirin stretched her arms and tried to shake out her legs to stay awake. Being lulled to sleep while on Drystan's back was surprisingly easy when he was in his Dragon form. His scales were warm and smooth, and his back was broad enough that she could hook one arm around one of his thick spines and hold herself in place comfortably as he plodded through the forest. The way he walked made a rocking motion that was far too easy to give in to.

When shaking her arms and legs didn't work, she shook her head, but it had little effect.

The temptation to wish for her mother's arms wheedled its way into her mind.

No. Eirin's shook her head to rid it of the thoughts. She wasn't going to think of her family. She couldn't. Because then she might begin to weep.

She was a mess.

She pulled the stone out from beneath her shirt, where it hung hidden, and pressed her fingers against it. Warmth preceded the vision of the Time Stones Room, where the remaining chunk of stone lay in the circle.

"You know you can nap," Nuru said in an unimpressed voice from below. Her question jolted Eirin out of the vision.

Nuru had spent the morning in her Sphinx form, flitting back and forth from the front to the back to the side of their traveling company. But now she was on Drystan's left side, looking up at Eirin as they walked, wings tucked neatly against her smooth furry back. "No need to be a martyr."

"I'm not trying to be a martyr," Eirin said, trying unsuccessfully to stifle a yawn.

And it was true. She wasn't. While it did seem unfair that all of her friends had to walk or fly, depending on the time of night they traveled, and that she got to ride, that wasn't the reason she was trying to stay awake.

"You can sleep," said a deeper, softer voice from below.

Eirin turned to look at Isayas, who gave her a sweet, sad smile from where he walked on Drystan's other side. "You'll wake up," he said softly. "I promise."

"That's the problem," she replied in a low voice. "I'm afraid you won't be able to promise that much longer."

She had meant it for the Wizard's ears only, but when Drystan stiffened beneath her, Eirin silently cursed his incredible hearing. She hadn't meant to share just how desperate her situation was becoming.

Of course, there were many things she meant or didn't mean that turned out the opposite of how she'd planned. For one, the feelings she was constantly battling about the Dragon she was riding now.

For more than two weeks, ever since their escape from Rangvald's fortress, she'd been forced not only to interact with him every day, but to accept his help and protection. Every night she had to stay in physical contact with him, and even when she wasn't right beside him, he was always near. And the conflict that raged inside her burgeoned by the day.

At the outset of their journey, Eirin had been sure she would be able to put off the feelings of frustration, pain, and longing she had for him. She'd accepted his admission that he had only pretended to be in love with Callispa with the sole purpose of protecting Eirin from the dangers of his own fire, as he had still been inexperienced in controlling it. Rangvald, Drystan's uncle, had somewhat confirmed the sincerity of that motivation when he revealed that Drystan was putting himself through physical pain to separate himself from her. And that pain was something Eirin had no desire to exacerbate.

And yet...

She glanced down at the beautiful Phoenix who walked just ahead of Drystan, talking to him in hushed tones.

It wasn't a secret that Callispa harbored feelings for Drystan. They'd spent so many hours together, training and attending Mhaedin's meetings. And Eirin didn't miss the way Callispa looked at him still when she thought no one else was watching.

Maybe Drystan *was* attached to Eirin for life as Rangvald had said. Supposedly, Dragons loved for life and didn't move on after their mate died. Many of them died from a broken heart. Even if that were true...was she what he really wanted? Did Drystan secretly wish he could return Callispa's affection? Rangvald had explained to her that once a Dragon chose a mate, he could never love again. And yet, there were so many moments when Drystan didn't seem like a Dragon, and seemed very much like the lonely man Eirin had refused so she could focus on the task at hand.

If only Eirin could ask her parents what to do.

But, no. This was exactly why Eirin had told Drystan they needed to wait. Eirin's distraction would help no one. All of Solevar and its inhabitants would die if she didn't fix the Time Stones soon. The curse was in its final days. She could feel it with every bone in her body, the imminent destruction of the entire world. She needed her head clear of worry about Drystan and

Callispa so she could focus on their mission. Everything else—heartbreak included—could wait.

They made good time that night, and the group was in good spirits by the time they made camp an hour before dawn. As usual, Isayas went about lighting his magical flames and uttering several incantations before taking off into the woods. What he did there, Eirin had no idea. But he would be back soon to speak his incantations over her and around her tent as she drifted off to sleep, just as he did every day before dawn.

"I have a question," Thane said as they set to erecting the tents. "Say we get to Iilaedin around the same time as Rangvald. What then?"

No one answered at first. Eirin could feel their eyes on her, but Drystan spoke before she did.

"I suppose we would both send our Seers—if he actually has Mannish—to the tower to see if they can fix the Time Stones."

"No."

Everyone looked over at Eirin.

"No?" Nuru asked.

Eirin shrugged. "No, it won't be that simple."

"How do you know?" Qeb asked in his deep voice.

Eirin fixed Drystan with a look. "The Time Stones weren't the only things that were misused when the curse fell."

Drystan's brow creased, but he held her gaze.

"I don't remember you mentioning anything else being broken when we were back in Mhaedin," Thane said. "What changed?"

Eirin sighed and touched the place where a headache was beginning to bloom. Both Drystan and Nuru handed her their waterskins. Unfortunately, they had run out of fresh, clean water from the mountain about a week ago, and Eirin was sure the groundwater she was now sharing with the others was a large part of why she was feeling so poorly. But going without water wasn't really an option either. So she accepted Nuru's outstretched waterskin and gave Drystan a weak smile before continuing.

"I've suspected it for a while, but the more I consider it, the more I'm sure I'm right," she said. "The Time Stones were how the curse began, yes. But there were other things that went wrong as well. Particularly with the Dragon princes." She frowned into their small fire. "I just wish we knew what happened that caused the rift between them. I feel like it would give us answers."

"But that doesn't tell us what else we'll need to do to break the curse," Nuru said. "If you haven't noticed, we're not excelling at this particular mission as it is."

"More like limping along," Thane chuckled.

Nuru rolled her eyes.

"I can't be sure yet," Eirin said slowly, "but I get the feeling that it has something to do with the Blood Fire Throne. And, unfortunately, I believe it will require Rangvald's participation."

Callispa gaped at her. "You mean you think we won't be able to break this unless we get Rangvald's cooperation? But why his?"

"Because he's one of the remaining princes," Eirin said, evenly meeting Callispa's gaze. "I believe Karolus would have been required to participate as well...had he survived." She turned to Drystan, but he was glowering into the forest. Not that she'd expected anything else.

Drystan had never been keen on being called a son of Oreck. Being part of the royal Dragon bloodline that had held the Blood Fire Throne conjured up enough conjecture at first glance. He was even less fond of identifying his lineage more specifically as a son of Kamon, the youngest Dragon prince who had unleashed the curse upon the world. The cruelty of the other Atharrachs at Mhaedin had taken its toll. And though Drystan had eventually won their favor, Eirin was only too aware of the doubt he secretly harbored about himself and his kin. Being a descendant of the prince who had brought the curse down upon Solevar haunted him. Getting him to act in the place of his ancestor was going to take a miracle.

"But," Eirin said, snapping herself from her reverie as she realized that the others were still staring at her, "that's trouble for another day. For now, we need to make our way to Iilaedin. Nothing can be fixed until we get there." She stood. "I'm going to sleep. Thank you for supper, Callispa." Then she headed to the tent that had been erected for the girls. Nuru followed her.

"You're not telling us everything, are you?" Nuru folded her arms after securing the flap behind her.

Eirin sighed as she climbed into her bed. "I have theories, Nuru. That's all they are."

Nuru frowned down at her. It was getting easier to see her expressions as dawn neared. "This isn't like you. Holding your thoughts back. Back in Mhaedin, we couldn't get you to shut up about what you'd learned. And you were an excessive showoff in Torbaine as well."

Eirin sat up. "Well, we're not in Mhaedin now, are we?" she snapped. "And if you had bothered to spare me a second glance at the Citadel, you would have known that I excelled at our studies because it was the one place where I could prove myself without someone making me bleed!" She threw herself back down and rolled over.

A long silence stretched out between them, long enough that guilt began to gnaw at Eirin's conscience.

"I may not have known you well in the Citadel," Nuru finally said in a low voice. "But I was aware." She gave a humorless chuckle. "After all, you were the enemy. And as you always placed ahead of me in our studies, my mother used your success to torture me into promising I would do better." Then she sighed. "I *also* know you used to confide in Alys. And...now I can't help but wonder." She paused. "I'm not Alys. But have I proven myself any less trustworthy?"

Eirin rolled over. "I'm sorry." She sat up and rubbed her eyes. "That was unkind of me."

Nuru came and sat at the foot of Eirin's pallet. "I want to help you. It's why I'm here. It's why we're all here. So if there's a way for us to fix this, you have to *tell* us."

Eirin nodded, the headache blossoming into full strength. She pressed her hands against her temples and spoke without opening her eyes. "I really am sorry. But this pain is just..." She shook her head, keeping her eyes closed as she spoke in a lower voice. "I didn't go into full details tonight because I know how Drystan will react. And it's about to drive me mad."

"He doesn't want to be king," Nuru said flatly.

"No. He thinks he doesn't deserve the throne after what Kamon did. And to make matters worse, Rangvald is *determined* to take the throne." Eirin opened her eyes to look at her friend. "He gave orders to kill Drystan and Karolus before our last attempt at going to Iilaedin."

Nuru stared. "You mean the whole thing really was a trap?"

Eirin nodded. "After lots of reading and a lot of thinking..." she paused. "I'm convinced that to fully end the curse, the Blood Fire Throne needs to be filled again. And it needs to be assigned properly, the way it was *supposed* to be inherited."

"Which means," Nuru said slowly, "now that Karolus is dead, that leaves only two people."

"It seems they're the only two descendants who survived." Eirin scoffed. "I'm also convinced that Rangvald is the one who killed Karolus's son."

Nuru nodded. "Getting rid of the youngest contender to the throne."

"Exactly. And if I learned anything in Mhaedin, it's that we can't cheat the magic. Not again. Everything needs to be as it was always supposed to be. The Time Stones must be restored by removing the foreign stone, and the Rite of the Blood Fire

Throne must be carried out to find the true heir to the throne." Eirin ran a hand through her hair. "But if Drystan refuses to take the throne..." She let the thought go unfinished.

"And," Nuru said, "has it occurred to you to talk to him about this?"

"In case you hadn't noticed," Eirin said, trying to make her voice sound light, "we haven't been talking much lately at all. Goblins and such."

Nuru rolled her eyes. "He's tried to talk to you. I've seen him try several times since I killed the Goblin." She tilted her head thoughtfully. "I don't know what's going on with you two, but you need to get it worked out before it gets us all killed."

"Actually, I'm not working it out for that exact reason." Eirin laid down again and pulled the blanket up beneath her chin. "I don't need any extra distractions right now. Trivial personal matters can wait for the time being." She expected Nuru to snort and tell her she was being stupid. But to her surprise, Nuru just nodded slowly.

"You're right. The quest does come first." She climbed into her own pallet and laid down as well. Before closing her eyes, though, she looked at Eirin once more. "But these matters might not be as trivial as you think." Then she rolled over and went to sleep.

Chapter Three

Three days after Eirin's announcement that they would need his participation to end the curse, Drystan was still trying to puzzle out how she had come to such a conclusion. That she was right, he had no doubt, much to his chagrin. Eirin had an uncanny ability to work out the puzzles their ancestors had left them.

But then again, she was a Seer.

A Seer that was dying.

His stomach churned every time he looked at her. It was like watching a flower wilt before his eyes. Everything about her was fading. Her color, her strength, even the light in her eyes.

He did his best to make her comfortable. Everyone did. Nuru, who was possibly the prickliest person Drystan had ever met—with the exception of her mother—had become a nervous nurse-maid around Eirin. It was like watching a mother badger with her baby, gentle and soft-spoken with Eirin one moment and ready to tear everyone else's head off the next. If the situation hadn't been so dire, it would have been comical.

"You need to talk to her," Qeb said as they prepared to make camp the next morning. It was an hour before dawn, and Drystan and his best friend were circling the perimeter of the campsite to check for danger.

"I would if I could." Drystan froze and sniffed the air. Then he relaxed. It was just an animal. A deer, most likely. He'd have to track it down when they were done. It would make a good dinner. Better than they'd had since leaving Mhaedin.

"And why haven't you?" Qeb asked.

"You've seen her," Drystan growled. "She's furious with me."

"I told you this would happen," Qeb said. Even in his Griffin form, he managed to look smug.

Drystan rolled his eyes. "Does it make you feel better?"

Qeb's smile grew. "Somewhat. Maybe you'll listen to me more in the future."

Drystan shook his head. "I just wanted to keep her safe."

"You know Callispa still harbors hope," Qeb said quietly, his smile now gone.

"I know." Drystan shifted back into his Human form just outside the camp, and Qeb shifted too. They could see the fire Isayas was building, but Drystan didn't make his way toward the light. Instead, he hovered in the shadows of the trees. "Eirin wasn't staying away, and Callispa offered her assistance. So I panicked and said she could help." He frowned. "I thought I made it clear that it was just for show. None of it was real."

"I think," Qeb said softly, "that she was hoping it would become real." His eyes narrowed slightly, and he gave Drystan a little shove. "Look. Eirin's over there on that boulder. Try to talk to her." His voice softened. "You don't know when you'll get another chance."

Drystan stared at his friend, aware of what he *wasn't* saying. But that wasn't Qeb's fault. So he swallowed and nodded before heading over to join Eirin at the edge of the clearing, where she watched the others set up camp, absently combing her hands through her long brown hair.

She looked so frail, and Drystan wanted very badly to fold her into his arms and hold her against his chest, safe from harm. But he knew better than that, so he simply sat on the boulder beside hers.

"Hungry?" he asked, hoping his voice sounded light enough. "I smelled a deer nearby. I could go get it."

She gave him a forced smile. "I'm not hungry, but the others would probably like it."

Drystan frowned. "Eirin, you have to eat, or you'll–"

"What? Lose my hair?" Eirin held up a small handful of long brown strands. Drystan usually tried not to draw attention to Eirin's weaknesses, but now he was unable to hide his horror. Not at the change in her appearance, but at this new irrefutable evidence that Solevar was killing the girl he loved right before his eyes.

"Eirin," he said quietly, trying to regain his composure. "Why didn't you tell me what you told Nuru about ending the curse? About me participating in an inheritance rite for the Blood Fire Throne, I mean."

Eirin stared at him long enough for him to realize he was referring to the conversation he'd overheard through her thin tent walls.

A conversation that hadn't been meant for him.

"I tried," she finally said. "Back in Mhaedin." She met his gaze, and for a second, her eyes flashed with their old fire. "You didn't want to hear it."

"But when you first told me," he said, fixing her with a frown, "you said it was just a hunch that we had to do something about the Throne. Now you know more, it seems, thanks to Rangvald. You have for several weeks."

"We weren't talking for several weeks."

"You know what I mean." He folded his arms. "If participating in this...rite...will save you, then I'll do whatever it takes."

Eirin didn't answer for a long moment. Instead, she studied him, and for a moment, Drystan was sure he saw affection in their depths. Then she shook her head and looked down.

"You mean well. But you can't just participate, Drystan. You have to *mean* it."

"I would mean to help you."

"You have to *mean* to aim for the throne." She quirked a brow. "Vying for kingship isn't something you can do passively."

Drystan stared down at her, weighing his response. Did he want to be king? Absolutely not. Without fail, it was the same every single time. No matter where he went or who he spoke to, his would-be subjects hated him the moment they discovered who his ancestor was. He doubted much would change as they got deeper into Solevar. And he wasn't necessarily convinced they were wrong either.

They were interrupted by a hiss from Nuru on the other side of the fire. Drystan and Eirin froze, and after a second of listening, Eirin's eyes widened at the same time Drystan's senses told him something was very wrong.

When he stood, he realized that everyone else was already in their Atharrach forms. Everyone, of course, but Isayas. Who was nowhere to be seen.

Fantastic.

Drystan needed to shift. He itched to shift as he sensed the danger growing closer by the second, a low hum now filling the forest around them. But he was too close to Eirin. Though he had better control of his fire now, his sheer size would injure her and the others. He had just begun to move into the trees when they were attacked.

Blurs of color streaked through the air, followed immediately by small, sharp pricking sensations all over Drystan's body.

Thane let out a curse. "Sprites!" he shouted. "It's a colony of Sprites!"

Drystan let out his own soft curse as he tried to bat the hand-sized creatures away. But they were too fast. And unfortunately, he figured out quickly, his Dragon form wouldn't help him much, even if he was able to shift. They wouldn't be able to bite him, but he couldn't do much to push them back either. The best he would be able to do would be to send a wall of flame at the pests, but as his friends were in the middle of the fray, that would hardly be helpful.

Blue, green, pink, orange, violet, and yellow blurs continued to whiz by him, striking him as they went.

Eirin screamed and dropped to her knees, covering her head with her hands. This awoke Drystan from his frustrated trance. With one arm over his face, he ran over to her and tried to shield her body with his.

"You fools!" Thane yelled. "She's Hu–" His word was cut off before he could finish it, though whether by his sense catching up with him or the swipe of Nuru's paw, Drystan couldn't tell.

The others weren't faring any better. Qeb was unable to use his weapons against them because of the Sprites' small size. Thane was trying to kick his strong legs into the air, but from the sound of his frustrated growls, he wasn't hitting much. Callispa was twirling her fiery wings in the air, and while the Sprites seemed to avoid her more than the others, she didn't seem to be accomplishing much else.

What use was there in having a Wizard if he simply disappeared?

The single member of Drystan's party that seemed to have the upper hand was Nuru, whose claim to fame in the Citadel had been outlasting her opponents.

"I got one!" she shouted, holding a small blue creature between her paws. She seemed to have it by the wings.

At the sound of their sister's cry, the cloud of color vanished as quickly as it had come. Half a minute later, the only Sprite left was the one in Nuru's paw. Nuru shifted quickly into her human form and grinned at the angry, cursing creature.

Small and sparkling blue, the Sprite looked a lot like a miniature version of a Fae Atharrach.

"The food!" Qeb growled. "They've taken nearly all the food!"

"You!" Nuru hissed at the creature. "Why did you take our food?"

The Sprite made an unintelligible noise.

"Tell me," Nuru said, switching to a purr, "or I'm going to eat you."

The Sprite quit struggling and stared at her. Then she—it appeared to be a she—looked over at Drystan. "She won't actually eat me, will she?" Her voice was thin and clear, like a strand of glass.

Drystan shrugged. "I honestly don't know."

The Sprite began to shake even harder.

"Please!" she cried. "Our food sources have been taken over by poison and thorns! Thorns in everything! Poison in the water! Poison thorns." She paused and looked at Eirin, tilting her head thoughtfully. "Is it true?" she asked in a reverent voice, her fear seeming forgotten. "Do you really have a Human?"

"If we let you go," Drystan said, yanking her attention back to him and away from Eirin, "you tell your friends not to let us see you again."

"Or what?" her voice became petulant. "You didn't stop us this time, did you?"

"That's because our Wizard wasn't here. But he'll be back anytime."

Drystan sent up a prayer of thanks as the little Sprite briefly lost her color before nodding quickly.

"Nuru," Drystan said, keeping his eyes on the Sprite.

Nuru scoffed loudly before letting go of the creature, who disappeared into the trees the moment she was free.

"I want to take this time," a deep voice from the trees said, "to point out that I haven't the slightest idea what to do about Sprites. They were pests back when my brothers and I roamed Solevar. And we couldn't get rid of them back then either."

Drystan gave Isayas a wry smile as the Wizard emerged from the trees. "They don't need to know that."

"What do you mean you can't do anything about them?" Thane demanded.

Isayas snorted. "You're a Centaur, one of the most revered military races. Do I shame you because you can't get rid of the mosquitos?" Then he turned back to Drystan. "I could technically destroy their entire race, but I'd prefer not to go to such extreme measures."

"More importantly, what do we do about our food?" Callispa asked, looking down at their sacks, which the Sprites had torn to shreds. "They've left us with barely enough for another few days. And that's *if* we eat and drink sparingly."

Drystan huffed. They'd taken several nights at the beginning of their journey to take turns flying to the outer edges of Mhaedin's farms at the foot of the mountain, gathering what they could without being noticed. They'd also hunted in turn. Unfortunately, Eirin couldn't stomach most of what they'd found for her that wasn't from the mountain or Mhaedin's farms. But then they'd run out of that, and she'd been forced to eat with everyone else. Still, they'd managed to keep a decent food store as they'd traveled, gathering what they could.

But now, all of that seemed for naught. For there was no telling when they would find drinkable water again, let alone something edible. As the Sprite had said, most of the food that grew in the wild was full of thorns.

"Isayas, your powders and minerals are still here," Qeb called out, holding up a partially shredded bag. "They must not have wanted those."

"Sprites despise Wizards," Isayas said, taking his bag. "We can't get rid of them, but if we choose to take revenge, we can make life very difficult." He rummaged through the torn bag muttering, "Which I will if they spilled my copper."

Everyone was quiet for a moment until Callispa finally broke the silence. "I know no one wants to consider it," she said hesitantly. "But we could go back to Mhaedin."

Drystan understood her suggestion. To Callispa, Mhaedin was home. The other Phoenixes were there, including her family, and home meant safety.

"I'm afraid we can't," he said, shaking his head. "As wonderful as Mhaedin was, its days as a safe haven are over." He gave her a sympathetic look, hoping she would understand. "If we can't fix the Time Stones, there will be no more safe havens soon enough. And Rangvald is sure to have spies there, waiting for news of Eirin."

Callispa frowned, but she didn't press any further.

"I'm afraid," Drystan said, looking at Isayas, "that our only option is to pray we find food and water soon and to move forward."

Isayas nodded. "We're too short on time to waste it going back."

With dawn just on the other side of the horizon, they settled into their tents after patching holes left from the Sprites, and laid down to sleep in the safety of the day.

As Drystan lay down, he tried to comfort himself with the knowledge that the Time Keeper had gotten them this far. He only prayed as he nodded off that the Divine would finish the job.

Chapter Four

The next evening was a somber one as the group packed up what little they had left and continued their journey. Thane was the only one who seemed unaffected by the Sprites' theft. He whistled as he tied up the men's tent, a strange sound against the quiet of the twilight as he ignored the pointed glares Nuru continued to send his way.

"We should be reaching Eedn in the next day or so," Isayas said, studying Eirin's map. He glanced up at their motley group, his gaze landing finally on Drystan. "Though I'm not sure they'll let us in."

Drystan felt his face heat. He knew what that meant.

"We have a Human," Thane chuckled, abandoning his whistling to speak. "I'm pretty sure that qualifies us to go anywhere."

"What is Eedn?" Qeb asked. "I've heard it mentioned several times in Mhaedin."

Isayas carefully rolled the map and placed it back in its leather tube.

"Eedn is a garden," Isayas said as he glanced at Drystan again. "And it's one of the last bastions of life for the people in lower

Solevar. It was built and kept by the Nymphs hundreds of years ago as a place to grow food for the poor and sick. They keep and guard it jealously."

"Does it still grow food?" Qeb asked.

Isayas sighed. "Last I heard. But so did Mhaedin. And as much as I hope Eirin's presence will buy us access, I'm afraid it will be very difficult to get everyone in."

"And by everyone," Drystan said, hoisting his pack on his shoulder, "you mean me." He felt Qeb stiffen beside him as he said the words, but he kept his eyes on the Wizard.

Isayas met his gaze unhappily, his blue eyes seeming paler than usual. "We'll see. No use borrowing trouble before we must."

After that, everyone but Eirin, Callispa, and the Wizard shifted. But before Eirin climbed on Drystan's back, she stepped in close.

"I've been thinking about what you said." She paused and swallowed hard. "And I think you're right. We need to talk." She glanced at the others. "Alone."

In spite of himself, Drystan's heart leaped in his chest, burning with pleasure as Eirin watched him. After being all but ignored for weeks, he craved her attention like a Merperson searching for water.

But she said no more, simply waiting for his nod and then climbing onto his back with Qeb's gentle assistance.

Drystan wanted to talk then and there. He knew, however, that he had no choice but to begin the trek.

The journey really was beginning to grow monotonous. The southeastern forests of Solevar didn't look nearly as large on the map as they did in person. When they'd first set out, He'd been sure, in spite of the Wizard's cautions, that they would be to the garden within a week at the most. But the pursuit of the Goblins and then Eirin's delicate condition had made travel painfully slow, and Drystan caught himself wondering often if they would ever actually reach Eedn.

Let alone Iilaedin.

The clouds obscured the moonlight that night, which slowed their progress even more than usual. Callispa mumbled often about not being able to see the way with her Human eyes until Qeb finally swept her up in his strong arms.

This, of course, made her protest more until he answered evenly, "You can shift, of course. But only if you want to draw the entire forest's attention."

"Fine," Callispa snapped, folding her arms across her chest. But at least let me ride on your back. You'll be bent like an old woman if you carry me this way all night."

When everyone was finally situated, their trek grew quiet as they walked. Drystan could feel Callispa's gaze on him whenever they had a brief glimpse of the moon as it peeked out from behind thick clouds. He kept his eyes on the path.

They were only a few hours from dawn when Eirin, whom Drystan had been sure was asleep, made a choking sound. Panic and dread coursed through him as he immediately knelt so the Wizard could yank her off. Everyone held their breath as Isayas whispered several rushed words over her, and the gem at the top of his staff lit with a soft glow. Nuru and Thane ran to hold her for him as he began rummaging around in his bag.

Though he worked quickly, every minute felt eternal as he struggled to uncork several of his little bottles of herbs and minerals. Drystan was about two seconds from smashing the glass with his teeth when Isayas finally got them open. Still muttering incoherently, he dabbed a little of each bottle into his hand, where he mixed them with his fingers and then blew the flakes onto Eirin's face.

A collective sigh of relief sounded when Eirin finally drew a jagged breath in. Then she began to sob.

Isayas put his bottles down and drew her into his chest. She let him, leaning into him limply as he whispered into her hair. But this time, Drystan knew he wasn't chanting incantations.

"We'll camp here today," Callispa said, hopping off Qeb's back. "I like these rocky outcrops. They'll be good for shelter in case it rains."

Taking her hint, Thane and Qeb began to help her set up camp. Nuru and Drystan remained, watching Isayas rock Eirin in his arms as tears still ran down her face.

"That's why I don't want to go to sleep!" Eirin whimpered. "It's coming soon! I can feel it. And I don't want to–"

"Shhh," Isayas said softly. His eyes met Drystan's, and Drystan could see that the Wizard was crying, too. "Shhh, it's not time yet. You're alive and with us, and you'll be all right."

In that moment, Drystan was seized by a sudden longing for his mother. It was a strange feeling. He'd spent his entire life believing his parents were dead, and he was the recipient of relatives' charity. Only in the last year had he realized his parents were not only alive, but people he saw every day. And while he hadn't been particularly close to her, he had a sudden sharp longing for her. Just having her near would have been a comfort. Someone safe with whom he could feel vulnerable.

"I'm scared," Eirin whispered, squeezing her eyes shut. "The darkness is cold. And when I'm asleep, I can feel its fingers around me."

"Nonsense," Isayas said, clearing his throat once, twice. "Even when death does take you, the Time Keeper won't allow the darkness to steal you away. His sons and daughters go to a place that's bright and warm."

"Speaking of darkness," Nuru said, clearing her own throat, "I think we should get you cleaned up and fed." She held her arms out, a soft affection in her eyes Drystan was sure he had never seen there before. Like a mother hen, clucking to her chick.

Eirin nodded and wiped her cheeks with her sleeve. She didn't meet Drystan's gaze as she let Nuru lead her back to the tent, which Callispa was holding open for them. Drystan and the Wizard watched them go. Then Drystan turned to Isayas.

"That's why you go every night, isn't it?"

"I don't know what you're talking about," Isayas grumbled as he bent to gather his bottles.

"You don't want to see what the curse is doing to her. So when we finally make camp every night, and you're done with all your spells, you escape."

"I gather herbs and minerals to keep her alive!" Isayas snapped, his eyes flashing in another brief moonbeam. They glared at one another for a moment until Isayas seemed to deflate. He looked down at his torn medicine bag.

"It's like watching Sarah all over again," he whispered. "And having Eirin..." He gave a shuddering sigh. "I never had a child. But I can only imagine her as everything Sarah would have ever wanted. Watching her fade is more..." His voice broke, and Drystan wanted to comfort him. But his own fear stuck in his throat, and he could only put his hand on the old man's arm and give it a squeeze.

Callispa was right. The rocky outcroppings were a welcome change from the never-ending forest they had been traveling through for nearly three weeks. The sharp rocks that edged a small stream stuck up out of the ground like slabs of tabletops that had been half buried on an angle. The one Callispa had chosen to make camp beside was large enough for them to all sit beneath it in a circle around the fire. And because they had made camp earlier than usual, they stayed up and talked about everything and nothing. Anything, it seemed, to not dwell on what had just taken place. Drystan was, as always, aware of Callispa's gaze, but his heart was with the girl in the tent.

An hour later, Nuru emerged.

"She's feeling better," she announced to the group. Then she looked at Drystan. "But she's asking for you." Drystan felt his heart both leap and simultaneously flop into his stomach as he nodded and stood. But as he made his way to the tent's entrance, Nuru grabbed his arm.

"Dragon or not. Prince or not, if you hurt her, I will make sure you hurt as well," she said through gritted teeth.

Drystan gave her a dry smile. "You'll have to get in line."

At the start of the journey, the Wizard had gifted Eirin a special rock that glowed when she spoke to it. A fireless light to help her dress and sleep by, as she lacked the shifter vision the rest of them possessed. It was a useful gift, as it didn't cast much light through the tent walls. Drystan was greeted by this soft light as he lifted the tent's flap.

"Nuru says you're feeling better," he said, forcing a smile as he stepped cautiously inside. Better to be lighthearted and cautious so as not to betray the depth of the fear that was eating him from the inside.

Eirin shrugged. She was lying back on her mat, a thin blanket rolled up like a pillow beneath her head. "I always feel better after a bath. I just hate that Nuru has to give them to me." She made a face. "It can't be very fun for her."

"Nuru knows," Drystan said, tucking the blanket up under Eirin's chin, "that the world needs you to survive. I think she'd chew your food for you if she thought it would help."

Eirin made a gagging sound, but it was sweet to Drystan's ears. Eirin was feeling well enough to make a joke, at least.

"But I'm guessing," Drystan continued, "that you didn't call me here to talk about the sudden appearance of Nuru's maternal instincts."

"No, I didn't." Eirin pushed herself into a sitting position. Then she put her hands in her lap and looked at Drystan. "We've danced around this issue enough, so I'm going to come right out and say it. You need to be Solevar's next king."

Drystan stared at her. "Well," he managed to say after a moment, trying to order his thoughts, "that's one way to get to the point."

A laugh sounded from outside. It was a sound they didn't hear much of these days. He wondered what they were talking about.

"I think," Drystan said after a moment, "that we need to focus on just getting you to Iilaedin. Then we can figure out what we need when we get there."

Eirin glared at him. "You said you wanted to hear what I thought."

"And I do," he said. "But I happen to disagree slightly."

"That's not good enough." Eirin shook her head.

"Very well," he said, folding his own arms to mimic hers. "Then tell me why I need to fight for a throne that I don't deserve and very few would want me to have."

"As long as the Time Stones have been standing, there's been a son of Oreck on the throne," Eirin said. "Isayas explained it to me the other day. In the Rite of the Blood Fire Throne, the princes all bleed onto the throne. The blood flows down into a special dais beneath the throne. The magic in the blood ignites in the dais, and the prince whose blood has the brightest flames is the one the Time Keeper has chosen as king."

Drystan's head swam. He'd often considered the possibility that his involvement might be required. But Kamon's sin had tainted his blood, and he was fairly convinced attempting to gain power would only make things worse, not only for him, but for Solevar as a whole.

But the way Eirin was glaring at him now made it quite obvious she would never accept such a theory. So he leaned forward and gently mussed her hair.

"True as that may be," he said, forcing a smile, "we still have to get there first."

Eirin shook her head. "We can't just fix the Time Stones and expect everything to return to normal. The Time Stones only stopped working because those who should have guarded the kingdom broke their vows. Fixing the Time Stones alone will help, but allowing the princes' vow to remain broken could make the curse final."

"Eirin–"

"Solevar has never been without a protector!" Eirin hissed. "At least...not before the curse. Do you really want to stake the fate of the kingdom and everyone we love on the idea that removing a broken rock is going to fix it all?"

Drystan tried to think of something to say to lighten the mood, or at least to deflect with humor. But all he could do was rub his eyes.

"Eirin, the people of Mhaedin didn't think I was worthy of living in their city, let alone sitting on a throne. In fact, I'm pretty sure that's what they were afraid I would try to do. I'm the embodiment of the curse itself."

Eirin's brown eyes burned, and her skin flushed, and for a brief second, she looked healthy and strong again.

"I never believed that for a second. Listen to me, Drystan." She leaned forward and took his face in her hands, pulling him close to her. Drystan's heart stumbled as her small hands gently pressed against his skin.

"You," she said in a whisper as she searched his face, "are not Kamon."

"No," he said with a sad smile. "But his blood flows in my veins."

She let go of his face, but her eyes stayed on his. "That doesn't matter."

Drystan let out a sigh. "Before we get ahead of ourselves, how do we even do any of this without addressing the mess we left behind?" He raised an eyebrow. "I didn't exactly leave my uncle on good terms."

Not on good terms was an understatement. Drystan's great-great uncle, Rangvald, had tried to kill him the last time they'd met. And then Drystan had succeeded in stealing his uncle's prized Human. Drystan's other uncle, Karolus, had sacrificed himself so they might get away.

Eirin frowned, and her shoulders drooped. "I haven't figured that part out yet." Her eyes met Drystan's again. "But what I can tell you is that Rangvald wants the throne, and he'll do anything to get it. You know that he killed Karolus's father and son, right?"

Drystan nodded.

"Right. And he can't be allowed to lay claim to the throne outside of the rite. We'll need to beat him to Iilaedin." She paused. "There has to be a way to get there before him. Or, if we don't, to outsmart him somehow."

"You don't think he'll simply concede if you sneak up and fix the Time Stones without him?" Drystan asked.

"No. He doesn't want the Time Stones fixed. Or rather, he wants them fixed, but he wants something else even more." Eirin's brow furrowed. "He's desperate to be king."

Drystan huffed and ran his hands through his hair. It had grown longer over the last few weeks. He'd have to ask one of the others to cut it again soon to keep it out of his face.

"Why do you think he's so determined to be king, even if it comes at the cost of Solevar?"

"I think," Eirin said slowly, "that he plans to fulfill his own desires by being the only heir alive left to claim the throne. Perhaps whatever he was doing was what led to the rift between the brothers before the curse fell." She paused. "Either way, there's no competition when all of your alternatives are dead. And if that were the case, he could simply carry out the rite on his own and be guaranteed to be chosen." She narrowed her eyes. "So think about it as you hesitate because it comes down to this. Karolus is dead. There are only two people left who can claim the throne in a way that will satisfy the magic." She raised her eyebrows. "Do you really want him to be king?"

"Maybe he'd be better. Who knows?" Drystan tried to give her a teasing smile.

But instead of smiling back, Eirin's eyes grew hard like steel.

"Good night," she snapped as she lay down and rolled over.

Drystan, not sure what else to do, stood to go. But at the foot of the tent, he turned and said softly, "I'll consider it. I promise."

"You'd better," Eirin said without turning.

Chapter Five

"Drystan! Drystan, wake up!"

Drystan bolted upright so fast that he nearly keeled over again at the sound of Nuru's terrified voice. The sun must have set over the horizon if Nuru was standing at the edge of his tent. For some reason, he felt unusually disoriented. What time was it?

"What's wrong?" he mumbled, struggling to his knees.

"It's Eirin! She won't wake up!"

Drystan's sense sharpened into focus at these words, and in seconds, he was out of his tent and inside of Eirin's. Isayas was already at her side. His hand was on her forehead, and his eyes were closed as he muttered inaudible words.

The moon hadn't risen yet, so Drystan was more thankful than ever for his excellent night vision. And though the colors weren't as bright as they would have been during the day, he could see that Eirin's face was an alarming shade of white. Her chest went up and down in quick, shallow movements, and her big brown eyes stayed shut.

"What do we do?" Callispa whispered. Drystan glanced back to see his other friends all peering over his shoulders.

"How about getting out of this tent and letting me work?" Isayas snapped.

Callispa's eyes widened, but Drystan motioned for everyone to leave.

"Not you, Drystan," Isayas said without turning his head. "I want you and Nuru here with me. Do exactly as I say."

And so Drystan and Nuru stayed. They washed Eirin's face with a damp rag, and moved her hair away from her face so he could press herbs behind her ears. They held her head up and her mouth open as he poured drops of water between her lips. For hours they labored over her, Drystan praying incoherently with each breath.

But nothing changed. And eventually, Isayas stopped working and rubbed his eyes.

"I have nothing else," he said, standing. Still, he hovered over her, a tortured expression on his face.

But Drystan didn't stand. He couldn't. He had her head cradled in his lap, and he was unable to pull his eyes from her face. Gently, he traced its curvature and angles with his fingers.

Nuru stood with Isayas, and for a moment, Drystan was sure she might cry. Instead, her jaw tightened, and then she stomped out. A few seconds later, Drystan heard her take her anger out on an unsuspecting tree as it crashed to the ground, followed by several of her favorite curses.

"You..." Isayas stopped and cleared his throat. "You might want to say goodbye," he finally said in a rough voice.

"I don't know how," Drystan whispered.

Isayas was silent for a long moment. Then he turned and stormed out. "I told you this was a bad idea!"

Drystan's hands shook as they continued tracing invisible lines on Eirin's face, and he found himself wishing they were real. Because if Eirin had lines on her face, that would mean she'd lived a long life. Children, most likely. Many seasons of planting and growing and harvesting. Years of love shared with whomever she handed her heart to.

A sharp stabbing in his chest made Drystan double over, nearly covering Eirin's face with his chest. He groaned as he clutched his chest with his free hand.

For all their fire, Dragons' hearts were fragile things.

Not even three seconds had passed before Qeb was in the tent beside him, his sharp Griffin eyes taking in the scene before shifting back into his Human form.

"What is it?" he asked, kneeling beside Drystan, his eyes searching Drystan's face. He had heard Drystan's groan.

Drystan struggled to inhale through the pain, but it was like sucking in a thousand needles.

"Nothing that can be helped," he said when he finally got enough air to speak.

"Drystan," Qeb snapped. "What's wrong?"

Drystan gave his friend a humorless smile. "Just something particular to Dragons, I'm afraid. Karolus told me about it before we left."

Qeb only raised his eyebrows. He wasn't going to let Drystan off easily.

Drystan sighed. "Dragons mate for life," he said, somehow managing to sit almost straight once more. When he talked, though, he still sounded slightly breathless. "According to Karolus, losing a mate is devastating for Dragons." He didn't add that many, apparently, didn't survive the deaths of their loved ones by many months.

"But Eirin..." Qeb frowned down at Eirin's still form.

"It has nothing to do with her. The moment I chose to love her–"

"Your heart!" Qeb exclaimed, his eyes nearly bulging. "Because your magic is in your heart!"

Drystan nodded and grimaced as yet another pang shot through his chest. "Break a Dragon's heart..."

"Break the Dragon," Qeb finished softly. "I heard that at Mhaedin, but I never understood it until now." He looked back down at Eirin with new alarm. "But she's not–"

They were interrupted by the sound of distant crashing. Qeb stood and shifted into his Griffin form as he exited the tent. Drystan nearly got up himself, but then decided to remain. Still, he placed Eirin's head on her makeshift pillow and gently laid her on the floor. He didn't have room to shift in her tent, but he could at least be ready if someone tried to enter. He stood just inside the entrance and drew his sword.

The crashing continued to grow louder and louder until Drystan made out the sound of thundering hooves. Whatever was galloping up–horses, or Centaurs, perhaps–was numerous. There were at least six or seven. No, more than that. Drystan soon stopped trying to count.

Why weren't his friends fighting to protect them? Not even Qeb was making a sound. Had they all been incapacitated? Drystan's stomach turned as he prepared himself to meet whatever had made his friends go silent.

"We're looking for the Human!" a strange woman's voice said.

Drystan wanted to faint with relief. The fact that the woman had spoken meant she was most likely talking to his friends, which meant they were most likely alive.

"Drystan!" Qeb, Callispa, and Nuru cried at the same time.

Drystan, sword still drawn, pushed through the tent's curtain door to find himself facing his friends and an entire herd of Unicorns.

Each one stood nearly as tall as Thane in his Centaur form. Their hides gave off, even in the weak moonlight, a silvery rainbow sheen, and their horns were even more colorful, veins of blue, violet, pink, green, yellow, and orange running all the way up to each shimmering white point. Their white manes were curled with locks of various colors in them as well.

Magnificent was an understatement.

"The Human!" The three Unicorns in the front of the herd stepped forward. The first shifted into her Human form, and the second and third followed suit. Two women and one man. The woman who had spoken looked at Drystan, a frustrated expression on her face. "Do you have a Human or not?"

That snapped Drystan out of his trance. He ran back into the tent and gently lifted Eirin before taking her back out again.

"She won't wake up," he said, his voice shaking as he came to stand in front of the woman who had spoken.

"Put her down here." The woman knelt with Drystan and immediately began to feel Eirin's face and neck and then pressed her hand against Eirin's chest. "She's barely breathing," she said to the two in Human form behind her. She turned back to Drystan. "When did she fall asleep?"

"This morning," Isayas said, stepping forward. "Along with everyone else. It was as natural as ever."

The woman paused and glanced up at Isayas. "I was going to ask how she made it this deep into the woods, but now I can see. Here, Wizard. I'm going to need you to take her hand and count her breaths for me." The woman turned and looked back at the Unicorns behind her. "Melody, come here."

"You...you all died!" Callispa burst out. "Everyone in Mhaedin knows you're gone!"

The woman gave her an annoyed look. "I can assure you we're very much alive. Whether or not we want Mhaedin tracking us down and forcing us to work in your healing rooms is another matter entirely." She turned back to the one she'd called Melody. "Three drops in her mouth, one on each eye."

The Unicorn named Melody nodded her head up and down, her mane fluttering in the breeze as she did.

"Lift her head and tilt her face up," the woman instructed Isayas. As Isayas obeyed, the Dragon within Drystan growled, his vision turning slightly red. He should be the one holding her, helping her. Eirin was his.

Thankfully, Drystan's Humanity held just enough control that he held himself in check. Of course, the Unicorns would trust the Wizard over him. They had no idea who he was, and if they did, they would probably trust him even less. He told the Dragon to sit down and shut up.

"Not too much!" the woman continued. "She's weak." But she needn't have worried. Isayas's hands were steady and gentle. Drystan's conscience smote him as he watched the compassion in the Wizard's face.

The Unicorn named Melody clopped forward softly and bent her head down until her horn was a handwidth from Eirin's upturned face.

"You're not going to do it?" Isayas asked, frowning. "Aren't you the alpha?"

"Melody is young," the woman said, still supporting Eirin's other side, "but her elixir is the most potent I've ever seen." Her voice swelled with pride. "She is also my daughter."

Melody, seeming to ignore the conversation, took in a deep breath, her sides expanding and then shrinking as she let it out slowly. Then Drystan heard his breath leave him.

Melody's horn had begun to glisten, and slowly, coalescing at its tip, a drop began to swell and quiver. Moonlight broke through the clouds as she did, and the drop shone like water in its light. Unlike water, however, it wasn't clear. Rather, it was like watching a rainbow grow and then rain onto Eirin's face. One drop. Two. Three drops landed on her slightly parted lips, and two landed on her closed eyelids. And instead of rolling down her face as water would, the rainbow drops were absorbed through her skin.

Melody took a few steps back, swaying slightly, the man putting his arms around her, steadying her as she began to shift back into her Human form. But no one else moved.

"Why did you stop?" Drystan whispered, watching Eirin's still form. "Shouldn't someone else take over?" He looked up, searching the Unicorns' faces. Were they giving up?

"Wait," the older woman said in a firm voice. "And watch."

Drystan didn't want to wait. He wanted to scoop Eirin up and press his ear to her heart to hear whether or not it beat. The Dragon within writhed as seconds ticked by.

As if hearing his thoughts, Isayas put his hand on Drystan's left arm, and Qeb came and stood at his right.

Sometimes, Drystan's companions really irritated him.

But as his Dragon was considering possible ways to force the Unicorns to give Eirin more elixir, her eyelids fluttered open, and she sucked in a sharp breath.

"Eirin!" Nuru cried, kneeling at Eirin's side. Their friends began to rejoice, but Drystan found that his feet wouldn't move, and he was suddenly too exhausted to do anything but watch.

"She needs water," the woman said. But when Callispa brought Eirin's waterskin, she shook her head. "I was talking to my people. Phillipe?"

The man who had steadied Melody removed a waterskin from his own shoulder and handed it to the woman.

"Your water is contaminated," the woman said, lifting the waterskin to Eirin's lips. "This is pure."

"Where did you get pure water?" Thane asked, his eyes wide.

The woman gave him a smile. "We purify it." She tapped her forehead, and Thane nodded slowly.

"I see."

"And you," the woman said, turning to Drystan, "can take her now. You've been chomping at the bit since you put her down." She raised a knowing brow. "But be careful not to squeeze her. I don't know what you are, but you're obviously something large."

As if in a daze, Drystan took Eirin into his arms. Her eyes moved to his face, but she was so tired that he couldn't tell what she thought about him holding her so close. That was well enough, though. She could order him to put her down later. Right now, when she couldn't push him away, he was going to hold her close.

"Wizard," the woman said, "If you could be so good as to enshroud us, we'll make our meal, and you can all ask the questions I know you're brimming with."

In the back of his mind, only then did Drystan realize that, supposedly, the Unicorns shouldn't have been able to see them. But perhaps in his worry for Eirin, Isayas had forgotten to set his protective spells around the camp. Drystan didn't care either way. He was only too glad that, for whatever reason, Isayas's spells had failed.

Drystan's companions seemed glad to have something to do. Minutes later, Isayas had finished expanding his protective spell, Thane and Qeb had caught several pieces of game, and the Unicorns were all gathered around the fire in their Human forms.

"Should he put her to bed?" Nuru asked the woman, whose name was Iris. Drystan glared at Nuru, but Iris just smiled.

"She'll probably be cold for a few hours, so being held will benefit her for the moment."

"Let us thank the Time Keeper," Phillipe said, his deep voice reverberating through the trees. The Unicorns nodded, but Drystan's company looked confused.

"Thank the Time Keeper?" Nuru asked.

Iris arched one perfect brow and looked at Isayas. "They don't know–"

"Callispa is from Mhaedin," Isayas mumbled. "The others are from inside the mountain."

Iris blinked. "The mountain I know little about. But don't tell me that they've ceased thanking the Time Keeper in Mhaedin as well."

Callispa blushed and looked at the ground. "We did it when I was small, but...my father says there's little to be thankful for now. Everyone says that." She shrugged.

Drystan was fairly sure he heard Phillipe mutter something to Iris about heathens, and it reminded him of the time he'd met Lady Seren, the Dragon lady his father had sent him to consult against the wishes of Torbaine's Elders. She'd called them heathens as well. As he clutched Eirin to his chest, Drystan was once again filled with the increasing awareness he'd felt more and more over the last few months–an ever-growing ache of loss. Loss of what, he couldn't say exactly. But he did know that he had been cheated of the rich culture and history and–it seemed–faith that his ancestors had held.

"You can learn now," Phillipe said, casting a stern glance at Drystan's group. Then he pulled something from beneath his shirt. Drystan nearly fell over when he recognized a stone very similar to the one Eirin was hiding as well. It was even hanging from a leather cord the way Eirin's was.

"Is that..." he began, but Melody, who seemed to have recovered, smiled and shook her head.

"No, these aren't true Time Stones." She giggled as if his question was incredibly foolish.

It probably was.

"These are cut to represent the Time Stones, though," Phillipe said, still solemn. As he held it up, Drytsan realized that this stone was larger than Eirin's, and there were little characters carved into its sides.

The other Unicorns all had one as well, and they were holding them up in front of their faces. To Drystan's even greater surprise, Isayas had pulled out his own stone. Its corners were nearly worn smooth, and the markings on its sides were barely visible. He now studied it with a frown. How long had it been since he'd used it, Drystan wondered. Before he could ask, however, the Unicorns began to sing.

Drystan's skin prickled as they raised their voices, which echoed through the trees. He didn't understand the language, but the meaning was clear. It was a song of thanks. For air and food, for water and light. For moonlight and stars. For love and for hope.

Hope.

Were these people still able to hope? Or were they simply echoing empty prayers up as the end came near?

"What was that?" Thane asked reverently when the song was done. "I've never heard that tongue before."

"It's the ancient tongue of the world before the Time Keeper created Solevar," Phillipe said, his chin held high. "Some prefer to sing it in their head. But we sing it for all to hear. Our faith is still strong."

Drystan looked down to see Eirin's eyes open wide. She still hadn't spoken since being awakened, but now she was staring at Phillipe with a look Drystan knew well. If she'd been feeling like herself, she would have pestered him until he'd told her everything he knew about the time before Solevar. If there was one temptation Eirin couldn't resist, it was the call of knowing.

"How did you find us?" Isayas asked a few minutes later when the food was being passed around. "I had several spells raised."

Iris put her food down and sighed. "I'm afraid the state of Solevar has made magic somewhat...unpredictable. Even our healing isn't always as successful as it once was. The Nymphs are about to work themselves to death trying to feed everyone else, and the Fae are nearly as scarce as the Humans were twenty years ago."

Drystan looked down to see Eirin frowning. He knew she was

thinking of her best friend, Alys, who had sacrificed herself so the rest of them could escape Torbaine again after being captured and returned against their will. Alys was a kind of Fae.

"Were you out looking for us?" Callispa asked.

"No," Iris said. "A colony of Sprites sought us out."

Drystan choked on the drink he'd just taken and started to cough and sputter.

All over Eirin, who gave him an irritated look.

"Sorry," he grunted, still trying to clear his airway.

"We were attacked by Sprites!" Thane exclaimed. "They took nearly all of our food and water!"

"Well, don't hate them too much," Iris said, looking somewhat amused. "Because after leaving you, they sought us out, claiming that they'd seen a Human who was near death."

"Yes. The Human they nearly starved to death by stealing all of her food," Nuru grumbled.

"Be that as it may," Iris said patiently, "they inadvertently saved your Human. If we'd discovered you any later, she wouldn't have awakened again."

The group went silent, and everyone turned to look toward Eirin. But Eirin just stared up at the stars, her face still too closed off for Drystan to read.

"So..." Callispa said slowly, "you're purposefully not coming to Mhaedin?"

Phillipe was the one to speak this time. "A few did several decades ago. My sister was one of them." He glanced at Iris, who placed her hand on his. "She sent word that Dragon lady who ruled Mhaedin wished for more Unicorns."

"A lot of people have been dying," Callispa said.

"I think," Phillipe said slowly, "that more would have come if your Dragon hadn't been planning to take us by force."

Callispa froze. "By..."

Iris nodded, her brows drawn together. "Yes. When none

answered her original call, she planned to come fetch us...with or without our consent. My husband's sister warned us early enough that we were able to work with some other races to stage our deaths. Then we made sure that we warned anyone we helped never to speak a word about us again." She looked at Phillipe. "In truth, I expected someone to find us long ago."

Isayas shifted. "Mhaedin is...not in a good way." He sighed. "It hasn't been for a long time."

"Well, you were successful," Callispa said stiffly. "Everyone thinks you're dead."

Phillipe raised one thick eyebrow. "And who is everyone?"

"Not many of us were willing or even able to follow the princes when they retreated from Iilaedin," Iris continued. "But there are hundreds of us living in Solevar now."

"But why?" Callispa asked, her voice shaking and her face red, and Drystan remembered her mentioning once how her people were dying out. The Phoenixes were nearing extinction.

As were many others. Including Dragons.

"Unicorns weren't meant to live in cages, my dear," Iris said with a sad smile.

"If Unicorns are alive then," Nuru said. "What about Humans? Are there more of them in Solevar, too?"

"There once were," Iris said slowly. "But none I've heard of in a long, long time." She turned and looked at Eirin. "Why do you think our search was so swift?"

Drystan didn't realize his grip on Eirin had tightened until she made a little noise and squirmed a bit.

"Sorry," he whispered.

She just rolled her eyes. But to his surprise, she didn't try to escape. She only nestled into a different position.

"We assumed," Phillipe said, "that you're heading to the Emerald Palace."

Drystan nodded. "We are."

"Then there are some things you need to know," Phillipe said with a nod. "For one, Rangvald is making his way there as well." He paused. "And he's acting very much as though he either has a Human or he plans to get one soon enough."

"We saw," Nuru growled slightly.

"We're better suited for healing than for protection," Phillipe continued. "But we'll accompany you as far as the first boundary wall of Eedn. There, we'll make sure the Griffins allow you safe passage through the orchard. It's the most direct path to the city."

"You can't accompany us further?" Isayas asked. "I assure you, we would–"

Iris interrupted him. "It's for your sake, Wizard, that we do not go farther. Our presence would draw too much attention. We rarely travel together as we have tonight. Only the fate of a Human could have brought so many together. The Unicorns are more highly sought after than ever. But," she motioned to Melody and nodded, "we will give you these."

Melody stood and removed the small bag she wore slung across her chest. From it, she removed two small vials. Both were made of a pearlescent stone, though one was white with rainbow reflections, much like the Unicorns' skin, and the other was a light blue.

"These," Iris said, taking the two bottles, "are worth more than anything else in Solevar, save your Human." She handed them to Isayas. "Give Eirin one drop from the white bottle before every sleep. Use the other to purify her water and food. They should last you your trip to Iilaedin." She glanced at Phillipe, who took her hand and squeezed. "Phillipe will do his best to meet you there. But even if he doesn't, these should ensure that Eirin makes it safely to the capital."

"How will you get there?" Callispa asked. "If you can't come with us?" Drystan was rather sure he detected a note of frustration in her voice, but Iris didn't seem to notice or care.

"We have certain ways of traveling known only to ourselves. Ways that would frustrate you. But we do promise to do our best to be there when you arrive."

The Unicorns all stood as if someone had given a command, and within minutes, they were ready to depart. But Phillipe approached Drystan.

"Eirin looks tired again," Drystan said in a low voice, frowning down at Eirin's fluttering eyelashes. "Should we give her the elixir?"

To his surprise Phillipe just smiled and gently closed Eirin's drooping eyelids with his large hand. "No. Melody's healing will be in her for two more days. She's safe now." Then he looked at Drystan, and his smile vanished. "But I have something to say to you that I didn't wish to address before the others."

Drystan tensed but handed Eirin to Isayas before following Phillipe into the trees.

Phillipe whirled about to face him. "I know what you are. And who you are."

"How?" Drystan asked, forcing the Dragon not to growl.

"Word spreads. And while we don't show our faces near Mhaedin, we have friends who do. And gossip has it that the youngest son of Oreck nearly killed Rangvald. And Rangvald is out for his blood."

The hair on the back of Drystan's neck prickled.

"I didn't say anything to the others," Phillipe continued, "because I believe you're doing the right thing." He glanced down at Eirin. "But there are many in Solevar who would not agree. The sting of your great-grandfather's folly cuts deep in this place." He paused and took a deep breath. "But many are also aware that Rangvald's desire is to rule. And those who recall his time as a prince in his father's court know that he ruled with an iron fist. There were rumors..." He paused then shook his head. "They can't be confirmed. But if you want to prevent Rangvald from gaining the throne, you're going to have to win the people over."

"But–" Drystan began to protest, but Phillipe held up his hand.

"Is there another son of Oreck alive? Does Karolus still breathe? Because my sources say he does not."

Drystan closed his eyes briefly, and the memory of his dead uncle's limp form played behind his eyelids. Finally, he opened his eyes again and sighed. "No."

Phillipe nodded once. "The choice is yours. But whichever choice you make, it won't affect you alone." He put his hand on Drystan's shoulder. "Such is the lot of a prince." Then he turned and walked away.

Chapter Six

Eirin felt oddly content as consciousness crept lazily over her. It was a faraway familiar feeling, one she hadn't felt since she was very small. Actually, no. The last time she'd felt this way had been when she was sick, and the Citadel had let her stay in her own home so her mother could nurse her to health. It was a lovely feeling.

And yet, in addition to this, she felt something more. Something strangely comfortable, though she couldn't say what. Whatever it was, she didn't want to open her eyes and chase it away. So instead, she let out a sigh and merely rolled over onto her other side.

As her consciousness began to return, she found words for the ways she felt.

Warm.

Fuzzy.

Safe.

Her hand brushed against her waterskin. A familiar vision jolted her awake, and her eyes flew open. It was day. And though the sun's rays couldn't reach her through their thick canvas tent coverings, she was distinctly aware that she'd been sleeping much longer than usual. She often woke during the day, as they could only travel at night due to the sun's poisonous rays. But every evening when she awoke, she felt exhausted, like there wasn't enough sleep in the world. Now, though...

For the first time since leaving Rangvald's fortress, Eirin felt *awake*.

Nuru was still snoring softly in the corner. That was normal enough. What was not normal was that Drystan was half-sitting, half-toppled over as he slept against the door of the tent. In spite of herself, Eirin smiled. As usual, taking up the role of defender. As she sat, watching him and wondering if she ought to roll up a blanket and stick it under his head, his eyes opened, and he bolted upright.

"Eirin!" he croaked, blinking hard and rubbing his eyes. "You're awake!" In one fluid movement he was at her side, his hands outstretched toward her. Eirin was annoyed with herself for noticing the flowing grace of his well-muscled limbs.

"Where are the Unicorns?" she asked in an effort to pretend he wasn't absolutely striking in every way a man could be.

Why was she so painfully aware of him today? What was wrong with her?

"Hold on." He uncovered a plate of food and handed it to her. "Callispa made this for you just before sunrise. It's still warm."

Eirin stiffened at the mention of the Phoenix, but then forced a smile as she accepted the food. Though she didn't want to admit it, she was ravenous. And it was kind of Callispa to make her a meal. Even if the girl was still making eyes at Drystan.

Even in her befuddled state, Eirin had noticed Callispa's longing looks over the past few weeks. And she'd appreciated none of them.

Eirin shook her head and took a bite. Why were there so many emotions rushing through her this morning? Maybe if she just ignored them and let them pass, they would leave, and she could return to sanity.

"What's wrong?" Drystan asked, leaning forward slightly.

Eirin swallowed. "I think...I don't know. I'm feeling better. But...I can't explain it. It's rather dizzying."

"I can tell you what that is," said a deep voice from outside the tent. Isayas pushed his way into the tent then shook his hood off. Usually, when one of them had to dart outside during the day to grab this or that or move from one tent to the other, they wore one of their special cloaks designed to protect them from the sun. But Isayas's tattered gray Wizard's robe either did the work, or he didn't care about the pain, as he always refused to don one of the heavy, black cloaks.

"You're feeling so strange," Isayas continued, seating himself beside Drystan, "because you're well." He beamed, but it quickly faded. "You've felt so poorly for so long that you forgot what it felt like to be alive and to contemplate all those usual pesky Human emotions." He indicated her plate. "And to be hungry. Keep eating. They brought this food knowing our situation. Iris said you needed food nearly as much as you did the elixir."

"Are the Unicorns gone?" Eirin asked as she dutifully took another bite of bread. Never had bread tasted so good. Never had they eaten this kind of bread. It must be another gift of the Unicorns.

"They are, unfortunately. Unicorns are in high demand in these parts." Isayas shook his head. "Well, everywhere in truth. They didn't want to draw more attention to you than they already had. It was dangerous enough for them to come together last night, but they were worried about being taken, should only a few come. It's safer for them to travel in a group, but it also attracts attention."

Eirin thought back to the Unicorns' pearlescent skin and

glowing horns and understood why. After seeing them once, she would be able to spot one anywhere.

She finished her bread and put down the empty plate. A third piece of the bread would have been delicious, but she knew as well as everyone else that they would need to ration their food, especially after what the Sprites had done.

"Here." Drystan handed her two small bottles. "This one's for purifying your water and food. We already treated this meal, but you'll need to add a drop to your food after this. The other is for you. You'll need to use one drop daily."

"How long was I asleep?" Eirin asked, tucking the bottles carefully into her bag, then thinking better of it and tucking them into her clothes.

Drystan and Isayas glanced at one another. "A day and a half," Drystan finally said.

Eirin nearly choked on the water she was drinking. "That long?"

"You were nearly dead, Eirin," Isayas said, his face ancient and pained again. "Healing takes time." He stood and pulled his hood over his head once more. Then he left.

Eirin shook her head. As she did, a wave of dizziness hit her. She swayed slightly, and Drystan caught her. As he did, she realized that she was already tired again. And in her exhaustion, she sent a brief glance at his wide chest. How nice it would be to lean against it.

He'd held her when the Unicorns had come. And it had felt good then. But no. She wasn't supposed to be thinking like this. She'd been nearly dead the last time, so her slip didn't count. Now, though, when she knew better...

"Eirin," Drystan whispered, his large hands on her shoulders and his voice deep and low. "Allowing me to help you doesn't mean you owe me your firstborn son."

There was laughter in his eyes, but Eirin could only stare at him as, against her will, she imagined handing him a son. But the heat that flared up in her chest at such a thought made her look down at the ground.

"I...um, need to relieve myself," she said, trying to stand on her own.

Drystan just chuckled. "Then perhaps Nuru would be a better help for that after all." He paused. "But Eirin? I meant what I said. I'm not here to hold you in debt. I'm here to be what you need."

Eirin gave him a sad smile. "That's the problem."

He frowned. "How so?"

Eirin didn't answer, though. She simply shook Nuru gently awake, then let Nuru help her don her sun cloak before they made their way out into the shade of the trees.

The problem, she reflected silently to herself, was that Drystan was everything she could ever need...if only Solevar weren't resting on their shoulders.

Chapter Seven

After what felt to Eirin like an eternal sleep, they were ready to move on that evening. A heavy cloud cover to the west allowed them to pack up sooner than usual as it hid the sunset behind thick blankets of gray. True, it might rain, and they could have to pitch their tents earlier than usual in the dark hours of morning, but nevertheless, Eirin rejoiced. For the first time in weeks, she felt alert and ready as she climbed up onto Drystan's back. Isayas said they should reach the garden either that night or the next. Eirin was ready for something new. They'd seen nothing but trees for what felt like a lifetime.

"You've barely slept in the last three weeks. How are you feeling?" a low, melodic voice said quietly. Eirin looked down to see Callispa looking up at Drystan in concern. Annoyance flashed through Eirin as Drystan brought his great shoulders up and down in a shrug, moving Eirin with them.

"I've slept more the last two days than I have in a long time," his deep Dragon tones rumbled. "Thank you, though."

Callispa looked as though she were going to say something else when her eyes moved up to meet Eirin's. Eirin sent her a cold smile. Callispa sent her a faint one back before taking her place at Drystan's side.

You don't own him, you know, a voice inside her head whispered. *He wanted more, and you told him no.*

I told him, "Not yet," Eirin argued back silently. *There's a difference.*

But the difference was negligible, and she knew it. Drystan was supposedly devoted to her for life. He had, unbeknownst to her, given his heart, the source of his magic, to Eirin. Could the-near-temporary, she reminded herself–rejection of his affections lead him to a new kind of desire for someone else? Someone who encouraged his affections?

Eirin's ruminations were interrupted by the sound of many hooves. Her mouth fell open, and she straightened as a familiar herd of pearlescent bodies stampeded into the clearing.

"Iris! Phillipe!" Isayas exclaimed, striding forward. "What's wrong?"

He didn't need to ask if something was wrong. The way the Unicorns were tossing their heads and stamping with their feet, snorting with arched necks made it clear that something indeed had gone wrong.

"We didn't get very far after leaving you before we were cornered by a group of Basilisks," the largest Unicorn said in Phillipe's voice.

Eirin felt her blood freeze in her veins. There were Basilisks nearby.

Which meant there were Manticores as well.

She shivered at the memory of their first and only encounter with a Manticore while in the mountain caverns. Bright red magic pulsing in its tail full of venomous spikes poised to launch into its prey. Feline, larger than even Nuru's Sphinx form. Sharp claws and piercing eyes. They'd only survived because Eirin had started banging pots together to overwhelm its sensitive ears. And even then, it had been close.

"Eirin, what's wrong?" Qeb asked. Everyone turned to stare at her. Her fear must be visible on her face.

"Um," she shook her head slightly. "Only...I remembered that Basilisks are the choice pets of Manticores."

Iris nodded. "That's right."

"How many Basilisks were there?" Eirin asked breathlessly.

A slightly smaller Unicorn glanced up at Phillipe. "At least seven."

Eiri closed her eyes. "Which means there are at least three."

"Three what?" Nuru demanded.

Eirin opened her eyes. "Manticores. They only ever keep at most three Basilisks each. They can't control more than that."

Thane let out an uncharacteristic swear word, and for once, Qeb didn't give him a dirty look.

"I understand why the Basilisks would attack," Nuru said. "They're not Atharrachs, just animals. But why would the Manticores attack *Unicorns*?"

"Since the curse, some Atharrachs have given into our more... creaturely side," Iris said. "Especially those who have cut themselves off from the world and lived in seclusion. The Manticores were one of the first Atharrach groups to do so. At this point, they're not interested in breaking the curse. They just want to survive as long as they can."

"We were able to hide in an abandoned building outside the garden walls," Phillipe continued, "but we were kept there all night and into the next day. We've only just escaped now because their masters called them off. But they can't be far. And a Manticore party that wants to hunt a pack of Unicorns–"

"Is more dangerous than most," Isayas nodded.

"We need to get Eirin into the garden," Iris said. "Drystan, you won't be able to carry her."

"I can fly her there," Drystan growled. Eirin could feel his scales grow warm beneath her. "It will take less than half an hour if the map is correct."

"No." Phillipe shook his head. "It's too dangerous."

"My scales–" Drystan began, but Isayas cut him off.

"They're right, Drystan. You could survive, but you would be limited in your ability to evade or retaliate."

"I could fly higher," Drystan snarled.

"We don't know how far their spikes go," Qeb said in a quiet voice, putting his large hand on Drystan's scaled shoulder. "Eirin is recovering, Drystan. If you had to evade, even if we were there to protect you, she might fall."

"I'm fine," Eirin called down, but everyone ignored her.

"I don't know if the Manticores in the mountains do so," Phillipe added, "but here, many of them create their own bows and arrows, and many fit their arrows with their own spikes. If they loosed one and it hit Eirin, it would be the end of her and all hope for Solevar."

"I'll fly higher," Drystan argued again, but Phillipe shook his head, his mane flashing in the moonlight.

"Griffins protect the garden, and since the curse fell, it's been law that nothing may fly into the garden. Not even them. They keep watch from the great wall that encircles Eedn. You must go through the gate. If you fly anywhere near the wall, you'll be attacked without question."

"Not just that," Iris added, "but the garden itself is enclosed with trellises above. The sunlight may get in for the plants, but nothing else. Not even Sprites may come through."

"I understand that," Thane muttered.

"What do you suggest?" Isayas asked. "We can't be that far."

"We're not," Phillipe said. "Only an hour at a slow trot." He looked up at Eirin, his horn pulsing white with flashes of the rainbow, similar to his skin. "I suggest Eirin ride Iris. The rest of us will surround them, and you all will surround us. We're not skilled as warriors, but we'll be one more thing between the enemy and Eirin." He looked at Drystan, whose scales were heating so fast that Eirin would have to get off soon if he continued.

"I know this goes against instinct," Phillipe told him, "but you'll be serving Eirin by protecting her. There have been recent sightings of Manticores often in this area. We just didn't realize they had come so close. A Dragon will be our best hope at surviving."

Drystan tried to turn his head to look back at her, so Eirin slid off his shoulder and put her hand on his thick, scaled forearm.

"They're right," she said, forcing what she hoped was an encouraging smile. "You'll be a lot more lethal without me." She gave him a light punch. "Besides, you'll be itching to take on the enemy. And you know it."

To her surprise, he pressed his large forehead against hers, managing not to poke her with any of his spikes. Eirin froze for a brief second before putting her hand up and patting his neck.

"Keep me safe," she whispered. Guilt tried to wash over her as she charged him with this. As if she had to remind him. His whole life now revolved around keeping her safe. But now that she better understood the Dragon within him, she was beginning to see that the Dragon had more base desires than Drystan's Human nature. The last thing he needed was the distraction his Human mind was likely to create. And Eirin wasn't unaware of her influence over the Dragon. If she gave him charge over Drystan's thoughts, he would rule with an iron fist until his mission was carried out, or she ordered him to do otherwise. And though she was loath to exercise that power, Eirin was more loath to watch him die.

"We need to go. Now." Iris approached Eirin. Thane knelt and helped Eirin mount the Unicorn's back.

"I've never ridden a horse before," Eirin said, looking down at her mount with sudden doubt.

"That's good," Iris said with a snort. "Because I'm not a horse."

The other Unicorns were already gathering around them in a tight bunch, which was then surrounded by Eirin's friends. Drystan took the lead.

"The closest gate is on the south side," Phillipe called to the front. "We need to make our way due west."

No one spoke as they began to trot. Eirin wasn't sure which was louder. The silence from the forest around them or the noise of the dozens of hooves and other Atharrach feet against the ground. Still, in the sporadic light of the moon, which had risen as they'd talked, they ventured west. Brighter than the moon, however, was the magic that pulsed brightly from within Eirin's friends and the Unicorns, and Eirin was glad as she often was that no one else could see the magic but her. The brilliance of their magic would be a dead giveaway for sure.

The first few minutes were torturous. But eventually, Eirin began to breathe a little easier. They had made it five minutes without being attacked.

Ten minutes.

Half an hour.

And then they saw it, and Eirin's heart nearly leaped into her throat. The great wall was as Isayas had described. Made of columns of thick, rounded stones stacked higher than the Citadel was tall, with rows of solid wood between, all covered in green, furry moss, the garden walls towered over everything around them, blocking out any moonlight that made it through the thick clouds.

Eirin jerked her head to her left. At the same time, Iris tensed up beneath her. Eirin's Human eyes never adjusted to the night the way her friends' did, but she didn't need to make out the creature's shape to know where it was. She could see the Manticores' lights from a distance. It was strange, though. They were a distance off yet, but there was another sound coming from the nearby brush. And as she listened, a tidbit of information she'd learned back at the Citadel returned to her.

"Basilisks are in the grass! Don't look at them!" she screamed.

"How are we supposed to fight them if we can't look at them?" Thane called, his voice thick and tight, but before Eirin could answer, Iris and the other Unicorns broke into a sprint. It was all Eirin could do to grasp Iris's mane and hold on for her life.

"She's here!" a harsh, gravelly voice tore through the night. "The Human is with the Unicorns!" Eirin couldn't see the speaker well, but she could see the red light of his spiked tail.

The Unicorns drove on faster, and Eirin could feel the fear thicken the air. But they weren't alone. Her friends were close. Dark shadows lit by familiar lights encircled them. But then she looked ahead once more. Where was–

A river of fire streamed down from the sky, and animal screams made Eirin's hair stand on end. Drystan turned and flew at them again, Callispa silhouetted on his back as he did.

"Stop!" Qeb shouted from the front of the pack where Drystan had been only moments before. The Unicorns came to such an abrupt halt that Eirin nearly flew off Iris's back.

When she caught her balance, Eirin realized that their way was blocked. Red lights dotted the shadows.

"Give us the Human," the gravelly voice said, though this time, it sounded out of breath, "and we *won't* release the Basilisks."

"Eirin," Thane said in a low voice from somewhere to her left, "why can't we look at the Basilisks?"

"Their gaze is poisonous," Eirin said as low as she dared. If he had been paying attention at the Citadel, he would know this.

"To kill them, you have to cut off their heads. And to do that, you have to be impossibly fast."

"Shut up!" the gravelly voice snapped. "No talking unless it's to me!" Several low growls sounded from the ground.

Eirin had studied Basilisks intensely at the Citadel, which was unusual. She usually studied Atharrachs, and Basilisks weren't Atharrachs. But they were some of the most dangerous animals in all of Solevar. Only four feet in length, much like a snake with the scaled legs of a bird, they had reddish-blackened crowns of horns on their heads. Their red eyes were so poisonous that, if one made direct eye contact, that person would be dead within an hour. The Manticores, for some reason, had learned to tame them long ago. But not even they could control the Basilisks in groups of more than three.

Where was Drystan? Fear flamed in Eirin's chest for both Drystan and her friends. The Manticores wouldn't hurt her. But the others...

"Leave us be!" she screamed. It came out so high-pitched that even she barely understood herself. So she tried again.

"We're going to Iilaedin! Let us go to the garden!"

"I don't think so, Human." The gravelly voice laughed. "No Human has been able to fix the Time Stones. But you'll fetch a high price from people who think you can."

"Stand down and call off your beasts," Qeb growled. Eirin knew he had his war hammer in one hand and his sword in the other.

"Or what?" another gravelly voice asked. "You'll sic your Dragon on us?"

"They'll sic their Wizard on you," Isayas called as he walked with his staff toward the front. He pointed the end with the gem at the Manticores.

"You can't stop all of us," the first Manticore's reply cut through the night with a growl. "We have you surrounded." He scoffed. "Unless you want to accidentally hurt your friends as well."

"No, but I can make life quite miserable for some of you," Isayas retorted.

Fear prickled all over Eirin's skin as she wondered again where Drystan was.

"My guess," the first voice said, as if answering her unspoken question, "is that your Dragon didn't pay attention to how close he is to the garden." It chuckled.

"Mighty good aim those Griffins have," the second added.

"So they do," a deep rolling voice called out from the right. Eirin and the others looked up to see the wall suddenly covered with the forms of Griffins. Orange light burst out from their wings, originating, Eirin knew, where their wings met their backs, around the shoulder blades. Their bows were held taut with flaming arrows nocked and pointed down at the Manticores.

The Manticores hissed and raised their tails.

A wave of fire rained down from the sky. Eirin whipped her head again around just in time to see Drystan fly over them, a shadow descending from the night, his gold and blue flame streaming from the heart. Screams went up again from the Manticores as fiery arrows flamed down from the Griffins on the wall. The Unicorns drew closer together, and Eirin's friends tightened their ring around the herd.

Though it felt like years, the conflict was over in less than a minute. Several Manticores ran away with their Basilisks, but between Drystan's flames and the Griffins' arrows, the area was soon nothing but charred grass and trees.

"Come!" a Griffin called, gliding down from the wall and landing in front of Qeb. "The gate is close by. You have no time to lose."

Chapter Eight

Drystan landed hard as soon as the Manticores and their pets were on the run.

"Careful," Callispa cautioned as he tilted dangerously to the side. "You'll be off-balance until your wing heals."

"Thanks," Drystan groaned as she slid off his back. Though he knew it was impossible for him to have been truly burned by the Griffins' flaming arrows, his right wing felt as though it were on fire. Most likely because it had a gaping wound that nearly went all the way through.

Drystan had smelled the Basilisks and Manticores just before the others had seen them. Callispa, who had been near, had seen him stop and had stopped too.

"What are you doing?" she'd demanded.

"I'm going to fly over so I can flame them," Drystan had murmured, preparing himself to take flight off the ground. He'd been getting better, no longer needing a cliff to jump off of as he had even a few weeks before. But it was still difficult and took all his concentration.

"You heard the Unicorns!" Callispa hissed. "The Griffins will shoot you down! We're right next to the wall!"

"I'll stay low!" he'd argued. "They're going to need someone from above." When she gave him another look, he scoffed. "Have you ever fought a Manticore?"

Callispa had glared at him a moment longer before letting out a huff. "Very well. But I'm coming with you."

Drystan had been thankful for her once he was in the air. He was getting much better at flying, but she had been assigned his trainer for a reason. She still knew far more than he did about his own wings and how to use them.

He didn't regret his decision to aid his friends from above. He even avoided the Griffins' initial attack once the Manticores made their move, but just as he'd been about to let forth his first stream of flame, he felt something sharp hit his wing. Then many sharp pangs in the same place.

A line of Griffins stood on the wall, so high they had been invisible when he'd taken off from the ground. They must have hit him when he was looking down.

"Not me!" Drystan had tried to call in a low voice. "The Manticores! They're after the Human!"

"There's no flying near the garden!" one of the Griffins had called. "Now land, or we will force you to!"

"There is a Human being attacked by a pack of Manticores!" Drystan shouted, no longer trying to remain stealthy. "They're going to kill her! And all of your Unicorns!" Then, without giving them a chance to respond, he'd darted off toward his friends, who were still running.

He managed to get several good streams of flame aimed at the enemy on the ground before having to fly higher once again to look for enemy reinforcements. As he did, he felt another sharp pain in his right wing, but this was ten times worse than the first. He looked back at the wall to see multiple Griffins nocking more arrows.

"Drystan!" Callispa had screamed, clinging to his back. "Land! Land!"

"Why won't you land?" a new Griffin, larger than all the others, shouted from the wall.

"Because my friends are being attacked by Manticores!" Drystan roared.

Another Griffin ran up to the first and whispered something in his ear. Drystan was breathing heavily by now, still flying but struggling more by the minute to remain in the air. He could just leave, of course. But that wouldn't help his friends. The Griffins would just target him again.

"We have men on it," the larger Griffin called. "But you cannot fly here. It's forbidden and has been since the curse fell."

"You don't understand!" Drystan shouted. "The Manticores are attacking a *Human*!"

The Griffin in charge stared at him for an unfathomable second. "A Human?" he echoed. He glanced down at the ground, which was difficult to see in the shadow of the wall, even with enhanced eyes. "Then...go. Go!" the Griffin shouted.

Drystan didn't have to be told twice. If he got to speak with the Griffin commander again, however, he would have a word with him about his underlings' listening skills.

When he'd caught up with the others, the battle was fairly short. Less than two minutes later, their attackers were gone, and it seemed as if no one had been lost.

"Shift back," Callispa said in a low voice now as Drystan's friends regrouped themselves. "They'll want to speak with you." She glanced up at him. "No need to flash your family crest."

Dragons, Drystan had learned, had particular markings on their backs that denoted their family lines. Each Dragon was born with one. And unfortunately for Drystan, his marking identified him as part of the once-royal family.

It didn't endear him much to the people of Solevar, to say the least.

"They won't hurt Eirin," Callispa continued, tugging on his left forearm. "Make yourself as non-threatening as possible, and they *might* let you stay with her."

Drystan glared down at her before nodding. As much as the Dragon inside hissed at switching to his more vulnerable form, Callispa was right. It was unlikely they would let him enter once they knew whose blood flowed through his veins, if they didn't already. No need to make the situation even more difficult than it already was.

Besides, his right wing was really starting to bother him.

"Drystan!" a familiar voice called from up ahead as he shifted forms. As soon as he was in his Human form again, Drystan looked up to see Eirin running toward him. Reassurance filled him as he noted that she was as healthy and whole as when he'd left her.

The relief on her face was replaced by alarm as she neared him. She stopped and stared at the front of his right shoulder, and she gasped. He followed her gaze to see sticky blood staining the shoulder of his shirt.

"What happened?" she demanded, looking from him to Callispa.

"I'd like to know that, too," demanded a much deeper voice from behind her. Qeb appeared in his Human form as well. Fury was written all over his face as he came closer to examine the wound.

"Nevermind that," Eirin said, taking Drystan's left arm and pulling him toward the gate. "The Unicorns can help."

Callispa, who had been standing at Drystan's left, put her hand on his lower back and gently pushed him forward. In normal circumstances, the literal push and pull of the girls would have amused Qeb, but he was a thundercloud now that Drystan was injured, and probably would be until he could, as he called it, redeem himself in battle.

"Drystan's injured!" Eirin called as they neared the crowd of Griffins and Unicorns standing around a towering metal gate that was built into the side of the wall. "We need to get him inside so you can heal him," she said to Phillipe as she came to stand beside him.

"I'm sorry," the tall Griffin pushed his way toward Eirin. "A son of Kamon cannot enter the sacred garden."

"How do you know who he is?" Eirin snapped, putting her hands on her hips. If Drystan hadn't been in so much pain, he would have shaken his head and sighed. The sight of the girl glowering up at the Atharrach twice her size reminded him too much of the time she'd slapped a Hibagon and gotten herself stuck in the healing room as a result.

Although, that had been largely his fault as well.

"Eirin," Drystan said in a low voice. "We need to get you out of the open. I can go around."

"I'll go with you," Callispa quickly added.

If Eirin had been tempted to listen to him before, Drystan could see the resolve to have her way burn in her eyes now. He sighed.

She whirled back around and faced the Griffin again. "Why can't he come in?"

"It's not personal," the Griffin said with a sigh, his great wings slumping as he rubbed his eyes.

Eirin tended to have that effect on people.

"This garden is the one sure source of food we have left for the people in this part of Solevar," he continued. "I saw his mark as he flew. That man has tainted blood within his veins. Bringing the sin of Kamon within the sacred gardens–"

"Will help me get to Iilaedin faster!" Eirin interrupted. "And *Drystan* didn't curse Solevar. Kamon did."

"She's correct," Isayas said. Everyone seemed to jump as he appeared in their midst. Drystan didn't know where he had been, but he could only guess that the Wizard had been laying spells to protect them as they bickered in front of the gate. "He's sworn to protect her as she ventures to Iilaedin. It is only because of him that she's made it this far."

"This is ridiculous," Iris snapped, shifting into her Human form as well. "Can't you see he's injured?"

"I wonder who could have done that?" Qeb growled.

The Griffin leader looked appropriately disconcerted as Iris came over to him. "Phillipe," she called.

Phillipe, still in Atharrach form, bent his head to Drystan's shoulder. Drystan steeled himself for pain as the sharp horn touched his wound. To his surprise, however, he felt nothing but cool relief, similar to the sensation of aloe to a burn. But even better.

At the same time, exhaustion nearly overwhelmed him. He nearly swayed as Phillipe withdrew his horn. Qeb grabbed him by the other shoulder and steadied him.

"You'll feel tired for several hours," Iris said apologetically. "It's a natural part of the elixir. It encourages people to sleep as they heal."

"I told you," the Griffin said, looking down at Eirin. "It's not personal. We feed people from Korach to the base of the Northern Mountains. Kamon was the bringer of the curse. If we bring that within these sacred walls–"

"I don't think you heard me correctly," Eirin snapped. "Drystan. Is *not*. His ancestor."

"Eirin," Drystan said, touching her shoulder, but Eirin shook him off.

"If you won't let him in, I'm not going in either." She folded her arms and raised her chin defiantly. "And you can explain to everyone within those walls why the curse will take..." She paused and looked back at Iris. "How long does it take to go around these walls?"

"At least three days," Iris said, sharing a look with her husband. "Probably four at your rate."

"And if we die," Eirin raised her brows, "you can tell them why."

"You seem convinced you can break this curse," the Griffin growled. Qeb, Drystan, Thane, and Nuru all took a step closer, and in response, the band of Griffins behind their leader straightened and drew closer as well, but Eirin kept her eyes locked with the Griffin's.

"I am."

"That's a lot of hubris, considering how many Humans died trying to do it before."

Eirin gave him a wicked smile. "That's because I have something they didn't."

Drystan cleared his throat, but Eirin ignored him. After escaping Rangvald's fortress, she had told her companions about the artifact she carried, so her friends now knew as well. They had all agreed to keep it secret from any strangers they might encounter. But it seemed tonight that she felt staying with him worth the gamble.

Why was that? Why did she push him away daily but cling to him in the face of any impending separation? Was it because she truly wanted him with her? Or was it because she was married to the idea that he was necessary to break the curse?

"Well, Griffin," Isayas said gruffly. "What say you?"

The Griffin raised his eyes to look at the Wizard. "You're not going to enchant me to give you what you wish?"

Isayas rolled his eyes. "Could I? Yes. But it would take too much time and cause too much trouble, and frankly, you're not worth that amount of trouble." He paused, and in a more placating tone said, "But we're on the same side, are we not?"

The Griffin let out a gusty sigh, then shook his head. "I'll regret this, I'm sure," he muttered before addressing them in a louder voice. "You may all enter the wall. If I'm convinced by your story," he gave a pointed look at Eirin, "I'll consider asking the Nymphs permission to let you cross through the garden."

Eirin looked as though she wanted to argue, but Drystan squeezed her hand. She looked back up at him. No words were exchanged, but Drystan could almost see her thoughts as they whizzed through her head. Finally, she huffed and nodded.

"Very well. But it needs to be in private. Away from any other listening ears."

"We won't be continuing on with you," Iris said, taking Eirin's hands.

"I wish you would," Eirin gave her a weary smile.

"I wish we could, too. But as we told your friends, we would draw too much attention." She nodded at Eirin's bag. "Use your drops. And though we can't travel the way you do—Unicorns aren't as hardy as your friends—we'll do our best to keep ears and eyes on you as well as we can."

She drew Eirin into her arms, and Eirin hugged her tightly back, looking for a moment like a lost little girl. Drystan was reminded of how fiercely Eirin had told him once that she missed her family. She hadn't spoken much of them in recent days, but then, neither had anyone else. Drystan hadn't, to be sure. They needed to focus on the task at hand, and thinking of the parents he had found and then lost was far too distracting.

Once the Unicorns were gone, the Griffin leader having given orders for their protection until they were safely hidden within the surrounding trees, the Griffin turned to Eirin and gave orders for the gate to be opened. The metal creaked as the gate, three times taller than Drystan in his Dragon form, swung open. Drystan placed himself on Eirin's right, and Nuru walked to her left. If Eirin was frightened, she didn't show it. She strode in with head held high.

* * *

The gate clanged shut behind them the moment they were all inside the wall. Drystan glanced back through the bars to see a number of glowing eyes peeking out at them from the forest. He looked down to see Eirin looking back, too.

"What are they?" he asked. He might have better eyes for the night, but Eirin's Human ability to see magic wasn't necessarily a gift he envied.

She shivered slightly before facing the front again. "You don't want to know."

"Where do we go from here?" Drystan asked, looking around what seemed to be an antechamber, an unwelcoming space that seemed to have been built to let visitors in through the gate but no further. There was nothing but several piles of weapons on the floor and several closed doors. Doors?

Only then Did Drystan understand. Everyone who worked in or around the garden lived within the wall. The wall itself was a fortress.

"Wait a moment, and you might see," the Griffin growled. The Dragon inside hissed, but Drystan forced himself to stay calm. Tensions were high. Making them worse wouldn't help anyone.

Everyone blinked and squinted when a door was opened in front of them, and light poured out. They were herded through the door, this one much smaller than the gate they'd entered through, into a wide room with many tables and several hearths. Men and a few women sat at the tables in various groups, eating and drinking as several women scurried about serving food and what looked like ale.

"The tavern," the Griffin grumbled. But now that they were in the lighted room, Drystan could see that he had shifted to his Human form, and he didn't look unlike Qeb. Broad-shouldered with swarthy skin and long black hair woven into tight braids. His dark eyes were a little too sharp for Drystan's taste. This man had shed blood. He was an ally, of course. Drystan knew that. But the Dragon's instinct to hide Eirin away from someone so dangerous was strong.

"Who lives here?" Eirin asked. "I thought it would be more of a military installation."

"Only people who contribute to the growing, harvesting, and protection of the garden, or who help run the entire establishment," the Griffin answered as he led them through the room toward a table in the back. "When the curse fell, we were hit by waves of people who wished to take shelter within our walls. We tried to take them, but the food production stuttered, and we had to become severe with who we allowed to stay." He glanced at Drystan. "Or pass through." He indicated the table in the corner of the room. "Sit here while I go see to something." He waved, and a woman came over, carrying a tray of drinks. "Get them supper," he said. "I'll be back soon." Then he glanced at Eirin. "Get her extra."

Eirin had removed one of her little bottles—the one for food—and was examining it closely. She looked worlds better than she had two days ago before the Unicorns had arrived, but she was still far too thin.

They were so hungry that hardly anyone spoke once their food arrived. Drystan could feel Qeb's frustrated gaze on his shoulder throughout the whole meal, and he knew that Callispa and Eirin were trading wary looks over the table but trying not to be obvious about it. Thane kept trying to catch Nuru's eye, but as usual, Nuru was ignoring him completely.

Drystan suddenly found himself hoping the Griffin would come back sooner rather than later.

His wish was granted more quickly than he'd anticipated. The Griffin returned and looked pointedly at the spot between Qeb and Drystan, but Qeb pretended not to notice, drinking his ale slowly as if the Griffin didn't exist. Thane, who was sitting to Qeb's left, scooted over, and the Griffin grunted his thanks as he sat.

"What's your name?" Eirin asked as the Griffin waved his hand at the serving woman.

"Stavros," he said.

"Who are you tied to?" Qeb asked in a gruff voice.

Stavros stopped and sized Qeb up before answering. "This garden," he finally said.

Eirin paused, a bite halfway to her mouth. She set it down. "But I thought Griffins only tied themselves to people."

"Usually, we do." Stavros frowned and took a swig of his drink. "My friends and I were young when the curse fell. We hadn't even reached full maturity, and my parents were adamant that I not tie myself down until I had found a mate to go with me." He sighed. "We were from one of the largest Griffin lines in the kingdom. Well organized and well-trained. Royalty and nobility alike came to us to find companions for their children from a young age. I received several offers, but my parents wouldn't hear of it."

"Do you regret that?" Eirin asked softly.

He studied her, his brow furrowing slightly. Then he looked down at his mug. "Sometimes," he finally said. "But then again, if I had, this garden probably wouldn't have survived."

Drystan could tell Qeb was fascinated, despite disliking the other Griffin. He was watching out of the corner of his eye while pretending not to.

"We lived not far from here," Stavros continued. "My father was tied to a wealthy Human judge, and my mother tied herself to the judge's wife. They both died, however, when the curse fell, so we flocked to the gardens, as did countless others. Many of my traveling companions died, however, before they even reached the garden. And within hours of arriving, we could tell the garden would be trampled in the chaos if something wasn't done. The Nymphs who cared for and lived in the garden were beside themselves with angst." He paused and took another drink before continuing.

"My father, having been freed from his bond by the judge's death, sought to organize the refugees. There were several families of Giants who had arrived, and he directed them to build this wall around the garden, something to protect the gardens and the people who took care of them. Then he oversaw the testing of the refugees. Everyone who lived within the wall had to be able to contribute something, with the exception of those who were in the infirmary. The Unicorns cared for them, but by the time several months had passed..." He sighed and shook his head.

"Such organizing and directing doesn't seem as though it would come naturally to a Griffin," Eirin said. "A Dragon, I would think, would have been preferable."

Stavros let out a humorless laugh. "Aye, a Dragon would have been preferable. My father hated every minute of it. Both my parents' hearts were in shreds after losing the family they'd promised to protect." He paused. "I suppose...I suppose it felt to them as though they were still doing their best. They hadn't been able to save the judge's family from the poison. But they saw countless others who were suffering from what would be the same fate. And it was their way of trying to continue what would have been their purpose, had the judge's family lived."

"Why didn't a Dragon take charge?" Thane asked.

"Many of the Dragons died before the curse ever fell,"

Callispa said, answering before the Griffin could. "A war that took place several years before had wiped many of them out."

Thane's eyes widened. "Who were they fighting? Each other?" He looked around, eyes wide. "I mean, aren't Dragons nearly impervious to most enemies?"

Drystan could understand Thane's skepticism. Dragons were nearly impossible to bring down. He'd been injured less than an hour ago. But even with his injury, sustained from multiple attacks by an enemy he was trying to befriend, hadn't kept him from putting about a dozen Manticores to death. And if he had desired to kill the Griffins? They wouldn't have touched him.

Nuru scoffed. "No, genius. Only some Dragons died in the war. But when they died, their mates died, too."

"Why did their *mates* die?" Thane asked.

Nuru glared at him for a long moment, then sniffed. "Unlike some races, Dragons aren't able to forget *their* allegiances."

"You mentioned friends earlier," Drystan said loudly in an attempt to rescue the conversation before Nuru tackled Thane from across the table.

"There were lots of Griffin families in the vicinity," Stavros said, watching Nuru warily. "My father organized us into groups to protect the garden. We've been here ever since."

"So..." Eirin said slowly, "you somehow transferred your loyalties to the garden and its inhabitants. Is that right?"

"I suppose you could say that. Although," he sighed, "it's more like drinking milk when what you really crave is meat." He waved to the high-walled room around them. "This isn't the way things were meant to be. None of it is." Before any of them could respond, he looked straight at Eirin and stood. "But enough of that. You promised me answers. And now that you're done eating, I think it's high time you give them."

Eirin nodded and pushed away from the table. "Very well. We had a deal."

Drystan stood as well and followed her to the door Stavros was now unlocking. Qeb made a move to follow, but Drystan waved him back. He would get a tongue-lashing from his best friend later, but he had a better sense of politics than Qeb did. There was no way Stavros would agree to be in the same room with a Human, a Dragon, and another Griffin without allies of his own. And he was sure that whatever Eirin had to say *needed* to stay hidden.

Stavros had the door half open by the time he saw Drystan. "Let me guess." He rolled his eyes. "This will include him as well."

"You are correct," Eirin said primly.

"Stavros–" one of the Griffins, who had been standing nearby, began, but Stavros waved him off.

"I get the feeling," he said, staring at Eirin as she passed through the door, "that I should worry more about you than him."

Eirin gave him a smug smile in return. "Do you find us amusing?"

He just shook his head as he closed the door behind them. "Not many Humans left around here. Much less one who's attached herself to a Dragon. You have to admit that would pique anyone's curiosity."

"Naturally, you're all agog."

He shook his head and gave her a dry smile. "I'm a hundred and eighteen years old, and I can say with absolute confidence that this is a story I never thought I'd hear."

Chapter Nine

The room wasn't large, and its ceiling was so low that if Drystan had jumped, he would have bumped his head on it. Based on the sound of footsteps coming from above, he could only guess the Giants had built several levels above them. There was a couch so worn that feathers were coming out of the cushions, a square table, and three chairs. A small hearth sat opposite the door, its flames just high enough to light the room.

"I'm going to be completely honest," Stavros said as he locked the door behind them. "Being locked in a small room with the most hated Dragon in Solevar makes me more than slightly uncomfortable."

Drystan hid the urge to wince. He was used to being disliked on first sight. He was incapable, it seemed, of being differentiated from his great-grandfather before people got to know him. But the most hated Dragon in Solevar? That was a new low.

"If you're finished insulting my protector," Eirin snapped, "I'd be happy to tell you what you want to hear."

"Not an insult," Stavros said with a shrug. "Just the truth." He gestured to the couch. "Make yourself comfortable, Human."

"Thank you," Eirin said, sitting on it and reclining against the back. Drystan had to resist the urge to tell her to close her eyes and sleep. If he was feeling exhausted from the Unicorns healing his arm, he couldn't imagine how tired she must be after being brought back from the brink of death and then running for her life from Manticores and Basilisks. She'd taken another drop of elixir with her supper just a few moments ago. Would that make her sleepy as well?

Eirin interrupted Drystan's internal fussing. "You want to know why I'm confident I can break the curse, do you not?"

"Yes." Stavros leaned back in the chair he'd plunked himself in, and he crossed his arms over his chest. "No offense, but you're not exactly the hardiest Human I've ever seen. And none of those who went to Iilaedin changed a single thing, no matter how big or strong they were."

"That is because it's not about being big or strong," Eirin said. She pulled the leather cord out from beneath her shirt, where she kept it hidden at all times. At the bottom of the cord was tied a broken stone.

Stavros squinted at the stone for a moment before leaping out of his chair so fast it banged on the floor. Stumbling backward, he pressed himself against the wall, his large chest heaving deeply as he kept his eyes trained on the stone.

Drystan was instantly in front of Eirin, his vision turning red and the fire flaming in his chest, but there was no need. The Griffin seemed to be trying to get as far away from her as the small room would allow.

"Is that what I think it is?" he gasped.

Eirin gently pushed Drystan to the side. Even in his half-Dragon form, senses and instincts pulsing, the feel of her small hand on his skin was distracting. "If you're thinking it's the half of the foreign stone that broke off in the Time Stones circle, then yes, it is," Eirin said, tucking the stone back in her shirt.

He stayed pressed against the wall for a moment, sending Drystan a frenzied look, then looking back at Eirin. "But how..." His voice trembled.

"It was my mother's," Eirin continued in the same even tone. "It's been passed down through my family for generations, since the fall of Solevar. None of us have been able to return to remove its other half, however, until now."

Stavros swallowed hard, then slowly, slowly peeled himself from the wall. "I'm... I'm sorry," he said, righting his tipped chair, his hands visibly shaking as he did. "I just wasn't expecting that."

"Understandably," Eirin said with a nod. "But you asked on what basis I had the confidence...or the audacity, perhaps," she smiled, "to think I could end the curse. This fragment is not only part of the foreign stone that's stuck in the Time Stones, but it also tells me where the other half of the fragment is, something no other Seer before me has been able to locate. Which means," she said, sitting straighter, "it's the key to breaking the curse. Well, and along with him." She nodded at Drystan.

Drystan bumped her boot with his. She may be right that he was also part of breaking the curse. He did have the founding king's blood after all. But that wouldn't necessarily endear him to people who already wished him dead.

Unfortunately, Stavros's sharp eyes didn't miss the interaction, and now they narrowed at Drystan.

"Are you aiming to retake the throne?" Stavros looked back at Eirin. "Because if he is, people aren't going to be happy."

"I'm here to protect Eirin," Drystan said stiffly. "I didn't even find out who I was until after this insanity had all been set in motion less than a year ago."

"I'll be blunt," Eirin said.

As if she was ever anything else.

"Drystan has no desire to be king," Eirin continued. "He

never did. I'm the one who has told him what he needs to do to break the curse."

"You mean *he's* a part of this?"

"Do you think I chose to be born into Kamon's line?" Drystan scoffed, his patience beginning to run thin.

"You can embrace it or not, but there are things that must be set in motion if the curse is ever to be broken," Eirin said, her voice hard. Then she leaned forward slightly. "Do you think Seers see only the stones? Or has it occurred to you that we might learn other things as well?"

In the Griffin's defense, Eirin had learned what she knew of Oreck's line from meticulous research back in Mhaedin and asking Isayas. None of it, to his knowledge, had been revealed to her in a vision. And as to her question, most Seers could only See using the Time Stones. Few could see memories in everyday objects the way Eirin could.

Not that Stavros needed to know that.

"Now," Eirin said, her voice calm but commanding. "Will you let us go through the garden, or will you delay our journey longer? Because I can tell you this." Her words grew low and hard. "I have Seen more destruction than you can imagine. And every day we delay is one day closer to the finalization of the curse. You're worried about providing food for the people now? You won't need to be, soon enough."

Stavros's jaw hardened. "And why is that?"

Eirin shrugged. "Because there won't be anyone left to feed."

In the dark it was difficult to tell, but Drystan was rather sure the Griffin paled.

"Very well," he finally said after seeming to recover his speech. "You can go through the garden."

"What about the food?" Drystan couldn't help asking. "Aren't you afraid I'll spoil it?"

The Griffin ran a hand down the back of his neck and let

out a deep sigh. "In truth, the food is already starting to fall to the curse. The fruit has begun to have thorns in it, and many of the vegetables and grains come up rotten. Not all. We would starve if it was all. And the Nymphs have come up with ways to pluck out the thorns, but..." He shook his head at the ground, then looked up at Eirin. "This is all on your shoulders now." He glanced at Drystan and gave him a wry smile. "Both of you, it would seem."

He motioned for them to go to the door. Eirin and Drystan stood and joined him there, but before he could open it, Eirin turned.

"I have one more question," she said.

"And that is?"

"Do the people still believe?"

Stavros frowned. "Believe in what?"

"The Time Keeper," she said.

He snorted. "With all that's going on in the world around them, they'd have to be blind fools to disbelieve. Now how they feel about him... that's another question entirely."

* * *

It was decided that because they were shaving several days' journey by walking directly through the garden, Drystan's group could afford a few hours' rest.

"You can journey through the garden during the day," Stavros had told them. "The trees are thick enough that they shade anyone beneath them from the sun."

The men were to sleep in a common room, and the girls were led off to the Nymphs' personal quarters. The two parties were a bit farther away from each other than Drystan would have preferred, but Eirin looked so exhausted that he swallowed his objections and nodded when she looked at him questioningly.

"The Nymphs will take better care of her than we will," Isayas said gruffly, watching the girls leave as well.

Drystan nodded, then forced himself to turn and join Qeb and Thane as they spread their sleeping rolls out on the floor in the corner of the men's common room that they'd been directed to. Sleeping with large groups of people had never bothered Drystan, as no student received his own room in the Citadel. Unfortunately, it was a room shared with the Griffins who were off-duty, which meant Qeb's hackles were already up.

"I thought you'd feel safer with us sleeping here," Drystan murmured to his friend. "These are your people."

"These aren't my people," Qeb said, watching those around them.

"No?" Thane snorted. "Who are your people then?"

Qeb gave him a look of disgust. "Not Centaurs, if that's what you're asking."

Thane sat back up. "And what is wrong with Centaurs?"

"Maybe it's not all Centaurs," Qeb smiled slightly. "Just the one I know."

Drystan smiled to himself as Thane gaped and began to protest.

"If you don't shut up, I'll put a silencing curse on all of you until morning," Isayas growled.

Drystan lay his own head down and closed his eyes. He meant to go over the plan one more time in his mind before falling asleep, but whether it was the Unicorn elixir still lingering in his body or the sheer need to escape, he was unconscious before he could finish the thought.

Chapter Ten

Eirin woke feeling as rested as she had the day before, prior to the disastrous run-in with the Manticores and Basilisks. Had that only been yesterday? She'd only been asleep for four or five hours, but she felt as though she'd rested for days.

Perhaps just as luxurious as the Unicorn elixir Nuru had helped her apply before going to sleep was sleeping in a real bed. The Nymphs had doted on her, many of them stopping at her bedside to run a long, graceful finger down her face. Their pale green skin had a cool, waxy feel to it, not unpleasant, and their dark green eyes were full of a longing Eirin knew words couldn't express.

What did Nymphs long for? What was the paradise they longed to return to? A garden where they could grow life-bringing food that didn't try to poison them or choke them with thorns?

Like the Nymphs' healing room in Mhaedin, the garden's infirmary was underground, and everything one could possibly need was growing directly out of the walls. The beds were made of ivy and clover, and the walls were covered in mushrooms and crystals of various colors and sizes, and there were even a few vines that hung heavy with fruit.

Eirin knew they were in a hurry, but she lay in bed a few minutes longer as Nuru and Callispa still slept. There were no windows in the room, but she knew in her heart that it was day. The chill of the night was gone, and she could feel the sun calling to her soul. Nearly every vision she saw when she touched various forest objects involved the sun. And she was getting rather tired of experiencing it only secondhand.

Or maybe, after getting spoiled in Mhaedin by all their canvas covers and being able to walk about during the day, her heart was unable to forget what it was like to walk, so to speak, in the light.

"Good morning," one of the chief Nymphs said, stopping at Eirin's bed with a smile. "I thought you might be hungry." She handed Eirin a plate of food. Eirin's mouth watered as the fusion of scents hit her nose. Fluffy eggs, thick slices of ham, and steaming bread, yellow with butter. They hadn't eaten like this since they'd first arrived at Mhaedin.

Eirin's conscience smote her as she realized no one else in the room was eating that way either.

"Don't feel guilty," the Nymph said kindly. Her eyes crinkled at the corners, and there were white streaks through her green hair. "If you're going to reach Iilaedin, you're going to need all the strength you can get." She gently tapped Eirin's nose. "So eat."

Knowing they were right, Eirin paused only to add a drop of the Unicorn elixir, then she ate faster than she'd previously thought Humanly possible.

"Hungry much?" Nuru asked from the next bed over, her mouth curled up in a dry smile. "Keep eating like that, and Drystan will have to enlist help carrying you to the capital."

"Shut up," Eirin said, taking a big bite of her bread. This made Nuru laugh, something Eirin wouldn't have thought her capable of a year ago. But then again, their entire world had turned upside down since last spring. Maybe, Eirin thought as she scraped the sides of her plate, not all change was quite so bad.

Of course, not all change was good, either. Callispa, who was in the bed on Eirin's other side, might have once smiled and chided Nuru for saying ridiculous things. But this morning, she simply pushed her food around her plate, eating mechanically as she did.

Unfortunately, Eirin was pretty sure she knew what Callispa was thinking about. And it wasn't something either of them wanted to address. They needed to save Solevar. Petty rivalries would have to wait until later.

As soon as the girls had eaten their fill, the Nymphs set about preparing them for the next part of their journey. A bath was poured for Eirin, one which, Eirin was assured, contained some of the Nymphs' own Unicorn drops. Along with the drops, however, were floating bits of lavender, rose petals, and a generous helping of salts. As Eirin sank into the deep stone tub, the combination of smells that rose on the steam filled her nose and her lungs and threatened to put her back to sleep. She'd never felt anything so delightful, so enveloping in her whole life as the hot water that covered her completely. It was even better than the bath she'd had in Lady Seren's castle.

As she relaxed in the tub, wishing she could stay there for all eternity, the Nymphs unbraided her hair and began to wash it slowly and methodically. A mask of clay was rubbed all over her face, and when it had hardened, was washed off, making her feel as though she had a new body entirely.

"Where are Nuru and Callispa and the boys?" Eirin asked as a potent aloe was rubbed through her hair.

"They're all getting baths as well," the Nymph said.

"Do you treat all your guests as kings and queens?" Eirin laughed.

"No," the Nymph said evenly. "But if you're going to walk

through the garden, you'll need to be rid of as much contamination from the outside world as possible. You'll be receiving new clothing as well as new boots and new bags. What can be washed will be, and shall be stowed in your bags. What can't be washed will be destroyed." She glanced at Eirin's necklace but said nothing.

Eirin froze. "My map—"

"Was cleaned and is back in its home," the Nymph said with a smile.

Nuru and Callispa seemed just as relaxed and refreshed as Eirin felt when they were all reunited in one of the main halls within the wall. The clothes they'd been given were lighter than the ones they'd worn in Torbaine and even Mhaedin on the mountain. They were softer and breathed better, and Eirin decided that the Nymph's style of clothing was worlds more comfortable than any she had ever felt before.

Drystan, who had always kept impeccable hygiene, probably thanks to his perfectionist grandmother, appeared little altered when he joined them. Qeb's braids were shiny and neater than they had been, and even Isayas looked slightly less irritable than usual. Thane, however, came out scowling.

"I smell like a girl."

Nuru, who hadn't spared him more than a glance or two since leaving Mhaedin, snorted.

"Just because you got used to Centaur stink doesn't mean the rest of us have to." Qeb smirked.

"The bath I was fine with," Thane snapped. "It's the roses I object to. Have you ever heard of a Centaur that smells like roses?"

"The rose oil and the oil from the other flowers have created a thin covering for your skin that will help protect you from further contamination when you leave," the Nymph said patiently. "Now, if you'll follow me."

She led them down the hall. There were doors on each side, making the hall largely dark and difficult to see. Sometimes, however, doors on the left would be open, revealing shaded windows much like the ones in Mhaedin, allowing light to enter without worry about any direct beams. Various people passed them. Many sent them gazes but seemed either too afraid or too well trained to stop them or ask questions. Eirin counted many Nymphs, a number of Griffins, several Brownies, which wasn't surprising, as they were known for their gardening abilities, a Giant, three Pegasi, a Roc, two Thunderbirds, one Fae, and a White Hart.

"How did the garden come to be?" Eirin asked, having to walk fast to keep up with the Nymph's long, graceful strides. "Isayas said it existed before the curse fell."

"It did," the Nymphs said with a sad smile. "It was a gift from the Time Keeper to one of the early cloisters of Nymphs who chose to focus specifically on food-bearing trees with which to feed the hungry. So the Time Keeper gifted them this garden in which to continue their work." She turned left and opened the door into a smaller hall, and Eirin's party followed. She stopped in front of a large wooden door.

"Before you enter the garden, there are a few things you need to remember. First, you can eat any of the fruit you find. We have packed you as much food as can fit in your bags, but it would not be bad to save those. You're free to eat whatever you find as you pass through. Be on the lookout, however, for thorns."

As she spoke, Eirin was reminded of why Stavros, the large Griffin leader, had at first refused to let them pass through.

"This place was once a sanctum," the Nymph said softly, running her hand down the door frame. "But the curse has crept in even here." Then she cleared her throat. "The trees are old and large enough that if you stay close to their trunks, which are laid in straight rows, you should be able to travel throughout the day.

Rest if you need to, but remain no longer than you must." She paused. "Not to add to the burden already on your shoulders, but if this garden falls as the rest of Solevar is doing, the vast majority of the valley won't live to see the day you may or may not fix the Time Stones." She looked at Eirin.

Eirin nodded. She understood the crushing weight of responsibility the Nymphs were bearing. She bore it, too.

Then, to Eirin's surprise, a gentle smile came to the Nymph's thin face. "My final piece of advice," she said, "is that while you're in this place, enjoy this little piece of paradise. Let it strengthen and nourish you. Draw from its well of peace, small as it may be. May it sustain you as you face the long road ahead." With that, her small smile became a beam, and she swung open the door, light flooding the corridor. "Welcome to Eedn."

The sunlight wasn't direct, but it was bright enough to make Eirin blink, and for a moment, she couldn't see anything. But then her eyes adjusted, and as she entered the garden, she felt her breath flee.

When Isayas had said they would be visiting a garden, Eirin had pictured something akin to their gardens back in Torbaine. Not that she'd expected them to be the same, of course, but something similar, at least. There, they had raised box gardens in some areas of the cavern. In others, there were fields specifically planted with wheat or corn. Everything had its neat little corner of the cavern, and changing the quota was not allowed. But here...

The garden itself was so wide Eirin couldn't see the other side. All she could see were trees, countless trees everywhere. And while they had been planted in neat rows, each kind having its own section, no space was wasted. Their new shoes tread softly over stepping stones, which were raised so that they wouldn't step on the flowering strawberry plants or the thick mint leaves that carpeted the garden floor. Above them rose a dome so high its heights were impossible to see. It was latticed, though with what materials, Eirin couldn't see.

The trees rose up in straight rows, majestic and enormous compared to any fruit trees Eirin had seen in Torbaine or Mhaedin's fields. They were decorated with thousands of pieces of fruit, bursts of color against their varying shades of green leaves. Between the rows of towering trees ran rows of smaller bushes carrying other varieties of fruits. Blueberry, blackberry, raspberry, currants, goji berries, and at least half a dozen others Eirin didn't recognize.

Along the wall were trellises and what looked like a small river of soil, in which grew pumpkins, tomatoes, zucchinis, peas, and carrots, and in the distance, Eirin could see the golden stalks of wheat and the green of corn. Rice grew in little round ponds.

Even more awesome than the food itself, however, were the clouds that floated around within the dome. Gentle showers made the leaves flutter as they traveled from one side to the other, and several rainbows arched high in their wake.

"What is this place called again?" Thane whispered.

"Eedn," the Nymph said with a smile.

"Wait!" They turned, and their reverie was broken by Stavros's urgent tones. "I need to show you something!"

"Stavros!" the Nymph snapped at him as she jumped in his way.

"I'm not going in," he snapped back. Then he waved frantically for them to return. Eirin took one last look behind her, afraid that he would reveal some reason why they shouldn't venture into this paradise after all.

Once they were gathered back in the hallway, he gestured to Eirin. "The Dragon said you had a map."

Eirin obediently removed the map from its tube and opened it for him to see.

"Oh!" she exclaimed. "It's different!"

"We took the liberty of adding several landmarks you were missing," the Nymph said. "I hope you don't mind. But as we were cleaning it, we noticed it seemed an older version of Solevar, and things have changed."

"We thank you," Drystan said with a nod.

Eirin nodded as well. Part of her prickled at the additions. Her father had made this map, and it was the only thing she carried from him now. But she couldn't really complain. If she wanted her father to live, she would need to survive the journey, and an updated map might save their lives. She realized as she touched it that it had been waxed yet again after the additions had been made.

"The exit you're looking for is here," Stavros said, pointing to the far side of the garden without touching the map itself. "There are other exits, though, so if you lose your way, walk along the wall, and you'll come to one sooner or later. But if you keep to this line of trees, you'll be on the fastest path." He then pointed to the other side of the garden boundary wall. "You'll walk due north through the forest for a while longer, though you should move faster than before, as the trees aren't as thick as what you were traveling through on your way to the garden. You'll come to a bridge here." He pointed to a river that ran northeast to southwest. "Once over the bridge, you'll be in Sphinx territory."

Eirin glanced at Nuru, but her friend didn't so much as blink.

"Besides the Sphinxes, there aren't many predators in that region. It's rather desolate and wild. You'll need to ration your food until you reach Mhira Lake. Now, if you don't heed anything else I say today, heed this." He looked around, making eye contact with everyone in the group. "The only way to get across the lake is by ferry. It's nearly large enough to be a sea, and trying to go around it would cost you weeks of travel due to the dangerous nature of the shores, not to mention that you'd have to go through the southern portions of Iilaedin, which means dealing with far more people and creatures than I can express."

"So we need to take the ferry if we wish to remain hidden," Isayas said.

"Yes, but I cannot stress enough the danger you'll be facing when you do."

Eirin sucked in a sharp breath. She felt the others looking at her, but she kept her eyes on the map, trying to regulate her breathing.

"The lake was once home to the Merfolk, but it's been taken over by their cousins, the Sirens, and whatever unholy creatures they've twisted with their songs." He paused and studied Eirin. "You're familiar with Sirens?"

Eirin swallowed and nodded.

"I don't need to warn you of the danger they pose to your friends then, do I?"

Eirin shook her head.

"How long would it take to go north of the lake?" Qeb asked, his thick brows furrowed as he stared at the map.

Stavros sighed. "A week at best. But you're traveling with a Human, so most likely longer. And your greatest danger there would be the lack of trees. There are some under which to make shelter in the Sphinx fields, but the area north of the lake is a dry salt bed, arid and unlivable. You'd be camping in the direct sunlight." He paused. "You'd also most likely meet a generous number of Grindylows. They eat the bones the Sirens throw up on shore."

Qeb cursed.

"And as I said, going south," Stavros continued, "would mean making your way through days and days of what's left of Iilaedin's streets, which—last we've heard—are full of starving people and desperate thieves. Cutting across the lake isn't ideal, but it is by far the fastest way to arrive at the Emerald Palace."

Eirin's heart sank into her stomach. Unimaginable danger no matter which way they went.

"I'll end with this," Stavros said, stepping back and gesturing for Eirin to roll up her map. "Without a doubt, it will make what you've been through look easy. And with stories of Rangvald making his way north to the east of here, I have little doubt you'll be watched as you go. The Sphinxes won't take kindly to your intrusion, and many hungry animals will be delighted to find you within their territories. But," he said, suddenly smiling. "If anyone can do it, that someone will be you. Just...don't judge the people you meet too harshly." He sighed. "They've lost everything that makes them Human."

After one more goodbye, he turned and went back into the hall, and the Nymph, after uttering her own blessing over them, followed. Eirin and her friends turned once more to face Eedn.

* * *

They'd been walking for about five minutes when Eirin glanced at Nuru, who was frowning.

"What's wrong?" Eirin asked her.

Nuru shook her head. "It's strange to be walking in the day again."

Eirin nodded. It was indeed strange. During their months in Mhaedin, they'd traded sleep schedules back and forth, but more than once, they'd spent weeks with their waking hours during the day and sleeping at night. Unlike most other places in Solevar, the elaborate overhead canvas system had allowed them to walk about during the day, as long as they stayed in the canvases' shade. But since leaving Mhaedin, they'd been forced to become nocturnal once again.

The rest of the group walked in reverent silence. The sounds of the garden sang of an alien peace, and it made Eirin's chest hurt in a strange way. Birds twittered in the distant treetops, and bees buzzed from plant to plant. Every now and then, Eirin would hear the gentle humming of a Nymph gathering food or tending to a plant.

"I wonder if this is what it was like," Nuru whispered.

"What *what* was like?" Eirin asked softly.

"Before the curse." Nuru's voice broke, and to Eirin's amazement, a tear coursed down her friend's cheek.

And yet, as surprised as Eirin was by her friend's uncharacteristic outburst of emotion, Eirin understood.

There was a longing inside her that had been building from the moment they'd stepped into the garden, one that wished to step out of the shade into the sunlight. She yearned to stretch her hand out and feel its rays. She longed for the freedom to go out of doors whenever she pleased.

That longing grew stronger with each step, and it stabbed at her chest like a memory that wasn't hers. It wasn't even a vision, though Eirin had felt the sun many times in visions of the past. She felt them every time she touched something in this new world, it seemed. And yet...this desire...this hunger wasn't from those visions. It was something new, an overwhelming sense that something precious was gone.

"It's all right to mourn what's been lost."

"What?" Eirin looked to her left to realize that Isayas was walking beside her. The look on his weathered face was unusually compassionate, and only then did Eirin realize she was crying as well.

"But I didn't lose it." She wiped her cheek with her arm and let out a tremulous laugh. "I never even knew it." Her chest constricted even tighter as she uttered the words.

"We all lost Solevar," Isayas said. He continued to walk, but his pale eyes grew distant. "My wife loved to sit in a field of clover blossoms. She would go outside and put a blanket down on the ground. Then she'd lie down and do nothing but close her eyes and inhale deeply." He smiled.

"I never knew that," Eirin whispered.

"Hm." He smiled and looked down, then at Eirin. "But don't let me fool you into thinking she was idle. She loved working at the Time Stones. They were smaller, of course, than the ones in the Emerald Castle. A mountain village surrounded by a handful of mining communities doesn't merit nearly as many stones as the capital did. But reading the stones was her passion. That's why I stayed, you know. I was guarding them."

"All this time?" Eirin asked.

Isayas paused to pluck a handful of cherries from a tree, then he handed half of them to Eirin. She took them gratefully. Struck by the beauty of the garden, she'd been walking nearly three hours by now and had completely forgotten she could eat of its fruit.

"My wife was afraid someone would try to abuse them as the first Time Stones had been. So she begged me on her deathbed to preserve them at all costs. And if I couldn't," his expression darkened, "to destroy them."

"Just those on the mountain, or..."

"All of them." He gave her a wry smile and lifted his staff slightly off the ground, the gem at its tip glinting in the light of the day. "You probably know this, but I can use this to see other places. It doesn't always work, especially if there's a great amount of twisted magic near the place I'm attempting to see, but I was generally able to watch the other Time Stone circles as well."

"And no one tried to abuse them?" Eirin asked.

"Oh, some tried." He chuckled. "I discouraged that quickly."

"But how? If you weren't there, I mean?"

"Oh, nothing very impressive. Earthquakes. Sandstorms. Great numbers of biting flies." He shrugged. "The usual."

In spite of herself, Eirin laughed. "I'm not sure that's usual for anyone but Wizards."

He smiled, but it quickly faded, and he looked ahead once more, his eyes turning misty. "Before I left my home, I knew I wouldn't be coming back." He swallowed hard. "Destroying those stones was like..." He sniffed and blinked hard.

"I'm sorry," Eirin whispered, putting her hand through the crook of his arm. "I wish I could have known her."

For a moment, she wondered if she'd gone too far. Not everyone liked being touched when they were in pain. But before Eirin could withdraw her hand in embarrassment, he put his free hand on hers and squeezed, keeping it there.

Eirin was sure the conversation was over, but he surprised her a few moments later by speaking again.

"When I heard that there was another who might restore her beloved Time Stones, I didn't want to go. I didn't want to leave Sarah behind. But," he sighed, then gave Eirin a tired smile, "it's what she would have wanted. And I knew that if I didn't help you down here, I'd hear an earful of it when I got to eternal bliss and told her about my time after she left."

Eirin chuckled along with him, but when she glanced back up at him, she saw him watching something up ahead. She followed his gaze to see Drystan staring at them from his place at the head of the group. Drystan's expression, as it often was, was inscrutable. But if Eirin had to guess what he was feeling, she would say that he was sad.

"Why do you keep pushing him away?" Isayas asked in a softer voice.

Eirin looked up at him in surprise.

"He's not as ugly as most of the men in this world. Most women wouldn't be running in the other direction the way you seem to be." Isayas continued with a sly smile. "Besides, he could be the next king, you know."

"Not if you ask him," Eirin grumbled. Then she sighed and shook her head. "All that aside, it's...it's not him I'm trying to push away. It's the Time Stones. I need to focus on them so we don't die. I'm afraid I'll lose sight of where I'm supposed to go and what I'm supposed to be. I can't afford a distraction right now. And Drystan is..." She glanced at him. "Definitely a distraction."

When she turned back to Isayas, she found him studying her intently. "What?" she asked.

"You might be surprised," he finally said.

"By what?"

"Magic and love are far more entwined than any of us can fully understand." He paused and glanced at Drystan again. "You might find you need it more than you think."

Chapter Eleven

Drystan snapped his attention away when Isayas and Eirin noticed his gaze. Embarrassment made his neck hot, but it couldn't rival the struggle his body was waging within him.

The longing in his chest was nearly painful. It was as if his body was drawn to her like the Dragon within him was drawn to blood. And yet, this pull was even stronger than that. His desire was nearly overwhelming, and he had no idea how to quell the emotions raging inside of him.

"What's wrong?" Qeb asked. Drystan smiled in spite of himself. As usual, his friend missed nothing, though sometimes, Drystan wouldn't have minded if he did.

Times like now.

Drystan shook his head. "Not here."

Qeb nodded, but when he looked back at Eirin, his furrowed brow relaxed. "Oh."

"I said not here!" Drystan hissed.

Qeb chuckled. "You're not fooling anyone, Drystan." He grew thoughtful. "Didn't you mention something about the Dragon heart–"

"Forget I ever said that." Drystan wished his friend would shut up. Qeb sometimes seemed to forget that they were surrounded by creatures of magic with incredibly heightened senses of hearing. The only person who couldn't hear them was literally Eirin.

"You think I don't understand the power of a magical tie?" Qeb asked quietly.

He had a point there. Complaining to a Griffin about the strength of a magical tie was like complaining to a Mermaid about being wet.

"Not that I ever wanted to marry you." Qeb chuckled.

"You at least had the chance to choose who you tied yourself to," Drystan pointed out.

Qeb raised his thick eyebrows. "And you didn't?"

Drystan huffed. Arguing with Qeb was like arguing with a brick wall. The brick wall always won. And in Drystan's case, the brick wall was usually right.

Drystan had chosen Eirin. He could look back on their journey from Torbaine to Mhaedin to Solevar, and he could point out which piece of his heart became hers when. Without a doubt, though, he had solidified the choice to love her the night they had danced under the stars in Mhaedin. But it had begun long before that. And Qeb was right, as much as Drystan hated to admit it. The choice to love her had been conscious and deliberate. And since making that choice, he hadn't regretted it for a minute.

He only wished sometimes that the strength of his heart—the part of him that housed the magical, legendary fire that was passed from one generation of royal Dragons to the next—wasn't quite so intense.

They stopped soon after that to eat a midday meal. Then they walked again until it began to grow dark.

"We should arrive at the northern door within an hour or so," Isayas announced as dusk fell. "Which means it would be prudent for us to eat our supper now and to use the remaining light to gather as much produce as we can fit in our packs. I, for one, will be searching the herbs." Everyone agreed that this was a good plan. The Nymphs had insisted they eat as much as possible while in the garden. Once they left the garden, the Nymphs had warned, food would become much scarcer and the road much harder. They would need as much nourishment and strength as was possible when they began the rest of their trek to Iilaedin. So everyone chose a spot beneath the trees and began to eat.

Drystan would have liked nothing more than to spread his cloak out upon the soft grass at the foot of the giant pecan tree he'd settled beneath and go to sleep. The peace of the garden, as nourishing as it was, had opened something open inside of him that had nagged at him all day, like a wound that refused to close. The faster they got out of the garden, the sooner they could resume their journey, and he could harden himself against the temptation to remain and allow fate to take them as long as he was at peace.

The sun had gone down by the time Drystan finished eating, so he shouldered his pack and went off in search of pecans he could stuff into the corners of his bag.

"Drystan?"

Drystan looked up to see Callispa standing beside him.

"Can I...Can we talk?" She glanced at the others, who had spread out to search for food as well. Nuru had joined Eirin and Isayas, and Qeb and Thane appeared to be deep in a quiet conversation of their own.

"Of course," Drystan said, resuming his picking. But before he could gather anything, she surprised him by placing her hand on his and pulling it down from the tree. Drystan stared at her as she held it for a long moment, staring down at his fingers as though they held the secrets of what was left of the kingdom, a slight furrow between her brows.

"Callispa," he said, gently extricating his hand from hers. "What did you want to tell me?"

She turned her large blue eyes up to his. They looked unusually vulnerable in the pale moonlight.

"I know that you've sworn to protect Eirin," she began, and Drystan's heart sank into his stomach. "And I know that you think you love her."

"Callispa–"

She held her hand up. "Just...listen." Then she drew in a deep breath. "I've kept quiet. I respect that Eirin is trying to put the Time Stones before everything else. But we all know that the likelihood of our success is small." She gave him a sad smile. "And I would always regret it if I didn't try."

Drystan was about to ask what she wanted to try, but before he could utter the words, she had wrapped her hands around his biceps and pressed her mouth against his. Her passion surprised him, and the way she clung to him made his attempt at retreat more difficult than he would have expected. He was forced to go against his better instincts with the force with which he had to use to pull free of her hold.

"Callispa!" he hissed, shock quickly turning to rage. "Why would you do that?" he whispered fiercely.

"I told you! I love you, Drystan. And facing death–"

"But what in Solevar made you think I would return your sentiments?" Drystan knew he was being rude, but he was too angry to care. "My heart is tied to Eirin. You know that. Everyone knows that!" And if they hadn't already, they knew now.

"You *think* it's tied to Eirin! But in Mhaedin, when we were together–"

"It was an agreement, Callispa! A farce! In fact, it was your idea! Even Eirin knows it was for show."

She blanched. "You *told* Eirin?"

"Of course, I told Eirin! There was no reason to keep up the facade."

"So..." Her voice began to quiver as her breath came in and out faster and faster. "All that time we spent together...and you felt *nothing*?"

Drystan rubbed his face with his hands. "All that time we spent together was your idea."

Callispa didn't answer at first. When he finally dared to look at her again, she was staring, unseeing, into the trees. "I had hoped..." she whispered.

Drystan wanted to growl. They were already in a race against time to break the curse. Rangvald was up to something. There were bloodthirsty predators waiting to kill them the moment they stepped outside the protective garden walls, and their only hope of survival lay in the hands of the most delicate, most stubborn creature in all of Solevar.

And now Callispa had laid bare her heart for him to break right as they were getting ready to venture back into it all once again. No wonder Eirin had desired to wait to discuss the tangled mess they were in.

"Look," he said, pinching the bridge of his nose. "It's not–"

"I don't understand!" Callispa was crying now. "She constantly rebuffs you. She's rude to you. She uses you when it's convenient, and–"

"Silence!"

Everyone turned to look at Isayas, who was holding his staff up high over his head. It glowed slightly.

"Do you smell that?" he whispered.

"Smoke," Thane said as he shifted into his Centaur form. Likewise, the others changed as well.

"Excuse me," Drystan said curtly as he stepped away from a tree to shift as well. Callispa nodded, but he didn't miss the heartbroken look she sent him as she stepped away from the tree her own wings of fire springing from her back.

"Why is there smoke?" Eirin asked, her voice edging on panic Drystan wasn't used to hearing.

"I don't know. Go!" Isayas shouted. As he spoke, he lifted his staff into the air, and muttering a few words, aimed its head in the direction they were going. A beam of light shot ahead of them, lighting the way.

"Eirin!" Drystan stopped and knelt so that Eirin could scramble onto his back. Nuru was right behind her and stooped to help her up. The group sprinted toward the north wall, which was getting harder and harder to see through the increasingly hazy air.

They'd been running hard for about ten minutes when a Nymph appeared out of the smoke in front of them.

"Quickly!" she shouted, then coughed. "There are Trolls clearing the forest just outside the garden, and they've set fire to the gate! We fear they'll break through the west edge of the wall if they don't stop!"

"Has this ever happened before?" Isayas asked her, slowing slightly so she could lead them.

"No! Never. When people try to come through, they attempt the gates. No one has ever tried to destroy the garden before!" Her green eyes blazed with anger and fear. "If they break through that wall–"

"What are the Griffins doing?" Qeb interrupted.

"They're sending volleys of arrows and hurling rocks at them, but it seems to be doing little."

"Wait!" Eirin called from above. Everyone came to a stop. "Did you say there's a *group* of Trolls? How many?"

"Oh, I don't know! At least six?"

Eirin looked down at Isayas, who also looked shocked.

"Have you ever–" she began, but he was already shaking his head.

"I only ever heard of the ones who served Faradoon staying in a group that large."

"Is this *really* important?" Nuru snapped.

"It is!" Eirin said. "Trolls can't stand other intelligent creatures in general. They try to stay alone as much as possible. So much so that they rarely procreate."

"Which means," Thane said grimly, "that something or someone has control of them."

"That's what the Griffins think," the Nymph said. "They think..." her face went to Eirin. "They think Rangvald sent them."

"Which means there will be reinforcements on their heels," Drystan growled to Qeb.

"You must follow me!" the Nymph called, turning again. "We'll try to get you out unnoticed!"

Drystan had little hope of that, but they had few other options.

"That's not the only strange thing we saw!" she called over her shoulder. "They traveled here before the sun set!"

Drystan didn't slow, but he wanted to stop and break something out of sheer frustration.

"Were they wearing a special covering of some sort?" Nuru called.

"Yes!" the Nymph exclaimed. "Thick black cloaks."

Drystan ground his now very large teeth. Whoever was after Eirin was risking a lot. Risky people were desperate people. And desperate people were dangerous.

They could hear the banging before they saw it. The sounds of thunderous explosions seemed to ripple the air as they neared the northernmost part of the wall. Nothing seemed to be crumbling, but Drystan didn't know how long the wall would last against six determined Trolls. For as the Trolls were nearly the height of Giants and about three times as heavy, dismantling the wall couldn't take long. They would need not only to slip out but to try to draw the Trolls away from the garden as well. Solevar did not need to lose its last main food source.

"Nuru! Help her down! I have to shift!" Drystan called over his shoulder. Somehow, Nuru heard him over the noise, and the moment Eirin was a safe distance away, Drystan shifted back into his Human form.

Once they passed through the door on the northern wall out of the garden and into the wall once more, there were Griffins running and shouting everywhere, and piles of weapons lay on the floor where smaller Atharrachs were preparing them.

"This way!" The Nymph motioned for them to follow her. "We have a secret door down here that the Griffins use to get out unseen." She opened a trap door in the floor, and grabbing a lantern that hung on a peg nearby, made her way down the descending steps.

"Thane, Qeb, and Callispa go first," Drystan directed. "Then Nuru. Isayas and I will bring up the rear with Eirin in the middle."

The tunnel was wide enough for Qeb, Callispa, and Nuru in their shifter forms. Eirin and Isayas fit as well, of course. But the trap door entrance leading into the tunnel clearly hadn't been built with Dragons or Centaurs in mind.

Drystan, who hadn't planned on using a cramped tunnel to exit,realized quickly that he and Thane would have to leave the fortress in their Human forms. This would make things difficult if they met with trouble on the other side. Thane must have also realized this, because he quickly switched with Qeb to let the Griffin lead the way.

"Shout if there's trouble!" Drystan called ahead, to which Qeb sent him a quick nod.

They obediently filed down after the Nymph. Drystan couldn't see much inside the tunnel, even with his sharper Dragon vision, but it smelled strongly of earth, and when he brushed his hand along the wall, he felt packed soil and a tangle of roots. He also heard Eirin draw her sword, and once again thanked the Time Keeper for his father's foresight to train her to fight.

Eirin might be weak compared to the Atharrachs, but she was not helpless.

The descent was longer than Drystan had expected, but eventually they began to go up once again and emerged within a small copse of trees. Though the sounds of battle were nearby, no one seemed to see them, much to his relief.

"Thank you!" Eirin whispered, hugging the Nymph tightly.

"Thank us by removing the stone!" the Nymph whispered back. She looked as though she was about to say something more when a deafening boom shook the ground, and she scurried back down into the hole, pulling the door shut behind her.

"We can't leave them like this!" Callispa said, peeking through the leaves.

"We also can't be seen," Nuru snapped. "That would make this entire venture in vain." She glared in the Troll's direction.

"Leave that to me," Isayas said. He reached into his robe and pulled out a small vial of powder. Unstopping the small cork on the top, he tipped it just enough to pour some on the jewel inside his staff's tip. Then, cupping his hand over it, he whispered over it. Stepping out of the trees, he aimed the end of his staff toward the sounds coming from the Trolls. A green light shot out of the end.

Drystan was about to peek through the trees to see the outcome of the Wizard's spell when a shout from behind them made him turn.

There was a slight break in the trees on the copes's west side, and through it, a man in his Human form was staring at them.

"I see them!" he shouted. "I see the Human!"

Drystan didn't even stop to think about what he was doing. He broke into a sprint. As he ran, the Dragon burst out of him, and in a moment, not only was he in full Dragon form, but he'd sent a well-aimed ball of flame at the retreating man. His sudden explosion of growth destroyed half the trees, knocking them all flat, and his fire incinerated the other half. But with the trees gone, he could see.

The man didn't get up. But Drystan couldn't have cared less. The man was the least of their problems. The greatest problem he could see now was that the man had fallen at the foot of a ridge. And at the top of the ridge were the beginnings of an enormous tunnel being built out of wood. Though it was night, the tunnel was plainly visible due to the hundreds of lighted torches that made it nearly as bright as day. Piles and piles of wood were stacked around the tunnel's mouth.

"How did the Griffins not see this?" Nuru hissed from behind him. Drystan turned to find that his friends had followed him.

"They don't explore the world around the garden," Qeb growled. "Everything they do is within or immediately outside the walls."

"Rangvald must be building the tunnel faster than we thought," Thane said, pointing. "We were told they were far away!"

"They must have been forced to move east because of the mountains," Eirin whispered.

Drystan, who had been considering taking flight to do some reconnaissance, saw something move. "Look!"

As he spoke, half-a-dozen Griffins appeared at the top of the ridge.

Chapter Twelve

Eirin was trying to remember the exact location of the river where they might throw their enemies off their trail, when Isayas's voice broke through her panicked thoughts.

"Back!" the Wizard hissed. "Into the forest!" He turned and hurried back toward the thicker trees just beyond the clearing that Drystan had inadvertently created. Qeb grabbed Eirin and tossed her up onto Drystan's back, then stayed on his heels beside Nuru. The others followed, angling north, away from the garden.

But as soon as they were in a thicker part of the wood, they had to stop.

"Where's Isayas?" Eirin whispered.

As if summoned, Isayas appeared. "Everyone spread out in a circle!" he said. "Keep it tight. But not too close. Drystan, grab Eirin and wrap your arms around her. Hide her as much as you can."

"In my Human form?" Drystan did not sound pleased.

"Yes!" Isayas snapped. "If you want this to work!" He began swinging his staff in a circle as everyone hurried to do as he said. If they'd learned anything since leaving Mhaedin, it was that orders from Isayas should generally be obeyed.

Eirin knew better than to argue. But amidst all the more important things going on, such as a band of enemy Griffins who were surely pursuing them by now, and probably a bunch of Trolls nearby, her heart beat erratically as Drystan wrapped his large Human arms around her. She could feel his breath against her temple as he pressed his cheek against the top of her head. His own heart was beating fast through his chest, the strength of its beat moving even through his chest armor.

What was the purpose of this? Much to her embarrassment, Eirin was suddenly aware that she wanted nothing more than to stay tightly wrapped in Drystan's arms.

Running was getting more than a little old.

But then Isayas was calling out incantations in the Wizard language, and swirls of green magic filled the air. It hovered slightly before moving into each of her friends. She watched in awe as the green light moved from the air into their skin as if the two substances were the same.

Then she nearly shrieked as Drystan's strong arms elongated and thinned. His skin grew gnarled and dry as his limbs knotted and twisted before her eyes, and a thick screen of green leaves began to sprout from his extremities. When she looked down, she realized that his feet were now buried beneath the soil and looked far more like roots than boots. Then it occurred to her to look up, and she gasped as she realized she was hidden as though she'd been placed within the hollow trunk of a great tree. Just a few natural openings remained, the kind that might be occupied by squirrels or an owl. Through these holes, she could see Isayas approach her.

"I can't glamour you directly because you're Human," he whispered, looking past Drystan in the direction from which they'd come. "The magic won't work on you."

"But you've been glamouring the whole campe for weeks!" Eirin whispered.

He gave her a wry smile and slightly lifted his staff. "And this is just that on a small scale. I can't glamour you directly, but I can place a glamour *around* you, and it works better if you have a sort of barrier between you and the magic. Now, stay as quiet and still as you can. I'll turn everyone back once they're gone. No matter what, do not give yourself up." Then he mumbled to himself, "As long as the blasted magic doesn't start going awry again."

Eirin had no intention of giving herself up, but she was thankful for his warning nonetheless as he, standing in the center of the circle, took the shape of a tree as her friends had. And he was just in time. Less than a minute later, the Griffins came crashing through.

"If you saw them with your own eyes, I'm not sure why you needed me," said a woman's voice. Eirin froze. That voice. She knew that voice.

"Rangvald was adamant," one of the Griffins grunted. "They have a Wizard. They could be trying to disguise her as one of the others."

"It would be incredibly foolish if they tried," the woman scoffed. "Humans can't be glamoured. And Rangvald should know that, injured or not."

"No," replied another Griffin, "but they could glamour one of her companions to look like her."

"Well, even if they did, it won't do us much good if we can't find them now, will it?" she snapped.

The memory hit Eirin like a training staff. It was the woman from the attack on the Citadel, the one who had first identified her as a Seer.

The Elf.

Eirin's already shallow breath caught in her chest. In a way, this was the woman who had started everything. If it hadn't been for her, Eirin wouldn't have been forced to leave Torbaine for Lady Seren's fortress.

Eirin wasn't sure whether she wanted to thank the woman or kick her.

They continued to bicker as they wandered, and Eirin was just about to relax when the woman's voice grew louder again.

"...something I want to look at once more." Eirin pressed her back against the tree—against Drystan—as hard as she could. Through one of the holes in Drystan's arms, she could see the woman walk over to the tree that was Callispa. As soon as the woman's violet light came into view, Eirin knew for certain that this was the Elf.

"This is the work of a Wizard," the Elf woman said, frowning.

"The tree?" Her companion sounded unimpressed. More Griffins walked up to where the woman was standing, but Eirin couldn't count how many.

"Look at these trees," the Elven woman gestured around the circle at them. "Do they look normal to you?"

The Griffin frowned then shrugged his massive, feathered wings. "Should they?"

The woman muttered something under her breath as she moved from Callispa to Nuru. Hopefully, Nuru wouldn't do anything rash. She wasn't known for being very patient with being poked or prodded.

"We can't very well take a bunch of trees captive, can we?" another Griffin said.

"No." The Elf woman stopped and then smiled. "No, but we can chop them down. They might make a nice addition to our tunnel, would they not?" This she said a little louder than necessary, and Eirin knew she was trying to draw them out. If she thought they were that easily duped, she had much to learn.

"Dregin, go get your axe and–" the Elf had been addressing one of the Griffins, but then her eyes moved over his shoulder. Eirin's stomach fell as she smiled.

But as she took two steps toward Eirin, Drystan burst out of his tree form, bark flying everywhere as he let out a shout, his sword out of its sheath and in his hand. He thrust it into the chest of the first Griffin to get in his way.

By this time, the rest of their companions had come out of their tree forms as well, and they encircled the Elf and the Griffins, closing in on them fast.

"Someone fly back to Rangvald!" the Elf woman shouted, putting herself in the center of the Griffins. "Now!"

Two of the Griffins lifted off into the sky. Qeb cut one down before it was even fully airborne, and Thane hit the other just when it seemed as though it would get away.

Drystan, unable to shift into his Dragon form due to the proximity of his companions, was forced to fight in his Human form. The others battled in their Atharrach forms, while Isayas, though he bore no sword, fought with his staff. This wasn't a problem, however, he brought several of their enemies crashing to the ground as stone statues.

Unfortunately, Griffins were known as a warrior race for a reason. Paying no heed to their fallen comrades, they pushed Nuru and Callispa back quickly, and though Thane joined them, he, too, was hampered by the lack of space. The trees grew close together, and in his Centaur form, he couldn't move freely. And though Eirin had believed there to be only five or six Griffins, she could see now that there were far more than she'd first guessed, as many came charging out of the trees where they must have been searching.

"You're coming back with me," the Elf's voice said, cutting through the chaos of the battle.

Eirin looked to her left to realize the woman had somehow broken away from the main fight. Eirin held her sword up, over-joyed she had it until the woman pulled her own blade, which was twice as long as Eirin's.

Drystan, however, hadn't forgotten Eirin. Seeing the Elf woman, he leaped and twisted in the air at the same time, bringing his sword down hard against hers. The Elf woman's sword was knocked to the ground, but she quickly pulled something else from her pocket. It glowed, a mix of magic swirling about inside of it.

"Drystan!" Eirin screamed. She yanked him back as the woman uncorked the small clay jar and the mixture of magic floated out toward Drystan. Eirin tackled him and stayed on top of him.

"Eirin, what are you doing?" Drystan shouted, but Eirin kneed him in the leg.

"Stay down!"

She could feel the magic hit her back as she spoke, but she stayed still until it was gone. Drystan looked like he might just murder her when she finally let him jump up. But as the Elf woman moved behind Eirin, he just yanked Eirin out of the way. His eyes went from blue to a glowing yellow and orange, and he sent a stream of fire from his mouth back at the Elf, who seemed to evaporate before their eyes.

Eirin glanced around to see with relief that every one of their party was still alive. But they weren't winning. If anything else, they simply seemed to be drawing out the inevitable. There weren't just Griffins in the fight anymore. Centaurs, a Fenris, and several White Harts had joined, and there were more on the way from the sound of it. They needed to get out into the open.

Drystan had resumed fighting, alternating between his Dragon and Human abilities, when a new group of Griffins burst into the small clearing. Eirin raised her sword again, but when she saw them in the light of the fires Drystan kept igniting, she nearly dropped it in relief. Stavros and his men had arrived.

Once their allies were there, the rest of the fight was over quickly. Short work was made of those who were still fighting for Rangvald, thanks to their new allies. But just when she was sure their fight was over, an unfortunate Faun appeared at the top of the ridge. Qeb grabbed him and carried him to where the others had congregated in the center of the clearing.

"Please!" he cried. "Have mercy!"

"What do we do with him?" Qeb asked, holding him by the scruff of his neck.

In spite of herself, Eirin pitied the young man. "Don't kill him," she called out.

Drystan turned to look at her, his eyes still blazing with the embers of the flames kindled during the battle. The sight was incredibly unnerving and attractive at the same time.

"He came here to kill you," he said in his rumbling Dragon voice.

"No!" the Faun called out weakly. "I just came to see what all the trouble was! Like many of them did!" He looked in terror at the fallen bodies. "We didn't come as soldiers. We were told to build. So we did."

"We'll take him," Stavros said, holding his large arm out as he folded his wings behind his back. "It would be good to learn what Rangvald is up to, and I get the feeling a meal or two will give us much in that arena."

The young man nodded vigorously.

There were so many fires burning the edges of the trees by now that Eirin could see that Stavros and his men were bloodied and their clothes tattered.

"Did you stop the Trolls?" she asked.

"We did, thanks to the Wizard." He nodded at Isayas. "Why didn't you do for yourself what you did for us?"

Isayas gave him a wry smile. "We were so closely engaged, I didn't think my companions would enjoy being punished with my enemies. But I would hardly call my contribution useless." He looked down, and for the first time, Eirin realized many of the enemies who remained alive were tied to the ground by roots that had come out of the ground and held them down tightly against it.

"After your help, we discovered that the Trolls had been instructed to dismantle our walls to use as building material for their tunnel." Stavros's companion spat on the ground while shifting to his Human form. "That fool, Rangvald, is so confident of his success that he thinks it's worth the sacrifice of the garden to construct his tunnel."

Eirin thought back to when Rangvald explained his scheme, and she shivered.

For years, while the leaders of Mhaedin, Lady Phaidra and Drystan's other uncle, Karolus, had tried again and again to transport Humans to Iilaedin, Rangvald had been making his own plans. He wanted to build a tunnel and a road all the way from his fortress to Iilaedin, one in which they could transport and shield a Human from the curse's poison so the Human would reach the Time Stones safely and in good health.

And she was his missing piece to the puzzle. Unless he had somehow gotten his claws on the other Human from Mhaedin, Mannish.

Eirin shivered again.

"With *fire*?" Thane was asking. "If they wanted your wood, what in the world–"

"Trolls are strong," Qeb said mildly. "No one said they were smart."

"You," Stavros said, pointing to Drystan. "I didn't get to speak with you earlier as you escaped. But hear me now."

Drystan let out a slight rumble, but Eirin was rather sure she was the only one who could hear him. Meek and mild he may seem to strangers, but Drystan was a Dragon, and he disliked being ordered about.

If Stavros heard his quiet complaint, however, he ignored it. "When I met you, I was horrified that a son of Kamon had survived the curse. For all we knew, your ancestor had died, and the hope of any offspring with him."

Drystan growled again, slightly louder this time.

"But you've proved yourself faithful in protecting your charge." Stavros nodded at Eirin. "And now that the madness of Rangvald has been confirmed, I'm convinced this world's only hope rests on your strength." He turned to Eirin. "And on you. Stay with him. Don't leave his side."

Eirin wondered what point Stavros was trying to make. They'd been on this journey for weeks. Did he think they didn't know this?

"But I'm also convinced of something more," Stavros continued, looking at Drystan again. "If, by some miracle, she fixes the Time Stones, there will be something still lacking."

Eirin felt herself beginning to smile. She got the feeling she knew what Stavros was going to say. And Drystan was going to hate it.

"The Emerald Palace will still need a king to sit on its throne," Stavros went on. "And that king *must* be a son of Oreck."

Drystan grunted an assent.

"I won't give you false hope. Convincing Solevar to follow you will be near to impossible. But if you can get her safely to the Time Stones, and if she can remove the stone, there is a chance... just a chance that the people would see you raised above these lands."

"We know–" Drystan began, but Stavros strode toward him until their faces were inches apart.

"You must," he growled, "at all costs, prevent Rangvald from taking the throne."

Drystan held his gaze for an eternal moment before glancing down at Eirin.

Eirin gave him a smug smile and a shrug.

But Drystan didn't smile in return.

Chapter Thirteen

The Griffins returned to the wall, which now needed to be repaired. Thankfully, Stavros said it seemed as though the Trolls hadn't damaged the garden itself, just the wall where they'd attacked. Unfortunately, however, that portion of the wall was also where a large number of garden workers lived. The Trolls hadn't actually deconstructed much, but the fire they'd set had left numerous charred gaps between the stone pillars.

"It would have been easier to just keep chopping trees." Nuru scoffed.

Stavros had grimly smiled. "At least their foolishness has halted construction for the time being. Trolls aren't known for their natural acumen. Rangvald must be getting desperate to have used them." He nodded in the direction of the wall. "But now that we know what they want, we'll be on our guard."

After Stavros and his men had gone, Eirin's friends talked, and it was decided that, as they were so close to the tunnel, they should stall Rangvald's efforts to give themselves a bigger lead. Drystan and Qeb, taking advantage of the thin clouds that darkened the sky, flew up and over the trees to where the tunnel was being built.

Drystan had expected to see a thin, poorly built wooden shaft stretching south. After all, Rangvald's men couldn't have built anything large in the short time since Drystan and his friends had escaped his fortress.

But he was wrong.

"How in the blazes..." Qeb left his words unfinished.

A tunnel wide enough to fit a cottage inside stretched south, where it disappeared among the trees. It was easy to see where the forest had been chopped down to build the monstrosity. Large patches of land lay bare, stumps sticking up from the ground all around the tunnel. And unlike the shoddy, uneven patchwork Drystan had expected to see, the tunnel itself was smooth and well-laid. The wood was cut evenly, and it looked sturdy enough to withstand a violent storm. Piles of matching lumber, which Drystan could only assume were meant to continue the construction, lay in even intervals near the entrance and slightly beyond.

"Eirin told me they've been planning this for years," Drystan said as they hovered over it. "Rangvald must have had at least some of their materials ready and prepared. There's no way it could have been built this quickly otherwise."

"I'll bet they started it the moment they found out about Eirin," Qeb said.

Drystan nodded grimly. Then he looked at Qeb. "Ready?"

Upon Qeb's nod, they floated silently down toward the now empty construction site. If there were any workers left, they were most likely either hiding or had fled.

"Should we torch the tunnel?" Qeb asked.

Drystan thought about this. Destroying the tunnel would give them a definite advantage.

"How many people do you think are in there now?" he asked,

nodding to where smoke came through the holes in the tunnel ceiling.

Qeb's face, though in its Griffin form, turned grim. "There's no way of knowing."

Knowing Rangvald, Drystan got the feeling that the tunnel was far from empty. Destroying the tunnel itself would be one thing. But destroying countless lives in the process was another. As little as Drystan cared for his uncle, he had no desire to kill the people under his thumb who were simply hanging on to life.

"I want a better look," Drystan said, flying south again. Qeb followed silently behind.

They didn't have to go far. Sure enough, there were chimney holes spaced evenly throughout the tunnel. Drystan estimated the distance as they flew, and sure enough, not far from the mouth of the unfinished tunnel, he discovered smoke coming out of the chimneys.

"We can't destroy the tunnel," he told Qeb as they flew north again. "Better do the supplies instead."

Qeb grunted, and Drystan understood his friend's frustration. Destroying the tunnel would have been a fantastic way to ensure that they reached Iilaedin first. But if Drystan knew his uncle, he knew there would be children in that tunnel. Rangvald wasn't stupid. He probably expected Drystan to try to attack it at some point. What better way to shore up its survival than to place families inside?

Still, Drystan's conscience was assuaged as he set every pile of lumber ablaze. Rangvald might still have the tunnel, but now his workers would have to chop down hundreds of trees to replace the ones he was destroying. And this time, the garden would be on the lookout for more attacks in the future.

When Drystan and Qeb landed again, they'd already lost half the night.

"That took longer than expected," Isayas said. Thane grinned at them.

"Gives a lovely orange glow to the night, doesn't it?"

"Let's go," Nuru said, helping Eirin put on her pack. "At this rate, the curse will fall before we ever cross the river."

Callispa didn't look at Drystan, and Eirin was silent as well. But Drystan had the gratification of seeing relief in her expressive brown eyes as she climbed up his shoulder to her usual perch on his back.

"Everyone hold still," Isayas grumbled as he fiddled with several little vials of powders. "Don't move until I say so."

"What are you doing?" Nuru asked.

"I'm going to place a cloaking spell on each of you. It's the same one I do every day when we make camp. So if you'd stop moving about, it would be helpful."

"I thought you said you couldn't shield me," Eirin said as Isayas began to sprinkle the powder on each person's head.

"No, I said I couldn't glamour you. There's a difference. This is more of a general spell around you. Not Fae magic to change your specific appearance like the one I used earlier. Of course, it would work better if we weren't all walking. But it should at least make us a little harder to see, should more enthusiastic road builders come our way." He tapped his staff on the ground and uttered a few quiet words. Eirin sucked in her breath.

"Can you see it?" Drystan murmured.

"I can," she whispered. "It's beautiful. Like being underwater."

"You could have seen it before, too," Isayas said, putting his powders back in his bag. "But it was large enough you notice. Now, let's move."

It was decided that, since they were short on time, they would keep up a light run as long as they could hold it. Everyone was beginning to tire, as they hadn't slept while they were in the garden and had then fought a battle, but no one seemed to suffer too much for it.

By the time the sky began to lighten, Drystan sensed a wave relief settle over the group. No one had made chase, at least to their awareness, and once the day came, they should be safe.

"Well, unless they decide to send more Trolls in cloaks," Thane pointed out as they feasted on fruit from the garden.

"They wouldn't send Trolls to find Eirin," Nuru scoffed. "The clumsy oafs might kill her by accident."

"My guess," Isayas said, studying the grape he had just plucked from a bunch, "is that they sent the Trolls in cloaks because Rangvald is a brute, and he doesn't care if they burn." He scoffed. "But if they do send someone, they'll send the Griffins most likely. Because if they had any doubts as to our whereabouts before, the Manticores and our work at the construction site have all been wonderfully informative."

"We'll keep two on watch for the next few nights," Drystan said. "Until we cross into the Sphinx fields. Stavros said he's rather certain they'll take the west side of the lake for their tunnel. They don't have to worry about running into people the way we do."

Everyone nodded assent, so Drystan announced that he would take first watch. Qeb immediately volunteered to join him. But once the tents were pitched, and the others began to settle into their beds, Isayas made his way back out to Drystan, who was sitting under a large tree in his Human form. They were still in the forest, but the trees were beginning to thin considerably. Which, if someone attacked, could be a good or a bad thing.

"You need to sleep," Drystan told the Wizard as Isayas shook out the folds of his robe.

Isayas snorted. "Yes, lecture the old man. He's so senile he doesn't know what he's good for."

Drystan just smiled and looked back out at the sky as it began to turn a thin shade of yellow.

"I didn't want to say it while the others were awake," Isayas said, his voice suddenly grave, "but while we were eating, I sent a wind back to Rangvald's fortress."

Drystan looked at him in surprise. "That's a handy trick."

Isayas waved him off. "It doesn't always work. Winds can be feisty. But I did learn something this time."

Drystan turned to face him. "What is it?"

"Rangvald has put a price on your head."

"That...complicates things," Drystan said slowly. "Is it because he wants Eirin?"

Isayas grimaced. "That's the unsettling part. It's not."

Drystan stared at him.

"He's determined to end the lines of all other possible heirs," Isayas went on. "If there are no others who can take the throne, he doesn't have to worry about being the most worthy at the Blood Fire Throne."

Drystan frowned. "*Worthy*?"

"Blast. It was Eirin I was talking to about this, wasn't it?" Isayas muttered to himself. He got a far-off look in his pale blue eyes for a moment before turning back to Drystan. "Eirin can tell you more in the future, but for now, suffice it to say the king is chosen by the Time Keeper Himself through a ritual at the Blood Fire Throne. The heirs present themselves, and the Time Keeper chooses the most worthy. Rangvald, I suspect, knows he will come up wanting. That is, I'm sure, why he killed Karolus. And why he now wants to kill you." Isayas's eyes were hard as ice. "Besides him, you are the only heir of Oreck left." His frown deepened. "And while putting a price on a Dragon's head usually would be a waste of time–"

"He knows that Eirin makes me vulnerable," Drystan finished.

Drystan chewed over Isayas's words long after the Wizard retired to bed. It was a good thing they were now shaded in part by the smaller mountain range to their east because Drystan probably wouldn't have noticed the sun rising until it was too late.

So many warnings he'd received. From Phillipe. From Stavros. Now from Isayas. And, of course, from Eirin. Always from Eirin.

"You look as though someone put you in a trance," Qeb said, settling next to him in the shade of the tree. He pulled off his thick hood and handed Drystan a roll.

"What kind of king do you think I would have been?" Drystan asked, turning the roll over in his hands.

Qeb, now in his Human form again, looked at him with wide eyes. "*Would have* been?" he asked.

"If we'd stayed in Torbaine. If everything had gone the way it was planned, and I'd become king, and the Elders had had their way."

Qeb leaned his head back against the trunk and let out a gusty breath. "I think you would have been as good a king as they would have allowed you to be."

Drystan quirked a brow.

Qeb gave him a wry smile. "You would have obeyed, for the most part, done your duties, and overseen the training of a talented generation of guards and SgaethOirs. But you were never meant to be docile, Drystan." Qeb's smile widened. "You would have rebelled in your own way, disobeying wherever you found the chance. Until, that is..."

"Until what?"

"Until they pushed you too far." He looked over at Eirin's tent. "Until they did something to her that you couldn't abide."

"You mean to Eirin?"

Qeb chuckled. "Drystan, you've been watching over that girl since the day she came to the Citadel."

Drystan snorted. "Because I couldn't believe they were stupid enough to let her in. It doesn't reflect well when first-year students die."

"No, it was something more." Qeb shook his head. "You've been drawn to her from the first day." Then he looked at Drystan again. "My question is what you're going to do about it now."

Drystan shrugged. "I've done what I can. I told her how I feel." He scoffed. "Callispa, too."

"I saw that," Qeb said. Then his voice softened. "Don't worry about Callispa. She'll see soon enough that you two never would have been good for each other."

Drystan looked at him in surprise. "You sound confident."

"Callispa is in love with the man she thinks you ought to be. But that's beside the point. I want to talk about you and Eirin before either of you do something incredibly stupid."

Drystan nearly laughed. Qeb was often quiet and generally gave off an unassuming air. But he was oddly nosy when it came to Drystan's personal life. But then again, Qeb was a Griffin. And Griffins, Drystan was learning, were concerned with every aspect of well-being when it concerned the person they were tied to.

Kind of like a mother hen. Not that Drystan dared make that comparison to Qeb's face. Qeb would not appreciate being compared to a chicken.

"Eirin knows how I feel, but she's trying to focus on finishing this mission. Not that I can blame her. I just..." He sighed. "I wish it could have become something real."

"What do you mean *could have*?" Qeb asked. "You speak as though that *could* never *will*."

"Rangvald has put a price on my head."

Qeb went still. For a moment, Drystan thought he might shift. His eyes took on that slight glow they always held when he was a Griffin, and his body rippled slightly. But then he seemed to get control of himself and leaned back against the tree again.

After a moment, he shuddered and blinked a few times before asking,

"Does he even give an excuse? Or is he being transparent about it?"

"According to Isayas, he wants to remove all possible competitors to the crown. Once the Time Stones are fixed, he plans to take the Blood Fire test unchallenged."

"Which means," Qeb said slowly, "he believes there's a chance he'll lose." Then a slow smile spread across his face. "Which is what Eirin's been telling you all along, is it not?"

Drystan rolled his eyes as Qeb continued to chuckle. "I don't know why you even bother arguing with her." He paused and looked at Drystan, his mirth fading. "What is it?"

Drystan stared down at his hands. They were Human now, scarred from his years of training as a Human warrior. And another reminder of just how little he knew about this world he was stepping into.

"They're not going to accept me, Qeb. You see it. Every time we go somewhere new, I have to prove myself. Again and again and again. I'm Kamon–"

"You are *not* Kamon," Qeb growled. "And you are not responsible for his sins."

"But to them I am!" Drystan hadn't meant to raise his voice, but his frustrations were about to boil over. "And while Rangvald might be bloodthirsty. And mad. And determined to take the throne at all costs, they *know* him. At least...their grandparents knew him. And if I learned anything in politics in Torbaine, it's that people crave familiarity and comfort, even when offered something better."

Qeb looked up into the sky. Silence stretched out between them for a long time. Long enough for guilt to creep into Drystan's conscience. His friend had only been trying to comfort him. Qeb didn't deserve his wrath.

"I'm sorry," Drystan said with a sigh. "It's not your fault."

"Not my fault that what?" Qeb arched one dark brow proudly.

Drystan gave him a wry smile. "That you sometimes shift into a really ugly version of Eirin."

Qeb gave him an odd look.

"I see your face," Drystan continued. "But it's Eirin's voice I hear when you open your mouth."

Qeb stared at him for a moment before leaning over and punching him in the arm. "Then for all our sakes, you'd better listen."

* * *

They walked through the thinning forest for two more nights before finally reaching the river. Each of them was jumpy, expecting attacks at any time, but none came. According to Thane, who had gone on a brief scouting expedition as they made camp early on the third morning, the progress on the road seemed to have stopped. He'd gone up on a ridge and had caught a glimpse of the tunnel in the distance. The entrance was still charred, and no new piles of wood lay around it. This brought enough comfort to the group that there was a good deal of pleasant chatter as they filled their waterskins in the river, excited to cross over as soon as the sun set again.

At least, that was how it seemed.

Drystan tried to take true stock of his companions' moods as they settled in for another sleep. In general, they appeared happy and relaxed, but he knew all too well how easy it was to pretend. Not that he suspected Isayas of pretending. He looked as ornery and grumpy as ever. And Callispa had hardly spoken to anyone since they'd left the garden. She sent Drystan injured looks when she thought he wasn't looking, which made it even more awkward when he had to assign her to this duty or that.

Nuru was still ignoring Thane, though with slightly more finesse than before. And though Drystan was no expert on females' feelings, even he had noticed that after Thane's brief abandonment in Torbaine, a light had seemed to go out of her. Thane had come back repenting on hands and knees, of course, but it seemed too late, at least by Nuru's standards. Before that time, she'd begun to open up to Thane's shameless flirting. But these days, her attentions were all for Eirin, and Drystan wondered just how deep her wounds really went.

Thane and Qeb continued to be their dauntless selves, Thane cheerful to a fault and Qeb unmovable as ever. Even Thane, however, was beginning to show his cracks. When he thought no one was looking, his smile often faded, and he stared out at the sky as though searching for something.

Then, of course, there was Eirin. It always came back to Eirin. Did she realize how close she stood to him these days? Like his second shadow, she rarely left his side unless Nuru drove her away to sleep or change. Her nearness made his chest ache even more, the pain of his heart bond threatening to strangle him each time she sat beside him, close enough to touch but not inviting him to do so.

He had hoped the intensity of his desire would fade with time the way the pain of a wound eventually became bearable if ignored long enough. But it didn't. Her mouth practically begged for him to trace it with his own, memorizing every curve and corner. He wanted to wrap his arm around her waist and draw her into him, and every time she came near, he felt as though his body had been set on fire, overly aware of just how little effort it would take to touch her.

And there were moments every morning, just as he was about to fall asleep, where he imagined her beside him. He thought of all the things he would whisper to her that no one else could hear. For one brief, glorious time in Mhaedin, she had been his confidante, the friend who drew out of him what even Qeb never had.

How he longed for that closeness again. Against his better judgment, he often let himself pretend she was. Because if she were his, he would draw her to him as he drifted off, taking comfort in her warmth and the satisfaction of holding her in his arms, safe from the world and safely pressed against his heart.

Perhaps it was better this way, though. Because if Rangvald had his way, Drystan wouldn't survive Eirin's triumph even if she did fix the Time Stones. Rangvald knew better than Drystan did what a Dragon's heart bond meant. If Drystan wasn't mistaken, Rangvald would gamble on the assumption that Drystan would sacrifice himself to keep Eirin out of Rangvald's reach without question. And if Rangvald did, he would be right.

Unfortunately, while Drystan would never hesitate to challenge his uncle for Eirin's sake, their last fight had inspired no confidence on Drystan's part. Yes, the longer he was in Solevar, the better he got at flying and using his Dragon reflexes. But Rangvald was over a century old. He'd had formal training for years, unlike Drystan, probably with the best Phoenixes Solevar could offer. He'd fought in battles, and though he was wounded now, Drystan had no doubt his uncle would heal quickly.

No, if it came down to it, for Eirin's sake, it was probably best that they keep themselves from falling too deeply. Because, knowing Eirin, she would most likely find some way to save Solevar and create a new world. If that were the case, it would be best for her if she didn't give her heart away just to live in that new world alone.

hey crossed the bridge the following evening. Eirin felt somewhat exultant as they passed over the sparkling waters. Finally free of the eternal forest, they were finally making progress. But what they met on the other side of the river brought her entire party surprise and dismay.

Several times in the forest, they had come across small groups of refugees who were moving south in hopes of finding respite in places like Mhaedin. But this group was the largest by far. Unlike the small family groups they'd easily avoided earlier, this was a massive wave of various peoples, from Fauns to Griffins, from Centaurs to Brownies, from Dokkaebi to Giants and Hibagons and Imps and Nymphs and Thunderbirds. There were hundreds of them.

Most of the crowd was thin and bedraggled, clothed in dresses and tunics and trousers that were threadbare and riddled with holes. They carried little and talked even less. The quiet was so heavy that Eirin quickly decided it was unnerving.

The group was so large that going around them was impossible. Eirin's group had no choice but to plunge on through the middle of them.

To her relief, no one stirred up any trouble. And yet, that in itself was troubling. The weary travelers didn't even seem to notice Eirin and her company. Their eyes remained downcast, and rather than quaking and running from the Dragon, they simply walked around Drystan as though he were a boulder that had been rolled in their way.

Eirin, unwilling to let such a mystery walk on by, slid off Drystan's back and touched the shoulder of one of the Brownies passing by.

"Pardon me, ma'am," she said softly. "But where are you going?"

The small woman eyed her suspiciously for a moment, but then the dead look returned to her face. "To Mhaedin. And you'd be going there, too, if you had any sense." She shook Eirin off and continued her slow march south.

"Should we tell them," Thane wondered quietly, "that Mhaedin is fallen?"

Isayas sighed and shook his head. "No. Let them hope."

"What–" Nuru began, but the Wizard shook his head again.

"Would staying here be any better?"

Eirin was forced to admit that he had a point. From what they'd heard, northern Solevar had suffered far worse than the south. Maybe...just maybe, their sheer will to live would keep them alive long enough for her to make it to Iilaedin.

Then what? a voice in her head asked. Eirin refused to answer it.

Once the great wave of travelers had passed, Eirin and her friends were able to go faster. The trees grew farther apart, dwindling until the fourth night after the river, at which point they were well into the Sphinx Fields.

"The southern tip of the lake should be that way," Eirin said as she looked at her map. "But we can't go directly there. We have to make it to where the ferry docks."

The others agreed, and their travel went as well as could be expected. Rangvald sent no more hinderers, and they slept safely during the day in their tents, knowing only a fool would venture out into direct sunlight, shielded not even as the Trolls were by the forest when they tried to destroy the garden. But there was an unnatural silence on the plains so loud that it hurt Eirin's ears. From what she could tell, though no one actually said it aloud, it made her friends uncomfortable as well.

To make things worse, Isayas was unusually grumpy, even for him. His staff had been damaged during the fight with the Griffins, and he needed a particular tool to fix it, one he didn't carry.

"The tool broke about thirty years ago," he growled. "And being the fool that I am, I didn't see a reason to make another." Every time they stopped to sleep, he fiddled with the staff, but nothing seemed to work.

Eirin's least favorite part of this leg of the journey by far, however, was Drystan's silence.

Drystan had always been quiet, less likely to laugh with his peers, even when he was a student in the Citadel. But many times throughout their acquaintance she'd seen him share quiet jokes with Qeb, one of them saying something to the other in a low voice before each of them grinned at the other. But now, even that seemed gone. Ever since Drystan's talk with Stavros at their parting.

Now, Drystan simply moved. Drystan was always moving, whether in his Dragon or Human form. He was rarely still unless he was listening.

Eirin also noticed the constant little looks that Callispa continued to send him. As did Nuru.

"I'm going to bite her if she doesn't stop moaning over him," Nuru growled. They had just finished their second night out on the plains, and Thane and Qeb had left briefly to hunt before the sun came up. They had discovered a narrow but deep ravine with a small stream on the bottom that hid them nicely from view, and it had been decided, on account of Isayas's broken staff, that they would remain there for the full day and the next night. Eirin, who had been growing tired again, could rest that way, and Isayas could try to find something with which to mend his staff.

Now, as the sky was just beginning to gray, Drystan was talking quietly with Isayas, and Callispa, who was supposed to be helping Nuru and Eirin erect the boys' tent, was staring at Drystan. Again.

"You should say something and make her stop before I do," Nuru said, bumping Eirin with her shoulder.

Eirin sighed. "I'm not about to get into a fight with a Phoenix. The girl is allowed to give her heart to whomever she chooses, even if he doesn't return it." It was a stupid thing to say, but Eirin was getting a headache, and she had the sneaking suspicion that the Unicorn elixir, as much as it was helping, wasn't chasing away her reaction to the curse entirely. She disliked Callispa's continued attentions more than anyone. But her exhaustion was real. And picking a fight with Callispa was the last thing she wanted to do.

Peace. Their goal was peace so they could get to Iilaedin and save the world. Even if Eirin did feel like telling Callispa to back off.

"Well, biting her would make *me* feel a whole lot better." Nuru gave a quiet snarl. "It would also make her take her eyes off of him for half a minute."

"I get the feeling there's someone else you'd rather bite instead," Eirin murmured. The moment the words were out of her mouth, she wished she could take them back. It was probably a really foolish thing to say. Thankfully, they were more alone than usual as they put the tents up without Callispa. "Why don't you forgive him?" Eirin asked in a gentler tone. "He really is trying."

Nuru's lips thinned dangerously. "It's not the forgiveness I begrudge him. It's the chance to play me for the fool again."

"Forgiveness might be a good place to start," Eirin said with a shrug.

Nuru looked at her and rolled her eyes. "You're one to talk."

"I'm not trying to punish Drystan. I'm trying to stay focused on saving Solevar." Eirin bumped Nuru's shoulder.

Nuru snorted and threw another thick sheet over the top of the tent. "You can tell yourself that, but it doesn't make it true."

Eirin felt completely drained as she snuggled into her sleeping sack an hour later. But sleep didn't come as easily as she'd expected.

Was Nuru right? Was she punishing Drystan?

No. At least, not the way Nuru doled out punishment. Eirin was talking to Drystan, at least. And she never tried to insult or hurt him. And yet...

And yet, she thought of all the times she'd pushed him away, keeping him at arm's length. He'd saved her life more times than she could count, but she refused to let him in. And when it came to Callispa...

Very well. Maybe she was still slightly jealous. A little. The memories of all those hours he and Callispa had spent together traveling, training, and that vile memory that continued to pop up of him holding her hand. And yes, he had assured Eirin it had been nothing but a ruse. And she believed him, only...

Then she'd seen Callispa approach him in the garden. Which Callispa technically had every right to do. Eirin had rebuffed Drystan's offer. But Eirin hadn't been able to watch. She'd looked away quickly and tried not to think of it again.

Though, of course, she had.

Memories were hard to banish, as were the feelings they evoked.

And Eirin would do well not to heed them. They could only detract from her focus and determination. So she used her Unicorn drops, said a prayer for her family back in the mountain, rolled over, and did her best to go to sleep.

* * *

Eirin slept for nearly a full day. She somewhat suspected that Isayas was responsible for this, as she woke up several times throughout the day and night, only to fall asleep again. But when she finally awoke in earnest, the sky—once again—was a mixture of yellow and gray.

Neither Nuru nor Callispa were in the tent, though Eirin knew from her brief moments of consciousness that they had slept there earlier.

Eirin rolled over and groaned slightly as her muscles protested. As much as she hated to admit it, she knew now that the Unicorn drops weren't a perfect cure. They'd severely lessened the symptoms of the curse. She was far healthier than she'd been when the Unicorns had first found them. But she could feel the pain returning, the fatigue and aches settling into her bones. At the moment, they were simply annoyances. But how long until they began to seep out of her bones and into the rest of her body once more? How long could she truly hold on?

Eirin sat up and paused. There was something else amiss, and it wasn't the curse. Eirin breathed in slowly, deeply, and tried to measure the change that had taken place around her. It was in the air. She was sure of it. The air was heavier. And so was the silence. When she'd fallen asleep, there had been the usual sounds of the breeze rustling the few trees in the ravine. Water had been rushing over the rocks in the stream, and animals had chattered around them. But now? Aside from the sounds of the water, there was nothing.

Eirin climbed stiffly out of her tent. Drystan was sitting just outside of it, examining one of his knives.

"You're awake," he said without looking at her.

Once again, Eirin was hit with guilt. But, as usual, there was no time for that now.

"Where's Nuru?" she asked. "And the others?" Now that she looked over their camp, she could only see Isayas, who was still muttering angrily over his broken staff, and Qeb kindling the fire.

"She's gone out to look for an herb for Isayas. Thane and Callispa went with her."

"This close to sunrise?" Eirin frowned, still scanning the horizon. There was little to see. Mostly plains with low hills and few trees. Dark clouds hovered to the northwest.

"They've been gone for a while." He finally put the knife down and looked at her. When she met his gaze, her worry must have been evident because his eyes widened, and he sat up straight. "What's wrong?"

She looked back out and tried to hone in on the air rather than the scenery. "It's...magic." She shook her head in frustration. But there! Dancing in the early morning light, she could see it. Like dust motes that sparkled brilliantly in the dull light of early morning, they filled the air. "There's too much!" She stumbled back, suddenly breathless. "Drystan, something's wrong!"

He was out of his chair and at her side in a flash, catching her before she could fall. His large, rough hands gripped her carefully, steadying her. She looked up at him, and she could see her fear mirrored as stress on his face. His blue eyes sparked amber as he held her gaze.

"Isayas," he called in a low voice.

"What?" They looked up to see Isayas frowning at the plains as Eirin had just done.

"Eirin says–"

"I know." Isayas looked down at them. "Take her back inside."

"But–" Eirin began.

"Now," he said firmly.

Drystan looked down at Eirin and gave her the ghost of a smile, but Eirin couldn't return it. Not for the first time was she frustrated by the knowledge that the world's future rested on her shoulders. Sometimes, she just didn't feel like being *safe*.

But Isayas was right, so she trudged back into the tent to wait. To her surprise, Drystan followed her inside and closed the tent flap. He'd been so aloof lately that it was oddly intimate to suddenly have him so close, his eyes on hers.

And for some reason, looking quite embarrassed.

"I...um." He ran his hand through his dark hair, making it stick up in every direction. "Since the Atharrachs are all out of hearing distance, I guess now would be as good a time as ever to confess something."

"No one but Qeb." Eirin gave him a wry smile. "But then again, he already knows, doesn't he?"

Drytan's eyebrows shot up. "How do you know that?"

Eirin rolled her eyes. "Since when does Qeb *not* know everything?"

Drystan smiled wanly as he looked down at his hands. "Well, not everything," he said in a quiet voice. "But yes, he knows this because he happened to see it."

Despite her determination to remain calm and detached, Eirin's heart fluttered. "And what did he see?" she asked, trying to maintain her air of detachment. But what in the world could he be looking so guilty about? The only time he'd ever looked so guilty--aside from the time he'd nearly eaten her after his first shift--was the time Callispa...

Oh no.

Eirin wanted to throw up.

"When we were in the garden," he said, still looking down at his hands, "Callispa kissed me."

Eirin flushed, and beads of sweat broke out on her neck and back.

That minx.

A sense of rage came over Eirin to a degree she'd never felt before. Yes, she might have told Nuru that Callispa was free to pursue Drystan. And she might have even pretended to believe that Drystan was free to pursue her. But in that moment, Eirin knew it was all a load of horse dung. Drystan had woven his magic around *her*. He had kissed *her*. And now, as they fought their way to the Emerald Palace, the Phoenix had had the audacity to seize for herself what—

"Well," Eirin said, trying to suppress the rage that wanted to come screaming out, "I suppose that's up to both of you." She began to gather up her sleep sack and roll it back up, though her rolling was so violent she had to start again.

A rough hand gently took her wrist. "Eirin," Drystan said in a voice so soft, so caressing that she had to look up.

"What?" she snapped, her eyes filling with traitorous tears.

He studied her for a moment before the corners of his mouth lifted slightly. "I pushed her away."

She stared at him for a long time, the stupid water in her eyes threatening to spill over rather than retreat like it was supposed to. Slowly, so slowly he reached out and caressed her cheek. Holding her gaze, he knelt before her so that they were facing one another. With his other hand, he gently cupped the back of her neck. His movements were so careful that Eirin felt as though she were watching from outside her own body. He leaned closer and closer until she could feel his breath on her skin. The hand with which he was caressing her cheek moved down and traced the outline of her jaw.

"Am I *distracting* you?" he whispered, his lips grazing her ear.

Eirin let out a shuddering breath and closed her eyes, drinking in his touch while trying not to give in. "Very much so."

He put one hand on her waist and moved the other back to her face. "You sure that's the only reason you're throwing up walls?"

Eirin scrunched her eyes shut. "That's the problem, Drystan."

"What is?" He ran his finger from her forehead down to her chin, tracing her profile.

Eirin dared to open her eyes, and she gave him a sad smile. "You're already in my head. And my heart. And day and night, you threaten to destroy every wall I've ever built."

"And what would be so wrong with that?"

To Eirin's surprise, she let out a small sob. At this, Drystan leaned back slightly, which was a relief and disappointment.

"Eirin–" he began, but she shook her head.

"You don't understand."

"I don't if you won't tell me," he said, looking slightly bewildered as he wiped away her tears with his thumbs.

Why did his voice have to be so warm? Like a gentle thunderstorm on a warm afternoon.

"I am doing everything in my power not to think of the people I've left behind," Eirin sniffed. "My family. Alys. The people at Mhaedin. Because I am terrified that I'm going to let them down. And the fear..." She had to stop and let out another sob. "The fear is paralyzing. To the point that I can barely move because I'm sure I'm going to fail." She shook her head. "Letting you in like that...like I want to..." She finally looked up to meet his piercing blue gaze. "I can't bear the weight of losing you, too."

He leaned forward and pulled her against his thick, warm chest. Unable to resist, Eirin let him.

"I'm going with you either way," he whispered into her hair. "I wish you would let me bear the weight with you, rather than shouldering it all on your own."

Eirin closed her eyes and leaned into him. He didn't understand. There was no way to make him understand. She wanted to let him in. With every fiber of her being, she wanted to be his alone and completely, body and soul.

But to have him entirely and then to lose him...she didn't think she could survive that. Even if she did survive in body, she would always feel as if she'd hacked off a part of her soul. It was better this way. Keeping him out meant staying safe. Because if he died, a part of her own self would die too until the day she joined him. But she wouldn't know what she had missed. She wouldn't know the true depth of what had really been lost.

He pulled back and looked down at her, and the bright light in his eyes dimmed somewhat. His smile grew sad as he played with a lock of her hair that had fallen from her braid.

"I understand," he said softly. "I just wanted you to know since..." Then he shook his head and stood.

Eirin narrowed her eyes and stood too. "Since what?"

"You're right. We both need to focus now. It's just that..." He took a deep breath and pressed his lips to her forehead. "I love you," he whispered against her skin.

Eirin clung to him against her better judgment, and for a brief moment, she let her mind take her where she'd not allowed it to go before.

What would it feel like to kiss him? Not the gentle, cautious kiss he'd given her as they danced back in Torbaine, when he'd enveloped her in his magic as if she were a part of him. No, she wanted a real kiss, one full of the same passion Drystan lived his life with. What if she asked Isayas to marry them on the spot without ceremony or tradition? Just their vows to love one another until death tore them from one another's arms? She could lie in his arms as she slept, warm and safe for those brief, precious moments when they stopped to rest. She could give him everything she was without reserve.

Eirin let out a small, sharp curse. Drystan, whom she was sure had never heard her utter such a word, looked at her in surprise. But before either could speak, they were interrupted by a shout from Thane such as they had never heard before.

Drystan and Eirin bolted from the tent to see Thane galloping toward them in his Centaur form across the plains, Nuru on his back. Callispa was flying behind him, her fiery wings spread wide. Qeb and Isayas had hurried to the edge of the ravine as well. Only as Eirin struggled up the ravine toward them behind Drystan did she realize something strange.

The sun should have risen by now.

When she reached the top of the ravine and could see the plains in full, her heart nearly stopped.

Where the dawn should be was a swath of monstrous, billowing black and blue clouds. The storm was headed straight for them.

Chapter Fifteen

"Ice!" Thane roared as they slid into the ravine. "The storm is filled with ice!"

"What happened–" Eirin stopped short when she saw that Nuru was in Human form.

"Nuru flew farther out than we did," Thane said as Qeb pulled her down. "She saw it first. She tried to fly back to us to warn us. And she made it but got hit by hail on the way."

"I still ran–" Nuru began, but Thane interrupted.

"We found her just as it got bad."

"You outran the storm?" Eirin asked, looking back up at the blue, black mass coming toward them.

"I could have made it back on my own," Nuru growled, her eyes still closed. "These idiots insisted on helping me."

"It's coming from the northwest!" Callispa gasped, her fiery wings disappearing back into her shoulder blades. "It's not as fast as we are in Atharrach form, but only just."

"Can you stop it?" Drystan looked at Isayas.

"Not with a broken staff," the Wizard said.

"Which means we need to get into our tents now!" Qeb growled, but Isayas shook his head.

"No tent will hold back this freeze. This is the wrath of the Ymir up in the northern mountains. Someone must have angered them."

"Further up the ravine," Thane said, still breathing hard. "We'll be better sheltered than we are here."

"It won't work," Isayas began to say, but Drystan shook his head.

"We have to try! Everyone, grab your pack and go!" Qeb began to pack a tent, but Drystan stopped him. "We don't have time. Just the essentials!" He whirled around to talk to Eirin.

"Can you hold onto me if it hits?" The temperature was already starting to drop, and the wind was beginning to bite.

Eirin really wasn't sure, but she nodded anyway. "Yes." As though they had another choice.

"Take her now!" Isayas called. "Don't worry about us! We'll follow!"

Drystan shifted, and Thane practically tossed her up onto his back. She grabbed the spines on the back of his neck and tried to position herself securely against them on his massive back. In seconds, they were in the air, and she watched as their friends quickly grew smaller behind them.

"There!" Drystan rumbled over the sound of the increasing wind. "I can see the spot Thane was talking about!" But as he began to descend, the wind began to howl, and his words were lost. Eirin glanced back once more to see her friends in the distance as they were swallowed up by the billowing white.

Even as she watched it, a white fog began to creep into the air they were now slicing through. The wind grew so cold it bit into her skin, and Eirin's hands began to hurt. She did her best to squeeze, fighting the numbness. She had not come this far to fall off a Dragon in a windstorm.

Despite her determination, her fingers were beginning to turn blue as Drystan dove toward the ravine. In one smooth move, he somehow flipped around and yanked Eirin against his chest as he hit the side of the bank with his back.

The impact jarred Eirin so hard her teeth seemed to crunch against one another. That was nothing, though, to the cold that settled in her bones when the wall of white devoured them. She hadn't imagined such cold could exist.

Before she could give in to it, however, the way she felt the cold wanted her to, Drystan used his thick scaled forearms to pull her tightly against his warm chest and wrapped his wings around her to shield her from the cold. He opened his mouth and breathed on her, the warmth making her skin prickle painfully. But it was better than the numbness that wanted to lull her to sleep, never to wake up.

They stayed that way for longer than Eirin could count. Drystan continued to breathe on her as the frost continued to creep in between the cracks.

"Fight it, Eirin," Drystan growled between breaths. "Don't let it take you. Don't go to sleep!"

Eirin tried. She really did. She flexed her muscles all over her body and wiggled slightly to try to keep her body awake. She knew what happened to Humans who were exposed to severe cold for any length of time. The Citadel might have lied to its students about many things, but the dangers to Humans had been thoroughly studied.

A sound jarred her from her musings. Drystan began shouting her name again, but for some reason, Eirin found she couldn't answer. She was just too tired. She tried to open her eyes, but her eyelids were so heavy. When had she closed them?

"Eirin! Eirin!" Drystan sounded frantic.

Eirin tried to answer him, tried to tell him she was finally comfortable. But she couldn't. She was just too sleepy.

Just before she started to doze, she realized she was moving. But she couldn't imagine why.

Chapter Sixteen

The Sphinxes stared at Drystan expectantly as he hugged Eirin closer to his chest, though their smug expressions were growing difficult to see through the storm.

"Didn't you hear me? Let me take the girl, and you follow us!" a male Sphinx hissed.

"I heard you," Drystan shouted over the sound of the storm. He could barely see the three Atharrachs now through the sleet and snow, despite being somewhat sheltered in the ravine.

"Would you like to put her in a proper shelter or watch her fall dead at the breath of the Ymir?" the second Sphinx, a female, snapped.

"I will take her into the shelter myself!" Drystan called over the wind.

The Sphinxes all looked at each other, and Drystan was rather sure they rolled their eyes at him.

"There isn't time for this," the first one snapped. "Nor is there space in the tunnel. You'll barely fit in your Human form as it is. Now give us the girl, and let us be done with this."

As if to punctuate his words, an icy blast hit them, nearly knocking Drystan back into the ravine wall. If he didn't get Eirin out of this soon, it wasn't going to matter who took her anywhere.

"Lead me to the tunnel!" he shouted. "Then I'll hand her over!"

"Fine. Whatever you wish," the third one, another female, scoffed. They turned and bounded back down the ravine. As he followed them, Drystan prayed to the Time Keeper that he hadn't just agreed to something very stupid.

The wind seemed to be getting colder by the minute. Drystan didn't mind much. His heart pushed its fire around his body, but he was sure he'd be shivering much the way Eirin was if he was in his Human form. And Eirin, it seemed, was fading by the minute. He'd been trying to get her to respond to his voice for several minutes by the time the Sphinx trio had found them. And as much as he hated not to have the upper hand, they were right. If kept out in this much longer, Eirin would die.

When the Sphinxes came to a stop, Drystan saw that they hadn't been lying about his size. The hole in the side of the bank was round and seemed just large enough to fit the Sphinxes' feline forms as they dove inside, their wings folding neatly against their backs.

Feeling very much like a traitor, Drystan handed Eirin to the last one, then shifted into his own Human form. The last Sphinx, holding Eirin tightly, quickly slipped inside, leaving Drystan out on his own.

Drystan had been correct in his guess. His Human form, though still warmed by his fiery heart, was far more susceptible to the storm than his Atharrach form. Shivering and unwilling to test how long he might last in the ice storm, Drystan tried to climb in after them. But he was dismayed to realize that the mouth of the hole was far thicker than he'd expected. Even worse, it grew smaller the farther in he got. Just as they'd predicted, his shoulders wouldn't fit.

He was stuck.

Frost began to creep up his neck and face, and panic threatened to take him. Quickly, he summoned his Dragon fire to warm the air around him. Simultaneously, he did his best to shove himself inside.

To no avail. And Eirin, his heart told him, was in there alone. Without him.

Drystan tried calling for the Sphinxes, but none answered. Desperately, he tried to shove himself inside. After all, it was only dirt If he could just break the mouth of the hole open a little wider...

The earthen tunnel around him exploded. Once. Twice. Three times. With each blow, the hole widened, and before he knew what was happening, someone took Drystan by the shoulders and yanked him through. The next thing he knew, he was on the floor of a dirt passage, looking up at Qeb, who was also covered in dirt and looked quite upset.

Relief flooded Drystan as his tired mind noted that his best friend wasn't dead. But Eirin's name was the first word to pass through his lips.

Qeb nodded toward the other end of the tunnel. "With the others."

Drystan nodded and thanked his friend as he stood. The wind behind them howled, and the cold still seeped into the tunnel, but not nearly with the strength it had outside.

"And everyone else?"

"They're safe, too. A Sphinx found us further down and brought us in through another passage. I came because I heard you calling."

"Thanks," Drystan said again, taking a step down the tunnel, which he could now see was lit with torches fixed on the walls. But before he took two steps, Qeb put his large hand on Drystan's shoulder and held him in place.

"Take care," he said in a low voice. "I don't think they wanted you to make it."

"That doesn't surprise me at all," Drystan said wryly.

The passage was winding and met many other winding tunnels along the way. The labyrinth was neat but not intuitively laid out. And the deeper they moved into the winding passages, the less Drystan trusted their hosts. Had they just escaped one horrible death for another?

Eventually, though Drystan couldn't tell how far they'd traveled to get there, he and Qeb entered a large chamber. At least two dozen Sphinxes lounged around the earthen room lit by a roaring fire in the large hearth. Some of the Sphinxes were in Human form, but they, too, sported the usual lazy smile Drystan had come to associate with the Sphinx. It was smug, as though they knew something everyone else didn't. Although, that seemed likely in this case.

More torches lit this room along with the fire in the hearth, making it nearly as light as day. The ceiling, walls, and floor were all earthen, and the ceiling was so low the top of Drystan's head nearly brushed against it. The Sphinxes in their Human forms wore loose, light clothing, the women in simple dresses and the men in loose-fitting trousers.

Drystan's own little group was huddled in front of the tall hearth, and he was once again nearly overcome with relief when he counted all members of his party safe and accounted for. They all sat before the fire except for Eirin, who was being tended to with what looked like warm bowls of water, and Nuru, who was having her wings examined.

"So nice of you to join us," said one of the males, who happened to be the largest in the room. He hopped down from his perch on the couch, which had been carved out of the wall, and padded toward Drystan.

The Dragon's blood began to boil, but he felt a staying hand on his shoulder. He turned to look at Qeb, who gave him the smallest shake of his head.

"Don't fall for it," he muttered quietly before going to join the others at the hearth.

Drystan coaxed the Dragon to back down. Qeb was right. They were goading him the way Nuru had once enjoyed goading Eirin. It must be a Sphinx thing.

The lounging Sphinxes were looking down on their visitors with pure, unadulterated scorn. The only ones they didn't seem to be glaring or smirking at were Eirin and Nuru. Three of the Sphinxes were tending to Nuru's wings which, Drystan gathered, must have been injured when the storm first hit, just before Thane carried her back. They seemed intent in their ministrations, murmuring to Nuru and to one another as they applied a waxy substance to what looked like ice burns.

Eirin was wrapped in a fur blanket and propped up on a couch near the fire. She was pale but gave him a small, relieved smile when he walked in.

Isayas, who sat closest to Eirin, was glaring at his staff. Thane glanced continuously back at Nuru, and Callispa was staring blankly into the fire.

A particularly large Sphinx, the one that had addressed Drystan in the ravine, settled himself close to Eirin, curling up on the end of her couch. Drystan knew instinctively that he was trying to push Drystan's boundaries to see how far he would let them go, but the Dragon writhed inside anyway.

Not now, Drystan told himself. They were in the Sphinxes' home. While he had no doubt he could effortlessly kill every Sphinx himself, Eirin wouldn't be safe in such an enclosed space if a fight broke out. She could easily be killed. So Drystan simply met the Sphinx's gaze evenly.

"Now that we've rescued you from the wrath of the Ymir," the Sphinx said with a slight purr, "I believe it's only polite for you to answer a few questions." He paused. "But I sense you wish to ask one of your own."

"I do." Drystan said, standing straighter. "Why did you help us?"

The Sphinx snickered and rearranged his large paws. "It certainly wasn't for you." He tilted his head to the side and studied Drystan before continuing. "We've been following you for several days."

"Why?" Drystan asked.

"You're in our territory." The Sphinx snorted softly. "You don't think we'd find it strange that a Wizard, a motley group of Atharrachs, and one Human were traipsing through our lands?" He paused. "It, of course, led to questions."

"Such as?" Drystan asked.

"What are you doing?" the Sphinx purred.

Drystan raised his eyebrows. "Excuse me?"

"As I said, we've been following you for several days now. And to see a Dragon, a Wizard, a Sphinx, a Centaur, a Phoenix, and a Griffin traveling *toward* the curse rather than away from it?" His lips slid into a leer. "Not to mention your Human."

Drystan's hackles raised at the mention of Eirin, but he couldn't really fault them for their curiosity. With only one, possibly two Humans left in all of Solevar, anyone would be curious. Not that such curiosity would dupe Drystan into trusting them.

"And all of this," the Sphinx continued, "at the same time Rangvald is preparing to bring his own Human to Iilaedin as well. At least, that's the rumor." The Sphinx shrugged his powerful shoulders.

Isayas looked up from his staff for the first time, and Drystan and Qeb exchanged a glance. His own Human? Did he mean Eirin, whom Rangvald desired to abduct? Or did he mean Mannish?

"What I want to know," the Sphinx continued, "is why another son of Oreck is making his way through the Sphinx Fields. And going the long way, too." His large eyes glinted. "Almost as if he wants to avoid the city at all costs." Getting up from his couch, he stretched and padded over to Drystan, and when he reached him, he began to sniff Drystan all over.

Every natural instinct in Drystan was dying to force the enemy away. But he remained still. If peace was at all possible, he had to try to maintain it. For Eirin's sake.

"Which son of Faradoon are you?" another Sphinx, this one a female, asked. "You're obviously of the line of Oreck, but Faradoon had three sons."

"And last we heard," the male Sphinx's eyes narrowed, "Demetrius's line has ended. You're not Rangvald nor are you his seed. Which leaves only one possibility."

"They're taking me because I don't trust Rangvald."

Everyone turned to look at Eirin, who was struggling to sit up while keeping the blanket wrapped around her.

The male Sphinx turned. "You don't trust Rangvald?" His eyes were bright and searching.

"I've been to his fortress," Eirin said, her voice slightly stronger now. Drystan longed to go to her and pull her against him to warm her, but he stayed put. One unexpected move from him might throw the place into chaos.

"What I saw there was disturbing," Eirin went on. "I don't trust his intentions."

The male Sphinx looked back and forth between Drystan and Eirin, his face twisting into one of confusion and disbelief.

"But you trust this man? Spawn of Kamon?" He looked back at Drystan, and his grimace grew. "And you, son of Kamon, you're telling me you lay no claims to the throne? You're only here to help her?"

Drystan felt every eye in the room fixed on him. He could also feel Qeb ready to spring up, prepared to move into action at the slightest provocation.

"My priority," Drystan said slowly, "is to get Eirin safely to the Time Stones so she can break the curse. I swore to protect her when we began this journey, and I intend to see it through." Though, for some reason, Eirin and a growing number of dissenters seemed to think that part of that duty meant challenging Rangvald for the throne.

"Wizard." The Sphinx turned to Isayas. "Does he speak the truth?"

"I can attest that he has sworn to protect the Human at all costs," Isayas said, sounding disgusted at being asked such a question.

The Sphinx turned back to Drystan with another slight smile, and Drystan knew immediately that he didn't believe them. But, to Drystan's surprise, he didn't challenge the claim either.

"How long do you think these winds will go on?" Nuru croaked from where she lay. She was in her Sphinx form again, but Drystan recognized her from the distinctive spot of white fur on her throat. None of the other Sphinxes in the room had it.

"No one knows," an older female replied. She was in her Human form and using her Human fingers to minister to Nuru's wounds. "It could be over in a few hours or three or four days. "The Ymir send winds that rage to match whatever had angered them." She shot Drystan a glance as though he was the one responsible.

"You must all be tired, though, so there's no use worrying about that," she continued. "You will all eat, then you'll be shown to a place where you shall sleep."

"Is food difficult to find here?" Qeb asked.

A young female in Sphinx form gave him a rather chilling smile, exposing her teeth to their best advantage. "Not when your food comes to you."

A shiver ran down Drystan's back. And when they were seated around a low table on the floor, he prayed desperately that they weren't about to eat anything...thoughtful.

Once the food was served, to Drystan's surprise, the Sphinxes left them on their own, choosing to eat in their own private corner away from their guests.

The food, to Drystan's relief, tasted like rabbit, and it was served with a wide variety of potatoes, onions, carrots, and other ground vegetables, similar to what families had grown back in Torbaine.

Eirin sniffed at her food and gave Drytan a questioning look. He knew what she was asking. Is the food safe to eat? He gave it his own sniff, knowing she was relying on his nose more than her own. When he nodded, she tucked into her food as if she'd never eaten before, nearly forgetting to use her Unicorn drops until Isayas reminded her. Qeb ate his food steadily. Callispa ate mechanically, as though it had no taste, staring down at her plate the entire time. Thane, who usually devoured everything in sight, was eating unusually slowly. Of course, this might have had something to do with his constant looks at Nuru.

Nuru had been instructed to stay in Atharrach form until her wings were more healed. That wasn't so unexpected, though. What troubled Drystan, and he guessed Thane as well, was how quiet she remained as they ate. There were no little sarcastic comments slipped in, no digs at their hosts or even at Thane.

Could it be the Sphinxes themselves who were affecting her? Drystan realized with a jolt that this was probably the closest to a home she would ever feel anywhere. It was no secret that she resented her mother, one of Torbaine's Elders, for the way she'd treated Nuru and everyone else around her in an attempt to gain power.

What if...was it possible that Nuru might choose to stay here?

The thought alarmed Drystan, and he studied her more closely as she picked at her food.

There must be a draw, of course, for her to want to be surrounded by what, for her, could be considered family, especially with the way her mother had treated her at home. The Sphinxes at Mhaedin had all but ignored her as well. Drystan wouldn't blame her for wanting to stay.

But somehow, in the course of the last year, Drystan had gone from being wary of her every move to relying on her completely. As much as it surprised him to say it, he wasn't sure he could take care of Eirin without her.

After supper, they were shown two chambers in a passage not far from the main room they'd eaten in, one chamber for the women and one for the men.

"We have more if Nuru or Eirin wish to rest alone," the female Sphinx said, eyeing the two girls. Her tone was just a little too accommodating for Drystan to believe she meant goodwill by such an offer.

"Just the two will be fine, thank you," Drystan said firmly. Once the woman had shrugged and walked away, he looked at Isayas. "I don't really like to split up even this much."

Isayas frowned, but instead of replying, he pulled something out of his bag. When he held up his hand, Drystan saw a pile of green glass balls, each about the size of a walnut.

"Every one of you, take one of these," Isayas said in a low voice. "If too many Sphinxes are near, your ball will glow and make a slight whining sound to wake you up. Not as useful as if I had my staff," he grumbled under his breath. "But better than nothing."

"Why do you think they've taken us in?" Eirin whispered. "I still don't understand their motives enough to trust them."

"Don't," Isayas whispered back. "Sphinxes are known for

serving their own interests before anyone else's." He paused and looked at Nuru. "No offense."

"You think I don't know this better than anyone else?" Nuru said with a dry smile. But it didn't touch her eyes.

Half an hour later after washing his face and arms, Drystan returned to the girls' room to check on them once more. When he knocked on the door, Eirin answered.

He was rendered briefly speechless as he gazed into the dark brown eyes that looked up at him, and he was reminded of the moments together before the storm. Even now, with the door mostly between them, he longed to reach out and pull her close again. But this wasn't the time or the place, so he simply leaned as close as he dared to whisper,

"Is everything well?"

Eirin glanced back into the room and then gave him a somewhat wry smile. "As well as can be expected." He sensed she wanted to say more but didn't want their friends to hear, and he was once again seized by the desire for the intimacy they'd shared back during those early days in Mhaedin, when they could talk about anything, those few sweet days before he had realized what a danger he posed to her. His chest ached even as she stood before him.

For a moment, he wondered if she would say something... anything about what had happened between them in the tent. But after a moment of hesitation, she sent him a tight-lipped smile and closed the door as she wished him a good night.

irin let out a deep sigh as she closed the door behind her. What had happened in the tent had been a mistake.

Not that anything had actually happened. They were in the same place they'd been before...waiting. But he'd gotten close.

And she had let him.

She looked down at the little glass ball in her hand. She likely wouldn't need it. Her head was pounding and her skin was crawling with the amount of magic in this place where so many Atharrachs surrounded them. She was used to her friends' magic. But not even in Mhaedin or within the garden's walls had they slept in such cramped quarters. She would know for sure if anyone came close to their door because her head might just explode. She rubbed her arms, trying to rid herself of the sensation.

Callispa was either sleeping or pretending to sleep by the time Eirin made her way to the bed that had been prepared for her, and Nuru was already in her own bed, staring up at the ceiling. Eirin went to where a bowl of water had been set out for them and added a drop of Unicorn elixir. Then she used it to wash her face, neck, and arms.

"I'm glad you weren't hurt."

Eirin paused, mid-scrub, and turned to face Nuru. "What?"

Nuru shrugged but didn't take her eyes from the ceiling. "I was a fool this morning. And I endangered everyone else because of it."

Eirin dried her hands and went back to her sleeping nook. Once she was nestled in her pile of blankets, she faced Nuru. "You didn't bring on the ice storm. I'm not sure why–"

"I shouldn't have strayed so far. Isayas told me not to, and so did Callispa." She snorted. "Even Thane was nervous. But I didn't listen, and I nearly got us all killed."

Eirin frowned. "I still don't see–"

"I smelled them, Eirin!"

"Smelled..who? The Ymir? I'm confused."

Nuru scoffed and sat up. "The Sphinxes. I smelled them."

Eirin blinked at her friend. "Oh," was all she could think to say.

"They have a distinctive smell," Nuru went on, her voice slightly softer. "I guess you wouldn't know that, though."

Obviously. Eirin shook her head.

"I knew better, too. That's the thing. I knew not to look for them. I've never met a single Sphinx who treated me well. But I couldn't help it. I was sniffing out one of their stupid burrow entrances–"

"Can they hear us?" Eirin whispered, glancing at the door.

Nuru shrugged. "Probably. They've probably heard almost every word we've said tonight." She smirked. "We have excellent hearing. Anyhow," her smile faded, "I'd followed my nose too far west. I was halfway into the hole when the initial burst of the storm hit."

"Is that why your wings were injured?" Eirin asked.

Nuru nodded. "We only got out in time because Thane found me. And because he's so ridiculously fast. He even dragged Callispa out far enough ahead of the storm that she could fly without freezing."

Eirin shivered. As much as she currently resented Callispa, she had no desire to see her die. Snow and ice could be lethal to a fully transformed Phoenix. It could extinguish their fire completely.

"I made an excuse and told Thane I was looking to make sure they weren't near enough to be a threat," Nuru whispered. "But I wanted to see..." She drew in a shaky breath.

Eirin got up and went to Nuru's bed. If it could be called that. It seemed as though the Sphinxes didn't have traditional furniture, for the most part. The beds and couches had been carved into the walls, and Eirin hadn't seen a single stool or chair since arriving. To her surprise, though, the nests of blankets laid out for them were quite comfortable.

Sitting beside Nuru, she put her arm around her friend and leaned her head against the taller girl's shoulder. A small voice in her head whispered that, had she been told a year ago that she would be *embracing* Nuru, she would have told the messenger to get lost. Another small voice wondered when Nuru would shove her away, as she generally did to anyone who got too close.

But to her surprise, Nuru simply leaned her head against Eirin's and let out a long, deep sigh.

"You know what scares me the most?" she asked.

"No," Eirin whispered.

"When this is all done...if by some crazy stroke of fate, we survive and fix the Time Stones and all..." She paused. "I don't know what I'm going to do."

Eirin turned to look at her friend. "What do you mean?"

"I mean," Nuru said, looking down at her, "that war was all I ever trained for. It's what I lived for. My mother wanted to be sure I was the smartest, strongest, fastest guard in Torbaine. And the only reason she's still not pushing that is because I left with you." She shrugged. "I've never known anything else."

Eirin gave her friend a sad smile. "Well, I hope whatever you decide to do, it's not too far from me."

Nuru stared at her for a moment, then snorted. "You know you'd rather have Alys any day of the week over a cantankerous Sphinx. Especially the one who tried to pummel you on a daily basis."

"I certainly miss Alys," Eirin said slowly. "But...if I made that exchange then I would miss you, too."

Nuru gave her a look so funny that Eirin laughed. Callispa moaned in her sleep, and Eirin clapped a hand over her mouth. Nuru rolled her eyes, but Eirin nudged her shoulder.

"Of course," she added in a lower voice, "I prefer the Nuru who doesn't try to kill me daily."

Nuru gave her a dry smile. "I guess I do, too."

The candle flickered, reminding Eirin that she needed to sleep. But just as she climbed into her own bed, Nuru sat up once more.

"But Eirin?"

"Yes?"

"Don't trust them. All right?"

"Who?" Eirin asked, glancing at the door. "Our hosts?"

Nuru nodded. "Sphinxes are known for being tricksters. It's like a game, part of the hunt."

Eirin glanced at the door once more, then it dawned on her. Nuru wanted them to hear her. She *wanted* them to know she was on to them.

Nuru was bold.

"I believe their intentions toward me are decent enough," Nuru went on. "I'm one of them. They even told me that. And they're not stupid enough to hurt you. But I don't think they mean to help us."

Eirin forced a grin. "Well then, it's a good thing we have you." She wiggled down into her blankets. But Nuru didn't smile.

"I mean it, Eirin. Don't let your guard down. These people are cunning. They asked me if I would..." She paused then cursed the Ymir before moving down into her own blankets and blowing the candle out.

Tired as Eirin was, she didn't immediately fall asleep. Instead, she digested what she'd seen and learned that day.

To begin with, there were the visions she'd seen when they'd first laid her on the couch in the main room. In her vision, the Sphinxes, as they had admitted, had been discussing Eirin and her friends. But no matter how many times Eirin had watched the scene over again, there had been no mention of their specific plans for Eirin's little party. As Nuru had warned her, they were sly, so sly as to not even reveal their plans in secret.

Then, of course, she wanted to consider her time with Drystan. But no, it was better to try and stow that away for later. Preferably after the curse was broken. Not now, when she needed all her concentration to focus on the task at hand, which, at the moment, seemed to be outwitting the people who had saved them.

Eirin did her best to consider their situation from every angle, but the wind was howling above them like a mad Wizard incanting against the world. And against her will, Eirin drifted off to sleep.

Chapter Eighteen

E irin scrunched her eyes shut and pushed back against whatever sensation had awakened her. Her blankets were warm and soft, and she was greatly relishing the feeling of sleeping away from the elements.

But there it was again.

And again.

With a groan, Eirin forced her eyes open to see the little glass ball glowing a bright green. And only then did she realize what sensation had awakened her.

Magic. Magic everywhere pressing in on her. After a moment of panicked confusion, Eirin then realized what the magic meant.

The Sphinxes were right outside her door. Eirin bolted up in her bed.

"Nuru!" she hissed as loudly as she dared. "Nuru! Callispa!"

But neither of them woke up. Their little glass balls glowed as well, however, and began to emit a strange whining pitch. But both girls continued breathing as deeply and evenly as before.

Eirin glanced at the door and hopped out of bed. She ran to Nuru and shook her shoulder.

"Nuru! Wake up!" But as soon as she touched her friend's

shoulder, she knew Nuru wouldn't be waking up anytime soon. A strange kind of magic tingled on her friend's skin.

Eirin stared at Nuru, fighting to keep her own breath even, rather than going into hysterics the way she desperately wanted to. Her friends had been drugged. Why she hadn't sensed it the night before, she couldn't...

Then she remembered how Mannish had told her once that there were certain kinds of charms Wizards, Elves, and sometimes Nymphs could create, charms that had delayed effects. The Sphinxes could have easily gotten hold of one of these charms. They must have drugged everyone at supper, knowing there would be less of a struggle if they were simply allowed to go to sleep as usual. Nuru had been right about everything, and this was far too much like their run-in with the Tsuchigumo named Shigeo for Eirin's comfort.

So what could Eirin do about it?

She was no match for a single Sphinx, let alone an entire Sphinx colony. They wouldn't hurt her, of course. Not on purpose. But if they decided to take her, she had no way to stop them.

A scratching sounded at the door, and Eirin bounded back to her own bed. Closing her eyes and trying to slow her heart, she did her best to look as though she were asleep. Seconds after she had yanked the blankets back over her body, the door opened, and she heard the sound of Human footsteps.

Eirin gripped the handle of the knife she kept sheathed beneath her blanket. It was the one Drystan had given her and, it seemed, the only help she would have tonight.

"We know you're awake, Human," the male with the deep voice said. Eirin tried to remember his name. She was sure he'd given it to her at some point. But the Sphinxes moved, acted, and spoke so much like they were all just parts of a whole that she had a hard time telling them apart.

"Magic draughts don't work on Humans," he continued. "And you whisper so loudly the entire colony hears it."

Eirin swallowed and continued to lie frozen.

"We don't wish to hurt you or your friends. We simply want some time alone with you, and we knew your friends wouldn't allow you to give it."

Eirin sat up slowly, keeping her hand clasping the knife handle under the blanket. "You won't hurt them?"

"That is not our purpose," one of the older women, also in Human form, purred. "We thought we would be able to coax Nuru into helping us, but she refused as well." She frowned thoughtfully at Nuru's sleeping form, as though this perplexed her.

"And don't bother hiding your weapon," the man said with a sigh. "We know it's there. We wouldn't be stupid enough to hurt you." His eyes glinted in the dark.

"It makes me feel better to hold it all the same," Eirin said, her voice wavering slightly.

One of the females chuckled softly. "You can't seriously believe you can keep us all from them should we feel provoked."

And there it was.

The threat.

"If you come with us, the female continued, "we can talk somewhere a little more comfortable," the female continued.

"I was comfortable sleeping," Eirin grumbled, but she climbed out of bed and went with them. And just because they had laughed at her, she kept the knife.

They gathered back in the main room. Eirin was seated by the fire, and though she didn't voice it, she was incredibly thankful. Even buried here in the earth, the air was freezing.

"Let's get to the meat of the matter," the male Sphinx said, sitting across from her. His long, thick braids swung back and forth, creating snake-like shadows in the fire's flickering light. "We know you possess something special."

Eirin blinked at him. "And what would make you think that?"

He smiled knowingly and leaned back. "The curse has raged for a hundred years. Hundreds of Atharrachs head south by the day, hoping to escape the doom that awaits us all. Knowing all of that, a ragtag group of outcasts wouldn't be traipsing through Solevar if they didn't think they had reason to do so. Humans are far too precious." Then he leaned forward on his elbows, his dark eyes bright. "Which can only mean that you carry something no one else has."

As though he'd snapped his fingers, the entire room converged upon Eirin. Though only Human fingers touched her, she saw and smelled fur everywhere. And she prayed they wouldn't find the stone.

But the prayer was not granted her. One young man somehow found the leather cord that was around her neck, and in his excitement, nearly choked her as he yanked it off.

"No!" Eirin gasped. "Don't touch–"

Before she could finish, he lay still on the floor. Someone let out a haunting scream, and two of the Sphinxes in Atharrach form leaped to his side, nudging him with their noses and whining piteously at his side.

"I tried to tell you!" Eirin cried. "You cannot touch it! No one but a Seer can!" She tried to push her way toward the stone where it had fallen when the young man had collapsed, but the head Sphinx was there first. Gracefully, he knelt and lifted it carefully by the cord.

"So it's true," he whispered. "The stones really are cursed."

"They're *sacred*!" Eirin snapped. "There's a difference."

"That's a dangerous thing to be running around with on your neck," one of the women said gently. She pulled an ornately woven pouch off her waist and handed it to the man. He dropped the stone inside and pulled it closed, then tied it around his own waist.

"I think this makes our way clear," the woman said to him in a low voice as some of the Sphinxes hurried to help the grieving parents carry their son's body away. The others sat back, watching everything with bright eyes.

"Which means?" Eirin interjected.

The Sphinx looked at Eirin for a long moment before sitting across from her once again. "It means you will be continuing your journey to the Emerald Palace with us."

"And my friends?"

He pursed his lips slightly before looking at the young man's body as it was carried away.

"You're going to kill them, aren't you?" Eirin said. Her heart pounded so fast she was nauseous. She could feel another one of her dizzy spells threatening to take her, and she suddenly wished she'd taken one of her Unicorn drops before they'd taken her from her bed.

"Your friends are...a liability," he said slowly, steepling his fingers in front of him.

"They saved my life more times than I can count," Eirin growled between clenched teeth.

"Saved you from what?" the man asked gently. "Danger they most likely drew to you in the first place. For example," he pointed back toward the rooms where her friends slept, "the son of Kamon. Surely you can see that his sheer presence will threaten every Atharrach within a ten plough radius. Even," he put up his hands as Eirin opened her mouth, "if he doesn't mean to."

"And what makes you think he's a son of Kamon?" Eirin asked. It was probably a stupid question. They'd obviously seen the mark of Oreck on his scales before he'd shifted back into Human form. There were only three Dragons who even bore that mark in existence.

Well, two now.

But still, there was a chance he was bluffing.

As if reading her thoughts, the man nodded. "Word has it that the second heir to the Blood Fire Throne is dead. Which leaves two." He chuckled. "And we all know that that young man is not Rangvald."

"Your friends are too blind to realize how they're endangering you," the woman said. She sat beside the man, her large dark eyes never leaving Eirin's. "Even your Sphinx friend is determined not to see."

"We tried to convince her," one of the young women piped up. "We really did."

No wonder Nuru had been in so much pain last night. They'd offered her everything she had ever wanted, and she'd turned it down.

For Eirin.

"We can do what your friends can't," the man said. "We have tunnels and places of rest for ploughs. You could make it nearly all the way to Iilaedin without having to suffer the winds above."

"And there are other colonies who have even more," the woman added, her eyes growing brighter. "We can escort you there safely, and you will remove the stone from the Time Stone circle under our protection." She leaned forward. "What say you?"

Eirin stared at the woman, then at the man, then she looked out over the many eyes that were watching her just as closely.

They really believed they were doing what was right. That much was clear. They believed they were going to save the world and themselves by killing her friends and forcing her to go with them. Nuru had believed them to be offering help out of selfish ambition, but Eirin sensed that they believed themselves to be offering far more. She licked her lips and did her best to order her thoughts.

"What if...you led all of us through the passages? Drystan would happily give you-"

But the man was already shaking his head. "I told you. That boy draws far too much attention to you without even realizing it. No, we are doing this without him."

Fire raged inside of Eirin, the anger inside her burning almost like a vestige Drystan's magic, a remnant from the night he had wrapped her in his heartfire. She lifted her chin.

"Then I don't know why you're even bothering to ask."

The man's face, which had been open and gentle, hardened, and his eyes seemed to darken as she watched.

"Then I am sorry, but-"

The air began to crackle, and tiny white lights exploded above them. Eirin ducked and covered her head as a deafening explosion rocked the room.

When she looked up, the Sphinxes around her were either unconscious or lying still on the floor, moaning. The explosion had been violent enough that it took Eirin a moment before she was able to stand. The magic hadn't affected her, of course, but the pure power of the explosion had.

By the time she managed to make it to her feet, Drystan and Nuru were at her side.

"You're awake!" she squeaked as they began pulling and tugging at her arms, turning her to examine her every which way. "And I'm fine." She brushed them off. "But my stone..." Her hand immediately went to her chest, where it always lay hidden beneath her clothes. Then she remembered. Whirling around, she looked for the man who had taken it. He was nowhere to be seen.

"The...the male. The one in charge," she sputtered, panic making it difficult to form complete sentences. "He took my stone! And now he's gone!"

"Nuru-" Drystan began, but before he could finish, Nuru

had shifted and was already sprinting down one of the many passages that led off the main room.

"Everyone stay down," Qeb growled. He, like Drystan, was still in Human form, probably because the ceiling was uncomfortably low for his Griffin form. He had somehow regained his weapons and was holding them at the ready as he walked around, scowling down at the dazed Sphinxes.

"Here, Drystan," Thane said, tossing Drystan his weapons. "They had them stashed in a room near ours."

Drystan accepted his weapons, as did Callispa. Isayas emerged, holding his staff and looking quite pleased.

"Well, this was convenient," he said to Eirin with a grin. Then he held up a small metal tool Eirin didn't recognize. "They had exactly what I needed. And now it's good as new." He tapped his staff on the floor, and it emitted a strong light, doubling the room's brightness.

"How did you all wake up?" Eirin asked. "Weren't you drugged?"

"We were," Thane called. "Nuru was the one who recognized it in our drinks. She managed to convey that to Isayas before the meal ended."

"Sometimes what you really need most is a clever Sphinx." Thane beamed as though he had been the one to relay the message rather than Nuru.

"The Unicorns gave us some of their hairs before they left," Isayas said. "Very kind of them, of course. Not that I expected to use them this way."

"We tied them all around our wrists before going to bed," Drystan continued. "The Unicorn hair counteracted the sleeping draught."

"So...you were just pretending." Eirin frowned. "How in the world did all of you get this sorted out without telling me? And also, why didn't you tell me? Do you have any idea how–"

"I do apologize for that," Isayas said, picking his way through the flattened Sphinxes to stand beside Drystan. "But they were watching you more than the rest of us. If we had told you, we would have been found out."

As he spoke, Eirin was reminded of the night before, when Nuru mentioned that their hosts were probably listening to every word they said.

"But why did you wait so long then?" Eirin wasn't ready to forgive this quite yet. Her backside still throbbed from being knocked to the ground.

"Isayas had to fix his staff," Drystan said, his eyes dangerously amber for his Human form. "He wouldn't let us interfere before then."

"I knew they wouldn't kill you," Isayas called. "But a brawl would have been dangerous if you were caught in it. This way, I was able to fix everything all at once." He looked around. "Well, close to. I see we're missing some people."

"So..." Callispa said in a low voice, "What now?"

"Once Nuru gets your stone back," Isayas said, "I'll put everyone to sleep. Just so we don't have any helpers on our tails, of course. By the time they wake up, we'll have reached the lake."

"What about the storm?" Eirin asked.

Isayas scoffed. "My staff is working. I'll have no trouble blowing the blasted thing out." As he spoke, Nuru returned, looking quite smug.

"You're right," she said to Isayas, tossing Eirin the bag. "Those glass balls are handy."

Isayas looked surprised. "You released the magic inside? Sfiaras are difficult to crack."

Nuru scoffed. "No. I threw it at his head."

"And I'm sure it made you feel much better," Thane laughed.

Eirin snorted, Qeb chuckled, and even somber Drystan's

mouth turned up at the corner. Only Callispa remained straight-faced.

"We need to go," she said, nudging someone's leg with her boot. "They're waking up."

Isayas tapped his staff once more, and another burst of white lights flew out of its gem and hit the Sphinxes on the ground. "Right, then." He nodded. "Makes it easy when they're all lying still. Now, is everyone ready?"

Eirin and the others nodded, so he made his way to the nearest tunnel. "Nuru, would you do the honors of sniffing out an exit for us?"

Eirin expected Nuru's nose to get them out quickly. But finding their way through the tunnels took far longer than she'd first thought it would. For hours they wandered, Nuru cursing slightly whenever they needed to turn around and change course, and Eirin knew she wasn't the only one who breathed easier when they finally came to a door at the end of the tunnel.

"Is this the tunnel you came through?" Drystan asked. "I destroyed the one they took Eirin and me through."

"They have tunnels all over the place," Nuru said with a sneer. "They took special care to cover our tracks from when we entered. That's why all the tunnels smell alike."

Now that they had found an escape, Eirin let herself smile. Nuru had been getting grumpier by the minute, muttering to herself about being outsmarted by a rabbit hole.

Thane cracked the door open. "It's day, apparently," he said as a thin beam of sunlight shot through the crack in the door. He immediately slammed it shut again.

"Did you not hear me say I could blow the ice storm away?" Isayas scoffed. "What do you think I was doing while we were wandering around?"

"So what now?" Nuru asked. "Do we wait here until night?"

"No, we do not." Isayas pushed everyone back into the tunnel with his staff, then turned to face the partially open door.

Then he began to chant. Words Eirin didn't understand, but that sounded familiar all the same. The gem on the end of his staff changed color several times before Eirin realized that it wasn't the gem changing color at all. Instead, the clouds that were gathering overhead had cut off the light that had been shining from its tip.

A crack of thunder made Eirin jump and stumble back into Drystan, who was annoyingly calm as he steadied her.

"Are we...going to go out under that cloud?" Nuru asked.

"A new cloud. Safer than the Ymir's. And we'll have to travel fast," Isayas said, his voice sounding somewhat strained. "I can't hold it all day." Even as he spoke, his hands shook slightly, and more thunder boomed. "But it should get us at least back to the cover of the copse of trees in the ravine."

"Then we can pack up our tents and all we left," Qeb said.

"Well," Thane said, stepping forward. "You don't have to ask me twice."

Eirin was the second-to-last to climb out. She had donned her black cloak, as they all had...all except Isayas, of course, who still insisted on wearing his tattered Wizard's cloak. And into the day they went. Until they came to the ravine and stopped short.

"What's wrong?" Drystan demanded as he helped Eirin over a large log.

"This isn't right," Nuru said, frowning at the scene before them.

Isayas, who trembled slightly, let out a moan and shook his head.

"What is it?" Eirin asked him.

He shook his head and closed his eyes. "We're nowhere near our camp. We've gone too far."

Chapter Nineteen

Drystan looked around, and to his dismay, he realized they were right. Nothing looked or smelled familiar. He was bombarded by the scents of animal dens nearby that he hadn't smelled when they'd made camp, and there were far fewer flowers.

No wonder their trek through the tunnels had taken so long. They'd come too far.

"Do we have time to follow the ravine back to look?" Thane looked at Eirin.

Eirin swallowed. "I don't..."

Drystan understood her hesitation. Now that they knew Rangvald was still making his way north, every second counted. But they would also need shelter from the sun. And Isayas was looking rather pale.

Eirin looked at Isayas. "You've been to Iilaedin. How many days do you think we'll have until we can find shelter?" Surely, there had to be some abandoned houses along the way that they could hide in. Too many people had been going south for them to all be occupied.

The Wizard drew in a heavy breath, his staff still pointed up toward the rumbling thundercloud that had gathered above. "Not many. If we make haste, we should reach the fishing village where the ferry is located by nightfall. Then we can sail across the lake after dark. Once on the other side, we're less than a night's walk from the city."

Eirin looked up at Drystan. He kept his face impassive. For some reason, he suddenly felt as though his struggle to keep his feelings to himself was a hundredfold harder than it had been before their run-in with the Sphinxes. After holding her close, willing her not to die in the ice storm, feeling the life drain out of her...

He just didn't know how much longer he could pretend.

So he met her gaze and said evenly, "It's your decision to make."

Eirin frowned but nodded.

"If we can make it without our things," she said slowly, "I think we should go on." She glanced back at the tunnel opening. "Especially with all of them so close."

Isayas nodded, but he looked weary, and Eirin looked as though she wasn't sure she'd made the right choice.

* * *

An hour later, they'd made it across the plain to a thick gathering of trees. They couldn't see the lake yet, but Eirin, still seeming oblivious to Drystan's frustration, whispered to him that if they pushed much harder, Isayas wouldn't last.

They all seemed to be thinking along the same lines, as everyone agreed that it was a good place to rest until nightfall. The Sphinxes, even when they did wake up, wouldn't be able to follow them through the sunlight, which shone brightly around the thick cloud Isayas kept above them.

Sure enough, as soon as they were in the shade, the Wizard's knees buckled, and Drystan and Thane had to help him to one of the larger trunks, where he could lean against it. His hands shook so hard that when he tried to get a drink from his waterskin, the water mostly spilled down the front of his robe. Eirin grabbed it as it tumbled from his fingers and held it steady for him as he drank in great, desperate gulps.

As she pulled the waterskin away when he was finished, she let out a cry.

"What is it?" Drystan hurried to her side, as did Qeb.

"Your magic..." Eirin whispered to Isayas, ignoring Drystan's question. "It's–"

"Just needs a rest, that's all," the Wizard retorted, closing his eyes. "Now, if you'd be so considerate–"

"No." Eirin stood up and put her hands on her hips. "Your magic is nearly gone. And I want to know why." Her dark eyes burned, and she wore a familiar look of determination.

"I don't know what you're talking about," Isayas scowled, leaning back, keeping his eyes shut.

"Yes, you do." She lifted her chin. "You can make it look like you have magic, but I just touched you, and I know a shell when I see one."

Drystan frowned down at the Wizard.

Drystan had seen Eirin touch Isayas far too many times to count. He often took her hand to help her climb onto Drystan's back when they were getting ready to travel, and more than once, the Wizard had taken her by the arm to point out certain magical aspects of the Solevarian landscape. If he was losing his magic, Eirin would know.

"Is it true?" Drystan asked him.

Isayas scoffed and tried to wave them away. "I'm well enough, so stop fussing."

"Eirin said you're running out of magic," Drystan said,

folding his arms across his chest. "Which means you're hiding something."

Isayas glared at Drystan through his big bushy brows. Then, after glaring at each of the others in turn, he huffed.

"Oh, very well. You might as well know."

As he spoke, Eirin dug through his bag and pulled out a small lock of Unicorn hairs, recognizable by their rainbow sheen. She carefully unwound one and began tying it around the Wizard's wrist.

As the hair touched him, he let out a deep sigh. He leaned back against the tree and sighed, his shoulders sagging.

"You're dying. Aren't you?" Callispa said quietly.

Everyone froze.

Drystan stared at her. "Dying?"

Isayas gave Callispa a look of annoyance, but he did finally nod. "Slowly. But yes. I am."

"What..." Eirin looked in horror at Drystan, but he had nothing of comfort to offer. He was reeling, too.

"When Wizards take on magic, we become like Atharrachs," Isayas said with a gusty sigh. "Our magic becomes intertwined with our lives. One cannot exist without the other. Of course, we're less vulnerable than Atharrachs in that our magic flows throughout our bodies. There is no particular area of magic where one might destroy us. And the magic lengthens our lives considerably." He put his hand to some of the wrinkles on his face and chuckled ruefully. "As you can see."

"But why now?" Nuru demanded. "Why are you dying now when you weren't back in the tunnels?"

Isayas gave her a wry smile. "We're always dying, Nuru. Every one of us marches closer to it with each second." He pulled a pecan out of his pocket and cracked it open. "Which is why I am taking care with how I live."

"It was the storm, wasn't it?" Eirin whispered. "You spent so much of your magic on the storm, protecting us from the sun–"

"Yes. And I would do it again."

"How long…" Drystan cleared his throat. "How much more do you have left?"

Isayas shrugged. "Who's to say? Only the Time Keeper knows when the days allotted me are gone."

"But say you were to try more big magic," Eirin said, her brows furrowed. "Something like what you just did."

"Then I would make sure it was the biggest magic of my life," Isayas retorted. "Really, you didn't all think I could live forever, did you?"

No one answered him. Drystan hadn't thought that, of course. But he hadn't wanted to believe the Wizard could be taken from them *now*.

"And this is why I didn't say anything about it," Isayas grumbled. "I knew you'd all carry on as though I were dead already."

The group stayed quiet that afternoon. Drystan and Qeb took watch while the others slept with their cloaks on in the shade of the trees. But about an hour after Drystan had taken watch, Isayas waved him over.

"You're supposed to be sleeping," Drystan said dryly as he went to sit at the Wizard's side.

"I am over four hundred years old," Isayas intoned. "One would think I might know how to take care of myself."

Drystan had to smile a little at this. "What did you want to tell me?"

But Isayas didn't answer him immediately. Instead, he looked out over the gently rolling hills they still had to climb. The grass was dry and yellow with little green left in it, and the sporadic groups of trees that created patches on the yellow landscape made it look somehow more desolate. The thundercloud Isayas had conjured was no longer in one piece, and fluffy white clouds blew silently across the blue sky.

"Why are you so reluctant to pursue the throne?"

Drystan, yanked from his daydreaming by these words, blinked at Isayas. "Excuse me?"

"You and I both know that you're doing everything in your power not to participate in the Rite of the Blood Fire Throne." Isayas drew his bushy eyebrows together. "We also know that kingship is your natural duty."

Drystan frowned down at the weed he'd pulled from the ground. It left a sticky trail of white foam on his hand where its stem had broken.

"I'm not trying to shirk my responsibility," he said slowly. "I was raised to be king. But that was before I knew what the world really was. What I am. Back when I was wrong about everything." He tossed the weed away. "And it seems as though the people of Solevar would really prefer that I not attempt to be king." He gave Isayas a wry smile. "Eirin says we have very little time before the curse is final. How am I supposed to unite a people that hates me?"

Isayas's eyes grew distant as he stared off into the waning afternoon light. "Life seemed to lose all meaning after I drank the Hidden Waters."

"How so?"

He sighed. "You wouldn't think it would feel that way. All the things I'd wanted as a boy were suddenly within my reach. I was one of the most powerful creatures in all of Solevar. Women threw themselves at my feet. I never lacked food or provisions." He paused for a moment to stretch out his hand. A butterfly landed on the back of it, and he gave it a sad smile. "And I hated it."

Drystan understood this. As a Dragon in the line of Oreck, he was arguably one of the strongest, most magical of all Atharrachs. But that alone seemed to bring nothing but trouble.

"Every time my brothers and I seemed to stave off some disaster, another would arise. And worse than the natural problems, such as plague and famine, were the ones caused by the Solevarians themselves. An earthquake is bad enough, but a darkness brought about by evil is so much more sinister."

Again, Drystan understood this far more than he wished to.

"But then I met Sarah." This time, Isayas's smile was genuine. He lifted his hand, and the butterfly flew into the tree. Still, the Wizard's smile remained as he watched it flutter away.

"She quite literally saved me from the despair that threatened to undo me."

"How?" Drystan couldn't help asking.

Isayas's smile widened. "She was good. And the way she looked at me made me wish to be the man she thought I was."

Drystan looked over to where Eirin was lying down. She had been sleeping, but now she was whispering with Nuru, giggling at something Nuru had said.

He missed the way she used to smile at him. "I had that," Drystan said softly, still watching her. "And in my desperation to save her, I lost it." Would she ever understand? Every mistake he'd made in Torbaine, foolish as it might seem now, had been out of love. The memory of her body, burned and bloody from his own flames, still haunted him in his dreams. And if he was honest, he couldn't promise he wouldn't make the same choices all over again if it meant she lived.

"So did I."

Drystan frowned at Isayas. "Your wife never left you." Technically, Eirin hadn't left him. But in a way, she had.

"No," Isayas chuckled. "You should, however, know that I failed her again and again. But..." He raised his brows knowingly.

"You can also believe I never abandoned her out of shame for those failures."

"What did you do?" Drystan asked.

Isayas shrugged. "There was nothing left for me to do but try again." Then he leaned forward, and his blue eyes became hard. "You have been faithful in many ways, Drystan. Not just to Eirin, but to Solevar. And if you ask me, being faithful in the small things is just as important as being faithful in the great. You can't tell me you mean to give up now."

"No," Drystan said, "but I'm not sure that my fidelity in the small things will be enough to win forgiveness for the sins I didn't commit."

Isayas put a hand on his shoulder. "And who says you need to atone for debts that aren't yours?"

Drystan gave a humorless laugh. "All of Solevar, it seems."

Isayas leaned back and studied him for a moment, all hints of his smile gone. "Consider it this way, then," he said. "Rather than trying to pay for Kamon's evil, which you will never be able to do no matter how hard you try, what if instead you focused on the road ahead?"

"But–" Drystan tried, but Isayas continued.

"Because if you don't do something, Rangvald is going to fulfill the requirements for the Rite of the Blood Fire Throne. He *will* take the throne, and whatever evil Kamon suspected him of doing will become real."

He was right. Drystan knew he was right. But what he was suggesting...

Drystan shook his head and forced a smile. "What about you? Are you going to take the easy way out with all this waning magic business?"

Isayas stared at him before scowling. "I'm going to die when I'm good and ready. And I can guarantee you that it will be spectacular."

Drystan chuckled. "I have no doubt of that. I only...I have a request, in that case."

Isayas quirked one thick brow. "And that would be?"

"If you can manage, maybe wait until we get to Iilaedin at least? Because if you don't, Eirin might just bring you back to life to let you know exactly what she thinks of your death."

Isayas snorted, but Drystan could see the light return to his eyes. "I suppose I'll consider it. We all know better than to kindle the Seer's wrath."

"Drystan."

Drystan looked up to see Qeb standing over him.

"You should get some sleep. We have about four hours until sundown. Thane says he'll take your place."

Drystan wanted to argue, but Qeb was right. Unlike his friend, Drystan couldn't live on two hours of sleep a day. A Griffin feat Drystan was quite jealous of.

"But Drystan?" Isayas said as Drystan began to stand.

Drystan looked at him in surprise. "Yes?"

Isayas paused before saying softly, "Don't give up before you reach the end, son. You can't know what it will be like until you get there."

Drystan thanked the Wizard and headed over to where the others were sleeping. Once the sun had begun to sink, several of the others had hung their cloaks from the lower tree branches to form a wall on the west side of the trees to protect them from its rays. Once he reached the spot Thane had deserted, he began to arrange his cloak in the best way he could beneath his head.

"Drystan?" came a small voice.

Drystan looked over to see Eirin an arm's length away. She was lying down, but her large brown eyes were wide open.

"Yes?" he asked.

"Thank you," she whispered.

Drystan stared at her. "For what?"

She shifted slightly and turned her eyes down. "For the way you sheltered me. In the storm, I mean."

"Any time," he said, forcing a smile. Did she know how difficult it was for him to lay here, close enough to touch? Had she thought about their brief time together before the ice storm a thousand times as he had, wondering where it would have taken them if they had been left alone?

Would she have let him kiss her?

He imagined slowly, so slowly touching his lips to hers, savoring the way her mouth felt pressed against his, the soft skin of her jaw beneath his fingertips. If he'd had just a few minutes more, would he have broken down the walls she continued building up?

But no. He grimaced, bringing the daydream to a halt before it could progress any further. Eirin was right after all, though most likely for reasons she didn't even know. Rangvald wasn't going to let him live past the Rite of the Blood Fire Throne. Drystan didn't know how he knew this. But he did know. It was better this way.

He might not be able to love her the way he wished, making promises of forever and watching the years pass by at her side. But he could make sure she got her chance to fix the Time Stones. That was how he could give her his love.

Chapter Twenty

She was supposed to be sleeping. After all, who knew when they would get another chance to rest? And yet, Eirin struggled more by the minute to remain where she was. Her instinct, which was getting harder and harder to ignore, was to get up and take Drystan's hand and tell him she had been wrong and that she needed him more desperately than he could ever know. Her will was crumbling, even as it considered the pain she would feel if she loved and lost him. This fight—both against time and the curse—was eating away at her, and Eirin wasn't sure how much longer she could go on like this.

Of course, Drystan had his own burdens to carry. But his shoulders were wide, and Eirin longed to hand him her burdens as she had back in Mhaedin. He would, she had no doubt, take them without complaint. Would the end result be worth it, though? Neither of them would escape the inevitable pain if she gave in. And judging by the way he'd been studiously distant today, she was sure he was aware of it, too.

"Prepare to feast!" Thane announced. He, Qeb, and Callispa had set out about an hour earlier, after the sun had finally set, and now they returned, Callispa bearing long, thick roots, and the men with fish.

"These," Nuru said, grimacing as she poked one of Thane's victims, "are the ugliest fish I have ever seen."

"Mudderots," Isayas said with a chuckle. He was already scraping the scales off the side of his fish with a flat rock. "None too tasty either, but they've got more than enough meat on them to satisfy."

"Do you think the Sphinxes will find us?" Eirin asked as she took her own fish to clean.

"No," Isayas said. "I had the back of my thundercloud rain to wash away our scent."

"Very clever." Eirin smiled.

"You didn't even ask where we got these fish," Thane said, pointing his little knife at her. "And if you did, I think you'd say I was very clever, too."

"Fine." Eirin rolled her eyes. "Thane, where did you get these gorgeous fish?"

"From the lake." He beamed, a lock of blond hair falling in his face as he did. "You should all be pleased to know that we're just a stone's throw from Lake Mhira."

"We must have come farther than we thought," Drystan said as he skewered his fish and set it over the fire.

"The town is abandoned," Qeb said, skewering his own fish on a stick. "But there is a boat still at the one dock. And it seems to be in better repair than the buildings."

"I'm sure people have been using it to come from the north side of the lake," Isayas said. "Some young sprout probably made some coin fixing the thing up and ferrying people across."

"If he did, there's no one there now," Callispa said. As usual, she was careful not to look at Drystan or Eirin, and her voice was low and subdued. "I can only guess it's because of the Sirens."

As much as it killed her, Eirin had to give the girl credit.

Callispa was obviously in pain. But she was still with them, and she was still doing her best to help.

At the mention of the Sirens, everyone seemed to pause, all except for Thane, who looked at Eirin.

"You studied all the Atharrachs in the Records Keep. What exactly are Sirens again?"

Eirin frowned at her fish. "To be honest, there wasn't much about them."

"That's because there weren't many when the curse fell."

Everyone turned to look at Isayas, whose bushy brows were now drawn together. He was staring into the fire, no longer seeming to pay attention to his fish.

"Then more have been born since the curse fell?" Eirin asked.

"More have come into existence, yes." Isayas scoffed. "But saying they were born, however... that's a gross misnomer."

"How so?" Drystan asked.

"Sirens aren't *natural*," Isayas said slowly. "They were once Merfolk. Mermaids, to be precise. There are no male Sirens."

"Why not?" Nuru asked.

"Because they rejected the natural way the Time Keeper created for the Merpeople. The first Siren realized what great power she had in her voice, and she convinced some of her sisters to experiment, to see just how low they could bring men, how hard and how fast they would fall to their knees."

"Their magic doesn't work on women," Eirin suddenly recalled from her studies. "That's why the ancient sailors used to take their wives with them on their ships!"

Isayas nodded.

"I don't understand," Thane said, waving his stick with its fish in the air. "How does one change from one thing to another? Wouldn't their choices just make them evil Mermaids?"

"You have to understand the...the power of misusing magic," Isayas said. "Twisting what is good to satisfy one's own desires changes the very fabric of the nature inside." He put his stick down and pointed at Eirin.

"Eirin does not change because she has no magic. Human is who and what she is at all times. But you all change forms based on the nature, or the bent of your magic."

"Their magic must have been heavily twisted indeed," Qeb said.

"It was. And with great purpose. More than any other creature has ever achieved."

"But I still don't understand what they *are*," Nuru said.

Isayas picked his stick back up. "Deformed remnants of what they once were. Their voices still hold their magic, as they did when they were in Mermaid form. And by the Time Keeper's mercy, like their Merfolk relatives, they still only maintain that magic when they're in water. But rather than bringing forth food and life from beneath the waves, they now bring death and destruction as they seek to mutilate the world as they have done to their own selves."

"How are more...made?" Thane asked.

"They can either make that choice on their own, singing the cursed song that will change them from one to the other, or," Isayas gave him a dark look, "a Siren drinks the blood of a man, and--"

"Do you know what? I really don't think I need to know after all," Thane said, making a gagging noise.

"How can they be stopped?" Drystan asked.

"Oh, that was always the work of the Merfolk." Isayas sighed. "There never were Sirens in the lake before the curse. Either they were brought in from the sea, which I doubt greatly, as they would have been free from the curse there. Or..." He let his words trail off.

"Or what?" Thane asked.

"Or," Isayas said slowly, "desperation has driven my noble friends of the waves to darkness."

"That still doesn't tell us how we can keep them away while we get across," Drystan said.

"Dragons can technically burn the darkness out of a Siren, but doing so is difficult and painstaking for all involved. Generally, it isn't recommended to take on Sirens without the help of the Merpeople. Even for a Dragon. But," Isayas smiled, "there are ways to remain out of their clutches." He reached for his bag and began to search inside. But after a minute, he let out a short oath.

"What is it?" Drystan asked.

"I must have left the beeswax at the camp!" Isayas then uttered a string of almost unintelligible curses. "That means you'll need to tie bands of cloth around your ears. The men, I mean. The girls are fine."

Eirin glanced at Drystan. She didn't know much about Sirens in detail, but she had read a few stories about them in the Citadel's records. And what she remembered most was their preferred taste for the blood of men.

If only Isayas hadn't used so much magic on the cloud! But then again, even if he could use that magic to save them from the Sirens, Eirin doubted he would. If they survived the lake, they would still likely have to face Rangvald, who had far more magic than the Sirens ever could.

The group was somber that evening as they packed up what little they had and set out for the lake. Eirin was tempted to tell Drystan what she had contemplated earlier. But as this seemed neither the time nor the place–nor did she wish to give in just yet–she talked with Isayas.

"You said the Sirens change because they twist their magic. Is there any way to change them back into Merpeople?"

"There is," Isayas said. "But it's unspeakably painful, and so far as I know, no Siren has willingly surrendered herself for it."

"But what *can* change them?" Eirin pressed.

He looked at her and raised his brows. "I told you before. Dragon Fire."

As he spoke, they arrived at the lake's edge. And the moment her feet touched its pebbled shore, Eirin's entire body went taut.

There was deep magic here, and it weighed upon her suddenly, threatening to crush her lungs.

Something was deeply, deeply wrong.

"Isayas–" she began, but he gave a sharp nod.

"I feel it, too."

"Feel what?" Nuru asked, and Eirin immediately felt Drystan's eyes on her as well.

"The magic on and in this lake is heavy," Isayas said slowly. Then he looked at Drystan. "Much has changed since last I was here."

"Is it safe to cross?" Qeb asked, frowning back at the lake. Nothing looked out of place. At least, not to Eirin's untrained eye. She'd never seen a real lake before. The one in Torbaine was a pond compared to this. The moonlight reflected on the small waves that crashed rhythmically upon the shore, and the constant sound of the water lapping at the shore was like a strange, enchanting rhythm.

"I don't think we have the time to go around either way," Eirin said. "I want to fix the Time Stones before Rangvald gets anywhere near Iilaedin."

"What if we flew?" Drystan asked Isayas. "Surely no one from Rangvald's camp would spot us if we stayed low."

But Isayas shook his head. "Flying near the Sirens is more dangerous than going in a boat."

"Why?" Thane asked.

"Siren voices travel far," Isayas said, still shaking his head. "If we have a boat, we have something sturdy to keep us on our path. In the air, there's nothing to hold you back." He looked at them. "And remember, your eyes will need to be covered as well."

"You're not making any sense," Thane complained. "How does a boat keep us on our path? And what do you mean holding us back?"

"We're going to have to tie you to the boat," Callispa snapped.

Thane's eyes grew wide. "*Tie* me to the boat?"

"Did they really teach you nothing of Sirens in the mountain?" Callispa asked.

"There aren't many oceans or lakes inside the mountain, if memory serves me," Nuru retorted. "Sirens are somewhat difficult to come by."

"That's enough," came a deep rumble.

Everyone turned in surprise to look at Drystan. His eyes glowed with flecks of amber, and he stood erect and indignant.

The picture of a king, Eirin thought smugly to herself.

Drystan turned to Isayas. "Tell us what we need to do."

Before Isayas could answer, a strange ringing filled the air. It grew louder by the second. When it changed notes, however, Eirin realized with dread just what they were hearing.

A Siren's song.

One look at Drystan confirmed it. His eyes had grown somewhat distant, though the embers in them hadn't burned out. If anything, they were brighter.

"Korenago Friterre!" Isayas shouted, pounding his staff once on the ground. Immediately the song ceased. But the Wizard looked graver than ever.

"They know we're here," he said quickly. "They were fishing for us then, but now their appetites have been wetted, and they'll be coming if we don't act soon."

"Are you sure we can't just go around?" Thane asked.

"No. Eirin's right," Qeb said. "I flew over the south end of the lake earlier this evening. Rangvald's people are close. They would see us if we tried to fly around. And going the north route would add at least two days."

Isayas looked at Thane. "You said there was a boat nearby. Where is it?"

Thane pointed to a small abandoned building just north of where they were standing. "On the other side. It should be big enough to fit us all. It won't be fast, though." His answer was natural enough, but his eyes had the same misty expression Drystan's had had a moment ago.

"Leave the rowing to me." Isayas turned to Drystan. "You, Qeb, and Thane will need to allow us to bind your eyes and ears. Then we'll tie you to the boat itself." He opened his bag and pulled out a little bottle. "And I'll need to give you each just a touch of bruthsi root–"

At the mention of bruthsi root, all three men began to protest, but Isayas glared at them. "Would you like to shift on the boat and sink us all?"

This shut them up, though none of the three looked too pleased.

"What will we do?" Nuru asked.

"You're going to help me push," Isayas said. He looked around and then pointed behind one of the abandoned buildings. "You see those oars? Get one for you and one for Callispa. And you, Eirin, will steer."

"Why do they get to row, and we get tied up?" Thane complained.

Isayas huffed. "You really *don't* know anything about Sirens, do you?"

"Remember, Sirens only affect men with their magic," Eirin said. "They can make you do terrible things." After shuddering slightly at the recollection of the stories she'd read in the Citadel, she turned to Isayas. "I've never steered a boat in my life." Unless she counted the time Benjamin had let her try. But that had been on a slow river with an experienced Merman standing behind her, laughing goodnaturedly at her mistakes.

Eirin suddenly wished Benjamin, their captain from the river within the mountain, was here now. But like many of their other former allies, Benjamin, too, was dead.

Another voice, though lower than the first, echoed over the water.

"We don't have much time!" Isayas hissed. "Now go!"

They all scrambled into action, Nuru and Callispa running to grab the oars, and Eirin tying the bandages over the men's ears.

"What about you?" Thane asked, scowling as Isayas rubbed a bit of bruthsi root on his temple.

"I," the Wizard said smugly, "am beyond such paltry tricks."

Eirin paused slightly when she came to Drystan. She wanted so much to draw him down and kiss his lips.

And not just a little peck.

But she shoved that desire down, working instead to tie the band around his eyes and ears as snugly as she could. According to Isayas, while Sirens' songs were their main form of magic, they could somewhat manipulate men's eyes as well, tricking them into thinking the Sirens the most beautiful creatures in the world.

Eirin gave the band of cloth one more tug.

The boat was much simpler than Eirin had imagined. It was literally a flat square made of logs tied together with several crossbeams beneath it. There were railings on each side, designed, Isayas explained quickly, so that many people could cross over at once. It should carry them all easily...as long as none of them tried to get off. If they put even one foot over the water, the Sirens would feast.

As they made their way onto the boat, a low moan rolled over the waters, and the girls froze.

"What was that?" Nuru whispered.

"There's no way to know." Isayas began to tie Drystan to one of the railing posts. "In the deeper parts of the ocean, the Sirens have been known to conjure up creatures just as dark and twisted as they are."

Five minutes later, Isayas pushed off with his staff. Silently, Nuru and Callispa began to paddle while Eirin stood at the rudder. Isayas had shown her how to guide the boat back and forth, and now, against every instinct in her body, she aimed them for the middle of the black lake.

Steering wasn't easy, but the more difficult struggle was ignoring the prickly darkness she could feel sweeping over the water. This magic was odd, however, in that it didn't glitter and shine like all the other magic Eirin had seen. Even Rangvald's had still glowed a vivid blue. This magic floated on the surface of the water like flotsam. In fact, Eirin would have dismissed the dull gray motes for something else entirely, except that they continued to emit a faint glow even when the moon briefly hid behind a cloud.

Just when they were far enough from land that swimming back would be difficult, Eirin heard it again.

Slick and cloying, the song rolled over her like oil. Eirin wanted to rub, to scratch it off her skin, and it was with great effort that she kept both hands on the tiller. Isayas, as though reading her mind, gave her a long look. She didn't even try to smile back. He nodded once, then returned to searching the waters, though for what, Eirin didn't know.

The deeper they went, the more Eirin began to regret their decision to cut through the lake. Yes, she did need to reach Iilaedin before Rangvald. But this—

Another song cut her thoughts short, and every hair on her body stood on end. This song was far louder than the ones they'd previously heard, and soon, the first voice was joined by several more.

The men, despite their bindings, heard the songs as well. Or, a hint of them, at least. Drystan, Qeb, and Thane all began to struggle slightly. Eirin gripped the tiller and silently pleaded with Isayas, Nuru, and Callispa to row faster. They weren't even to the center of the lake yet.

Drystan in particular was struggling the hardest, and with each passing second, his attempts to escape his bonds became more urgent. But just when Eirin was sure he might break loose, a new voice boomed through the air.

Eirin looked over to see Isayas singing. His voice, a deep baritone, was surprisingly powerful, and if Eirin hadn't been scared senseless, his song would have been pleasant to hear. His words were foreign to her, but somehow, she understood what they meant.

Precious were the days of sparkling blue, which glittered in the sun.
    Clear and gentle were the waves bearing us safely home.
    We were content and felt no fear of poison in our run.
    Naive and blissful, we went, like children pressing on.

At the sound of his song, Qeb and Thane began to calm and relax against their posts.

But not Drystan.

Drystan began to jerk harder and harder at his bindings. Somehow, he managed to work his blindfold off, revealing eyes that were an alarming amber.

All of this happened just as a creature with skin as white as the moon appeared on the side of their boat opposite Drystan. She must have been beautiful...once. Her hair was as black as her skin was white, and her eyes had no whites in them at all. When she smiled at Eirin, it was to reveal perfect, pointed teeth. Then she turned her gaze to Drystan and let out a song much louder than any they had heard before.

At the same time, several other Sirens appeared in a circle around the boat, closing in slowly as they sang. Isayas continued to boom his own song as the end of his staff began to glow yellow. He swung the staff from side to side, his song never faltering as he walked from one side of the boat to the other. But Eirin could see beads of sweat dripping down his temples, and his hands shook slightly.

He wouldn't last much longer.

Drystan let out a snarl and swiveled his head from side to side like an animal.

"Isayas!" Eirin screamed, but it was Callispa who dropped her oar and ran to Drystan. She begged and pleaded for him to stay with them, using tones that were pleading and sweet, staring into his eyes, her face inches from his.

"Callispa!" Eirin called, letting go of the tiller. "Let me–"

"Stay there!" Callispa snapped. She turned back to Drystan, but before she could speak again, he struggled so hard to free his hands from the railing that he knocked her to the ground.

Looking stunned and confused, Isayas watched Drystan for a moment before grim determination settled on his face. Slowly, he raised his staff.

No. Isayas would not sacrifice himself this way. Eirin wouldn't let him. After throwing down the tiller once more, Eirin stepped over Callispa to stand before Drystan. His eyes still glowed amber, a hunger in them Eirin had never seen.

"Eirin, no!" Isayas shouted.

Eirin ignored him. Instead, she took Drystan's face in her hands, a face that was looking less and less Human by the second, and willed him to look into her eyes.

While Eirin knew less about Sirens than Callispa seemed to, and far less than Isayas, she knew how their songs worked and why they worked only on men. Their songs, though unintelligible to the female ear, were ones of seduction and temptation. They appealed to the darkest desires of the soul, charming the lusts good men did their best to subvert. They sang promises of pleasures and delight, of hopes and dreams fulfilled in the realization of those base desires.

And Eirin was not about to let them destroy the man she loved.

Over the past weeks and months, she'd done her best to keep her heart separated from Drystan's. She had hoped to spare them both the inevitable pain of what she felt was a final separation, striving to focus on the goal before them both instead.

But her decision was made even before her hands had left the tiller. Drystan was a good man. Too good to fall into such darkness. And no scum-sucking Siren was going to have the satisfaction of bringing him to a watery grave. Solevar needed him.

And so did she.

Drystan's eyes blazed with fire, but Eirin yanked him down and pressed his lips against hers.

At first, he was unresponsive. She had to use all of her strength to keep his face in her hands as he writhed and fought against her. But then, for the first time since his blindfold had fallen off, his eyes focused. And they focused on her.

Eirin closed her own eyes and smiled into the kiss as soon as he relaxed, knowing the danger had passed. He deepened the kiss, and she happily allowed him to lead. When he finally pulled back, it was only to whisper her name before kissing her again.

Eirin could have lived in that moment forever, but she wasn't given the time. The Sirens' song changed, and she felt the boat beneath them dip dangerously. She grabbed onto Drystan to keep her balance and looked around to see what had happened.

"Cut them loose!" Isayas was yelling as he sliced through Qeb's bonds. Nuru freed Thane, so Eirin yanked her knife from her boot and cut Drystan's bonds as well.

Nuru began to shift, as did Callispa, but Eirin realized with dread that none of the men would be able to shift along with them. They still had bruthsi root in their systems.

The water began to swirl, a vortex opening in the water beneath them. Giant tentacles, each thicker than Qeb's broad shoulders, broke through the water's surface and slapped Nuru and Callispa down, Callispa's wings sputtering and fizzing dangerously as she fell back down onto the boat, shifting as she hit the wood. The Sirens sang gleefully from the sides of the maelstrom as the boat began to tip.

Drystan reached out for Eirin, but the boat jerked to the side, and he missed her. Eirin screamed as she slid down the wet wood and into the frigid water.

Hands broke the surface, reaching, searching for her, but something strong grabbed her ankle and dragged her down below their reach.

Her chest felt as though it were collapsing as she fought uselessly for escape, and she watched helplessly as the moonlit surface grew farther and farther away.

Chapter Twenty-One

S trong hands grasped Eirin by the upper arms and pulled. But as her captor still pulled her down, she felt like the rag doll her brothers had once destroyed by stretching its arms and legs too far. She screamed in protest, only to suck in a mouthful of water. Choking on the water, she began to panic and flail as she tried to clear her lungs. Clearing her lungs underwater was impossible, of course, but it did free her ankle of whatever was trying to pull her down.

As soon as her captor let go, whoever had her arms sped toward the surface as though they had been catapulted up. But even as they neared the surface, she could feel herself beginning to go in and out of consciousness. Her vision became murky. She did, however, make out voices. Lots of voices. A cacophony of music and song. And the harmony was wrong.

But as she broke through the surface, one song seemed to triumph over the other, growing stronger even as the other one faded.

If she had been fully conscious, Eirin would have asked Drystan why these voices sounded so different. Something about them was...foreign, like nothing she'd ever heard.

No. She'd heard a voice like these once before.

Before she could work out where she'd heard it, though, a new icy fear gripped her. She should have felt fear before. She'd been drowning for a while. It hadn't seemed real, though, until now.

She did her best to reach out. She wanted Drystan. She needed to touch him, to know he was there. But she was fading too fast.

She was going to die all alone.

Then something hit her chest. She wanted to complain that it hurt, but she couldn't. It hit her again. And again.

Then she was coughing up water, gagging and choking as it came flooding back up. Had she drunk the entire lake?

"She's coming to!" called a familiar voice over the din.

Drystan. That was Drystan. If Eirin had had the strength to try, she would have reached out to find him.

"Tip her to the side so she doesn't suck the water down again. There, just like that. She'll be fine. She'll be fine," said another man in calm, confident tones. His voice was unfamiliar. No, she'd heard it before, too. But where had she heard it?

"Come on, baby," Drystan said, his voice husky. He was close, and Eirin felt familiar hands on her face. "Breathe. Just breathe."

"Give her time," said the familiar voice.

Eirin did her best to open her eyes, but she was still coughing and gagging on the lake water that seemed to have filled her chest completely.

Someone had tipped her on her side, but now she put her hands down to steady herself. Her fingers touched solid rock. She tried to press against it to push herself into a sitting position. Her arms shook so much, however, that she would have toppled over again had Drystan not been holding her.

When she was finally somewhat able to breathe again, she opened her eyes. She was lying on a dark rock, though the water was only a few arm lengths away.

The song that had been echoing over the water changed again.

Eirin and her friends were sitting on what appeared to be a small, rocky island in the middle of the lake. In the distance, she could barely make out pale figures bobbing at the surface of the lake. She was fairly sure from their pale complexions and dark hair that they were Sirens.

Nuru and Thane were nearby, watching her anxiously, while Isayas, Callispa, and Qeb stood guard, their eyes fixed on the distant Sirens.

That wasn't what made her stare, though. For surrounding them were countless Merpeople. Mermaids and Mermen singing with a power Eirin had never heard even from the trumpets in the Citadel. It was their song that had won out, and the haunting melody of the Sirens continued to recede in the wake of the Merpeople's song. The monster that had smashed their boat was writhing in the center of the lake, no longer in the center of a vortex but seeming to struggle just as Eirin had moments before. As they sang, some of the largest of the Mermen nocked bows nearly as tall as Eirin. On a particularly powerful note, the arrows were loosed, and they sailed straight toward the monster. It let out a high-pitched scream as more and more arrows assailed it until it finally sank beneath the waves.

Eirin blinked and looked around once more to study the people who had saved them. But it was only then that she realized who else was at her side.

"Benjamin!" she cried, throwing herself into another coughing fit.

"Whoa, there," he laughed, slapping her on the back several times. "I know I'm exciting, but I'm not worth choking over."

She stared at him again as soon as the coughing subsided. "But you...in the river..." She started coughing again.

"I was in the river, yes." He laughed, then turned to Drystan. "Can you fly her to shore?"

"I can." Drystan's eyes were still bright with glowing embers, and Eirin wondered if it was from the Siren songs or because the Dragon was ready to fight.

"But the brushsi root," Eirin began, but Drystan's eyes just flamed brighter.

"It's all gone now."

Benjamin seemed as though he was unsure as well, though whether for concern about the bruthsi root or any lingering effects of the Sirens' songs, he didn't say. Only after he studied Drystan for a moment did he finally nod. "Very well. But stay low and fly behind our lines. Rangvald is near, and though he'll know of the battle, he won't necessarily know you're involved unless you show him. He has spies everywhere, though, so take care to land behind the buildings on the other side. Wait for me there."

"I'm coming, too," Nuru said, taking a step forward.

"Are you?" Benjamin raised his eyebrows. "Well, that's a change, isn't it?"

Nuru rolled her eyes, but Eirin had to smile. The last time they'd seen Benjamin, Nuru had recently tried to do Eirin permanent damage. No wonder Benjamin was surprised.

"Actually," Isayas said, his staff still raised, "I need Nuru here with me. Callispa should go with you."

"But–" Callispa began to argue.

Isayas cut her off. "You're a Phoenix, Callispa. You don't stand a chance if one of the Sirens decides to set one of their water monsters on you."

Eirin didn't want Callispa with them either, but Isayas had a point. It would be deadly for Callispa to accidentally shift and then be dragged down into the water. Her wings–and her magic–would be extinguished forever. She would die.

The Merpeople surrounding them continued singing as they made space for Drystan to shift. As soon as he was in his Dragon form, Eirin climbed on, and Drystan, Callispa, and Qeb took flight.

The lake was much larger than Eirin had anticipated, though she should have expected it, based on its size on the map. Still, she was even more amazed at the number of Merpeople that filled it, their torsos rising out of the water as they continued to sing at the Sirens. They made the Sirens look few and weak in comparison, and Eirin cheered in her heart as Drystan passed over them.

Several minutes later, they landed on the west side of the lake. There was what seemed like an abandoned town at the dock here, too, though Eirin wondered now if it really was abandoned, or if the Merfolk just kept it looking that way.

As soon as they landed, Drystan and Qeb, who had wordlessly followed them, decided to skirt the immediate perimeter to ensure they were alone.

"Watch her," Drystan ordered Callispa. Callispa nodded unhappily. Drystan shifted back into his Human form, as his Dragon form was too large to be stealthy, then he and Qeb left.

Eirin had felt increasingly uncomfortable around Callispa since the beginning of their journey, but she hadn't realized the full extent of the awkwardness until they were alone. The Merpeople's song echoed off the water and onto the land, but nowhere near loud enough to cover up the dreadful silence.

"It's not fair."

Eirin looked up at Callispa, who was staring down at her own hands.

"Excuse me?" Eirin asked, doing her best to sound polite.

"He loves you," Callispa continued. She finally met Eirin's gaze. "And you're pushing him away." Her last word ended in a sob.

Eirin stared at her, unsure of how to answer. This was not the conversation she'd planned on having right after drowning.

"I don't want to," she whispered.

"We were a good team," Callispa said, tears still running down her cheeks.

"I know," Eirin said softly.

What was happening? She shouldn't feel sorry for Callispa. She should be angry. This girl had tried to steal Drystan. She'd tried to lure him away from what Eirin and Drystan had. But...

Eirin couldn't. She couldn't be angry with the girl who was breaking in front of her. Because she knew exactly how she felt.

"I...never wanted to push him away," Eirin said. "But this... saving Solevar. Saving my family..." She paused. What *was* she trying to say? "I never thought the world would need me. I was always the weakest. The slowest." Fantastic. Now she was babbling. But for some reason, she kept on. "And...being told everything rested on me was more than I ever expected. More than I ever wanted. I didn't think I could hold it all up. Both Drystan and the mission, I mean."

"I would have given him everything," Callispa said, staring back out over the water. "And yet he chose you." She gave a humorless laugh and wiped her face on her sleeve. "I can't trick myself into believing otherwise now. I suppose I knew the whole time. But..."

"I'm sorry," Eirins said softly. And to her surprise, she was.

"That's the hardest part of all this," Callispa continued. "You're right. You're right about everything. He always loved you. I just deluded myself into thinking I might find love before the world ended, too."

Eirin didn't know what to say to this, so they waited in silence until Drystan and Qeb returned.

"We'll stay here until the Merpeople are finished with the Sirens," Drystan said, seeming unaware of Callispa's tearstained face or Eirin's discomfort.

"I don't think we were seen," Qeb said, coming up behind him. "But I'll remain on watch while you all stay hidden here."

Drystan, who had been examining a nick in his sword, finally looked up and caught Eirin's eye. She must have looked anxious because he raised his brows in question.

Eirin's heart nearly stopped at the concern in his gaze. After the way she'd kissed him on the boat, there would be no pretending ever again. And she knew it.

Chapter Twenty-Two

Drystan needed desperately to talk to Eirin about that kiss.

For a brief time, he'd been sure the Sirens would be his downfall. Even now, as he recalled them, he was hit by an avalanche of shame. He'd known, of course, that they would call to him. Still, he'd been sure he would be able to block them out. After all, he was in love with Eirin, and a Dragon's heart could only be won once.

But he hadn't been counting on the strength of the desire those songs had awakened in him, and even as they'd encircled him, making their way through the bindings tied over his eyes and ears, he'd realized just how deeply he'd underestimated the call of temptation. Shameful, dirty desire that had nothing to do with love and everything to do with the dangerous games the Sirens bid him play. Shame had burned him from the inside out as the songs had come, louder and louder, and yet, he had still felt himself struggling against his bindings, trying to wrench himself free.

If Isayas hadn't insisted on giving him the touch of bruthsi root, Drystan had no doubt he would have done exactly as the Sirens had bid him. He would have drowned himself with outstretched arms. As it was, he'd nearly burned through all inhibition, bruthsi and otherwise, by the time Eirin had come.

But Eirin...she had released him. Her kiss was like pouring cool, soothing aloe on the evil the Sirens had ignited within him. And there had been no hesitancy the way he might have expected from the girl who had held him at arm's length for weeks.

Her kiss had been purposeful and passionate, and it had wrought within him a new desire. But this desire was like gold compared to the rusty iron wrought by the Sirens. He'd drunk desperately, hungrily, deeply of the escape she gave him.

And from the look on her face now as they spoke silently on this lonely pebbled shore, Eirin had been affected by the kiss, too.

But they weren't alone. Callispa and Qeb were here. And Drystan could hear the approach of the Merfolk as they sang their triumph. Benjamin, of course, was leading the way.

"You're here!" Benjamin shouted, grabbing Eirin by the arms and lifting her into the air. Eirin looked surprised, but she laughed as he swung her around. Drystan usually would have been annoyed at any man taking such liberties with her, but he was too relieved both at Benjamin's survival and his people's rescue to be vexed. Besides, Eirin hadn't been Benjamin's object of attention back in the mountain. That honor had belonged to Alys.

"Are you all here?" Benjamin asked, glancing around their group as Isayas, Thane, and Nuru joined them. The smile remained on his face, but the second look he sent Eirin was telling.

"She didn't come with us," Eirin said gently. "It's a long story."

"I see," Benjamin's smile faltered slightly, but then he grinned even wider. "Well, stories are best told over supper. We have little, but what we have, we're happy to share. Come! Let us break bread together, and we can tell one another of all that has happened since we parted!"

"Who is he?" Drystan heard Callispa ask Qeb as they followed the hundreds of Merfolk who began to fill the village.

"He was one of our guides when we first left Torbaine," Qeb answered in a low voice. "We believed he had died after Rangvald sent a horde of mercenaries to bring us back."

"He looks rather alive to me," Callispa said.

Nuru snorted. "Stunning observation."

Drystan sent her a look, but Nuru, as usual, ignored him.

Supper was already being set out on a row of tables as they entered what seemed to have been the village square.

"That was fast!" Eirin said.

Benjamin nodded with a grin. "Aye. We've been waiting for you, you see."

Eirin turned to him with wide eyes. "Waiting for us?" she asked.

As torches were being lit around them, Drystan could see their old captain better. Benjamin still had the long hair, a mixture of brown and gold, and his face was as scruffy and unshaven as ever. He wore no shirt, only trousers, which Drystan would have accused him of doing so to boast his obviously impressive frame, had all the other Mermen not done the same. Even the women, though they were more clothed, wore simple, light garments that Drystan could only guess allowed them ease in the water.

"Word has it that the two remaining heirs to the Blood Fire Throne have been racing north to the Time Stones." Benjamin gave a great laugh and slapped Drystan in the back. "You may not have known what you were on my boat, but I've been around long enough to have had an idea. So when we heard that someone was challenging Rangvald, we agreed that, should you come our way, we would help in any way we could."

"A most useful decision if ever one was made," Isayas said.

"You tried to warn me," Eirin said, looking as though she'd just remembered something important. "And you tried to hide us from Rangvald!" She grimaced slightly. "Sorry about your boat, by the way. But why didn't you let us take you with us? We would have tended to you!"

"Especially Alys." Thane smirked. "Despite the fact that she's terrible with binding wounds. Worse than Eirin, actually."

Qeb punched Thane in the shoulder.

Thane scowled up at him but didn't say anything else.

"No offense intended," Benjamin smiled, "but you didn't even know who you were or what you were capable of, with the exception possibly of the Elf woman."

Drystan's heart twisted. He'd been doing his best not to think of his mother, not to mourn her in the midst of all that was important. But it still hurt to think that she'd been so close...and he'd had no idea.

"I knew I needed the healing of my people," Benjamin went on. "I also knew that the river would eventually lead to the waterfall, which would lead to rivers in the valley below. And though it might come as a surprise to you," he wiggled his eyebrows, "Merfolk heal best in water. So I slowly made my way back to my family."

Drystan wondered just what had driven him away from them in the first place, but now was not the time to ask.

They came to a wide circle of large stones that surrounded a bonfire in the center of the square. Benjamin seated himself on one and indicated for the others to follow. Drystan could feel the eyes of everyone around them trained on his little party, but for once, he didn't feel threatened by the attention.

"I do wish to know, however," Benjamin said, turning to Eirin, "what happened to Alys." His voice became more gentle. "You two were very close, were you not?"

Eirin blinked rapidly several times, and once more, Drystan's chest tightened. Eirin had been torn from her family at a young age and then again just as she thought she was getting them back.

It seemed unfair that she should have lost her best friend and childhood protector as well.

"We are," Eirin said softly.

"Is she well?" Benjamin's eyes were clear and earnest, and he leaned toward Eirin, who was seated beside him, as though she had a secret to share.

"I wish I knew," Eirin said with a sad smile. "She sacrificed herself so we could escape when we were captured by our Elders and brought back to Torbaine." She shrugged, and her eyes grew troubled. "I would have hoped her connection to the Elders might have saved her, but her father..."

Her father had tried to take Eirin, and Drystan had killed him for it.

"Ah," Benjamin said. He sighed and then squeezed Eirin's knee. "She's clever and strong. Let us hope the Time Keeper guided her to use her many talents to save herself."

Eirin gave him a grateful smile, her eyes glistening, and Drystan was grateful for his kindness. Few people at the Citadel had understood Alys's choice in befriending Eirin. Alys was beautiful, popular, talented, and the daughter of an Elder. She could have chosen anyone in the entire Citadel to be her companion and ally. That she had chosen the Citadel's least talented student mystified and even angered many. But Alys had seen the same thing Drystan saw the first time he met the small girl. She'd seen the fire in Eirin's eyes. Drystan only wished Alys could see how far that fire had brought Eirin now.

He also wished he could find somewhere private to talk with Eirin about that kiss.

"If you don't mind me asking," Qeb said when they were finally served a very late supper, "Why would the Merpeople desire so much to help us?"

"Not that we're complaining!" Thane hurried to add, his mouth stuffed full of food.

"We've had few welcoming receptions since venturing into Solevar," Drystan explained, giving Thane a look. He did have manners when it suited him. The Citadel had seen to that.

"Rangvald has never been a friend of the Merfolk," growled an older Merman, his thick hair snowy white.

"How so?" Drystan asked.

"Rumor had it," interjected Isayas, "that he employed Sirens when it was useful to him."

"Not a rumor!" cried a woman. "It's true! He used them against our fathers and mothers when it served him, and he even took them to other bodies of water, polluting the waters there with their magic as well!"

"There are many who are not loyal to Rangvald," Benjamin said, turning back to Drystan. "And many who remember his treachery from prior to the curse."

"What treachery?" Nuru asked with a frown.

Benjamin paused to thank the young woman who spooned a second serving of supper onto his plate. A strange mix of fish, mushrooms, and what looked like a green weed, it was oddly tasty.

"He was often at odds with his father," one of the older gentlemen said. "And he would neglect his duties if he felt his heart dictated otherwise."

"Did you see this for yourself?" Nuru asked.

"Aye. We did," the woman said, seeming slightly affronted by Nuru's question.

"Merfolk have an average lifespan of one hundred and fifty to two hundred years," Eirin whispered to her friend.

"The other sons," the woman snapped, "were more dutiful. Until the end at least." Then she snorted delicately. "Not that we've ever believed that to be the full story. Prince Kamon would never attempt what he did with the Time Stone unless he believed his actions warranted."

"He always was the more impetuous one," another man said,

shaking his head.

"I am glad to know this," Drystan said slowly, sending a glance at their uncharacteristically quiet Wizard. "I'm not sure what you wish for me to do yet, as I haven't tried entering the city. But I'm grateful for your help and support."

"You wish to know what we desire?" the old man said tartly. "Challenge him at the Blood Fire Throne. You'd have far more support than you believe."

"We haven't had a grand show of support, unfortunately," Thane said.

But the old man shook his head. "There are many in Solevar who do not trust Rangvald. They fear speaking up, however, because those who trust him are quite loud about it. It makes their numbers seem to swell."

"Not that we wish to leave you," Eirin said, "but is there still a chance to make it to the city before dawn?"

"There is," a younger woman said. "We can escort you after everyone has eaten. It's not very far to the edge. You can shelter there until tomorrow eve."

"Rangvald isn't there yet?" Eirin asked, still seeming uneasy.

Benjamin gave her a crooked smile. "We might or might not have some friends who wished to make the journey a bit more difficult for him. Word has it that the White Harts have suddenly become very dull and stupid when it comes to following directions." At this, a chuckle rippled through the assembly, which was now silent, save those directly participating in the conversation.

"But take care," the older man said in a more sober tone. "Your welcome won't be as warm as it was here." He turned, and his vivid blue eyes bore into Drystan. "We knew who you were because Benjamin figured it out as word leaked from Torbaine. For them, however," he pointed west, "you'll have to convince them that you can be king. Benjamin has done what he can to prepare the way for you. But our neighbors will not be so easy."

Chapter Twenty-Three

A s the others finished their meals, Drystan touched Eirin's elbow. "Walk with me?" he said quietly. Her eyes grew wide, and he thought he saw a touch of panic in them, but after a moment, she nodded and stood.

They made their way quietly through the crowd, which was still finishing the rest of the food laid out on the long tables in the center of the square. There were countless other circles formed around fires, just like the one they had been led to. By now, so many people had crowded into the square that it took them longer than Drystan had expected to escape, but they did eventually make it back out to the quiet streets that ran between the dilapidated houses.

Drystan chose a small bench on the side of a two-story house and seated Eirin upon it. Then he walked a quick round to make sure they were alone. He wasn't too worried, though. Qeb would follow soon enough, if he wasn't already lurking in the shadows, and Nuru would be sure to appear sometime as well.

When they were both finally seated, Drystan took Eirin's hand in his, and for once, she didn't pull it away. He had planned to ask her about the kiss. Where did it leave them? What were they supposed to do now? But after the Merfolks' warnings, he suddenly felt as though he had run out of words. The enormity of what they were about to do settled on him and made him want to hunch with its weight. So he wasted precious minutes in silence, rubbing the backs of her knuckles with his thumb.

"Tonight feels like it's lasted three days," Eirin whispered. "What time do you think it is?"

Drystan looked at the horizon and gave a humorous chuckle. "At least three more hours before sunrise." Then he let out a gusty sigh. "How am I going to do this, Eirin?"

"To be honest, I don't know." She shrugged her thin shoulders.

That did not make him feel better.

"But..." she continued slowly, "this isn't the first time you've had to do something impossible. You've won people over before. More times than I can count. And, if I may remind you, you've been a prince most of your life."

He shook his head. "That was different. I was handed that role. I didn't have to convince anyone."

"That's not true." She pulled her hand out of his and crossed her arms. "You were given the role of the Heir because you were stronger and faster and more qualified than any other student in the Citadel. No one else even came close."

"But–"

"And it was all because you're a Dragon. Dragons were meant to rule. To defend. You've done that over and over, again and again."

"I can't do any of that, though, if they won't give me a chance. We don't exactly have eons of time here. Nothing like what we had in Torbaine. I don't know how to prove what I am overnight."

"You changed their minds at the garden," Eirin reminded him. "In two nights, if I must remind you."

"*You* changed their minds." Drystan tapped her nose. "They eventually decided to believe you."

"I wasn't the only one," she said, bumping him with her shoulder. "Destroying Rangvald's forces helped more than a little. Besides," her voice became softer. "I'm not going anywhere."

They were quiet again, and a few moments later, he felt a pressure on his shoulder. He looked down, and his heart nearly broke as he realized she'd laid her head on his shoulder. If only he had the time to show her how he really felt, to take her in his hands and hold her close and kiss her until she was dizzy. But they didn't have time for that. He could hear a change in the hum of voices and activity coming from the square. They would be leaving for Iilaedin soon.

And yet...he wanted to show her how much he loved her. How much he *needed* this fragile girl's strength.

"I still don't know how I'm going to do this in such a short time," He murmured, turning his head until his mouth was against her forehead. To his chagrin, Eirin leaned back. But then she surprised him by taking his face in her hands and forcing him to look at her.

"Do you know why I struggled so much with what happened when you shouted at me, back when I was thirteen?"

A sharp flash of shame cut through him. "I humiliated you in front of everyone. It was cruel."

She shook her head. "It tore me apart because I had always respected you. You were there from the first day, watching over me. You rarely spoke to me, but I knew you were there. I always thought of you as my secret guardian, a quiet protector in the wings."

"Eirin, if you're trying to make me feel better, this isn't the way to do it."

She rolled her eyes and took his hands in hers. "Just listen, all right? I saw your fidelity. You were faithful. You were a faithful friend to Qeb. The king trusted you implicitly. You always kept your word. So the night that you screamed at me in front of the rest of the Citadel, I felt as though you'd betrayed me and only me."

More regret crashed down on him, but Eirin just smiled, her brown eyes searching his face. "But now I know I was wrong. You were faithful, even when it hurt."

"I was cruel," Drystan said stiffly.

"Perhaps. But you were *trying* to protect me. I had done something foolish in going out alone that night, and you reprimanded me for it. And...I understand that better now."

"Eirin—"

"I would rather have a king," Eirin said, her voice growing stronger, "who does what is right than one who works to please."

Drystan felt his throat growing tight. A burden lifted from his shoulders that he hadn't even realized was still there.

"For some reason," she continued, "we have been placed here and now in a time of pain and suffering and confusion. And I don't know why. But here we are." She reached up and wiped something wet from his cheek. "Be faithful. As you always have been."

He reached up and tucked a piece of hair behind her ear, but he still couldn't find any words. He wanted to tell her he loved her, that she, even here and now as they were, was more than he had ever thought he would have. But he could hear their friends walking toward them, and he knew that if he spoke now, he just might crumble.

She studied him back, tilting her head slightly as her large eyes searched his face.

"Hmm," she said. "Well, if that doesn't convince you, then maybe this will." Taking his hand, she moved off the bench and knelt down beside it on one knee. Then she pressed his fingers to her soft lips, sending his heart into spasms.

"Drystan, son of Egan, son of Kamon, son of Oreck, I pledge my heart and mind to you. My fealty and honor are yours. My life is forfeit to the needs and call of my prince."

Drystan stared at her as she uttered the words of the oath the Citadel students pledged to the king when they became Sgaeths. Somehow, this beautiful, fragile creature had decided that she trusted him. And not only did she trust him with her life, but with the lives of her family and the rest of the kingdom of Solevar.

What had he done to earn such respect? Such loyalty? The child he had broken seven years before with his callous words and cruel, humiliating shouts was tying herself to him in a way that could only be undone by death.

Why? he silently asked the Time Keeper. *Why me?*

But before he could consider a coherent response, Qeb strode around the corner and stopped when he saw them. Drystan was caught between embarrassment and annoyance, but Qeb swept both emotions away when he stalked over to them and knelt beside Eirin. And to Drystan's amazement, his friend began to utter the vow as well.

As Qeb spoke the words, their other friends appeared, as did countless Merfolk. One by one, each knelt and began to repeat the same vow, a vow that must have originated in Iilaedin, rather than Torbaine, for everyone seemed to know the words by heart. Drystan looked around in amazement until he met Isayas's gaze. The old man didn't seem surprised in the least. He simply smiled at Drystan and nodded once.

"It would seem," the Wizard boomed when the vows had all been said, "that the Time Keeper has found it pleasing to once again give us a prince worth following." He walked over to Drystan, grabbed his hand, and held it in the air. Then the Wizard let out a deafening shout, which was immediately echoed by the Merfolk. Then he turned to Drystan.

"Your Highness. It is time we brought you home."

Chapter Twenty-Four

Their progress across the expanse between the Merpeople's village and Iilaedin was slower than Eirin had anticipated. It was also unnerving. There were fewer trees than Eirin's friends were used to, and their party had swelled with a contingent of about a dozen Merpeople as well. The king of the Merpeople, one who considered himself subservient to the High King, he assured Drystan, had sent a group of delegates to talk with the leaders in Iilaedin.

Benjamin's younger sister, Elizabeth, had wanted to make it thirteen. "Please let me come!" she had pleaded with her brother. "I want to help, too."

Benjamin had kissed her on the top of her head. "Sorry, love. Owen is already coming. You can't leave Father and Mother all alone."

She glared up at him, her pale eyes bright with indignation. "I'm seventeen, Benjamin. And that's old enough to--"

"Be responsible," he said, putting his hands on her shoulders. Then he sighed, his face suddenly looking much older. "This will be dangerous. And if something happens to your ugly older brothers, you would leave our parents empty and alone? Not to mention our people?"

Elizabeth's eyes grew wide as if she hadn't considered this. Then she threw her arms around her brother and squeezed her eyes shut.

"Stay safe," she whispered.

"Of course," Benjamin said, his usual humor returning to his face, "while danger is possible, I'm sure it will be utterly dull, and someone will have to come rescue me from the ridiculous meetings their committee will insist I attend. Listen for my voice in case I need rescuing."

As she watched this exchange, Eirin realized Drystan was standing beside her. She looked up to see a curious expression on his face.

"Is that what having siblings is like?" he asked.

"Sometimes," Eirin said with a shrug. "It can also mean having little terrors who shadow your every move."

"I'm glad I don't have any siblings," Nuru scoffed.

"That's only because the world wouldn't survive another Nuru," Thane said, just dodging Nuru's attempt at a shove.

When they finally set off, Eirin found that she had more hope than she'd had for a long time. For while the larger group made them more noticeable as they made their way across what had once been fields, their new numbers also bolstered Eirin's confidence. They weren't alone any more. They had groups of people all over Solevar who supported them. Most importantly, who supported Drystan.

Benjamin walked beside Drystan, chatting amicably with everyone around him. As Eirin was riding on Drystan's back, now that Drystan was back in Dragon form, she wasn't on the level to participate in most of their conversations, but she enjoyed listening to the way Benjamin made everyone smile.

"Eirin?" he called up to her.

"Yes?"

"Tell me. Back in Torbaine, does Alys have...admirers?"

Qeb snorted, and Nuru grinned wickedly.

Eirin schooled her features to look utterly serious. "Oh yes. Dozens."

Benjamin's eyes widened slightly, then he frowned. "Oh."

"She is beautiful, after all," Eirin continued. "Though many think it's a shame that she shows a preference for none." She glanced down at Benjamin. "It seemed to me that she's recently developed a preference for...fins."

Benjamin stared at her, then broke into a grin, and Eirin laughed as he launched into a spontaneous song proclaiming the beauty of Alys's left foot. Even out of the water, his voice was quite good.

"Say," Thane said when Benjamin had finished. "Your voice is different in the water than out. Does it have the same power?"

Eirin studied Benjamin as he answered. Now that Thane mentioned it...

The Merpeople's lights were in their throats. Their blue-green magic shimmered there, and when they sang, it moved out through their mouth. At least, it had in the water. But just now, when Benjamin had sung, it had barely trickled out at all.

"Our magic is enhanced a hundredfold by the water," Benjamin said. "We have a little on land, but if faced with an enemy, we're not much better off than the Humans." He grinned up at Eirin. "No offense intended."

Eirin waved him off. "If you're going to try to insult me, you'll have to do better than that."

They walked this way for a while, talking about various topics and sharing stories in low voices, the Merpeople randomly breaking into low rounds of song now and then. Eirin noted that the sky was definitely getting lighter, but Benjamin promised that dawn was still another two hours away.

Then Thane came to a halt. "What's that sound?"

Everyone else stopped and listened, too. The distant sounds of hammers echoed through the valley.

"That would be Rangvald's builders," Benjamin said with a frown. "It seems the White Harts weren't able to delay them after all." He nodded toward Iilaedin, which was barely visible in the shadows. "Let's keep going."

The lighthearted banter that had been passed around before was gone now, everyone watching and listening for more sounds from the south.

"We won't be long now," Benjamin said some time later. "About half an hour's walk if we continue at this pace."

"Perhaps we should attack now," Nuru growled slightly. "They would be unprepared."

"No," Drystan said, shaking his large head, his voice deep with the Dragon's timber. "There are people living in the tunnels. Entire families. Best to stay the course and make it to the Time Stones first."

As silence fell on them again, Eirin thought back to a few hours before, when she'd sworn allegiance to Drystan. She hadn't planned to do it. But her sudden conviction that she simply needed to had taken her in the moment, and she was very glad she had. Still, she wished she could have read his enigmatic expression as all their friends and the Merpeople fell to their knees in swearing fealty to him as well.

"There," Isayas's deep voice broke the silence as they came to the top of a low hill. "Up ahead."

Eirin strained to see through the dark gray of the early morning. And just as Isayas had said, there rose Iilaedin.

The outlying houses were nothing impressive. Most of them looked just as ramshackle as the Merfolk's village. But beyond them rose taller buildings of three, four, even five stories. Many were interconnected. And beyond those was the Emerald Palace.

Eirin had seen the palace before in her visions. But now that she saw it with her own eyes, those visions paled in comparison, like murky brown water compared to a crystalline stream straight from mountain snowmelt. Countless towers pierced the sky, so high that some of them were lost in the clouds. Even in the low light, she could see that its stone was white, and from her visions, she knew it was marbled with shining black, silver, and gold streaking through it. In intricate designs running up and around each tower like ivy were stones of green that reflected what was left of the stars. And, of course, at the very top, which was rapidly disappearing into the clouds, was a tower Eirin knew well.

The tower that held the Time Stones.

Eirin touched her stone where it lay beneath her shirt, warm against her chest. Soon, this would all be over.

A slight movement to Eirin's left caught her eyes, and she looked down to see Isayas stumble.

"Are you well?" Eirin asked.

"Just tripped on a rock," the Wizard answered sourly.

Eirin watched him a moment longer before deciding not to ask if he would like to ride with her. Drystan wouldn't mind. He could easily carry two. And Isayas looked fatigued. When he spoke, he sounded winded. But she knew him well enough by now to know that any offer to help would only be met with a scowl.

"I have word from the wind," Isayas spoke again, more quietly this time. "Rangvald is still in his fortress. And he won't bring Mannish through the tunnel until it's finished."

So he did have Mannish, after all. He wasn't planning on trying to abduct Eirin after all. Eirin gave a small sigh of relief.

"So that should give us about four days even if the builders finish tonight," Drystan rumbled in his Dragon voice.

"We'll reach the city by morning," Benjamin broke in from Drystan's other side. "So you shouldn't have any trouble making it to the Time Stones tomorrow evening." Then he frowned slightly. "The city is vast, though. So you'll want to hurry either way."

"Who goes there?" came a shout from somewhere in front of them. Eirin squinted into the dark, but she couldn't see the speaker.

"I am Benjamin!" Benjamin called out just as loudly. "Son of King Ohkeanos. I come with friends who seek shelter in the great city." He paused and glanced up at Eirin. Knowing what he was asking permission for, she gave him a nod.

"They bring a Seer," he added.

Before he could finish speaking, light flashed on Eirin's left, and she let out a shriek as two of the Mermen fell and the battle cry of a horn echoed around them.

Chapter Twenty-Five

Drystan couldn't see who was attacking them. Only that they were being attacked from all sides and from above. His first instinct, as arrows—some flaming—rained down on them, was to shoot up into the air and go after the attackers.

But with Eirin on his back, that was out of the question.

"Hang on!" he growled before taking off into the sky as fast as he dared.

Unfortunately, there was fighting in the sky as well. He passed Qeb, who was fighting two Griffins at the same time. Again, he had to ignore the instinct to fight by his friend's side. As he hovered above the fight, trying to make out which direction the attack was really coming from, and more importantly, who their enemy was, a flash of blue raced across the sky to his left, reaching out its translucent arm toward Eirin. Drystan jerked around, making Eirin shriek.

"Don't pay it heed!" she shouted as soon as she'd steadied herself on his spines. "It's a Spectre! He can't hurt me!"

"Then why is he trying to take you?" Drystan shouted back.

"He's trying to distract us!" Eirin adjusted her position again.

Several more of the Spectres floated by, and it took all of Drystan's willpower not to jerk away. Eirin was right. Spectres couldn't hurt her. They weren't even really alive. Just magic dust gathered from the bogs off the distant Dead Sea, Eirin had once told him. At least, that's as legend had it. But that didn't mean they weren't incredibly distracting, as it seemed they were intended to be.

Intended by whom? If Drystan knew who was attacking them, he would know what to do with Eirin. If it was Rangvald, he would fly straight west toward Iilaedin. But if it were Iilaedin's forces attacking them...

They would have to go back to the Merfolk's village. And that would not bode well.

"Look!" Eirin called. "Down by that old storehouse."

Drystan searched for a moment before he saw what she meant. There was a dilapidated storehouse that had most likely once housed corn or wheat, just to the south of the battle. Anger and relief filled Drystan as he watched the group of military leaders gathered behind it, speaking to one another as the battle raged on. After a moment of study, he realized with triumph that he recognized their uniforms.

"Rangvald," he growled.

Another shape launched itself at them. Too late, Drystan realized that this one wasn't a Spectre. It was a Pegasus. And with an expert knock of its hooves, it sent Eirin flying off Drystan's back. Another Pegasus hovering below caught her on its back and bolted south.

Drystan gave full reign to the Dragon within as he chased the Pegasus down. Several other flying creatures rose to get in his way, but for a Dragon, these obstacles were easily dealt with. As they fell helplessly to the ground, he charged on.

Now that they were flying south, he could see where Rangvald's road was headed, and that it was nearly finished. And the Pegasus was heading right for it.

Unfortunately, while the other offenders who rose up to oppose him were little to no trouble, Drystan had a problem. All he had to do was flame, and his opponents scattered, either by fear or by force. But how was he supposed to get Eirin back without hurting her? More and more of the enemy continued to flock toward them, and while he was able to clear them quickly, it seemed as if two appeared for every one he got rid of. He could barely see Eirin through the suddenly dense sky.

His best choice was to fly above the Pegasus and gently lift her off. But he would have to take care. It would be incredibly easy for one of the other creatures to yank her away from him. Or worse, for her to fall.

If he could just reach the Pegasus, he could simply take hold of the Pegasus with both claws and kill it, allowing Eirin to climb up his shoulder and onto his back as they flew. That would put a lot of strain on his wings, however, and he would have to focus to remain aloft as he combatted the other creatures who continued to get in his way. He could knock them out of the sky with his wings, but doing such would make sustained hovering difficult.

They were running out of time, and the closer the enemy clustered, hiding her from his view, the more he feared accidentally hitting Eirin with his fire. He would have to act now.

With one measured arc of flame he was able to clear enough space to catch a glimpse of her. And his heart nearly stopped.

Her knife flashed in her hand, and she wound her arm back. Drystan knew what she was about to do. He dove beneath the cloud of Atharrachs that surrounded her, taking care to angle his body correctly. If he didn't, she could be impaled on one of his spines.

No. It was too risky. He slowed. He would have to catch her with his forearms. Letting her land on his back was a gamble he wasn't willing to take. His heart pounded with fear as he prepared himself. This was a trick he'd never practiced with Callispa.

Sure enough, a second later, there was a blood-curdling scream from the Pegasus, and Eirin came tumbling from the sky. Drystan dove down after her. Only when he'd caught her with his forearms and held her safely against his chest did he dare breathe again.

"A little risky, don't you think?" he shouted above the wind.

"I got tired of waiting!" she shouted back.

In spite of himself, Drystan smiled.

But his smile didn't last long. They were bombarded on every side as Drystan flew them back north. Not with arrows and blades, as doing such a stupid thing could result in the death of the Human, but by more and more bodies crowding around Drystan, making it hard for him to fly and trying to yank Eirin from his arms. Drystan flamed, doing his best to fly faster, trying to stay balanced as his powerful wings knocked creature after creature out of the sky. Eirin did her part in keeping them away from her, drawing her sword and slicing at anything that got too near, and she drew blood several times. But without space to move his wings, flying became increasingly more difficult.

Drystan saw his friends far before he could reach them.

"No!" he heard Eirin cry.

Over half of their convoy of Merpeople had been slain. Qeb and Thane had teamed up and were trying to protect Benjamin and three of his friends. Nuru and Callispa had done the same. The Merpeople were singing and holding their weapons out, but just as Benjamin had said, their power wasn't the same as it had been in the water. Drystan's friends had been trained for war on land, but the Merpeople were meant for the sea.

"Can you climb on my back?" Drystan shouted over the wind.

"I can!" Eirin called back. "But I'll need help!" With Drystan's aid, his fire keeping their attackers at bay, Eirin scrambled up and over his shoulder. He heard her draw her sword once she was safely nestled beside his spines. A moment later, a Roc, who had apparently gotten too close, fell from the sky.

Drystan dove down and flew in a low circle over the battle, flaming at his friends' attackers. But just as it seemed he'd stopped most of their attackers, a new wave appeared on the horizon in the ever-lightening sky.

"Isayas, no!" Eirin screamed.

Drystan jerked around to see the Wizard walking slowly, carefully to the center of the fight. Few of the enemy, it seemed, cared to attack him, so he made it safely to the middle of the carnage. As he raised his staff above his head, Drystan could see why Eirin had screamed at him. And Drystan's heart fell.

He landed as the Wizard, in a voice that rose in volume and strength until it rumbled through the valley, began reciting words that Drystan couldn't understand, but he knew instinctively that they were as ancient as the world itself.

Tuehtuhim clakan diskrios!
    Tuehtuhim colbhan dicolkete!
    Tuehtuhim Firu di ligesse!
    Ahre colkete kien uhrang!

With these words ringing through the valley, Isayas smashed the end of his jeweled staff down upon the ground. Drystan pulled Eirin tightly against his chest and wrapped his wings around her as a wave of sound and magic fizzled through the air. And as the wave rolled away from them, out into the distance, Drystan felt consciousness follow.

Chapter Twenty-Six

When the Wizard raised his staff and began uttering his incantations, Eirin felt as if time had slowed. She knew what was coming. The amount of magic he was drawing and pulling through his body was incomprehensible. She could see it, magic of all colors and kinds. It amassed around and then into him as if being sucked in by a vortex, so much magic it would be impossible for one man—even a Wizard—to hold it all.

And it was impossible. Isayas knew it. Eirin knew it. She didn't miss the look he gave her as he brought the staff crashing down. Through the hole between Drystan's wings, she saw the world transform into a flood of stars as it flowed out of him into his staff and then into the world. Eirin heard herself scream as he drained all of his own magic to guide it, molding and shaping it so it would resist friend and wash over foe. Not that it didn't touch Isayas's friends. Eirin could feel it, even sheltered by Drystan's thick wings. To exist near Isayas's final blow felt like trying to inhale while being pummeled by gale-force winds.

And then it was done, and Eirin alone was left standing as Drystan fell away from her, hitting the ground so hard it shook.

She felt rather numb as she turned slowly in a circle. She should do something, she knew. Bodies, familiar and unfamiliar alike, were scattered around her. She was aware of that. She should remove her friends from the ground. But how?

"Eirin?" came a hoarse call.

Eirin looked around dumbly until she realized it was Isayas calling her. He, too, was on the ground. Eirin stumbled over to him.

What was wrong with her head?

"What..." she tried, then scrunched her eyes shut and shook her head. "What's wrong with me? What happened?"

"Eirin. Eirin, look at me. You'll be fine. Look at me, girl." His voice was gentle but commanding. "You're just dazed, that's all."

"What?" Eirin asked, still looking around until he reached up one hand and touched her face.

"You're a Human. The magic you just felt was a shock to your senses, but only for its potency."

Human. That's right. She couldn't be cursed.

"But what..." She looked around again. "What about them? What about you?" She felt as though someone had put a large ball of cotton in her brain.

He chuckled slightly. "I did my best to alter the magic's path so it wouldn't touch our friends. But I'm not as young as I used to be." He stopped to catch his breath, and Eirin had a sudden moment of clarity. She yanked her pack off and offered him the waterskin. He drank thirstily, then let his head fall back to the ground.

"But they'll—"

"They'll be well enough in a few hours." He closed his eyes and took a long, deep breath.

"But what about you?" Eirin felt her senses beginning to return, and with them, a sense of urgency she had lacked moments ago.

"Eirin, love," he said with a sad smile. "You, of all people, should know."

As he spoke, Eirin finally noticed the magic within him. It was still moving through his body as it had before, but there was much less of it. In fact...it was all draining out.

"Don't cry, Sarah," he said, his grin now wide. "I'll be there soon. Why are you crying, love?"

Eirin stared at him before she understood what he was saying. Then it dawned on her, and she cried even harder.

How long she sat there holding his weathered hand, she didn't know. He closed his eyes and breathed in and out. His eyelids fluttered now and then, and he mumbled sometimes. But just as the sky was beginning to pale noticeably, his eyes cleared, and he opened them fully once more.

"Ah," he whispered. "I see. Sarah wasn't crying. You just look so much...so much like her." He touched her face. "Just the daughter she wanted..."

He never finished his words. His eyes closed, and his head rolled to the side. His breath didn't return.

Eirin stared at him, panic threatening to take her completely. Her mind was clearing, but not enough to know what to do. She still had to get her friends to safety. That much she knew. But she didn't know how. She didn't even know how many were alive.

Before she could think in useless circles for too long, however, she heard a new noise. People were coming, some flying, some running, and a few galloping on horseback toward her. She counted twenty before giving up as more continued to approach.

She stared stupidly at them as they rode up. A man who looked to be in his fifth decade with a head of thick, curly hair approached her. His inner light told her he was a Faun.

"Are you the Human from Mhaedin?"

Eirin stared at him for another long moment before slowly nodding. He closed his eyes and sighed. "Thank the Time Keeper.

Come now. I didn't have time to fetch a saddle, but the way back is short. We need to get back to the city before sunrise." He glanced nervously at the sky as he spoke.

The mention of the sun broke Eirin from her stupor.

"My friends!" She looked around her in horror. "We have to get my friends!"

"We will," the man said gently. "That's what my friends are here for." He indicated the group around them, checking the dead bodies for survivors.

"Here, let me show you!" Eirin said, running around and pointing out her companions. She was a little nervous about finding all the Merpeople in her muddled state, as she'd known them for the whole of one night. But in the end, thanks to their lights, she found everyone, and to her great relief, her own party had lost only Isayas. But Benjamin, who was beginning to awaken, had lost seven.

"Come," the man said again. "My friends are here for yours. But you must come with me. The commander will want to escort you back personally."

"I don't want to leave them," Eirin whimpered, watching as a Nymph somehow returned Drystan to his Human form.

"Considering how far you've come," the man said, eyeing the carnage around them, "I think they would agree that your safety is by far the most important part of this mission." He glanced behind him at the pale horizon, which was quickly turning more yellow by the minute. "Meaning we must get you out of the open."

Eirin looked at her friends once more as they were being loaded onto some of the larger Atharrachs, then nodded and allowed the Faun to help her up onto a Centaur's back.

There was little else she could do.

* * *

"My name is Marcus," the Centaur called back to her over the wind. "And you must be Eirin."

Apparently, more than Eirin's race was being spread around the kingdom. "How did you know who we were?" Eirin called back. Riding a Centaur was far faster than she had anticipated and was surprisingly loud, thanks to the wind that blew past them as he raced toward the city. This shouldn't have been a surprise. She'd seen Thane run, of course. He'd been known as the fastest student in the Citadel during his final two years. But she'd never ridden him.

That would be, if she was honest with herself, rather awkward.

"There are a few who go back and forth over Solevar," the Centaur called back. "They've been bringing tidings of two parties traveling north for weeks now, each one with a Human. Or, in Rangvald's case, preparing the way for one."

"But after the battle?" Eirin asked.

"We noticed the battle several hours ago, but your Wizard sent word on the wind to wait until he was finished."

Eirin closed her eyes. Dratted Isayas had known he was going to die.

A loud sound echoed around them, and Eirin jumped. It was somehow familiar, but eerie all the same.

"Not to worry," Marcus said. "It's a wailing song. One of the Mermen, from the sounds of it."

Then Eirin knew where she'd heard that sound. It was Benjamin. He must be mourning the loss of his people.

His brother lay among the slain.

Eirin's heart ached for him.

As the light grew, Eirin realized just how close to the city they had come, and in spite of herself, she gasped. Never, even in Mhaedin, had she imagined that so many dwellings could be packed together in one place. As she'd guessed earlier, the outer buildings were the smallest, no bigger than cottages, not dissimilar in size to those in Torbaine like the one her parents lived in. But the deeper the city went, the larger the buildings grew.

A crowd of people was waiting at the edge of the city where the outermost cottages met the fields. A single figure broke away from the crowd and ran toward them. It was a woman with long, graying reddish-gold hair.

"Mother," Marcus said, coming to a stop.

"Marcus!" she cried. "You were successful!" She gaped at Eirin as though Eirin might grow a second head.

"There were more survivors than I would have imagined," Marcus said as he came to a stop before the woman. "Probably all thanks to their Wizard."

The woman's eyes somehow grew even larger. "But–"

"More are coming," he said. "Please send word to the Merpeople that we have some of their wounded."

"But the sun is about to rise."

"Send an Elven messenger on the wind then. I have a few left in the drawer in my quarters beside my bed. Send Simon to get one and send it off. This is important." He lowered his voice. "We were right. It *was* Rangvald who ordered the attack."

"But *why*?" she whispered. "If he has his own–"

"He wants to be king," Eirin mumbled. They both turned and looked at her in surprise.

"Well," Marcus finally said, turning slightly to glance at Eirin. "That doesn't change the fact that you need water and rest. Come. I'll take you to the healing rooms." He studied her for a moment. "When was the last time you had Unicorn elixir?"

Eirin gave a start. Then she yanked at her bag and pawed around inside it until she found the little bottles. She nearly fainted from relief as she took one of her drops.

"You need to be seen by the Unicorns," the woman said, frowning at Eirin. "You look fatigued."

Watching one's friend die was likely to make one that way, Eirin thought, but she was too polite to say so out loud.

After that, Marcus did as he said he would. Eirin was quickly delivered to a healing room, where she immediately spied a familiar face.

"Iris!" she cried with joy. She was tired, but she ran toward the Unicorn, who was currently in Human form, with open arms. Iris embraced her and squeezed her tightly back, and Eirin felt a pang of emptiness as she was reminded of her mother's arms.

"But how did you get here so fast?" Eirin asked when they finally let go of one another.

"It's amazing how fast you can travel when half the kingdom isn't hunting for you," Iris chuckled dryly. "You forget. *We* aren't hiding from Rangvald."

"You were able to take the west side of the lake," Eirin said.

"That's right." Iris's smile faded as she looked Eirin over. "Have you been using your drops? You look weary."

Eirin was tired, but not wanting to worry Iris, she simply nodded. After all, she hadn't slept in nearly a full day and had then survived a battle. Who knew what a good sleep might do for her?

Though, deep down, she knew sleep wouldn't cure the ultimate exhaustion that always lingered in her bones these days.

Iris still frowned. "We'll need to increase your drops. I can supplement whatever you have left in the bottle. So can Phillipe."

"Where are the others?" Eirin asked.

"They're...elsewhere," Iris said carefully. Eirin understood. She got the feeling that the Unicorn herd received little respite these days, always at the beck and call of others who were suffering the effects of the curse.

"Where are your friends?" Iris asked.

Eirin's elation quickly melted. "They were in a battle," she said. "Rangvald attacked, and Isayas..." Her throat grew thick, and she couldn't finish.

"But they're all well?" Iris asked. "Did they make it?"

"All but Isayas," Eirin whispered.

Iris closed her eyes and sighed. "I'm sorry."

"We'll be bringing them in soon," said a deep voice from behind her, making Eirin jump. She turned to find Marcus still in the doorway. "We'll need all the beds you have."

Iris began walking about the room, instructing the Nymphs to prepare all the spare beds. This healing room was like the one in Mhaedin, its walls and ceiling covered with moss, crystals, mushrooms, and all sorts of vines, flowers, and herbs, anything the Nymphs might need for their cures. The main difference was that this particular healing room was much larger than the one in Mhaedin. And unlike Mhaedin's, it was not underground. They were in a tower, and its many windows were covered by thick curtains that shut out all light. Eirin did her best to touch as little as possible with her hands. She was too weary right now for the inevitable visions of generations of patients suffering and dying in this room.

Iris and the Nymphs' preparations were finished none too soon. Eirin's friends were delivered less than ten minutes later, putting the entire place in an uproar.

Eirin was relieved to see them all breathing soundly. They had been put to sleep, she was told, so they could heal. She wished to remain at their sides, ideally running between their beds to watch for their awakening, but the Nymphs gently shooed her away. Her friends would awaken anytime, and the Nymphs assured Eirin that she would be notified the moment they were ready for visitors.

All except Benjamin.

Benjamin was fully awake, staring off into the distance. He had been awake enough when help arrived that he had refused to let them put him to sleep. He was now wearing a thin tunic over his trousers, but it was still unbuttoned at the top and hung loosely off his shoulders as though he couldn't stand wearing it. His hair, which was always gathered neatly at the nape of his neck, was limp and undone. His brilliant blue eyes were downcast and looked gray in color. And he was still humming the haunting melody he had sung on the plain.

Eirin didn't have the words she knew he would need, the kind that could heal. So she threw her arms around him and hugged him. And though he didn't lift up his eyes, she felt him hug her back. His arms trembled.

"My brother," he whispered. "My brother has been silenced."

"Benjamin," one of the Nymphs said. Eirin let go of him and stepped back so the Nymph could come closer. "You might not have died, but you are wounded, too."

Eirin hadn't noticed the wound in his side, but now she gaped as the Nymph began to unwrap the binding that had hidden it beneath his shirt. Before she could ask him about it, however, Marcus reappeared.

"Seer," he said, bowing his head. "I am sorry, but if I could have a moment."

Eirin nodded and followed him into the hall.

"I know you've traveled long and hard to come here," he said when the door was shut. "We've been tracking your progress from afar. But I think you should know that we have word Rangvald's tunnel was finished this morning."

Eirin sucked in a breath. "We were told they weren't ready-"

He shook his head with a grimace. "Whoever told you that was mistaken." Then he paused. "There is also the question of what to do with Kamon's heir."

What to *do* with him? Eirin stiffened. "He is the reason I've made it this far. They all are."

"I understand that. But be that as it may, his lineage does pose...challenges."

Eirin lifted her chin defiantly. "What *kind* of challenges?"

"You surely know by now that many will blame him for his great-grandfather's actions."

Eirin opened her mouth, but Marcus held up his hand.

"And," he continued, "as fair or unfair as that may be, many will side with Rangvald over him. It will cause society to crack even more than it already has."

"What are you really saying?" Eirin asked, folding her arms across her chest the way Drystan did.

"I'm simply asking...if you could possibly convince him to remain quiet until after the Time Stones are fixed–" But Eirin was already shaking her head.

"No. He needs to be present at the Blood Fire Throne as soon as possible. *All* the heirs must be."

Marcus frowned. "How do you–"

"Because that's what the Time Keeper instituted when Oreck's son was made king," she interrupted him. "It's not just tradition. It's required. All able-bodied heirs must be present at the Rite of the Blood Fire Throne. Always."

Marcus put his hands on his hips. "True as that may be, how do you suggest you get Rangvald to participate? Especially as word has it that he wants your friend dead."

Eirin felt herself pale slightly. "I... haven't worked out yet. But I *know* Drystan will need to be there." In truth, she'd been trying to figure out just how to fulfill the requirements of the rite. Especially as she knew one of the two required parties would be less than cooperative. How to involve Rangvald...that was still a riddle she was hoping the Time Keeper would reveal the answer to.

Quickly.

"Do you even know what the Rite of the Blood Fire Throne entails?" The Centaur asked.

Eirin tried to look confident. "Somewhat."

"Well, I can tell you. The participants must swear to honor the Time Keeper and serve Solevar all the days of their lives, whether they win the rite or not. Then they pierce their hands on the Dragon's tooth that adorns the throne. Their blood flows down the side of the throne and empties into the channels that run between the stone mosaic at the foot of the Emerald Palace. Then the blood alights with fire according to the strength of that Dragon's heart. The blood with the brightest flames indicates who has been given the greatest heart with which to lead. Then the other Dragons must serve their brother for the rest of their days until his death when the rite must be initiated again."

Eirin was no stranger to blood. She'd bled more than enough when at the Citadel. But the thought of a hand letting enough blood to fill the channels of a stone mosaic made her stomach turn slightly.

"That," she said slowly, "was one of the reasons we tried to reach the city first. To have the upper hand. Perhaps he will be more willing to participate in the rite if he sees that we are already here." She took a deep breath. "With the city's help, of course."

Marcus watched her silently for a moment before slowly echoing, "Of course." But his manner was not encouraging.

Eirin had to try harder. "I don't know what power you have here, but it's clear you wield some influence. And I must implore you to listen to me now as a Seer if nothing else. I can promise you that I have known Drystan my entire life. He knew nothing of his legacy until this last year. And in spite of that legacy, he has sworn to protect me, and he has done that faithfully day in and day out." She met Marcus's gaze. "Do you know how Karolus died?"

It was Marcus's turn to look troubled. "Word came to us that Rangvald killed him."

"Your spies were right. I watched as Rangvald broke his neck. And my visions revealed to me that Rangvald wished to kill

Drystan and Karolus long before he succeeded. In fact, he attempted to kill them before the battle under the guise of an ally." Her face flushed as the anger was revived within her. "He betrayed us on more than one occasion."

Marcus was silent for a long time. But eventually, he took a deep breath. "You are correct in that I do have some say in the committee's decisions. But I am only a military commander. There are other, more powerful voices than mine. I will share with them what you have told me." Then his pale eyes softened. "But you are tired. And your companions should be waking soon. Go to them. We will speak of this again after you have had some rest."

* * *

Eirin did a quick sweep of the room when she returned, and to her relief, her companions were indeed waking. Her heart clenched when she saw only five instead of six. But she wasn't surprised. She never had been surprised, really. The more she thought about it, the more she was sure Isayas had never meant to make it to the war's end.

Eirin tried to greet each of her friends as she went to their sides, but not all of them wanted to greet her. Nuru was cranky and wanted to be left alone. Callispa was staring listlessly at the ceiling. Her face was unusually pale, and one of the Nymphs was fawning over her so much that Eirin decided not to interfere. Thane was still snoring, though it was clear from the half-eaten plate at his side that he had already awakened once, and Qeb was already up and examining some of the herbs. Drystan, who was in the back of the room, lay facing the wall.

"Drystan?" she called softly as she approached his bed. "Drystan, are you awake?"

"Unfortunately, yes." He rolled over, and Eirin could see heavy rings beneath his eyes. "They wouldn't let me see you."

"You needed rest," Eirin said gently. "And I was just outside the door with the Centaur, Marcus."

He glared at her. "How was I supposed to know that?"

Eirin stared at him, unsure of what he was so angry about. Then she stepped closer and stopped. Weak as her Human nose was, even she could smell the scent that practically wafted from him.

"Bruthsi!" she exclaimed. "But they only said they were giving you a little...so you wouldn't wake up on the way back!"

He gave her a humorless smile. "Apparently, Dragons require more than most other creatures. Especially when they wake up to find their Seer gone, and no one can tell them where she is."

Eirin closed her eyes. "I'm sorry, Drystan. They were worried about the sun rising, and they begged me to go to safety while they prepared the rest of you to be carried back."

Drystan didn't smile. Instead, he took the end of her braid in his hand and fingered it. "Eirin, you don't know what that was like, waking up and finding you gone. Surrounded by a bunch of strangers, everyone simply saying over and over again that you were with Marcus." His jaw tightened. "Someone said I had gone mad. And I nearly did."

Eirin reached out and touched his face. Stubble grew thick on his jawline, and he closed his eyes as her fingers traced their way down to his chin.

"I'm sorry," she whispered.

"It's not your fault."

"I thought you would want me to go into the shade."

He took her other hand in his and squeezed it, and Eirin wanted to faint with relief. He wasn't angry with her. He was just scared. "I want you to be safe. Always." He gave her the slightest hint of a smile. "I suppose...I can be a bit of a beast where you're concerned."

She quirked an eyebrow. "One would almost say Dragonish."

He gave her a weak smile, but it faded quickly. "He's dead, isn't he?"

Eirin nodded, her throat constricting and making words impossible.

He nodded and closed his eyes again.

"Then it looks like we're on our own."

Chapter Twenty-Seven

Drystan stared at the ceiling, which was covered in moss, mushrooms, crystals, and plants, long after Eirin went to talk with Nuru. He had dreaded, of course, Isayas's revelation that his time in Solevar was limited. But he hadn't realized just how much the Wizard's death would shake him. He hadn't realized just how much he'd come to rely on the old man's wisdom and strength.

Isayas's absence hadn't affected him much at first, of course. Waking up and finding Eirin gone had nearly stricken Drystan mad. He didn't remember it well. Qeb had, at some point, attempted to calm him, but even he hadn't been able to succeed. Then there had been some sort of tussle, though he didn't remember much of that either. According to Eirin, the fog in his memory was a residual result of the Wizard's magic.

But now his mind was clear enough to feel the echoing loneliness and fear without impediment. The responsibility he had shared with Isayas, his ability to lean on the Wizard's vast experience and knowledge, was gone.

How in the world had he begun to think he could lead Solevar as king? He couldn't even get a group of less than twenty from the lake to the city without losing almost half of them. Who was he fooling to think he could command a kingdom?

"You look terrible."

Drystan looked over to see Qeb approaching him.

"You don't look so gorgeous yourself."

A smile briefly turned the corners of Qeb's mouth up before disappearing. "You had me worried back there. The way you fought..." He left the thought unfinished.

Drystan raised his eyebrows. "What exactly did I do?" Iris had been the one to awaken him. And it was Iris, unfortunately, who had been forced to tell him the brunt of what he'd done. But she hadn't gone into detail.

Qeb's frown deepened. "You took down about a dozen of their best fighters before they hit you with bruthsi. And even in Human form, you took down nine more. Would have killed them, too, if I hadn't jumped in."

Drystan closed his eyes. That was not how he'd planned to introduce himself to the people of Iilaedin. "I didn't know where Eirin was."

"I know. And that's what I told them. They tried to tell you, but you said you had to see her before you would believe them." He let out a gusty breath. "I'm not going to lie. It's complicated things here. Significantly."

"Do you trust them?" Drystan asked.

"I don't think we really have a choice. We need them if we're going to challenge Rangvald."

Drystan closed his eyes. "And I ruined that."

"I don't know," Qeb said quietly. "I wish I did." That was one thing Drystan had always appreciated in Qeb. Qeb told the truth. He'd been criticized often for his bluntness. But Drystan never had to doubt a word his friend said. Unfortunately, in this case, if Qeb said their situation was precarious, Drystan knew it was bad.

"Drystan, son of Kamon?" A Centaur approached them. His

hair was blond like Thane's, but it was threaded with silver and a few streaks of brown.

"Yes?" Drystan asked.

"Are you feeling well enough to walk?"

Drystan resisted the urge to groan as he pushed himself up. His body had never felt quite so breakable. Isayas's power must have been heavy indeed if he could make even a Dragon suffer.

Slowly, Drystan got to his feet and nodded for the Centaur to lead the way. Qeb began to follow, but the Centaur held up his hand.

"I'm afraid this meeting is for the Dragon. Alone."

Qeb looked as though he were about to say something, but Drystan just shook his head. He had made this situation bad. It was up to him to clean it up.

"I promise," the Centaur said with a small smile. "We'll do him no harm."

Qeb didn't look happy about it, but he agreed to go sit by Eirin until Drystan got back. A few minutes later, Drystan was following the Centaur down a set of polished stone halls. The stone hall echoed with the clip-clop of the Centaur's hooves and the quiet tap of Drystan's boots.

The Centaur didn't attempt to speak with Drystan until they were alone in a well-lit passage.

"My name is Marcus," the Centaur finally said. "I am the high commander of His Majesty's armies."

"Which Majesty?" Drystan asked.

Marcus gave him a wan smile. "That is a good question. And not one I know the answer to." They turned down another hall and exited through an open door to a large garden.

"Is this part of the palace?" Drystan asked, trying to see where the long, thin building ended.

"It's an outbuilding but not a part of the palace itself. We have several other buildings like it here," Marcus said. "They house provisions, weapons, and healing rooms like the one you were in." They walked along the edge of the building then entered another, careful to stay within the shadows, as the late morning sun was now high.

"We have an army of about two thousand here," Marcus said.

Drystan's ears perked up. "An army to do what?"

"Keep the stragglers alive. Which," Marcus took a deep breath, "is why we need to speak now."

Drystan nodded. "Of course."

Marcus nodded but didn't speak for a moment. Finally, he began walking again. "I've spoken with Eirin. And I believe that what she says is true, particularly pertaining to you." He turned and looked Drystan in the eye, and Drystan knew what he wasn't saying. "But before I can offer my official support, I need to know what you're planning to do. Rangvald is on his way already, and we just received word that he's escorting his Human. Which, we're told, means that they will be here within four days."

Drystan's mouth went dry. "Four days?" He was familiar enough with politics for this to make him wary. The Elders in Torbaine had once argued for four days about whether or not they should rename one of the Citadel's final tests. Four days was nothing.

Marcus nodded slowly. "Or as soon as two, depending on how fast he can actually travel within the tunnel. His people control the southern half of the city, so when he arrives, we will have no way to stop him. If we try, there will be a war. And once his Human breaks the curse, Rangvald will initiate the Rite of the Blood Fire Throne on his own. If he spills his blood on the stone in front of the palace without any competitors, it will all be over. The time to challenge him will be gone." The Centaur sighed and rubbed his eyes. "In truth, I'm somewhat afraid it already is."

Drystan stood taller. "Then we should go to the stones now.

Eirin can break the curse! We can be ready for him when he arrives."

But Marcus held up his hands. "Rangvald's men have already blocked the main path to the palace. There are some back alleys, of course. But remember that as the eldest prince, it was Rangvald's duty to guard the palace. It's unlikely we will know of an entrance, secret or known, that he does not."

Drystan studied the Centaur for a moment. "Something else is wrong. What is it?" Drystan knew Rangvald was resourceful, but he doubted his uncle could prevent them from entering the palace. Something else was bothering Marcus.

Marcus closed his eyes and muttered something, pinching the bridge of his nose as he did. Then he huffed. "I...I believe you and your friends have done a good thing. A monumental thing, really, in bringing her here."

"But," Drystan said, a slight growl slipping out. No matter what he did, there was always an exception.

"You haven't lived here, so you can't understand just how deep the resentment and hatred for Kamon goes. You haven't survived the curse, watched your home crumble, or stood by as your children starve." He shook his head. "I'm just not sure it would help your cause to have Kamon's heir present when the Time Stones were fixed."

"So you wish for me to wait in hiding while Eirin braves the way to the tower without me," Drystan said.

"I don't *wish* for you to do anything of the sort," Marcus frowned. "But it's not my decision to make. And before you say I don't understand, you should know that there are many who are furious that you've been allowed within the city at all. Especially after what happened this morning. Word moves quickly here, and the families of the soldiers you injured are out for your blood."

Drystan did understand, unfortunately. Torbaine's gossip chain had been strong.

"You injured many good men," Marcus continued. "My captain has called for your removal. And many others..." He paused and shook his head. "Removal is pure play concerning what they desire for you."

Drystan nearly allowed himself a bitter laugh. It was ironic. Drystan was talking to a man he could annihilate in seconds if he wished. He could destroy any and all of them without a second thought. But they knew he wouldn't. They knew he was a restraint unto himself, which gave them the courage they might have otherwise lacked to order him gone.

"You know," Drystan said slowly, "that the reason I'm here, besides providing Eirin protection, is that she's convinced I'm necessary to fulfill the Rite's requirements. That if I'm not here, it will somehow anger the Time Keeper again."

"And you believe her?" the Centaur asked. It wasn't a mocking question. Marcus really did seem curious to know what Drystan thought.

Drystan allowed himself a sardonic smile. "I've learned not to question Eirin's judgment." He paused. "And if you don't believe me, you can ask her about her continual visions of rot and death. I'm sure she would be happy to elaborate on those."

Marcus shuddered slightly, to Drystan's delight. Then he looked up at the tall building beside them. "The committee is going to hold a meeting tonight. I will discuss what you and Eirin have told me. But I need to know now." He stared hard at Drystan. "If we choose to ask you to leave for the sake of the peace... will you go?"

Chapter Twenty-Eight

After a day of eating, bathing, new clothes, and rest, Eirin, Nuru, Qeb, Thane, and Callispa waited in a circular antechamber as Iilaedin's committee of the various race representatives finally gathered and began their talks. Now that Eirin understood Torbaine's true history, she could see that this committee was the one on which Torbaine's city council of Elders had been modeled.

The committee members, representatives of the various Atharrach races from around the city, had been forced to delay their meeting's beginning until nightfall. The tall buildings blocked much of the sunlight during the day, which meant those within the city were generally able to travel from one part to the other without danger. But those who resided outside the city's shadowed protection had to wait to cross the fields under cover of nightfall. And though Eirin had been excited when the talks had begun, her enthusiasm was all but gone.

The night was nearly gone.

No one but Drystan had been invited into the committee's official chamber. This wouldn't have been quite so suspect, except that a contingent of guards made up of various large Atharrachs stood at attention around the circumference of the antechamber. They were simply present for protection for the committee, Eirin had been assured by Suri, a female Manticore. But, as Thane pointed out after, just whom were they protecting?

Qeb was on edge and paced the entire time Drystan spoke with the committee members, stopping from time to time to whisper with Thane. Nuru continued muttering a steady stream of colorful insults under her breath, and Callispa, though slightly less pale, still looked lost.

Eirin, unfortunately, was a victim of her own ability. She tried not to touch the cool marble floors, but she couldn't help it. From time to time, especially when she dozed, her hand would brush the floor or the column she was leaning against, and visions of the past flashed behind her eyelids.

She should have enjoyed seeing glimpses of ages gone by, nods to what had been. But this antechamber had seen countless dignitaries and heroes pass through, and Eirin was forced to note the magnificence of each. Everything from their embroidered silken robes to the shine of their boots to the glitter of their weapons and the gold glint of their crowns made her hurt inside. It was painful to see just how far Drystan's line and all those under his care had fallen.

"What do you think he would do?" Nuru asked, coming to sit beside Eirin. Her voice was pitched low, and she kept her eyes on the guards around them at all times.

"What would who do?" Eirin asked.

"Isayas. What would Isayas do?"

Eirin sighed. "I wish I knew."

"They're talking about breaking us up," Nuru said in a quiet voice. "I can hear parts of what they say if I tilt my head the right way."

Eirin frowned. She and her friends had come so far...only to lose Isayas and now to have others attempting to make their own decisions for them. Unfortunately, surrounded as they were, it was too late to make a run for it now. They were at the mercy of the people of Iilaedin.

Eirin's annoyance began solidifying into anger. This wasn't how it was supposed to be. They had come here to save Iilaedin. Not to be its prisoners.

The scrape of the large stone door made them turn to see Drystan exit the meeting room. He wore a cocky look Eirin wasn't used to seeing on his face, and he walked as though he hadn't a care in the world. This Drystan looked smug. Reckless. Arrogant.

What in Solevar was he up to?

Still, in spite of all the more important things going on, Eirin couldn't help noting that the new clothes Drystan had received made him look different, similar to the kings of ages past that continued to assault her mind every time she touched the floor.

More than that, though, there was something else that had changed since she'd seen him last that morning. She couldn't say what it was exactly. It wasn't even the oddly nonchalant expression he was wearing. It was something deeper, something only someone who knew him well would notice. Something...a strange glint in his eye, perhaps, was different. And Erin wasn't sure whether she liked it or not.

"We will call you back in when we're finished deliberating," Suri said, using her spiked tail to close the door behind her.

"Well," Drystan said to his friends when the door was shut. "Now we wait."

Eirin continued to watch Drystan as he sauntered over to Qeb. He smirked at the door and whispered in Qeb's ear. Qeb looked just as confused as Eirin felt for a moment. But then, as Drystan continued to whisper, his brow smoothed, and he snorted at something Drystan said.

Eirin wasn't the only one watching them. She noticed that the guard nearest them also seemed to have taken a keen interest in their conversation. His look of concerned focus, however, turned to one of disdain as the two young men snickered.

Drystan straightened and sauntered over to where Eirin was sitting on the floor. Eirin blinked up at him. He sat down beside her and put his arm around her waist, pulling her close. She sucked in a sharp breath as he ran the tip of his nose down her jawline and pressed his lips against her ear. She sat frozen as he continued pulling her body more tightly against his. What was he doing? Not that she minded being pulled close. But right now?

"Giggle," he whispered. "Flirt with me."

It took all of Eirin's willpower not to turn and stare at him. She knew Drystan well enough to have confidence in whatever he was doing. But first, she needed to get over the shock his proximity had placed on her senses.

A nervous giggle burst out of her.

"You'll have to do better than that," he said, skimming his nose down her cheek, then back up. "Make it believable."

Eirin allowed herself to lean into him and tilted her head to the side, feeling his hot breath against her neck and cheek. Then she deliberately unbraided her hair and began to run her fingers through it. He played with the ends of her hair, keeping his mouth against her ear.

"Giggle while I tell you this," he whispered. "Do you know where the Time Stones are?"

She giggled again and poked him in the side. "Obviously." She gave him a look that she hoped could pass off as alluring and not like she had gas.

He pulled her back against him and nuzzled her cheek again. Did he have any idea how difficult he was making it to concentrate?

"Where?" he whispered.

She turned her mouth to his ear, giving him a saucy smile as she spoke. She knew she must be at least somewhat convincing when one of the guards watching them rolled his eyes.

"The tallest tower," she breathed before laughing again.

"I'm going to get you into the palace," he replied in a sultry voice. "But we're going to have to go fast. When I shift in a moment, make sure you're not standing too close."

"What about the others?" she said, letting her lips touch his ear as she spoke. Actually, this flirting stuff wasn't half bad.

"Qeb will make sure they help us," he said, his voice barely audible as he trailed his fingers up the side of her right arm. It felt so good that she could only nod in reply.

"What about it?" he asked, his voice slightly louder. She knew that meant the end of their whisper session. And though she was glad they were finally making their move, she immediately felt his absence as she stood and left him on the ground. For good measure, she gave his shoulder a playful swat.

"If you can," she giggled before walking over to Nuru. Nuru was staring at her like she'd contracted a disgusting disease.

Eirin kept the saucy smile and whispered into Nuru's ear, making sure to glance pointedly at Drystan several times as though she were simply indulging in some tasty gossip.

"Be ready. Drystan's about to make our escape."

Nuru blinked at her once, then donned her own flirty smile.

"Oh, *really*?" she intoned, drawing the word out suggestively. When she did this, Thane turned around, took one look at her, and nearly fell over, and if Eirin hadn't been preparing herself for Drystan's shift, she would have laughed.

Drystan stood and gave a leisurely stretch. Then he clenched his hands, closed his eyes, and his body went taut.

And nothing happened.

Drystan's eyes flew open and met Eirin's, panic evident in them. Eirin stared at him in horror as the door opened and the committee members spilled out.

A large male Elf stepped forward and sighed. "And that," he said sadly, "is unfortunate."

"What do you mean?" Drystan demanded.

"You failed the test," Marcus, who was standing to the Elf's right, replied unhappily.

"What test?" Qeb demanded.

"We had hoped you would trust us enough to let us help," Suri said. "We wanted you to rely on us so we could rely on you." She shared a glance with the Elf. "Unfortunately, you failed."

"Wait!" Thane yelled. "You gave him more bruthsi root, didn't you?"

"He's right!" Nuru added. "It should have been out of his system by now."

Eirin studied her friends' lights with growing dread. Their lights were all still there, ebbing and flowing as they ought. But each light was slightly dimmer than it had been. She'd thought it an effect of the dimly lit room at first, as their lights were all slightly duller than usual. But now...

She should have seen it coming.

"You gave them all more bruthsi, didn't you?" she asked, turning to Marcus. "Without telling us."

Marcus looked at the ground, but the male Elf answered for him. "It was a test. One, unfortunately, that you failed."

"But that's not fair!" Eirin cried. Angry tears threatened to spill down her face, but she willed them back. "We came here. We lost friends coming here. *We* did it. Not you. And you think you have the right to stop us when we're–"

"And we're very grateful," said a soft voice. A female Roc said, stepping forward from the back of the group. "But this is our home. And we have sworn to keep it safe."

"We're not going to hurt him," the Elf said gently, turning his attention to Eirin. "The others can remain here in the quarters we give them, and he'll be sent to a waiting place in the mountains.

It's a comfortable little cabin, and he'll be safe there until this is all over and we have the time to make the decision of what to do with him."

"I'm not a pet," Drystan snapped. "You don't get to make decisions for me."

The male Elf ignored him and continued addressing Eirin. "I swear no harm will be done to him. And there's time enough for him to be taken safely to the mountains before sunrise if we leave soon."

"He can't leave!" Eirin thundered, stomping her foot. "I *need* him!" She looked at Marcus. "Did you tell them *anything* I said about the rite of succession?" She returned her attention back to the others. "I have studied the ancient ways, and I have seen death and destruction in vision after vision–"

"Seer visions don't tell the future," the female Roc said, her voice still soothing.

"And I have seen the *result* of violating the Time Keeper's created order!" Eirin continued. "It's nothing but death and destruction, and if I know anything about breaking the curse, it's that we won't succeed by breaking the ordinances further!" She pointed at Drystan. "He needs to be present at that rite!"

The tall Elf closed his eyes. "I am sorry. Truly I am." He gestured to the ten people standing around him. "We do not love Rangvald. We do not want him as our king. But the people of Iilaedin cannot overcome their distrust of Kamon's heir. And Kamon's heir has proven tonight that he cannot overcome his distrust of them either."

"But–" Eirin began, but he shook his head.

"If there were any other way, we would fight with you." His voice became weary, and he finally faced Drystan once again. "We truly believe you have the best intentions at heart."

"Then–" Drystan tried, but the Elf held up his hand.

"But the stain of Kamon's sin runs too deep."

Chapter Twenty-Nine

Drystan ran through every scenario in his head as he and his friends gathered around Eirin in the center of the room. They were surrounded and outnumbered. None of them could shift. They didn't even have weapons because those had been removed while they were being treated in the healing room.

He wasn't about to leave Eirin to these people, that was for sure. But how was he supposed to fight when his strength had been subdued, they were outnumbered, and he had no weapons?

"It doesn't have to be difficult," a Fae woman said in a soothing voice. "We don't want to fight you. We want peace."

"You're choosing death if you take him!" Eirin's shrill voice pierced the air. "I may not be able to see the future, but I have seen the past. And departing from the Time Keeper–"

"We know the past, child," the Fae woman said placatingly. "Many of us were there."

Drystan made his decision.

"You'll take care of them?" he asked. He could feel his friends turn and stare at him, but he kept his eyes on the tall male Elf.

The Elf studied him for a long moment, his eyes searching

Drystan's. Finally, he nodded slowly. "We will. We are truly thankful for all you have done in bringing the Seer here."

"You have a funny way of showing it," Drystan said with a scoff. He looked at Qeb and narrowed his eyes slightly. Hopefully, his friend would understand what he meant. Then he held his arms out in front of him, wrists together.

"One would think you'd wish to listen to the Seer," he said as Marcus came and bound his wrists together. "If Eirin says–"

"Eirin, from what we understand," said the Fae woman, "seems to be quite gifted. But she is young." She studied him, her brows knitting slightly. "As are you."

Drystan simply met her gaze. He couldn't allow his Dragon to reign right now. He needed to convince the committee that he was going to go quietly. They couldn't know how he planned to come back the moment he was free of the bruthsi root and steal Eirin back. Then they would take to the sky and enter the tower from above.

These people needed to believe he was beaten. None of them could know how his fire had flared in his chest while they interviewed him in the committee hall, looking down at him from their raised thrones. They couldn't know how his hesitance to accept his place as prince had been hardened by their questions, their doubt, and their inability to take action. They denied it, but they were determined to make Rangvald their king. Drystan was sure of it.

Determination to crown a madman would have been bad enough on its own. But even worse than their rejection of Drystan was their insistence that they knew better than the Seer, the one person in the world who seemed to have any inclination of how to fix things. And Drystan, who had for a long time wanted nothing more than to abandon his blood and legacy, had suddenly been struck by the conviction that he needed to stay. He *must* stay.

This left him but one choice. He would have to wait until the fire in his heart burned through the bruthsi root. Then he wouldn't rest until Eirin was his once again, and they were in the tower. To do this, he would have to convince them that he had given up.

Unfortunately, he would have to do the same to Eirin.

"What about the rite?" Eirin protested as Drystan allowed himself to be bound in chains. "We need *all* heirs present! You know this!"

"One heir is enough," the Manticore woman said patiently.

"You saw what Rangvald's people did to us!" Eirin shrieked. "They killed Isayas!"

"He sacrificed himself," the Elf said.

"They forced his hand!" Eirin argued. "They attacked us without warning or pity. Regardless of the curse, you're ushering in the reign of a ruthless dictator, and you're sending away the remaining heir?"

"The people's hatred of Kamon is too strong!" the Elf thundered, sounding very much like a father who was tired of his child's antics. "More blood will be shed if we allow him to roam the city. Pandemonium will ensue! Do you want more people to die?"

"You want peace. But at what cost?" Eirin snapped.

The male Elf turned and bent so his eyes were level with Eirin's. Drystan's Dragon hissed inside as this stranger got in Eirin's face, and Qeb and Nuru immediately pressed in closer against her, the ferocity on their faces showing clearly that they would have shifted long ago if they could have.

"We *could* kill him," he hissed. "But we're doing everything we can not to. *We* hate the unnecessary spilling of blood. Unlike you seem–"

But Eirin, being Eirin, didn't blink as she faced the angry Elf down. "I want this curse to *end*."

"We are choosing mercy!" the Elf replied.

"You're just assuaging your consciences!" Eirin looked at Qeb and then Drystan. "You know I'm right! You can't let them do this!"

Drystan hated the pain in her eyes, the frustration and disappointment. She thought he was giving up. Not just on their mission, but on her.

"Eirin," Qeb whispered, but Eirin shoved him back with her shoulder, edging a half-step closer to where Drystan stood flanked by guards ready to lead him away.

"You promised!" she sobbed through tears. "You promised you would stay with me!"

Drystan felt his heart rend in two as he watched the tears stream down her face. But there was no way to tell her, not with the entire committee and their guards watching. Hopefully, she would let Qeb tell her after he was taken.

Before she did something stupid.

"It's better this way," he said in a soft voice, pleading with his eyes for her to understand. "Stay with Qeb. He'll keep you safe." He tried one more time. "Please."

But Eirin was too angry to hear him. Her face was red, and her eyes burned like coals into his. And as he allowed the guards to lead him away, Drystan prayed she would wait.

Chapter Thirty

As soon as Drystan was out of the room, the Elf turned to Marcus. "Escort her to the green room in the palace."

Eirin wanted to snarl at him. So Rangvald hadn't cut off all the entrances to the palace like she'd been told. And they wanted her friends to trust them.

"Have the others placed in the dungeon," the Elf continued. He'd barely finished uttering the words when Qeb slammed into him, knocking him to the ground so hard Eirin heard a bone crunch. The Elf let out a shout as Qeb began to pummel him with both fists.

Nuru and Thane took advantage of the guards' momentary shock by grabbing weapons off those nearest them. Then they knocked the nearest guards over like the little stone blocks Eirin's younger brothers used to build up and push down.

Unfortunately, unlike the council back in Torbaine, the committee members weren't hesitant to shift. Those who weren't already in their Atharrach forms took them in a flash. The female Manticore bared her spiked tail at Nuru. Marcus took on Thane as the guards rushed to their assistance, each already in his or her own magical form.

"Eirin!"

A hand grabbed Eirin by the wrist, and Eirin turned to find Callispa behind her.

"There's a window in the next hall behind that door," she whispered. "If we can get there, I can fly you through it."

"What about the bruthsi?" Eirin whispered, watching as the room erupted into full chaos.

Callispa gave her a wry smile as the fire burned briefly in her eyes. Eirin understood immediately. They had dosed Drystan with far more bruthsi than the others because he was a Dragon. Because fire could burn through bruthsi faster than regular magic.

Apparently, they had underestimated the Phoenix.

Eirin gave her a nod, and they slipped between the ensuing fights toward the door. They even succeeded in getting through it, and were halfway to the window when Eirin felt herself yanked back by her cloak.

"Callispa!" she screamed.

Callispa turned just to be knocked down by four guards. She hadn't shifted yet, so subduing her was unfortunately easy.

"Get her to the palace," the Elf growled at Marcus, who came up behind him. Eirin noted with smugness that the Elf held his left arm tightly against his side. Qeb must have done that.

"I don't like this." Marcus shook his head. "She won't be secure there. You know what Rangvald–"

"Rangvald can do what he pleases if it means we break this curse!"

"I agree with Marcus," the female Roc said, appearing at Marcus's elbow, ruffling her feathers, her sharp avian eyes resting uneasily on Eirin. "We don't know what his men were told to do."

The Elf snorted. "You might be too young to remember, but I

remember Prince Rangvald. And Prince Rangvald expects obedience before he has to ask."

"So you're his lapdog then?" Eirin muttered.

The Elf shot her a glare. "I'm doing what will get our city free from the curse."

"You didn't consult with us on that," the Roc snapped.

The Elf ignored her, motioning to someone behind them. "You and Marcus and a contingent of guards take her to the green room in the palace. Stay with her until further notice. Take the others to the dungeons."

Marcus gave Eirin an apologetic look as he took her from the Elf's vice-like grasp. Another committee member, a male Fenris, appeared on Eirin's other side.

"Many apologies, Seer," the Fenris said through gritted teeth.

Eirin could tell they were trying to spare her frail Human form from injury as they took hold of her arms and began to drag her toward the window. And she was going to take full advantage of their caution. But first, she would allow them to take her outside. She had a better chance of escaping in less crowded quarters.

She tried to cast one last look at her friends, but they were all bound and had been dragged back to the antechamber, and she couldn't see them because the door had been shut. Saying a prayer for them, she coiled her muscles to spring the moment she was on the Roc's back.

She had expected the Roc to take her down to the doors on the lowest level, but then again, she forgot that she was no longer in Torbaine. They didn't have to walk. The Roc simply climbed out the window and perched on the balcony.

This would make escape more difficult. Eirin didn't have wings. But she had come too far to allow them to take her anywhere against her will. And if there was one thing Eirin had excelled at in the Citadel, it was getting away.

A Pegasus, a Griffin, two Sphinx, and a Fae accompanied them as the Roc took to the skies. Eirin took a quick look around to orient herself. Though it was dark, in the very early gray of morning she could see the open space that stretched between the city and the mountains, and it was smaller than she'd imagined. That was good.

After straining for a moment, she realized she could see several minuscule figures beginning to cross the expanse.

It had to be Drystan's party.

She wondered at first why they weren't flying, but as she continued to study them, she realized that Drystan was covered in chains. They were terrified he would escape. As they should be.

Eirin looked ahead. They were headed straight for the palace. To Eirin's relief, they weren't flying high. The rooftops were passing just beneath them. But she would have to take care. She didn't have the quick healing her friends possessed, nor was she particularly hardy. Her bones were like twigs in comparison to theirs.

After passing several spires and being able to grab hold of none of them, Eirin nearly despaired. Until, however, she realized where they were headed. And her heart leaped in her chest.

They were quickly approaching a palace balcony, one large enough to accommodate her family's cottage several times over. It had once been a beautiful garden covered with vases, pots, and raised soil beds. There were trellises covered in ivy and several rows of small citrus trees. All of the vegetation was dry and dead or dying, but it was an ideal place for her to make her escape, as there were several rooftops on each side that she could easily jump down onto, and one very long ladder.

Eirin meant to run the moment she saw an opening. But she stumbled as she climbed off the Roc's back, and she reached out to grab hold of the little ledge that faced south to steady herself. When she grabbed it, she found herself looking down over an enormous town square, large enough nearly to fit the majority of Torbaine's cottages. At the foot of the palace overlooking the square was a semi-circle dais. On the dais was an intricate mosaic made up of various stones in all shapes and sizes. And at the very back, facing the square, stood a large stone throne.

Eirin wanted to study it further, but the early morning scene before her was suddenly gone, and Eirin sucked in a sharp breath as the sensation of ancient magic overcame her. A vision filled her mind, and suddenly, it was night. Several young men stood before the throne. Eirin couldn't see their faces, but she watched as the tallest pressed his hand against the corner of the throne. One by one, their blood flowed into the channels between the mosaic stones. Each time, the channels of blood grew bright with flame.

In accordance with what Eirin had been told, the Dragon with the brightest flame arose, stronger and bigger than before. But not only did his flame change the dark of the night. It changed *him*.

Eirin returned to the real world with a gasp.

"Seer?" the Roc asked, her voice taut. "Are you well?"

Eirin blinked at her and then back down at the empty throne. "Don't you see?" she asked, her voice hardly more than a whisper. "We must have Drystan."

"Excuse me?" the Roc asked. The guards were now staring, too.

"The Rite of the Blood Fire Throne!" Eirin cried, pointing down at the palace steps. "You will not appease the Time Keeper by breaking more commands. Send for Drystan! Get him back so we can break the curse rightly!" She looked around, willing someone to hear her. "If you go through with this, you'll not only break the Time Keepers' ordinances further, but you'll be making Rangvald stronger!" She looked around again. "We have to get Drystan back! We *need* him!"

The Roc's expression, avian as it was, turned from anxiety to pity. "I'm afraid it's too late," she said gently. "He should be near halfway there by now. But if you just–"

Eirin was done with *just*.

Just sitting.

Just waiting.

Just listening.

Eirin was going to *do*.

The guards were now talking amongst themselves as two of them unlocked the balcony door. The other three failed to pay heed. They probably expected little trouble restraining a Human, especially one so small.

Fortunately for Eirin, they had never met a Human who had survived the Citadel.

Eirin bolted, ducking beneath the surprised Pegasus, and diving behind a thick, unruly rose bush. Knowing they would catch her within seconds if she stayed in the garden, a landscape she neither knew nor desired to know, Eirin raced to the corner where she'd seen the ladder.

She sent up a praise to the Time Keeper when it appeared, and she hauled herself over the little garden wall and began to make her way down as fast as she could.

Her heart was threatening to choke her as she fought down her fear while also trying to focus on the steps beneath her. She slipped in her haste, stifling a cry that would have given her away. But she continued her descent until she came to the end of the ladder and hovered above the nearest rooftop.

The distance was just far enough that any Atharrach, with the possible exception of a Brownie, could have easily made the jump. But Eirin was not an Atharrach, and the pitch of the roof, while not steep, would make it easy for her to roll off the edge.

"She's here!" someone yelled from above.

Eirin let go of the ladder and felt pain shoot up her knees as she hit the rooftop. That was the least of her worries, though. She began to slide down the sloping roof tiles, unable to find something to hold on to. She screamed as the roof tiles slipped out of her fingers, and she headed straight for the edge.

Then her left hand grasped something sharp. It was a broken tile, and Eirin was vaguely aware that her hand was bleeding as she clung to it. But she ignored the blood as she came to a halt.

She dangled, unsure of what to do for a long moment before deciding to try to climb back up. But it was a moment too long. A pair of strong hands pulled her from her precarious position and lifted her into the air. It was a Griffin. To Eirin's annoyance, he turned her so that she was facing him, pressed against his chest as he held her tightly, rising back into the air toward the balcony once again.

"Let me go!" Eirin screamed as she twisted back and forth. "I need to find him. It won't matter if we fix the Time Stones if he's not there!"

"Stay still, please!" the Griffin who had caught her grunted. "You may speak to Suri when we get–"

He didn't finish because he found that the blade he'd worn in his belt was now pressed against his neck.

"Put me on the ground," Eirin spoke through gritted teeth. "Or I will kill you, and we'll both die."

"You would risk Solevar like that?" he looked horrified.

Eirin gave him a fierce smile. "My family is not going to die because of your committee's stupidity."

He searched her eyes with his dark ones for a long moment before he started to rise again. Eirin nicked his wing with the knife. The cut wasn't deep enough to bleed his magic out, but painful enough to shock him. The Griffin cried out, and in jerky, lurching movements, they began to fall.

It had been a risk. Cutting the wing of the creature who was keeping her afloat several stories above the ground wasn't necessarily the smartest thing Eirin had ever done. But she was desperate, and she had done her best to cut him only enough that he would have to land.

Her gamble paid off when he hit the ground hard and she rolled out of his arms. By this time, others had realized what was going on, and they appeared in the sky, looking down at her.

"She's there!" Eirin heard from above. She paused only to pull the Griffin's sword from his scabbard before turning and sprinting up the street.

They should have caught her quickly, but Eirin had chosen her route well. The buildings had been built in close proximity, and there were enough people out in the street that Eirin was able to use them to her advantage. She could hear her pursuers behind her, chasing and calling for her to stop, but she didn't dare. She had to get to the expanse.

From what she had seen during her ride on the Roc, they were already near the northernmost part of the city. She should have only three or four streets to navigate before reaching the southern edge of the expanse. But the sky was growing ever lighter, and she could hear their voices growing louder from behind.

As she ran, Eirin was hit with regret. She regretted ever putting Drystan off. She should have told him how she felt from the beginning. She should have let herself love him. She should never have denied him her affections. And if she, by some miracle, got him back again, she would make sure she never denied him her heart again.

Heartache be hanged.

By this time, Eirin's chest was burning, and she knew from experience in the Citadel that she was going to see spots soon if she had to keep running this way. So she slowed and ducked down into the crowd, allowing it to push her along. As soon as she found a dark alleyway, she cut around a corner, hoping to find that the alley went all the way through. The alley did, in fact, lead to the next street, but Eirin was unable to reach it. Because she found herself face-to-face with a Centaur.

"Marcus," she gasped, so out of breath that speaking the word sent her into a fit of coughing.

"You're trying to reach him," he said.

Eirin nodded.

"Why?" he asked, taking a step toward her. Eirin raised her sword, and he held his hands up. "I just need to know why you would risk everything to get to him."

"Because," Eirin rasped, "if I don't, this curse will never be broken."

Marcus glanced up into the sky with a worried frown. "I will probably regret this, but I believe you." He swallowed hard and knelt down on his front two legs. "Get on my back. I'll take you."

Eirin hesitated only a moment, before doing as he said. Of all the committee members, she trusted him the most. And at this point, she had little choice, for two more pursuers appeared behind her.

"Marcus, you found her!" Eirin heard one of the Sphinxes exclaim. "Geoff will be—"

Eirin didn't hear the rest of whatever the Sphinx said because Marcus had whirled around and bolted in the opposite direction. Distant shouts sounded behind them, but the sound of his hooves and the wind in Eirin's ears quickly drowned them out.

"Dawn is coming!" he shouted over his shoulder. "I don't know if we'll make it in time!"

"We have to try!" Eirin shouted back.

Marcus was infinitely faster than Eirin would have been running on her own two feet. Not only was he a Centaur, but he knew the streets. It was only moments before they reached the northernmost edge of the city.

"It's too late!" He shook his head, looking at the pale yellow sky. "They're too close to the other side. I can't reach them in time." He looked down at Eirin. "Won't you come back with me? Can't we—"

Eirin had raised the hood of her cloak while he spoke. It wasn't the same thick black cloak she was used to wearing, but it would be better than nothing. It had to be.

And then she was running. Running as fast as her legs could carry her toward the figures in the distance.

"No!" she screamed. "Drystan, no!"

Someone grasped her arm from behind. Eirin turned to find a Griffin.

"You must come back!" he shouted. "The sun will rise in minutes!"

"I'm not leaving him! I can reach them if you let me go!" Drystan's group had been walking slowly, thanks to the chains, not running across the expanse. Their progress, from what she could see, was sluggish at best. Eirin might not be strong, but she was fast. Faster than Drystan's party had been going, in any case.

She had spent her whole life training for this.

"Please don't do this to my family!" the Griffin pleaded. He was not as tall as Qeb, but he was slightly bulkier. "We need you!"

"You need him, too!" Eirin grunted. And with a sharp twist of her wrist, a move she'd perfected back at the Citadel, she freed herself from the Griffin's grasp.

Eirin sprinted into the expanse. She fully expected him to grab her again. To her surprise, however, she remained free. She wondered why until she cast a glance over her shoulder and saw the Griffin struggling in a battle of his own.

With Qeb.

"Run!" Qeb shouted at her. "Before it's too late!" he cast a worried glance at the horizon, which was getting lighter by the second.

The distance wasn't so great. Eirin had run its length many

times over. But she was tired now, and her strength was lagging. Still, she ran.

She heard the sound of wings behind her and turned to find the Sphinx. Eirin grasped the sword more tightly and waited until the Sphinx had stretched out one long paw. Only when the Sphinx was about to grasp her arm did Eirin strike. The Sphinx let out a cry and yanked his arm back, and Eirin began to run again.

Several more times did various Atharrachs try to take her, but Eirin used their fear of the sun to her advantage. She learned quickly that if she wounded one, he or she would scramble back to the shelter of the city rather than staying and fighting. They were being gentle with her for fear of injuring the Seer, and she used this to her full advantage.

One more look over her shoulder sent a chill down her spine. A crowd had gathered at the edge of the expanse, waiting in what would soon be the shadows of the buildings. She glanced at the sky. The clouds above were glowing orange now, and she was just over halfway across. No one else came out to take her this time.

No one else was that foolish.

"Drystan!" she screamed again. If only the clouds would shroud her way. She would still burn through them, but the pain wouldn't be nearly so bad as that from direct sun.

Feeling as though her lungs might collapse, she pushed harder.

But the distance proved wider than she first expected, and though there was a fog floating on the horizon, it began to quickly clear. Screams sounded from behind her, but Eirin was now too tired to look to see why they were screaming.

Deep down, she knew they were screaming for her.

She tried to pull the hood of her cloak over her head again, but that was difficult to do while running, and the effort nearly made her trip.

"Drystan!" she called again, but without vigor.

But Drystan somehow heard her. He turned, as did his

guards. She continued to stumble forward as he started toward her. But his wrists and ankles were bound by the chains, and his guards, who had reached a shaded place, refused to let him go.

Eirin heard her name on his lips as the sun broke on the horizon. Then her world flooded with light, and she screamed as the pain from its rays brought her to her knees.

Chapter Thirty-One

Drystan watched in horror as Eirin raced toward him. What was she thinking? The sun was too close. She was too slow.

He had to get to her.

He couldn't shift and fly to her as he ought to have done. Unable to break free, the Dragon within writhed and roared, fighting to escape. The bruthsi, however, was still too potent for him to shift. So he did the next best thing. He broke the chains that had held him.

His captors might have believed they were capable of holding him captive with the bindings, but Drystan had known better all along. Going with them had been a way of maneuvering his position so he could get the bruthsi out of his system and fight his way back with the least bloodshed as fast as possible. But he had never been under the illusion that he was bound to their whims.

Even under the influence of bruthsi, he was far more powerful than they could imagine.

And now he disillusioned them as well. With a shout, he broke free and began to run. They wouldn't follow him out into the expanse. He knew that. They would remain safely in the shade as he ran out into what would very soon be direct sunlight.

Drystan ran as he never had before. *She's not going to make it,* a voice in his head whispered. *And neither will you.*

That was beside the point. Without Eirin, there was no living. The world would collapse, and he would prefer to die with her than to watch it burn.

But if he could only go faster. If the bruthsi within would burn up, perhaps he could save her yet. Drystan pushed himself harder.

It was all in vain, though.

The expanse exploded with golden light. Drystan knew somewhere in his mind that he was burning. But he couldn't feel it. All he could see was Eirin collapsed on the ground. Her piercing scream would haunt him forever. She was so close. Despite her weakness. Despite her Human fragility, she had nearly made it.

As if to add to his pain, he saw Qeb fall behind her. As always, his faithful friend had acted faithfully. And he would die for it now, too. The two people Drystan loved more than his own life were dying in front of him. And the fire burning within his heart, the one he'd spent the last year trying to learn how to control, how to repress, seemed to burst open, the flame beginning to consume him from within as the sunlight ate at him from without.

And it drove him forward.

Finally, after what felt like eternity he reached her. Drystan threw himself over her, doing his best to shield her small frame from the sun. He was all too aware now of the searing pain all over his body. Everything hurt, and there was a dull roar in his ears.

"Drystan?" came a small whimper.

The roaring ceased slightly.

"What, love?" he whispered.

"It hurts." Her voice was fading, a sob dissipating into near nothingness.

"I know, love." He searched with his mouth until he found her face. Kissing her temple, he pressed himself harder against her. "I know." The pain was so intense now that he knew he would soon lose consciousness. How she'd stayed alive this long, he didn't know.

Tears burned his face as they rolled down onto hers. "What were you thinking? Sacrificing yourself to reach me?" he whispered.

"You don't understand," she panted. "Solevar *needs* you." She paused, her breath rattling as she drew air in. "I need you."

"I'm here," he said, pressing another kiss to her forehead. The sensation of fire meeting fire, the burning from within and without, overcame him, and Drystan let himself go.

Chapter Thirty-Two

Eirin yawned and stretched, but she didn't open her eyes. Not yet. She *should* open them. Something important had happened, though she couldn't recall just what. She ought to wake up and find out. But she was too warm and comfortable where she was, and she couldn't remember the last time her sleeping mat had felt so good. So she rolled over, pulled the covers up to her chin, and sighed.

But no, that wasn't right. It was far too bright. Eirin scrunched her eyes to block out the firelight. The light, however, didn't dim.

Eirin cracked one eyelid open. And she froze.

Eirin awkwardly leaped to the foot of her bed, which was still in shadow. She stared in horror at the open window above her bed. Bright sunlight flooded over where she had lain. Who had been so irresponsible as to leave the window open? It must have been on purpose. No one would be that heedless.

Eirin held her hands up and turned them over and over again, searching for burn marks. But they looked...healthy. They weren't even pink. She gazed back at the sunbeams, dustmotes floating lazily from one to another.

If that were the case, though...if she wasn't burned now, then why did she remember burning? She closed her eyes and grimaced, doing her best to remember.

She *had* been burning. And so had Drystan. Now she remembered running after him, chasing him across the expanse. She had nearly made it. But then the sun had risen, and Drystan had thrown off his chains and tried to cover her.

Her heart stopped. Where was Drystan?

"You're awake," said a familiar voice. Eirin turned to see Nuru leaning against the doorpost of the healing room, arms crossed and a smug smile on her face.

"Someone left the window open!" Eirin pointed back at the sunbeams. "And where's Drystan? Is he–" she gagged on the word. She couldn't say it.

Nuru's smug smile softened slightly. "Drystan is fine."

Eirin stared at her. "But...how?"

"Here." Nuru nodded at the sunbeams. "Stick your hand out."

Eirin gawked, so Nuru rolled her eyes, grabbed Eirin's hand, and yanked it into the sunlight. Eirin's immediate reaction was to yank it back, but Nuru was stronger than she was, and her hand remained.

After the panic subsided, Eirin felt herself relax. Feeling the sunlight was...everything she'd felt in visions and more. She felt as though a warm blanket had been draped over her skin.

"Nuru?" Eirin whispered. "What happened?"

Nuru's smile was more genuine this time. "Come with me. There's something I want to show you." She took Eirin's hand and led her from the healing room.

As they made their way up several flights of stairs, Eirin felt the eyes of every Atharrach on her as they passed.

"Aren't they angry at me?" she whispered as they made their way out onto the fourth level. "I did run away."

Nuru nodded once. "You did. But then, as usual, you turned

everything upside down." She came to a set of glass doors and threw them open, then stepped out onto a balcony that must have been beautiful once. Rose bushes covered every wall and trellis, their colors faded and old. Eirin hesitated on the threshold.

"Eirin," Nuru said, beckoning. "It's safe."

Eirin slowly stepped into the sun. Immediately, the warm blanket enveloped her again, and she had to shield her eyes from the blinding brightness.

"You'll get used to it," Nuru laughed, indicating a stone bench partially in the shade.

"How long have I been asleep?" Eirin asked, slowly making her way to the bench as though in a dream.

"Just one night." Nuru closed her eyes and inhaled slowly. "But it doesn't take very long to get used to it."

"Nuru!" Eirin exclaimed, catching her friend's arm and holding it up in the sunlight to see. "You... you're so beautiful!" It sounded silly, of course. Eirin had seen Nuru every day of her life since they were six. But her skin...Eirin had never seen anything like it. It glistened, rich and brown, in the sun, and for the first time, Eirin realized that her friend's dark eyes were flecked with gold.

Nuru snorted and pulled her arm away, but Eirin could tell from the way the corners of her mouth turned up that she was gratified.

"Sit down," Nuru ordered, "and I'll tell you what happened if you shut up and quit asking questions."

Eirin nodded and did her best to prepare herself for whatever new insanity she had accidentally set off.

"After they took you, Qeb was the first one to break his bonds. We still couldn't shift, but Qeb is...well, Qeb. He freed Thane and then took off to find you. Thane freed me and Callispa, and we did our best to follow him."

Her brow furrowed slightly. "We didn't arrive until you were well over halfway across the expanse. And Qeb was running after you as fast as he could go."

"I was afraid their people would try to follow me," Eirin said, shifting uncomfortably.

"Oh, they did. But Marcus and Qeb stopped the fastest ones. And when we arrived, we helped, too. A few got out before we did, but you injured enough of them that the brave ones could only limp back in fear of getting caught in the dawn, and the others hovered in the shadows." Nuru tossed her head. "Cowards," she muttered under her breath.

"I remembered burning," Eirin said, closing her eyes at the visceral memory. "What happened after that?"

Nuru opened her mouth, then paused. "I'm...not really sure of the particulars. The committee is still trying to figure it out. But to make a long story short, something weird happened with Drystan's Dragon fire, and one minute, no one could be in the sun, and the next minute, he was fine." She sat back and studied Eirin. "And though you two were unconscious for it, you and Qeb were fine, too."

Eirin stared at her. "But we *were* burning–"

"And then you weren't. I told you, I don't understand it all. But we do know this now." She grinned. "Everyone who swore fealty to Drystan is now immune to the sun. It's like the curse never happened."

Eirin took a deep breath. "And Drystan...how is he now?"

Nuru's looked toward the door. "Why don't you ask him?"

Eirin turned to see Drystan standing in the doorway, watching her. He was wearing new clothes again, similar in style to what he'd worn the night of the dance in Mhaedin, the white shirt loose around the chest, shoulders, and arms, with a band of fabric wrapped neatly around the waist. His trousers were a dark blue, and a matching cloak draped around his wide shoulders.

He looked every bit a prince.

Before she knew what she was doing, Eirin was off the bench and had flung herself into his arms. She sobbed all over Drystan's clean shirt, but he didn't seem to mind. Instead, he lifted her gently in his arms and carried her back to the bench, where he set her in his lap and tucked her firmly into a strong embrace.

"I'm going to head out," Nuru said, making her way toward the door. "Qeb probably needs help getting on someone's nerves."

"Hey, hey," Drystan said softly, wiping her eyes with his thumbs. "What is this?"

That only made Eirin cry harder. "You...I didn't know why you left me! And then you were in the sun with me. And I didn't–" She hiccupped. "I'm very confused."

Instead of answering, however, Drystan simply cupped her chin in his hand and studied her face. Slowly he bent until his lips brushed hers. Eirin put her arms around his neck and steadied herself against him as he kissed her senseless. His hands, large and strong, held her waist, and he shuddered slightly when she touched his face with her fingers. She had only kissed him twice before, but she felt as if she had known his kiss all her life.

Too long had she pushed him away out of fear, unsure whether she could go on if she lost him. But she knew better now. This, feeling like the most precious treasure in the world as he caressed her face and whispered her name again and again...

This was too good to lose to fear.

Finally, much to Eirin's chagrin, Drystan pulled back. He was breathing hard as he pressed his forehead against hers. "Eirin," he groaned. "You're killing me."

Eirin leaned in again. "I beg to differ," she said, her lips brushing his as she spoke. "I can see the fire in your heart, and it's never been brighter."

He laughed slightly but pulled back again. "Usually, you're bursting with questions after anything important happens."

She gave him a pout that she knew was utterly ridiculous. "Usually, I get what I want."

Drystan laughed again, his voice low and throaty, and his eyes gleamed slightly amber. "The problem isn't giving you what you want. It's not taking everything *I* want."

Eirin made a face at him, but then she ran her fingers over his hand, which was wrapped around her. "You're sure you're well?"

He smiled and traced her bare arm with his free hand. "What do you think?"

Eirin thought she wanted more kisses. But he was right. She did want answers as well. So she decided to set aside time later to steal more kisses. Now, she would ask.

"What happened?" she asked. "Why aren't we dead?"

Eirin had seen people die in the sun before. Everyone in Torbaine had. It was gruesome, and it had left her with nightmares for weeks every time she witnessed another. She had felt the pain of the sun's burn. She had passed out, thinking it would be the last thing she felt.

"It's difficult to explain," he said slowly, a slight frown furrowing his brows. "But I'll try."

"That's what Nuru said."

He tweaked her nose. "That's because it *is* difficult. The committee members were still arguing about it last I heard. But from what I understand, they're now convinced that your theory about the kings abdicating their place on the Blood Fire Throne holds true. They believe--although they aren't sure, that when I sacrificed myself to cover you from the sun..." He huffed and shook his head.

"We believe," a man's voice said from the doorway, "that our knowledge of magic has faded more than we believed possible. And for that, we are sorry."

Eirin and Drystan looked up to see a number of the committee members crowding in the balcony doorway. The male

Elf, the one who had sentenced Drystan to exile, gave a slight bow, his long hair moving gracefully with him. The others behind him bowed or curtsied as well. Then, slowly, as though the group was still unsure, they finished filing out, their clothes reflecting the sun so brightly Eirin had to squint until they joined Eirin and Drystan in the shade.

"Thank you," said a Faun standing beside the Elf, "for opening our eyes. You do your title justice, Seer."

"Do you always make decisions the way you chose to cross that salt flat?" the Elf said, his mouth slightly curved at the corners.

"Usually," Eirin said curtly as Drystan snorted. Drystan may think it funny, but she wasn't quite ready to forgive the Elf for sending Drystan away. Not yet, anyways.

"We didn't know what to do," a Nymph from the side of the group said. "We have ways of going out into the sun, and some of our warriors were preparing. But it's not a quick process of preparation, and you ran out far sooner than we were ready."

"Your friends also made our decisions rather difficult," the Elf said with a grim smile. "Rather resourceful, aren't you all?"

"I remember the pain," Eirin said. "Then I passed out, and I don't remember what happened beyond that."

"We were confused as well," said the Nymph. "Then Prince Drystan was the first to rise."

Ah, were they using Drystan's proper title now? How respectful of them.

"He carried both you and the Griffin back, after which he informed us that he had stopped burning," the Nymph continued, "though he didn't know why. He flew you back, and then his friend, the Griffin. And to our surprise, though you and the Griffin were both injured, neither of you was dead." She nodded at Eirin's hand. "And then it was a rather simple healing process. Nothing the Unicorns couldn't fix."

"It took us a great deal of questioning," chimed in one of the Sphinxes, "but then one of the Merfolk mentioned that both of you had pledged fealty to the prince before leaving the lake."

"And sure enough," the Nymph added, "both your friends and the Merfolk who had also pledged loyalty are now immune to the sun as well."

"Benjamin was the first one to try," Drystan said, amusement dancing in his eyes.

Eirin rolled her own eyes. "Of course he was." Then she turned back to the committee members. A few more had joined them, and there were now at least eight. "But what changed?"

"That," the Elf said slowly, "we believe is owed to the prince." He paused and eyed her curiously. "Although... I'm somewhat surprised you haven't noticed it already."

Eirin blinked at him. "How so?"

"You can see the magic in all Atharrachs. I," he held up his hand, "must touch someone before I can see their magic. And when I touched those of your group who were immune, I realized something." He held out his hand toward Eirin. "What do you see?"

Eirin studied his arm. Elven magic was a silvery purple, and it ran from their heads down to their arms and into their fingers. She squinted at his fingers and tried to study the magic.

At first, she saw exactly what she expected, metallic purple light running up and down his fingers. But then, after another moment of study, she sucked in a sharp breath.

"Is that..." she began.

He pulled his hand back and nodded. "Does it look familiar?"

Eirin whipped her head around to stare at Drystan, who gave her a slight nod.

"It's in you as well," Drystan said.

Eirin stared down at her own hands. She shouldn't have any magic. Humans didn't have magic. And yet...

There it was. The slightest shimmer of gold, tinged with blue.

"It's... it's *your* fire," she breathed.

"It seems," a tall Fae woman wearing an elaborate headdress said slowly, "that when the curse fell, it wasn't the sun that changed after all."

Eirin stared at her for a moment before understanding dawned on her. "It was us," she whispered. "We changed."

The Fae woman nodded. "The toxin wasn't in the sun, but in everything it touched. When the curse fell, it affected everything in Solevar, from its people to its flora and fauna, even the water and air. The darkness wasn't in the sun. It was in us."

"When the prince sacrificed himself for you," the Elf said, "the fire of his heart–the fire given only to the sons of Oreck–combined with the sun and finished what the sun had been trying to do since the curse fell."

"It burned the poison away," Eirin finished, looking at Drystan with wide eyes.

"Not in everyone," the Elf gently corrected her. "Only in those who had sworn fealty to him."

"In sacrificing himself for you," the female Fae said, "he shouldered the mantle that the sons of Oreck had long abandoned. He allowed himself to suffer as the poison was burned out of him like dross in a flame. And those who had sworn their allegiance to him were gifted his magic's purity."

Eirin lifted Drystan's hand and studied it. His fingers, which were rough and calloused from years of combat, were nearly twice as large as hers. "But...there were only a few who swore fealty. And we did so before we came here." She looked back up at the male Elf. "How is it that you are protected now, too?"

"It seems," the Elf said, cracking a small smile, "that the purification wasn't limited to those who gave him their allegiance before the incident." He turned and nodded toward the center of the city, though Eirin couldn't see it through the vine-covered wall. "Since the news spread, people have been flocking here to pledge their allegiance to the prince. And we've received countless smoke signals and other messages promising that as soon as night falls, more will come to declare their service to this son of Oreck who can deliver them from the wrath of the sun." He gave Drystan a wry smile. "It seems you shall get all you asked for and more. An army of three thousand and growing."

Eirin's mouth fell open. "Three *thousand*?"

"We do, however," the female Fae said, stepping forward, "wish once again to beg your forgiveness." She sighed, her straight shoulders drooping slightly. "As we said, our knowledge of magic seems to have fallen far beyond what we ever imagined."

"We've been over this," Drystan said. "You asked forgiveness once. You need not continue." He looked down at Eirin and smiled. "We've all doubted this one at some point. And we all paid the price."

Eirin held his gaze, unable to let go. Then she gave a little start. "What about Rangvald?"

Drystan frowned slightly and looked up to meet the eyes of the male Elf. "He's still waiting. But it seems we have postponed his immediate plan for action."

"The city is enthralled with Prince Drystan," the female Fae said. "He had been traveling ahead of schedule, but now we believe Rangvald will wait at least two nights before he attacks. Many whom he believed would be in his ranks have abandoned him, and our spies believe he is delaying to rebuild."

"Solevar doesn't seem to have healed completely," Eirin said, looking at the dying roses. "I suppose they didn't heal with Drystan's sacrifice?"

"No," the male Elf said grimly. "We believe that to be because the Time Stones haven't been fixed yet."

Eirin drew in a deep breath and nodded. "And a son of Oreck still must be chosen as heir to the throne."

"Correct," said the Elf.

"Rangvald's forces have taken control of the main entrance to the Emerald Palace," the female Fae said. "We can challenge him, but we believe it would be wise to wait for the reinforcements who have promised to come."

"Perhaps," Eirin said slowly, "if we have enough support, we could convince Rangvald to simply participate in the rite without battle." She looked at Drystan.

"Perhaps," he said, but his eyes didn't smile.

"We're preparing for a battle but hoping Rangvald will see sense," a Griffin said, stepping forward.

"Unfortunately," Marcus added, stepping forward from the rear of the group, "we aren't optimistic."

"We do, however," said the female Fae, "have maps of old, secret entrances to the tower. Our hope is that Rangvald won't have them all covered. His forces would be spread too thin."

"If we have to," said Drystan, "I will fly you up to the top myself. It would risk confrontation, but it would be the safest."

"I'm not convinced of that yet," said a female Brownie, who pushed her way through the group. Then she looked up at everyone else. "We can continue speaking of this elsewhere. Give the Seer a few moments to catch her breath." She shoved uselessly at the great legs that surrounded her. A few of the taller Atharrachs chuckled, but they did as she bid and went back into the building, leaving Eirin and Drystan alone on the balcony.

Alone. Eirin turned back to Drystan and let out a sigh. She suddenly felt as though she'd been holding her breath since they'd left Torbaine.

"Eirin." Drystan took Eirin's hands in his. Pain filled his eyes where joy had been minutes before.

Eirin frowned. "What is it?"

He took a deep breath and blew it out slowly. "I know you're hoping that Rangvald will listen to reason."

Eirin nodded. "If we have larger numbers on our side–"

But he was already shaking his head. "I'm... I'm going to be completely honest with you."

Eirin raised her eyebrows. "Are you ever anything else?"

He gave her the ghost of a smile, but it disappeared almost before it had begun. "I'm going to do everything in my power to ensure the rite takes place. But I am...I know in my heart that Rangvald does not intend to let me survive to that point."

Eirin went still. "But surely–"

"What I *am* going to do is make sure I take him with me."

Eirin's eyes began to sting. "Drystan if this is like your stupid plan to let them take you–"

"That," he said, giving her a knowing smile, "wasn't the plan. The *plan* was to let the bruthsi burn through my system, then race back as fast as I could and take them by surprise."

Eirin stared at him blankly. "You mean you weren't giving up?"

"No, I wasn't. But that's not what I want to talk about right now." He brushed a piece of hair out of her face. "Now listen, please. Because we both know we don't have much time left."

Eirin was about to argue, but the misery in his voice made her hold her tongue. So she took a deep breath and nodded.

"Very well, I'm listening."

He stood and pulled her up to stand with him. "Eirin, I spent most of my life thinking I could never let myself fall in love. And then I had a taste of what could be. And as soon as I tasted you," he brushed his lips across hers, making her legs tremble as his mouth lingered against hers, "I knew I would never know how to live without you again." He drew in a sharp breath. "So I'm going to ask something extremely selfish. Something I have no right to ask of you. But I'm going to anyway."

Eirin placed her hands on his chest in a feeble attempt to brace herself. Her body shook with anticipation and hope. But not fear. Fear was nowhere to be found.

"For just one night," he said, his voice breaking on the last words, "would you give me what I long for most?"

Eirin licked her lips, which suddenly felt impossibly dry. "And what would that be?" she asked, her voice barely a whisper.

"Marry me."

Eirin looked up into his eyes. They were a vivid blue today, the amber flecks in their blue depths bright. This didn't worry her, though. It wasn't the amber of his flame. Rather, it was the same color as his heart fire had been when it had enveloped her while they danced under the stars. Even now, she could see that same fire striving to burst from his chest, swirling and tumbling against his ribs. She traced it from the outside, her fingers skimming his chest, and he closed his eyes and let his head fall back as he sighed deeply.

There was no question now as to what her answer could be. She couldn't say no, even if she wanted to. Over the last year, she and Drystan had grown closer and closer until she had begun to think of them as a single unit. Even when she had fought her natural pull toward him, she had known deep down that it was because she loved him so much. She had never loved so deeply before. And it had terrified her.

The fear returned, rushing back in like a thunderstorm. He was certain this was only for a night. He was certain she was going to lose him. But there had to be a way. She silently pleaded with the Time Keeper to give her a way...any way to keep him with her. Then she received an answer to her unspoken prayer in the form of sudden inspiration.

Of course.

Eirin closed her eyes and smiled to herself before opening them again.

"I'll marry you," she said softly. "But on one condition."

Drystan's blue eyes widened. "Oh?"

Her smile grew. "Give me your first scale. So I can have what I've always wanted as well."

The fear which had filled his eyes quickly became sharp interest.

"I'd love to know what that is," he said, nuzzling the side of her face. "Seeing as I told you." Then he pulled back. "But...just so you know, Dragon scales have been all but ineffective in recent months. It's why I never gave any of mine away. Both Phaidra and Karolus said I would be better off keeping my magic to protect you."

Eirin only grinned wider. "Well, then. Give me yours, and we can both see if my wish is granted."

"But—"

"If it is, you'll know." She patted his chest. He shook his head, and with a slight growl, leaned down for another kiss.

"Deal."

Chapter Thirty-Three

News came later that day that Rangvald and his Human were on their way to the Emerald Palace. They should, by all accounts, arrive in two days. So it was with more than a little concern that the committee, the city, and its surrounding inhabitants heard Eirin and Drystan announce that they would wed the night before what was assumed to be the great battle.

"We have no objection to the actual match," the male Elf—who Eirin eventually learned was named Aodhan—explained, steepling his fingers thoughtfully. They were back in the committee's meeting room, but this time, Eirin and Drystan had been given chairs of their own in the great circle. "We're simply...not sure that this is a good time."

Eirin blinked a few times, willing herself to pay attention. Her hands, though they were clasped tightly in her lap, itched to touch her chair again, which had hit her with a hundred interesting visions the moment she'd first sat upon it. But this wasn't the time for that now. She needed to focus.

Being a Seer could be such a distraction.

"We have thousands of people who wish to kneel at your

feet," added the female Fae, whose name was Maeve. "Now is the perfect time to build your army while they wish to come. Incite bravery and hope!"

"Battle is inevitable now," said a Dwarf, though Eirin still didn't know his name. "We've just received word that Rangvald refuses to meet for diplomacy."

Eirin's stomach turned. That was not good. Rangvald, Drystan was convinced, did not mean to leave him alive. And if he was going down, Drystan was determined to take Rangvald with him. So what happened then when there were no more sons of Oreck to hold the Blood Fire Throne?

They had to continue drawing support. If they could gain enough followers, Rangvald's men wouldn't engage in a hopeless cause.

Would they?

"His people did withdraw from the palace, did they not?" Drystan asked, a frown on his handsome face.

"They did," Aodhan said slowly. "They held the position for less than a day. But they still wait at its base."

"And now that we know," added the Roc, "that Rangvald himself *and* his Human are on their way, our time to recruit has been cut short. Two days from now, his forces will be able to rally behind their leader and his Seer in person."

"I'm not greatly concerned about Mannish," Eirin said, sitting taller. "I'm the only one who knows where the stone is that must be removed." The stone, which had been hidden beneath her clothes for these last months, now rested openly against her chest. She and Drystan had revealed it when they knew they had the committee's loyalty. It had been a gamble, but Eirin knew they needed every bit of support they could get. If they didn't win this battle...they didn't win at all. "I'm more concerned with the fact that the curse could become finalized if the Rite of the Blood Fire

Throne isn't conducted properly according to the Time Keeper's requirements."

"If that is true," ventured the Nymph, "wouldn't it be possible to wait until after the battle to wed? Why must you wed tonight?"

Eirin felt Drystan stiffen in his seat.

"What better way to win support," he said, his words sharp, "than inviting our people to watch the prince who fixed the sun's burning wed the Seer who will fix the Time Stones?" He was beginning to run out of patience. Eirin could relate.

A few committee members murmured agreement with this, but Eirin knew they weren't all convinced. "Besides," she added gently but firmly, "a Wizard once told me that love might be more necessary for this quest than we once believed." She smiled at Drystan. "I'm convinced now that he was right."

There was a long silence. The members exchanged long looks, particularly Aodhan and Maeve. Eirin glanced at Drystan, who kept a stony expression, and she was glad again that he had been raised for a life of diplomacy. She couldn't imagine the weight he must be carrying.

"Very well," Aodhan finally said, turning back to face Eirin and Drystan. "We believe you are right. Giving the people one more night to gather will allow us to better match their fighting forces. And," he smiled slightly, "perhaps bring a new kind of hope. One we haven't seen in a long time."

* * *

Drystan, who was joined by Qeb soon after, stayed to discuss strategy with Marcus and the other committee members, but Eirin was whisked away to prepare for her wedding.

She was taken to a large room on the northwestern side of the building the committee used. The wedding itself would take place on a large terrace covered with flowers that could be witnessed by thousands of spectators on the north side of the city. In the room, Nuru, Iris, and a host of other women awaited her.

"Where's Callispa?" Eirin whispered to Nuru as the women fussed over the clothes that were being delivered to the room.

Nuru opened her mouth to speak, but a low voice interrupted from behind. Eirin turned to see Callispa. Her bright red hair was tied back in a braid, and she wore her travel clothes.

"Callispa," Eirin said quietly with a glance at the other women, "what are you doing?"

"I'm going..." Callispa stopped and swallowed. "I mean, I'm going to find anyone who will come to aid us. Anyone not close enough to hear the bells." Her hands shook slightly as she tightened her grip on the bow slung over her shoulder. "I'm hoping I can find more support..." She closed her eyes. "I'm sorry, Eirin. I tried. I really did. But I just can't..." She shook her head as if that explained everything.

And to Eirin, it did.

Eirin, much to her own surprise, found herself wrapping the other girl in an embrace. "Stay safe," she whispered. "Come back when you're done. Please."

Callispa gave her what was probably an attempt at a smile but came out more like a grimace. "And...and you. Have a good..." She looked at the window. "Goodbye." Then she was gone, out the window, her wings catching fire midair before she shot off into the afternoon sun.

"Don't tell me you feel sorry for her," Nuru said in a dry voice as they watched her go.

"I actually do," Eirin said quietly. "She never had a chance."

"I don't believe that," Nuru scoffed. "No one forced her to fall for him."

But Eirin shook her head. "They matched her to him with the express intent of marrying them off."

Nuru rolled her eyes.

"Seer."

They both turned to see a young girl, a Unicorn by her light, standing behind them, smiling shyly.

"It's time to prepare," she said in a high sing-songy voice.

Eirin smiled at her. "Thank you."

Eirin hadn't even thought about what she would be married in until she was informed something special was being brought up. She had assumed it would be some sort of gown, but the moment the white silk was held up before her, she knew exactly what it was. As if in a daze, she moved forward slowly to touch it.

"Is this..." She looked up at the roughly dozen women who were standing around her.

"It is new," said a tall woman. Eirin studied her for a moment until she recognized that the woman was a Tsuchigumo. "I have made it for you."

"That was fast!" Eirin exclaimed as she ran her fingers through the robe's folds.

"It was my honor," the woman bowed slightly. "To make a royal Seer's robe was every Tsuchigumo's dream in ages past."

"I've brought flowers," said the young Unicorn.

"And I have gems," declared a Dwarf woman proudly.

"And I," said a Brownie woman, "have found the princess's crown!"

Eirin blinked at her. "Wasn't that in the palace?"

The little woman simply smiled and winked.

"Which means," said Iris with a clap, "that it is time we began. I have drawn a bath for her. We will begin there."

And so, the women descended on her like a cloud. Eirin was undressed, which was slightly uncomfortable in front of such a crowd, and forced into a bath. But the moment she was in the bath, which was steaming hot and smelled of lavender, rose hip, and chamomile, she relaxed. She hadn't felt so good since staying at Lady Seren's castle during their first escape from Torbaine. Even better were the Unicorn drops that she could feel Iris had mixed in.

The bath, much to her chagrin, was over too soon. She would have liked to stay in it right up until it was time for her to be married. But she was bullied out far too soon, after which she was patted dry and her hair brushed and yanked every which way before being attacked with pins and sprayed with what seemed every oil imaginable. Finally, she was dressed in the soft, silk robes, after which she was sat upon a stool and forced to undergo more ministrations.

"Are you nervous?" Nuru asked in a low voice. She seemed on the verge of laughing the entire time.

"I might be if I wasn't so terrified now. Is it possible to die from too much fussing?" Eirin muttered back as one of the Brownies fought with a knot in her hair.

"I heard that," the Brownie, who was standing on a stool behind her, mumbled through a mouthful of pins.

Nuru snickered until Iris announced that Nuru should be Eirin's lady-in-waiting and forced her to undergo a similar preparation to Eirin. It was Eirin's turn to snicker when Nuru was sat down beside her, scowling as though she'd drunk sour milk.

"You look lovely." Eirin grinned.

"I'm not getting married," Nuru hissed.

Somehow, the preparations lasted yet another hour. But when they were finished, Eirin was pushed in front of a mirror. And she blinked at herself in shock.

Her hair, which had always been straight as a stick, much to her younger self's chagrin, had been swept up into a twisted knot at the back of her head. A few straight locks had been allowed to escape and rest at the edges of her face.

She had never used rouge or any sort of enhancing paint the way she knew some of the noble ladies used in Torbaine. But someone had darkened her lashes and colored her eyelids, and the enhancements made her brown eyes seem larger and brighter than they ever had before. Her lips were a shimmering pink, and diamond drops hung from her ears, their sparkle matching the tiara that had been placed on her head.

More striking than all of these, however, was the shining white robe she now wore. She recognized it from the books she'd read in Mhaedin as the traditional garb of the royal Seers. It was so white it nearly glowed, even in the evening light of a quickly approaching sunset. A thin cloak of the same white raiment was draped over her shoulders and clasped at the neck with a ruby pin, and beneath it, the long robe was gathered in at her waist by a silken ribbon.

Oh, how her mother would cry if she could see this. And her father... Her father would cry just as much as her mother. Maybe more. And her brothers would kick up a fuss and stick their grubby little hands all over the white silk.

Eirin closed her eyes. She could cry later. Later, when Drystan was no longer waiting for her. When the blood had been shed, and the kingdom was set to rights.

Then Eirin would mourn for all she was worth.

"Eirin," Nuru said from behind her. "You look like a queen."

Eirin turned and faced her friend, having to blink hard several times. "I don't know if I feel like one," she whispered. "I feel like a little girl playing dress-up."

She wasn't even going to think about Alys.

"I have a feeling Drystan might change that," Nuru said with a wry smile. "But we have to get you to him first."

As soon as the sun set, Eirin was bustled out of the room, down several flights of steps, and then down behind some large bushes to await her appearance during the ceremony.

"We could just fly you down," Maeve said, a twinkle in her eye. "But it might muss your hair from this height. And it's tradition to hide you from the groom until the ceremony calls for you."

Tradition, Eirin learned, meant that Drystan was to be brought out in front of the people before the ceremony began. Many who had not yet pledged fealty had to wait until the sun had set to come out to watch. Hence, the delay until evening. But, as with the weddings at home, Eirin was to be escorted by the groom's man of honor.

Eirin smiled when she was greeted in her hiding place by Qeb.

"Is it time?" she asked with a smile as a woman's voice pierced the hush of the evening in song.

"It has been for a while," he answered with a grin of his own. He held his arm out, which was now covered with new armor, and Eirin took it. He walked her to the edge of the garden, where they stopped and waited for the signal.

"You know this is it, don't you?" Eirin said quietly. "After this, you're stuck with me."

"A better vantage point for when you get into mischief."

She gasped. "I never get into mischief."

He simply raised one brow. "I hope you have a child one day who is just like you. Then you can..." His smile faded. "Truly, though. Thank you."

She blinked up at him. "For what?"

He gave her a sad smile. "For bringing him happiness."

Eirin held his gaze a moment longer. Neither of them wanted to say it. Drystan was convinced this marriage would last one night. And though Eirin prayed to prove him wrong, she knew Qeb felt the weight of this knowledge as well.

Any sadness that lingered, however, disappeared when the blow of a horn echoed over the salt flats, which the garden bordered, and which the crowds were using to witness the ceremony. Butterflies erupted in Eirin's chest as she and Qeb stepped around the corner, and she got her first sight of Drystan.

Standing tall beside Marcus with Thane standing a little ways behind, he was no longer wearing the white shirt and blue trousers he'd worn earlier that day. Instead, he was wearing what appeared to be a robe, gathered at the waist with armor pieces that were a part of clothing itself, their silver reflecting a faint blueish tint. Symbols Eirin couldn't read were etched into the breastplate and shoulders. A new sword hung at his hip. Its hilt was a silver dragon with sapphire eyes and golden teeth.

His hair had been cut, and his face was smooth and stubble-free. It would have made him look younger, except for the number of scars that crossed his face.

Eirin loved every one of them.

A new circlet hung on his brow. Eirin recognized it from her past visions, and it made her catch her breath to see it with her own eyes. It was the crown that always belonged to the third son. Apparently, Kamon had left it behind. Perhaps there had been some regret in him after all. It was made of silver stars with bronze flames behind them. Sapphires dotted each star, making the circlet twinkle.

But most mesmerizing were Drystan's eyes. They blazed as they never had before, bright blue with bursts of amber within, burning and changing even as she watched. And the way he was looking at her made Eirin ache, wishing she had married him the moment he'd declared his heart to her at the beginning of their arduous journey through Solevar.

A moment passed before Eirin realized Qeb, with an amused smile on his face, was gently tugging at her arm. They crossed the wide terrace in front of what seemed to be thousands of people. After one glance, Eirin couldn't look again. So much magic made her dizzy. So she kept her eyes on the man she was going to marry.

Her keeper.

Her protector.

Her friend.

Qeb carefully transferred Eirin's hands to Drystan's. They were hands she knew well. They were hard hands, covered in calluses and scars. And yet, she was amazed at the gentleness with which they took hers.

How could she hold onto him for only one night?

More voices joined the sole singer as Marcus, smiling, held out a long, thick braid of ribbons. Each ribbon had a different color, but they all ended by being threaded through a bead of like color, creating a tassel of gems that hung from the braid's end. Sapphire, ruby, topaz and more. To Eirin's amazement, the ribbon hung in the air when he let go, suspended before them as if invisible hands were holding it from above. Eirin had been told how the ceremony would work. It wasn't so different from weddings in Torbaine, but there was more to it than she had known. She was thankful now that they had prepared her, for nearly all rational thought fled as she allowed Drystan to place her hands at the top of the braid, where he then placed his hands over hers.

The singers' voices began on a high note, and with each of Marcus's terms, they fell a half-step.

"Today is the birth of something new," Marcus began.

Eirin slid her right hand down the ribbon braid.

"A joining of gifts. Of power and flame."

Drystan grasped the braid, placing his right hand below hers.

"From this day forth, until the Time Keeper deems your time done, you are henceforth one."

Eirin moved her left hand one space below his on the ribbons.

"In fire and ice, in drought and in rain, in sun and in maelstrom, you will never again be your own."

Drystan moved his left hand below hers. They were nearly to the end of the ribbons.

"Blessed by the Time Keeper you will be, cherishing every year, every day, every hour, every minute you share together..."

Eirin placed both hands over the gems at the bottom. And once again, Drystan placed his hands over hers.

"In the name of the Time Keeper and before this people and this kingdom," Marcus said, raising his voice, "I declare Prince Drystan and Eirin the Seer one!"

A roar went up from the crowd as Drystan let go of the ribbon braid. His hands slid to the sides of Eirin's hips, and without hesitation, he pulled her close and captured her mouth with his.

The gold and blue flames in his chest, which had engulfed her briefly during their dance under the stars in Torbaine, burst out of his chest and wrapped them in a cocoon of magic once again. But this time, they didn't let go. Blue stars like the ones in his circlet exploded from within the flames. Eirin pulled away from Drystan briefly to look up and gasp, and Drystan gave her the most beautiful smile she had ever seen before pulling her back to him.

The Time Keeper seemed to have heard her prayers, for in that moment, time seemed to stop. Eirin put her hands on his face and relished the way it felt as he bent over her, his large frame embracing her small one, his large hands pressing gently against her hips, holding her secure. She felt cherished. Beautiful.

She felt safe.

"Attention!" came a shout from Eirin's right. She and Drystan looked up to see Marcus standing between them and the audience, his sword raised high. He had shifted to his Centaur form.

"Unlike the Seer, we cannot see magic," he called, his voice echoing over the crowd that pressed in at the edge of the salt flats all the way up to the edge of the platformed garden. "But I would chance that even we, with our dull senses, were *all* able to sense the prince's magic just now." He walked to the other side to address the rest of the audience. "Some of you remember Rangvald's time as prince. And though we would not for a moment repeat whatever evil his brother Kamon brought upon us, I would not choose another day of Rangvald's rule either. We have been given a gift!" he cried, "in a new prince, one who has risked his life time and time over to bring us this Seer. One who, by throwing away his own life, has delivered us from the sun. At least..." He paused. "Those of us who have pledged our loyalty to him."

To Eirin's surprise, she found herself being towed by Drystan up to the front of the platform, where he, too, addressed the crowd.

"I do not wish to force my way onto the throne," he called, his voice echoing over the silent crowd. "I wish to do as the Seer..." He gifted Eirin another beautiful smile. "As *my* Seer has claimed. I wish to restore the Time Keeper's ordinances. I wish to participate in the Rite of the Blood Fire Throne as it was meant to be."

His smile faded. "But I have faced Rangvald before, and he is an enemy like no other. He has also raised up an army to stand beside him. I cannot face him alone."

"And if we don't challenge him," Eirin spoke, her voice surprisingly clear, "Solevar will fall. The curse will be consummated. Everything we love will end."

"So will you stand with me?" Drystan asked. "Or will you watch Solevar fall?"

Eirin held his hand tightly, her stomach just as tight as she watched the people. No longer was she made dizzy by the sight of so many Atharrachs with all their magic. Somehow, as Drystan seemed to have come into his position, so had she. She searched the face of all, silently begging each to join them.

The group of Griffins, who had been standing at the edge of the crowd, were the first to kneel. They were followed by a number of Centaurs on the other side, probably placed there on guard. Then the entire gathering seemed to kneel in waves. A roar of voices filled the air, and Eirin gazed in amazement as over three thousand strong pledged their loyalty to her husband.

Her husband.

Eirin, of course, was more grateful than she would ever be able to express for their confidence and support. If they could get enough support, they might be able to stop the battle before it began. But even now, as the people continued to utter their fealty, row by row and led by Marcus, there was only one thing Eirin wanted at that moment. And when she caught Drystan's eye, she smiled.

She could tell he wanted the same thing as well.

Chapter Thirty-Four

Eirin and Drystan were shown to a room in the large building that the committee seemed to use for everything. It was clear the room was barely used, as the servant who guided them there had to force his way inside the unwilling door with his shoulder. But once the servant left them, Eirin could see it had been well-dusted, and someone had taken great pains to make it beautiful. Dozens and dozens of candles covered every flat surface in the room. Someone had spread what was left of the living flowers on the single chair and little table, and rose petals, though faded, had been sprinkled on the bed.

Supper was on the table too, but as soon as she saw the bed, Eirin lost her appetite. Nerves attacked her, making her hands shake as she walked around the room, studying it as though it was the most interesting place she'd ever seen.

What had she been thinking, asking for a scale? Such a wish had been audacious at best and dangerous at its worst. After all, Drystan's heart scale, as he had promised her, was his most important scale and held more magic than all the others. What if he needed that magic tomorrow when he fought Rangvald?

And yet, even now, she couldn't come to regret her request.

There was nothing else she wanted more. If she was going to have him and then lose him in the span of one day, as he seemed convinced she would, Eirin was surely entitled to this one last request. Wasn't she?

Eirin didn't have time to ponder this because Drystan, once the door was shut and locked firmly behind him, swept her up and carried her over to the bed. He laid her down gently, then, pausing only to remove his sword and armor, he bent to kiss her. But Eirin, her heart thudding in her throat, pressed her hand against his lips.

"I believe you have something of mine," she said, hoping she didn't sound nearly as nervous as she felt.

He stared at her for a moment in confusion until his gaze cleared and he stood. Reaching into his tunic, not breaking eye contact, he pulled out a scale. It shone deep blue and pearlescent in the low light of the candles. Then he studied it a moment before giving her a probing smile.

"Are you going to tell me what you're going to wish for with this?"

Eirin grinned and shook her head, then held out her hand. He gave it to her, and she ran her thumb over it, admiring its smoothness. It was still warm from being close to his skin.

He placed one hand on each side of her head and knelt over her. "You're sure you won't tell me?" he whispered, his lips caressing hers as he spoke. One hand reached up and played with a piece of her hair. His eyes blazed blue with streaks of amber running through them, and it took Eirin's breath away. She had to shake her head before she remembered how to speak.

"I told you," Eirin said, butterflies in her stomach fluttering around distractedly. "If I get it... you'll know." She reached up and touched his face, memorizing the shape of its silhouette.

"And if I'm not here to see?" the words were whispered, but they stuck in her heart like a knife.

She had to fight to keep her voice from breaking. "I refuse to let that be a possibility."

"Eirin–" he began, but she reached up and pulled him down into a kiss. And this time, when he wrapped her in his arms, he didn't let go.

* * *

A bell tolled the second hour of the morning in the distance, but Eirin was wide awake. She looked over, as she had been for the last several hours, at her sleeping husband.

Her husband.

Her chest swelled with pride before she had to resist the urge, as she had many times since he'd fallen asleep, to crumple into a ball and cry. She also had to resist the urge to kiss his face. He needed his sleep, and they would be waking early. Eirin might not be fighting for her life, but he would be. He was so handsome, his jaw strong and his cheekbones prominent. And it was killing her not to look into his eyes.

So instead, she took the scale out from where she had tucked it under her pillow. It was almost as beautiful as his eyes. She still struggled to believe that he had once feared she would think him hideous in his Dragon form. It was as much a part of him as his Human self. The Dragon and the son of kings were inseparable.

She knew what she needed to do. She had no Seer premonition to guide her, no visions or strong feelings one way or the other. But she needed this. And so would Solevar. If they managed to survive the curse, they would need it, too.

And so, as she had with Lady Seren's scale, she pressed it to her chest. Closing her eyes, she whispered her wish into the night.

Then, a feeling of peace enveloping her, she snuggled up against Drystan and let herself slip into precious slumber beside him.

Chapter Thirty-Five

Drystan wanted to lay beside his wife forever. It broke his heart to wake up so early. She looked so soft and fragile beside him as she slept. He wanted nothing more than to wrap her up in his arms and hide her away from the world, away from anyone who would hurt her.

And yet, as he brushed her hair away from her face, he said a prayer of thanks to the Time Keeper. The privilege of loving her had been his. She was his wife.

His.

Even if only for one night.

But perhaps that was part of the beauty of it all. Fleeting, fleeting, everything was fleeting. But he had been given a moment of indescribable beauty that shone over the entirety of his life like a shooting star. The memory of her eyes, her lips, the feel of her hands against his face were etched indelibly on his mind and heart and would be until he gave his last breath. She was worth every bit of sacrifice and more.

But it couldn't last. Soon Qeb was knocking on their door, and Drystan knew they must rouse themselves for the day. There would be no more sleep after this.

"Eirin, love," he whispered, leaning over to kiss her temple, her cheek, and then turned her face gently to kiss her mouth. "It's time to get up."

Eirin stretched adorably and then blinked at him several times before she seemed to realize where they were.

"Good morning," he said, trying not to let sorrow slip into his words.

"Good morning," she croaked, rubbing the sleep from her eyes. Then she sat up and looked around. And he knew the moment she recalled the day. A shadow, visible even in the moonlight streaming through the window, tinged her face with sadness. He couldn't help leaning in for another kiss.

"It's today, isn't it?" she said quietly as he pulled away.

He gave her the best smile he could muster. "It is."

Another knock from Qeb interrupted him. "Sorry to say it," Qeb called through the door. "The committee wants both of you. Rangvald is on the move."

This announcement cut off the many things Drystan wanted to say. He wanted to gather her in his arms once more and tell her everything he loved about her. He wanted to apologize for every way he'd ever hurt her, and he wished most of all to tell her all the things he would have done had their ways not been parted so soon.

When his armor was on again, he looked back to see Eirin staring at herself in the full-length mirror in the corner of the room. Her brow was slightly furrowed, and her eyes looked almost alarmed.

"What is it?" he asked, wrapping his arms around her and kissing her ear.

"I just want you to know," she said, before pulling out of his grasp and turning to face him, "that I meant what I said."

"Which was?"

"You are my husband and my king." She took his face in her hands and looked fiercely into his eyes. "And I will follow you to the end."

Drystan felt as though he'd stepped out of a dream and back into reality when they left the room behind. It had been beautiful and surreal. And now, it was over.

Marcus looked up when they entered the committee's strategy room. A large table stood in the middle of the room, drawings of the city spread out on top of it. Thane and Nuru were already there, and Qeb trailed behind Drystan and Eirin, so all their friends were present. All but one.

Drystan looked down at Eirin. "Callispa?"

Eirin gave him a sad smile. "She went to find reinforcements."

Drystan held her gaze for a moment before nodding. He understood. And though it was probably selfish, he was glad of it.

"Rangvald has been gathering his forces to meet at the foot of the Blood Fire Throne," Marcus said, pointing to the large square in the middle of the city. "We didn't think he would be here quite so soon. From what our informants tell us, we believe he means to speak to you before the melee begins."

"Coverings were also erected all over his side of the city last night," one of the Griffins said. "Raised canvases and awnings high enough to fly beneath. It seems he's caught wind of our people's newfound abilities, and he desires to fight us from the safety of the shadows."

"I thought he was planning to wait until tonight," Drystan said, frowning.

"We did, too. But he appears to have sped his plans up," Marcus said, frowning at the maps. "Still, the plan remains the same for the Time Stones. He hasn't tried to recapture the palace itself, so we should be free to fly Her Highness up to the Time Stones tower."

Her Highness. In spite of himself, Drystan nearly smiled. That's right. Eirin was a princess now.

"He won't attack me," Eirin said quietly. Everyone turned to look at her.

"He has Mannish," Eirin said, "but he knows I'm the more likely of the two to break the curse. In fact..." She leaned forward and studied the map more closely, her thick braid falling in front of her face and blocking it from Drystan's sight. Drystan resisted the urge to move it back.

"I believe he's still hoping I'll choose to side with him. In his opinion, it's the only choice that makes sense."

"I know he wants to fight." Drystan said, "Still, I still think we ought to make the request once more that he fulfill the rite with me."

"He'd as likely kill you as listen to you," Qeb growled.

Drystan gave him a smile. "I agree. Which is why I have a little surprise of my own. Someone I met last night. But we'll discuss that later."

"But why ask him if we know his answer is no?" a female Roc asked.

"For the sake of his men," Drystan said. "They need to see that we made every possible effort to do what is right." He looked down at the map and shrugged. "Who knows? Perhaps some will change allegiances when they see who they're truly serving." He paused. "How many does he have?"

Marcus winced. "Seven thousand. And though more and more fighters have continued to arrive through the night, we're not quite yet to four."

Those numbers were bad. "I wish we'd had more time." Drystan grimaced. "Our numbers would have been larger."

"I agree. But we have what we have, and Rangvald is forcing our hand," Marcus said.

They continued to speak. As they did, Drystan donned the

mask of stone he'd perfected while the Heir at the Citadel, the one that sealed in every emotion and reaction that might even hint at chinks in the armor. His heart sank as he realized he had been nursing the secret hope that they might avoid this battle after all. The numbers were too uneven. Rangvald's forces were too great.

They spoke for another half hour, but almost everything had been decided the night before. It was a losing battle. Drystan knew this. Everyone knew it. But they weren't fighting for victory. They were fighting to break the curse. And everything came down to Drystan and Eirin.

Eirin had to fix the Time Stones.

Drystan had to stop Rangvald.

But all too soon, it was time to go. Sunrise would come within the hour, and it would be best to get Eirin to the tower undetected.

"I expect to see you again tonight," Eirin said. She and Drystan were standing beside Nuru, who was in her Sphinx form. The committee had insisted that one of their Rocs deliver her, but Nuru had refused to allow this, and Eirin had sided with her friend. They had come so far together, Eirin had insisted. She wasn't about to finish her journey with a stranger.

Qeb and Thane stood a respectful distance off while Drystan said goodbye to his wife. She gazed up at him with her large brown eyes, and he ran the back of his knuckles down her soft face.

"Are you sure you won't tell me what you wished for?" Drystan said softly.

She raised her brows in a challenge. "Return to me tonight, and I'll tell you everything you could think to ask." Then she threw her arms around his waist and clung to him tightly. "Come back safely," she whispered, her voice thick with tears. "Please."

Drystan squeezed his eyes shut and gritted his teeth as he held her against him. He hated telling her no. But this was one promise he couldn't make.

"Eirin," Nuru said quietly. "We need to go."

Eirin nodded, tears running freely down her face now. "Safely," she told Drystan, her voice suddenly fierce. "I mean it!"

He pressed a kiss to her forehead and closed his eyes. "I love you."

And then she was gone.

Drystan watched until he could no longer see her against the growing gray of the sky.

Thane, who stood on Drystan's right side, said nothing. He simply clapped Drystan on the back. Qeb, who stood on his left, squeezed Drystan's shoulder. "I'm sorry," he said simply.

Drystan swallowed the pain of goodbye and turned to face his friends.

"I'm not," he said, allowing the Dragon's growl to seep into his Human voice. Red filled his vision, and the beast inside purred with desire. "We will not fear tomorrow. We will fight for today."

* * *

Drystan peeked out from his hiding place. His forces were hidden with the exception of a small contingent, which was to go forth to act as his escort during the confrontation with Rangvald. Qeb, who had been given a place with them, hadn't liked this at all.

"You'll be without me," he had grumbled.

Drystan had given him a look. "I won't be that far, and you know it."

"I don't know," Thane had said, scratching his head. "I'm actually with Qeb on this one. This is a pretty risky venture."

"This entire venture is nothing but risk," Marcus had said, joining them. "Drystan is right. This is the best way."

Drystan had secretly wondered if Rangvald would actually

appear for the meeting. His uncle wasn't above playing games. But an hour after dawn, when Drystan's men had marched out into the open sun, Rangvald did indeed come. Forced to remain in the shade of a canopy that had been erected the night before, he stopped just short of the morning light.

Their forces halted behind them. Separating the two armies was the dais upon which the Blood Fire Throne sat.

Karolus had his long, dark hair pulled back at the nape of his neck, its streak of gray lending the appearance of wisdom to his face. He removed his hood and studied Drystan.

"Hello, young nephew," he called.

Not so young. Still, Drystan felt as though he'd aged two decades in the last year.

"Uncle," he said with a shallow nod.

"I see you made it," Rangvald said politely. "Welcome to Iilaedin."

"I thank you," Drystan called back. "Now I can ask you what Eirin has wanted me to ask this long while since we were separated."

"And what would that be?" Rangvald answered in a pleasant voice, as if he hadn't tried to kill Drystan the last time they'd met.

"That we would avoid this fight altogether by waiting until she has time to fix the Time Stones. Then we might carry out the Rite of the Blood Fire Throne together as the Time Keeper ordained."

Let him say yes, Drystan prayed. *Let him simply say yes.*

But Rangvald only smiled cordially. "As kind of her as that is, and while I do intend to take part in the rite, I don't think Eirin needs to worry that pretty little head of hers."

Drystan bristled, but he held his stony expression in place. "Oh?" he called back.

"No. You see, I have my own Seer who's on his way up into

the tower now. Eirin mustn't feel as though she has all the pressure on her."

The Dragon's first impulse was to fly right up to the tower and protect Eirin from the man-boy who had pined after her not so subtly in Mhaedin. But he forced himself to stay in his place. Mannish would hardly be a threat to Eirin. And, as much as it drove Drystan insane, Mannish's affection for her would probably work in her favor. Besides, even if Drystan had wanted to join her, as someone who was not a Seer, he couldn't enter the Time Stones tower. He would be killed instantly, according to Eirin.

He would help her best by fighting here.

"We don't have to fight," Drystan called back. "We could do this the way it was intended."

For the first time, Rangvald's polish cracked as he sneered. "What would you know of the way it was intended, boy?"

Drystan gave him a grin in return. "I know only what my wife has told me."

Rangvald stilled, and for a long moment, he stared at Drystan. Then he began to clap. "Very good, I must say. I didn't think you would ever muster up the courage." Then he sighed. "Unfortunately, that will make this far more difficult to explain to her in the end. Which really does make me sad."

He made a flicking gesture with his hand, and out of the shadows of the canopies over a dozen bags soared through the air toward Drystan's escort as a near deafening shout was loosed from Rangvald's army.

Drystan's men scattered out of the way, though some were more successful in escaping than others. As soon as the small bags hit the ground, a white powder flew out of them, making Drystan's small forces cough and gag.

Bruthsi root. Drystan let a curse slip out as the dust cleared from the air. Leave it to Rangvald to spread bruthsi root against his enemies. But they had expected something like this. It was nearly time to reveal the truth behind his deception.

"As you can see," Rangvald called over the roar, "it might benefit us all if you forfeited." He paused. "Promising, of course, not to pursue the thr–" He froze, then his eyes narrowed. "What is this?"

Where Drystan had been standing, another man now stood.

"I would consider making that decision," he called with a grin. "If it was mine to make!"

Rangvald stared, then Drystan saw his mouth form the word. *Kitsune*. His face twisted with fury.

Marcus, who had, like the real Drystan, been waiting in the wings, pulled out a horn and pressed it to his lips. A long, baritone note rang out, and a moment later, a similar note echoed through the air. Seconds later, the great, violent crashes sounded from a distance. Drystan couldn't help smiling at Rangvald's look of surprise. A Phoenix raced toward them from the protection of the canvas.

"My lord!" the Phoenix panted. "The Merfolk have destroyed the bridges over the fjord!"

Drystan allowed his smile to grow. The Merfolk were fast. And now, one of Rangvald's paths of retreat was cut off. Even better, Rangvald's men were now an island of their own, surrounded by Drystan's men as they stood in the sun. Rangvald would have to fight his way out.

Drystan nodded to one of the soldiers who was standing nearby. Moments later, the air whistled with bags of bruthsi as they hurled toward Rangvald's army. Unlike Rangvald's bags, however, they were not allowed to hit the ground. Arrows, loosed immediately after, pierced the bags midair, sending bruthsi powder flying everywhere.

Rangvald's army cried out as it rained down on them. Drystan's men had aimed true. Soldiers aside, Drystan watched hopefully as the purple and white dust neared Rangvald. Unfortunately, Rangvald met the dust with a burst of flame, destroying any that came anywhere near him. Drystan sighed. It had been worth a try.

"We didn't have as much in storage as we had hoped," Marcus grunted.

"It's the best we can do," Drystan replied. Once their forces mixed, which was inevitable, they wouldn't be able to use bruthsi root for fear of hitting their own soldiers. Unfortunately, using it at the beginning of the battle meant they were wasting it on Rangvald's weaker troops. Rangvald would be hiding his stronger troops toward the back of his forces. Drystan knew because he was doing the same thing.

The skies, which had dawned perfectly clear, were suddenly filled with thunderclouds just as thick as the ones Isayas had cast.

The man beside him whistled. "That's a lot of magic."

"He must have Thunderbirds hidden nearby," Drystan growled. "Which means we'll have to try to outlast them. They won't be able to hold it for long." Unless they had hoards of Thunderbirds taking turns. He really hoped that wasn't the case.

As soon as the clouds were in the sky, Rangvald shouted, and a wave of soldiers rushed forward.

Small soldiers, just as Drystan had predicted. He hadn't spent his entire life training in tactics for nothing.

Part of him groaned as the two forces met, the sound of metal on metal ringing in his ears like screams. Drystan hated to kill those who should have been his family's subjects. But their attempt to incapacitate him and stop Eirin lowered his objection to their deaths tremendously.

Once the first batch of Rangvald's soldiers had passed through Drystan's own front line, mostly Brownies, Dwarves, Pegasi, and Impundulu, he could see the heavier forces behind them.

The Brownies, Dwarves, and Pegasi were not too difficult to

deal with. His fire sent most of them running. The Impundulu, however, were an interesting group Drystan hadn't expected to have at all. There weren't any, to his knowledge, in Torbaine, and he'd only learned they existed because Eirin insisted on reading some of her books aloud while researching in Mhaedin. About the size of a turkey, the Impundulu looked much like any other bird, except that their blue and silver feathers gave off a metallic shine in the light.

And, when they desired to, they could strike any object–or person–with a bolt of lightning.

The front lines of both sides quickly disappeared into one another. Most of them, as Drystan had commanded them earlier, fled to higher ground once they had engaged the enemy once or twice. Their purpose, he had explained to the rather indignant Dwarves and Brownies, wasn't to destroy the enemy. It was to test the enemy and to trick them into thinking the battle would be easy.

But now, as Rangvald's forces began to push forward, Drystan decided he'd seen enough. He leaped out of his hiding place, shifting as he went. His heavier forces, the majority of whom had been hiding in the cottages and houses nearest the battle, leaped out as well.

It didn't take Rangvald long to spot him.

"There you are," he shouted as their forces clashed. "I was wondering when you would appear."

"My reluctance seems to have been justified," Drystan said, gesturing to where the bags of bruthsi still lay on the ground. "You'll pardon me, of course, for taking precautions."

"Of course," Rangvald said, beginning to shift into his scaled form.

Drystan expected Rangvald to attack him then and there. But instead, Rangvald rose into the air and flew...away. Back to the rear of the battle.

Drystan wanted to follow him. But with every minute, more hordes of Rangvald's soldiers were rushing in. And these soldiers were not Brownies or Dwarves. They were Griffins and Dokkaebi and Manticores and their Basilisk pets. There were Centaurs and Cecrops, and even a few Fae.

So Drystan ignored the urge to chase after Rangvald, and instead, he turned his attention to the fight at hand. He moved his way down the line, spraying fire and swinging his heavy, spiked tail in tandem, taking care not to injure his own soldiers.

Qeb was never far, always fighting his own fight while somehow keeping an eye on Drystan at the same time, and Drystan could hear Marcus shouting out orders on the other side of the square. Thane, though barely visible, was making more headway than anyone else as he pushed through Rangvald's lines in the direction of where Drystan assumed would be the Thunderbirds.

At first, despite their heavy disadvantage, Drystan began to wonder if they might really stand a chance. But the longer they fought, the more his hope began to die. He had hoped the Thunderbirds would tire as Isayas had. But Isayas had been an old Wizard drawing from his nearly depleted store of magic. The clouds, much to Drystan's dismay, remained. He could only assume that when one Thunderbird would grow tired, another would take its place, strengthening the clouds above yet again.

The sun, Drystan's greatest asset, did nothing to push the enemy back. Marcus said they had several Thunderbirds of their own, but not enough to dissipate the thick clouds the enemy had conjured. And while they did their best to locate Rangvald's Thunderbirds, not even Thane could penetrate the enemy ranks deep enough to reach them.

"Your Highness!" Drystan looked up from the Dwarf he had just hurled against a wall to see Marcus hailing him. Drystan flew to him, ignoring the thin arrows that bounced off his scales as he landed.

"What is it?" Drystan asked.

Marcus's face and long hair were matted with sweat and blood, and he was breathing heavily. "We can't continue like this," he gasped. "There are too many!"

Chapter Thirty-Six

Eirin shook as she climbed from Nuru's back through the window of the highest tower. It was, as Aodhan had said, filled with a visceral darkness. No wonder no one but the Time Keeper and a few unsuccessful Seers had been here since the curse had fallen.

But she was here now. And she had no choice.

"Stay safe!" Nuru called. "I'll be down at the battle. But you know how to call me."

They had worked out a special whistle in case Eirin needed her. Nuru couldn't come into the tower with her, and she couldn't hover outside the window all day. Secretly, Eirin doubted very much that Nuru would hear any whistle she sent out. But that was well enough. It made Nuru feel better. And Eirin had to do this on her own.

As soon as she had taken two steps into the room, the dark smoke cleared, and she could see the room in its entirety. And for a moment, she stopped breathing.

It was just as she had imagined it.

The room was round, and its diameter was at least as wide as three of Eirin's old cottages put together. This was impossible, considering how much thinner it had looked from the outside.

But then again, this was the Time Keeper's domain. Surely, nothing was impossible in the sanctum.

The tower also rose far above her head, again, much higher than it had appeared to be from outside. The walls doubled as bookshelves, and volume after volume of leather-bound books and scrolls filled them. Four writing tables were placed evenly about the room against the walls, one to the north, one to the south, one to the east, and one to the west. Three of the writing tables were empty, but on the one to the west lay open the thickest book Eirin had ever seen, along with a large supply of quills and many bottles of ink. Though she couldn't see what it said, half the first page was filled by a neat, flourishing hand.

Sconces covered by rainbows of stained glass dotted the walls, and tapestries that had once been made of the finest silk and stitched with colorful threads were moth-eaten, torn, and faded. They swayed in the breeze coming through the window Eirin had climbed through. Still, they somehow maintained a sense of majesty despite their damage.

But more overwhelming than any of these were the Time Stones.

Eirin had seen the Time Stones, of course, in her visions. She couldn't touch the stone at her neck without seeing them. But never had she realized that the circle could be so vast. Nor so beautiful. For while none of the stones were special in and of themselves, their dark and light tones were lovely as they criss-crossed over the length of the floor. Some were laid north-south, while their neighbors pointed east-west, just as she had seen in her visions. There was no real pattern to them, but they were complex and as lovely as they were varied.

She was also struck with the realization that the longer she stood there staring, the more aware she was of a physical desire to *touch* the stones. It was nearly overwhelming as soon as she recognized it. And innately, she knew that it was the power of the room. It was calling her blood. For she was a Seer.

And she was finally home.

The echo of the sounds of battle reached Eirin's ears through the open windows, and Eirin shook her head to clear her thoughts. She needed to focus. People were dying, and the Time Stones had to be fixed. So she pulled the stone free from her tunic and gripped it tightly with her left hand.

As soon as she touched the stone, she could see the vision in her head, the one she'd seen a thousand times. But this time, she concentrated harder than she ever had before. She knew what the broken stone's mate looked like. And there were so many stones in the circle! No wonder no one had been able to find it before.

Slowly, while revisiting the vision over and over again, she removed her stockings and boots and knelt down on her hands and knees. Crawling across the stones, she allowed her vision to guide her. She could feel the hum of the other stones beneath her hands as she crawled, and she had no doubt that if she weren't holding her own stone already, she would be assaulted by a thousand other visions at once.

Unfortunately, the number of stones was so great that her progress was painstakingly slow, and Eirin began to be plagued by doubts. So many Seers had failed before her, searching for the broken stone until they died. What if, even with the help of her stone fragment, she still didn't find it? Or what if she was too late, and Rangvald was the one to greet her when she emerged?

Eirin squeezed the stone until her hand hurt. *Please,* she prayed to the Time Keeper. *Please let me find it. Fast.*

She knew by the change in the sun's light that an hour had already passed. Then two. Her heart beat so fast she became nauseated. She had nothing to do about it, however, but swallow her fear and continue.

And then, as if her torturous morning had never happened, she found it. Her hands trembled as she placed her fingers on the broken stone. Her nerves made her clumsy, and she had to take several steadying breaths before she was ready to pull.

This was it. All she had to do was remove the stone.

Eirin dug her hand into the little hole where her broken end of the stone had been and tried to pull the remaining shard out.

It didn't budge.

Eirin began to send up a stream of endless, almost incoherent prayers as she continued to pull. She tried using one finger. Two fingers. Two hands. Even the other stone. But soon, all she had to show for her pains were bleeding hands.

Eirin sobbed as she stared down at the stone. So little a thing to damn so many...

I don't know what else to do.

Eirin placed both hands down on the stone to pull again. But before she could try, she was assaulted with another vision. This vision, however, was so clear it made all her previous visions look as though she'd viewed them through murky water. This time, she could really *See*.

Eirin was suddenly in a world that wasn't her own. It was foreign yet familiar. There were lords and ladies, palace guards and civilians, craftsmen of all kinds, in both Human and Atharrach forms. Great crowds of people filling markets overflowing with fat, juicy fruits and vegetables. Farms covered the countryside, green and lush, and the forests were thick and crawling with life.

There were the Dragon kings and queens of old, stately and ethereal in their beauty and majesty, their richly dyed robes long and silken, and their bearing proud and powerful. Seers, too, garbed in snow white robes such as Eirin wore now, but offset with gems of this color or that, and sashes sewn with gold and silver threads. And in the streets, Giants and Brownies traded, and Manticores and Sprites ate and drank as friends.

At first, Eirin wondered what time she was viewing, but soon it was apparent that she was not seeing any one time in particular. Rather, the years flew by as each ancient Dragon king was replaced by a younger one, and soon, that one grew ancient as well.

Eirin was seeing the story of the world.

Her cheeks felt wet and cold, and reaching up to touch her face with her free hand, she realized she was weeping. So much beauty had been Solvar's. So much had been lost. She was nearly overwhelmed by it.

Inattentive to her sorrow, the ages continued to speed by until she felt as though she might pass out. All her people had lost was nearly too much for her. It was almost more than she could bear.

And yet, in spite of her angst, she began to feel as though a puzzle was coming together. She'd seen bits and pieces of the puzzle in her travels, but now she found pieces that had been long missing, and the mottled, incomplete picture she'd begun to form in her head these past months began to make sense.

Unable to help herself, greedily, almost feverishly, Eirin ran her hands over the other stones as well. Vision after vision assaulted her. People of long ago. Their celebrations and traditions, their joy and friendship. Sorrow. Terror. Relief. Birth. Life. Love. Death. The full spectrum of life as it had been.

And there was suffering. So much suffering.

As the years became more familiar, marked by the unmistakable signs of the curse, meaning they were speeding closer and closer to Eirin's own time, Eirin expected the visions to end. She rather hoped they would. She wasn't sure she could continue to witness so much pain. And yet...as she searched the epochs, the story went on. People continued to appear. Some strangers, and others familiar.

And then it hit her. A realization so strong she nearly removed her hands from the stones.

The Time Stones may have stopped moving. But they hadn't stopped collecting memories. They had never stopped. The Time Keeper had continued to add the stories of Solevar to the stones even after they ground to a halt. He must have. Eirin cried again, but this time with joy as she was hit by a particularly strong vision of her own family that must have taken place after she had escaped Torbaine. Her mother was now large with child, and her brothers at least another handspan taller than they had been the last time she'd seen them. Her father seemed much grayer around the ears than when she had left him, but she didn't care. It was them.

The Time Keeper had never abandoned them after all.

And then the scene changed again, and Eirin stiffened. Before her was the whole of what she'd seen in partiality before. Finally, she would know what had really happened the night the world had begun to end.

A Seer knelt on the Time Stones as Eirin was kneeling now. But instead of touching the Stones, he held a small stone in his hand. Almost as if he was waiting.

But what was he waiting for?

A near deafening grinding rent the air, and Eirin gasped as the Stones began to move. Magic of every color flew up from between the stones, and it was by far the most beautiful thing Eirin had ever seen.

The man, who was still kneeling on the stone, did not seem mesmerized as Eirin was. A look of complete focus on his face, he let out a shout and slammed the small stone down into the Circle.

The moment the stone was inside the circle, a blinding flash was accompanied by the crackle of thunder. When Eirin could see again, the man lay dead in the circle. The Stones had come to a halt.

"No!"

Eirin turned to see a young man who looked vaguely familiar

standing at the door. His mouth was open, and his eyes were wide.

"Prince Kamon!" Several Seers, who must have been in the hallway outside the door, ran up behind him, and one of them, a man, pulled him back. "You'll die if you set foot in there!"

But Kamon, easily overpowering the Seers, fought blindly to get back inside. "It's my fault!" he shouted. "I told him to put it in!"

A young Seer, who had been gawking at the body, whipped her head around. "You told him to do *what*?" Her voice was thick with dread.

"The stone!" Kamon cried, guards now coming to aid the Seers in keeping him back. Eirin would have expected the prince to shift any minute but for the tears running down his face. He was fighting blindly but without conviction. "He suggested we force in a stone," Kamon sobbed. "So we could change the course of fate. I told him to do it, and–"

"Oh!" the woman breathed. "Oh, no!"

The Seers who weren't aiding the guards in keeping the prince out paled as well. For a moment, they stood in stunned silence, staring at the dead man and the Time Stones.

"We...um," one of them began, clearing his throat. "We should take his body down to..." He let the sentence die, but the others seemed to understand him. Two other male Seers went over and bent carefully to pick up their fallen brother's body.

No sooner had they lifted the body from the stones than a dark mist began seeping out of the Stones' cracks where magic had been before, and the air began to thicken with what looked like ash.

Most of the Seers accompanied the prince as the guards led him away, and others bore the body, but one Seer still remained, fixed as if frozen at the door.

"Talia..." an older female came up behind her, her voice wary. "What are you considering?"

"I need to get that stone," Talia said.

"Talia, no!" the woman snapped. "It's too dangerous! Wait for the others. We need to talk–"

"We can't leave it there!" Talia answered. "We have to get it out!" She darted into the room, coughing as she ran. When she reached the Stones, however, she paused, her eyes trained on the large book lying open on the writing table. But then the Stones shook, and her attention returned to the Stones beneath her. Hesitating only a moment, she ran to the edge of the room. Eirin struggled to see what was in the trunk Talia was searching, as the air was getting thicker and harder to see through and the mist continued to pour forth from the stones.

After a moment of searching, Talia held up some sort of tool and a mallet, and running back to the foreign stone, stuck the end of the tool beneath it. She hit it again and again with the mallet, coughing until blood stained her arm when she wiped her mouth. Finally, a piece of the foreign stone was removed.

But only a piece.

The tower shook again as though the earth beneath it was moving.

"Talia!" The other Seer ran to Talia and tried to pull her toward the door. Talia, still coughing violently, dropped the tools and grabbed the piece of the stone she'd chiseled out. Then, coughing violently, she let the other woman lead her away.

"We have to go back!" she coughed as they moved into the hall. "We can't leave it there!"

"You have this piece," the woman said. "At least we'll be able to find its match when we return."

But, as the same black mist filled the palace, chasing its terrified residents from its halls, Eirin knew they wouldn't go back.

The black mist wasn't content to stay within the palace walls.

Instead, it leaked out of the windows and doors and spread itself over the entire kingdom. Over houses and fields, lakes and rivers, on the mountains and in the valleys. Nothing was left uncovered.

The scene changed again, and when it cleared, Eirin could see three men gathered around a table in an ill-lit room. Kamon was there, as was Rangvald. Eirin had never seen the third young man, but she knew from her time with Karolus that this must be his father, Demetrius, the second of the three princes.

"You did *what*?" Demitrius gaped, his voice a whisper.

Kamon hung his head. "Johann convinced me it would be for the best. And I believed him."

"The best to play with the Time Keeper's circle?" Rangvald snapped.

At this, Kamon's eyes flashed. "I wouldn't have felt the need if it hadn't been for *you*."

"You speak of what you don't know!" Rangvald hissed.

"Stop!" Demetrius held up his hands. He turned to glare at Kamon. "Now what's done is done. The question is what to do about it."

"He can't just–" Rangvald began, but Demetrius held up his hand again.

"We need to let the Blood Fire Throne decide. We'll participate in the rite, just as we had planned." He eyed Rangvald. "The Time Keeper will choose."

"The Stones have stopped moving!" Rangvald shouted, making his brothers flinch. "The Time Keeper has abandoned us, Demetrius! All because this little imbecile believed a rumor–"

"It was no rumor, and you know it!" Kamon roared back, his eyes glistening dangerously with amber.

"And even if the Stones were moving," Rangvald continued, jabbing a finger at Kamon, "he's gone too far. He cannot be allowed even the chance to be king!"

"I'm not sure what you think we should do then!" Demetrius

raised his voice as well, his own eyes flaming. "It's been three days! The rite must be conducted tomorrow according to the law!"

Kamon took a deep breath. And when he spoke again, his voice was lower. "I talked to Talia. She was able to remove part of the stone. She thinks if she can get back into the room, she could find and remove the other half."

"And then what?" Rangvald asked, his eyes still dangerously bright. "We can all go back to the way things were?"

Eirin, though still stuck in the vision, felt the hair rise on the nape of her neck. She'd seen enough of Rangvald over the last year to know that he had two dispositions. Calm and controlled on one hand, and on the other–

"Don't act as though you're blameless in all this," Demetrius warned Rangvald, putting a restraining hand on his chest. "While Kamon's claims may be overblown, it *has* come to my attention that you've been building secrets of your own."

"My mistake," Rangvald hissed, scales beginning to appear on his face as his voice dropped into its Dragon depth, "was not carrying out my own justice last night!" A chilling madness settled into his features––a madness Eirin knew all too well––just before he sprang at Kamon.

Eirin flinched. But Demetrius was in the way before Rangvald reached Kamon.

"Go!" he barked as he held his older brother back, already shifted into his own Dragon form. "Get away from here!"

Kamon evidently listened because the next scene that flashed before Eirin's eyes was one of escape. The black mist still flowed out of the castle windows, continuing to coat the world in its shadow. Countless people stood in line at the edge of the city, their goods packed on carts, donkeys, horses, carriages, and their own backs. It was evening, which Eirin guessed meant they must have already realized the danger of the sun.

"How many do we have?" Kamon asked a man who stood beside him. The man looked at the parchment he held.

"Somewhere above fifteen-hundred, Your Highness." He looked up. "And you're certain you wish to go to the mountains?"

Kamon turned and looked back at the palace. Pain lined his face. Then he closed his eyes and nodded. "If we stay here, we'll die."

"The forest would be closer," the man said hopefully. But Kamon shook his head.

"I have word from the Unicorns that the forests are just as bad. But the Dwarves report that the caverns are still safe."

The man sighed but nodded. "Then to the caverns, we shall go."

The days that followed sped by quickly, and Eirin was glad of it. She had no desire to watch the pain of those early days as Solevar's people died in droves.

Soon she saw Rangvald and Demitrius leave with their caravans, heading southeast instead of east as Kamon's band had done.

Then the visions were over. And Eirin was kneeling on the stone circle once more. The story had come to its end.

It was confusing, really. Eirin knew enough to understand that the Time Keeper had continued adding stories to the Stones even after the curse had fallen. But it felt so abrupt, so incomplete.

A snap sounded from the Stones. Eirin looked down to see the hole give a little crackle. Magic, small but undeniable, sparked slightly. Eirin stared at it, understanding suddenly coloring her world.

She had to complete the story.

The story was not a clean one. It was filled with darkness and suffering and angst. Evils had been wrought, and mistakes had been made. And yet...

And yet, beauty had come from darkness. Beauty in the faces

of her parents and her brothers and Drystan. The sacrifice of Alys and the redemption of Eirin's animosity with Nuru. Help from the Merfolk and the Unicorns and the Griffins and Nymphs and everyone who had given of himself to get them this far. *This* was all a part of their story. And it had to be completed.

With shaking hands, Eirin slipped the cord from her neck and untied the knot that held it there. Then, as the Seer had done a century before, she held it high above her head.

"What are you doing?"

Eirin jerked her head up to see Mannish standing in the doorway. She blanched a little.

He was different than the last time she'd seen him. His shoulders had filled out some, and his face was slightly haggard. He looked older.

Harder.

His face was pale as he stared at her. "What are you doing?" he repeated.

* * *

Eirin searched for words, which seemed to have fled her. "I'm... fixing the Time Stones," she managed to croak out.

"By putting it back in?" Mannish turned an accusing gaze on her. "We're supposed to take the stone out. Not repeat what started this mess!"

Eirin shook her head. She hadn't expected to see the other Seer for another day. She wasn't prepared for this.

"I see now," she said after swallowing. "The Stone has to remain in the circle! It's a hideous part of our story, but it *is* part of our story. We can't just pretend it didn't happen." Eirin looked back down at the hole and moved to put the stone in again, but before she could, the end of a sword appeared inches from her face.

"I can't let you do this," Mannish said, his voice trembling nearly as much as his hand. "We *have* to remove the stone."

Anger flared up in Eirin, but she shoved it back down. When he became angry, Mannish became as dangerous and unpredictable as a cornered animal. It would be better to try and try to win him over to her point of view.

"I thought that too," she said carefully. "But it never worked. I've seen it in the stones. Seer after Seer trying to remove the stone. Using their hands and tools and..." She took a deep breath. "Remember when you always used to say that I was good at Seeing? Well, trust me now. I know how to fix this. No one else has been able to, but I can." She hesitated. "You need to trust me." He had to believe her. He'd always believed her before. Why should he doubt her now?

"I thought this might happen," he said after a moment of hesitation, keeping the sword pointed at her.

"Thought *what* might happen?"

"That spending so much time with Drystan...that that Dragon might corrupt your mind. I thought you might come up with a new idea together that would gain Drystan the crown, and I was right."

Eirin stared at him, dumbfounded. What was he talking about? He had been the one to conjure up new ways to get power. Why would he–

Then Eirin understood. "You're angry that I went with Drystan and Isayas. Aren't you?"

"You left me!" Mannish snapped. "In the middle of that horrid battle, you left me behind!"

"You weren't even supposed to *be* there!" Eirin retorted.

Mannish winced slightly before tightening his grip on the sword again. Then another thought dawned on Eirin.

"What did Rangvald promise you if you fixed the Time Stones?" she asked slowly.

Mannish's nostrils flared. "That's not your business."

"Oh, I think it is. Especially considering you nearly cursed us again trying to steal a Wizard's staff!" Eirin had been slowly, slowly moving her hand toward the hole, but the sword came closer, and she had to stop once again. "Look, I'm telling you now. No matter what we thought back there, the Time Stones never stopped working! Touch them and see for yourself! They were here all along, recording everything that has happened since the curse fell!"

Mannish shook his head, his jaw trembling. "I don't believe you. In fact, I think you're trying to trick me into putting myself in a vulnerable position."

Eirin wanted to retort that she would indeed disarm him if he gave her the chance, but she swallowed the words back down.

"Every Human who tried to remove the stone didn't have this!" Eirin held up her portion of the broken stone.

With a surprising quickness, Mannish slapped her hand with the side of his blade, and Eirin's stone clattered across the floor several paces away. Eirin dove after it, but Mannish was suddenly in her way, his sword out again.

Eirin rolled away from him on her shoulder and whipped her own knife out of her boot, cursing silently that she had left her sword behind. There had been no way to secure it to her robe, and she hadn't foreseen any company once she was in the tower.

They began to circle one another slowly, each with blade drawn. And then Mannish attacked.

Though he was bulkier than the last time she'd seen him, he was still clumsy with the sword, and Eirin, for all her years of training, was far quicker. Unfortunately, her blade paled in comparison to his, and she was suddenly engaged in a sword fight with a knife.

"Eirin!" he pleaded as she dodged another attack. "Let's just take the stone out and be done with it like every Seer for the last hundred years has attempted to do!"

Eirin didn't answer. She was too busy dancing away from the end of his blade.

"I love you!" Mannish cried, his voice breaking as he went on the offensive again.

"You have an odd way of showing it," Eirin hissed, poised to spring.

At this, Mannish let his sword drop to his side. "Think of what we could do together!" he pleaded, a lock of his pale hair falling in his eyes. "You don't need to do whatever the betrayer's descendent has told you to do! You don't have to make him king!"

"I told you!" Eirin said, panting. "Drystan doesn't have anything to do with this! I just discovered it!"

"He's manipulative and conniving," Mannish snapped, his face darkening like a thundercloud. "And I know he's convinced you to repeat the same kind of mistake his ancestor made." He looked at the stone again. "Even Isayas said it had to be removed! Does Isayas approve of this?"

Eirin glared at him. "I never had the chance to ask him. He died when *Rangvald* sent in his forces." She scoffed. "Not that you care, seeing as you tried to kill him yourself."

"I didn't mean–" Mannish drew in a shaky breath. "But if he were here, you *know* what Isayas would say to all of this! What any Wizard would say!" He paused again to sneer. "But all that Dragon wants is to trick you into marrying him, making you queen and him king. He doesn't care–"

Eirin couldn't help the small laugh that escaped her. Mannish gave her a strange look.

"Didn't you hear?" Eirin said, coiling her muscles again. "I married him last night."

From the look on Mannish's face, it was clear he hadn't heard of their nuptials. And Eirin was ready. Using his shock, she dove toward the broken stone once more. This time, she got it.

But Mannish's rage had boiled over, and he came after her with a renewed strength.

His slashes were violent, but, to Eirin's relief, they were inelegant. And after a moment, Eirin was finally able to knock his sword out of his hands. But before she could dart over to the hole again, Mannish grabbed her wrist.

Eirin hadn't thought he could be any more surprised than he already was. But as soon as their skin touched, he gasped. And she realized what he had seen.

Magic.

"You... you're...you have–" he stuttered. Eirin yanked her hand away and sent him flying against the wall with a strong kick. Then, before he could get up, she plunged her dagger into his shoulder.

He screamed as blood pooled around him, but Eirin didn't stop to watch. Instead, she ran back to the center of the floor and slammed the stone into place.

But nothing happened.

Chapter Thirty-Seven

Eirin panicked.

The stone was in the circle. So why wasn't the circle moving? Why hadn't it come back to life? Where was the magic?

Eirin glanced over at Mannish, who was slumped against the wall. He seemed to have passed out, which she was thankful for. She just needed a minute to think.

Had he been right? Had she been mistaken? Perhaps she should have tried harder to get the remnant out instead of making it whole again. As Mannish had pointed out, all the Seers before them had striven to remove it.

Had she just doomed them all?

Eirin felt sick. She wrapped her arms around her nauseous stomach, closed her eyes, and drew in a long, deep breath. When she opened them again, her gaze alighted on the writing table where the open book still lay. And she remembered Talia.

She, too, had gazed at the book.

The story was in the circle...but the Seers hadn't merely Seen the visions.

Eirin ran to the table, fear making her clumsy. She accidentally knocked over the stool and nearly upset the open bottle of ink in her haste. With trembling hands, she grabbed the ink bottle and dipped a quill inside.

It was dry. Of course.

Swallowing down one of Drystan's favorite curses, Eirin looked desperately around the room for some sort of water. There was none, so she spit into the bottle. After a moment of stirring and breaking three quills in the process, Eirin managed to get the fourth quill to make a mark on the paper, albeit a poor one.

She paused then, her pen hovering over the parchment. What should she write? How far back should she go? She skimmed the last section that had been recorded. Then she read it again. Whoever had written here, whether it had been her great-grandmother or someone else, had been succinct and neat. Thanks to her vision, she knew without a doubt that the last record had been made the day of the curse.

So with a sharp breath and a prayer, Eirin began to write. And as she did, she felt her body begin to change. Every hair felt as though it were standing on end, and she felt charged, electrified as though she'd been struck by lightning.

Yes. This was what she'd been waiting for. As Eirin watched the visions in her head once again, she knew she had finally found it.

Eirin Saw what she'd been looking for.

Chapter Thirty-Eight

Drystan signaled for Qeb to join him in the sky. There were a number of other soldiers engaging each other in aerial battle, but few were foolhardy enough to attack Drystan as he hovered there.

"We're going to find the Thunderbirds," Drystan told his friend. "It should distract them enough that when they pull back to fight me, the others can move in."

Qeb gave a nod and clacked his sharp beak before flying back down to relay the message to Marcus and then Thane.

The battle had been raging for hours. It was nearing midday, and as Rangvald had never reappeared on the frontlines, Drystan should have been able to attack the Thunderbirds sooner.

Unfortunately, his forces had come upon an entire neighborhood of civilians, mostly made up of elders, mothers, and children, who had been too frightened to escape when they should have, and Drystan had been forced to provide protection for them as they fled. It had cost his soldiers time and blood, and the battle was beginning to look dire.

Drystan dove in the direction he guessed the Thunderbirds were in hopes of taking them by surprise.

His guess wasn't off, and his direct tactic worked. Their protectors were caught in the rush of soldiers trying to run back to protect them, and Drystan was able to release stream after stream of fire. As he did, holes began to open in the clouds above.

The Thunderbirds, suddenly unprotected, began to take flight, and Drystan smiled to himself as he gave chase. Down below, he could hear screams as Rangvald's men flocked to take cover from the sunbeams that pierced the sky.

One by one, he took the Thunderbirds down. But when he looked up from his last kill, to his amazement and horror, the clouds were back in the sky.

"They must have several Acalica hiding somewhere."

Drystan turned to find that Qeb had joined him in the sky.

Drystan cursed. The Thunderbirds had been a distraction. And he had fallen for it.

"Blast the weather Faeries," he muttered.

"Drystan!"

Drystan turned to see Thane calling up to him. The Centaur looked as though he'd aged a decade since the battle had begun. Blood and sweat matted his fair hair, and there was none of his usual joviality on his face.

"We have to pull back!" Thane continued. "I suggest the alleyways!"

Only then did Drystan realize what had happened. While he was attacking the Thunderbirds, Rangvald's strongest fighters had crept into Drystan's own ranks. His forces were being cut into two. Drystan gave him a nod. "Do it."

Thane blew several short notes on a horn, and Drystan's forces began to retreat. Drystan took the opportunity to cut across the two armies, loosing rivers of fire down upon Rangvald's men as they made chase, preventing them from following as Marcus and Thane urged their men back.

The plan worked. Drystan's army was able to regroup in the

alleyways that had been designated for such a retreat, while Drystan continued to pick off those of Rangvald's forces that were trying to follow. Unfortunately, when he was forced to focus his efforts on one particularly nasty Giant who was determined to follow Marcus and his men, Drystan forgot to look up.

Rangvald slammed into him from above, the impact so hard that Drystan crashed into the ground.

Drystan, remembering the injuries Karolus had inflicted upon Rangvald before Rangvald had killed him, bit down on Rangvald's left wing. Rangvald let out a shrill howl of pain, and Drystan rolled out from beneath him.

The area quickly cleared as the two Dragons faced off. Drystan had barely escaped his uncle's claws when a wall of flame engulfed him. Unlike other attacks Drystan had endured during the battle, this fire hurt. He gritted his teeth and let loose his own fire.

Stinging, he and Rangvald both rose into the air, circling one another warily. Lightning struck so close to Drystan that his ears rang, but he didn't break eye contact with his uncle. To do so would surely mean death.

Rangvald tucked his body and rolled in the air, flinging himself at Drystan. Drystan managed to dodge him, barely escaping the sharp claws that stretched out to slice his scales. Then, taking advantage of the other Dragon's momentum, he flamed Rangvald as he came out of his mid-air roll. Rangvald hissed, and Drystan dodged a swipe of his tail.

A scream pierced the air from below. Drystan looked down to see that Rangvald's forces had rounded up a large number of his smaller soldiers and were preparing to execute them as they knelt on the ground, their hands on their heads.

Where were Thane and Qeb?

Unfortunately, whatever worry Drystan had for his own soldiers was not shared by Rangvald. He took advantage of Drystan's distraction and sliced through Drystan's thigh with his back claws. Drystan roared in pain and flamed back. He missed.

As Rangvald drew slightly back to attack again, Drystan hesitated only a moment before diving down to lay fire upon the Griffins who were about to kill those of Drystan's soldiers who had surrendered. But before he could reach them, he felt Rangvald hot on his tail, and he pulled up sharply, maneuvering just in time to get his own claws into Rangvald's shoulder.

Rangvald's roar was joined by another sound. A horn, loud and long. But this horn, Drystan had never heard.

Or had he?

Suddenly streaming into the battle was a new set of creatures. Creatures that were led by a red-haired Phoenix, a blond Faerie, and a copper-scaled Dragon.

But that was impossible.

Yet, as they drew near, Drystan knew his eyes didn't deceive him. Callispa, Alys, and Lady Phaidra were indeed leading fresh troops into battle. Mhaedin *and* Torbaine had come to their aid. Drystan briefly wondered how they'd come so fast until he realized that Phaidra was missing many more scales than the last time he'd seen her.

It was Rangvald's turn to fall prey to distraction. Drystan, recovering from his shock faster than his uncle, took the opportunity to land on Rangvald's back, his claws digging into Rangvald's scales. He managed to bring his mouth down upon Rangvald's neck, but Rangvald jerked and shook him off before he could sink his teeth in all the way.

Rangvald then whirled around and flamed at Drystan as Drystan caught himself in the air. The fury on his face and the fire in his eyes were like nothing Drystan had ever seen before, and he knew that Rangvald had only just begun. He braced himself for the wrath of the madman, but as Rangvald prepared to spring at him, a voice like thunder and rain boomed over the sounds of the battle.

"Stop!"

Everyone, including Rangvald, obeyed.

There, on the palace steps, stood Eirin.

Her eyes were a milky blue, no hint of their usual brown within them. Her white robe glowed as she slowly made her way across the dais to where Drystan and Rangvald still hovered.

Admiration and fear battled within Drystan. She was beautiful and terrible, and he felt as though he were seeing the true Eirin for the first time. *But,* a voice inside him wondered, *how much of the old Eirin is still left inside?*

As Eirin walked toward them, people scrambled back to give her room. All fighting had ceased, and when Rangvald tried to take a step toward Drystan, Eirin gave him a look so fierce he froze where he was.

"I have touched the Time Stones, and I have Seen," Eirin said, danger still lingering in her voice. "And you will listen."

Chapter Thirty-Nine

Eirin looked down upon the carnage below her. And she knew they were listening.

Finally, they were listening.

"There were three sons of Faradoon," she said, her voice echoing over the vast square. "Two of them were noble in heart and eager to serve."

"We know which–" Rangvald began, but Eirin fixed her gaze on him, and he fell silent. She turned back to the crowd.

"It was not Kamon who was prepared to betray his people," she continued. To her satisfaction, both sides let out an audible gasp.

She turned once more to look at Rangvald. "It was you, first son. For years before your father breathed his last, you had vowed that you would never be servant to either of your brothers no matter whom the Time Keeper chose. They would be yours. You wished to give up neither your immortality nor your power. Serving as a lesser prince would force you to give up your scales and your power." Her voice sharpened. "And anything less than king would never be good enough for you. So instead of preparing to serve your kingdom in whichever way you were called, you

355

decided you would rule it with an iron fist. To accomplish this, you spent years secretly gathering supporters and rallying them to your cause as you waited for your father to die."

Rangvald snarled, but when Eirin glowered at him again, he stayed put. Whatever change had come over her in the tower seemed to have, for the moment, cowed him.

She hoped he would stay that way.

"My lady!"

Eirin turned to see Rangvald's Griffin, his first-in-command, step forward.

"If you please...tell us...where does Kamon come in? We know he set the curse in motion." A chorus of nervous murmurs in the affirmative went up from the crowd.

"Kamon caught wind of what his brother was planning," she answered them. "He tried to convince Demetrius to stand with him against Rangvald, to confront him together. And he was not alone. Many of their loyal subjects were concerned as well and pleaded with Demetrius to listen."

She looked back at Rangvald in disgust. "But Demetrius was convinced you could never do such a thing. That you would never betray your family or your people. So when Demetrius refused, Kamon grew desperate, and on the advice of his friends, decided to act."

The people staring up at them were deathly silent. No one moved. So Eirin went on, unsure of how long she would be able to command their attention.

"Kamon gathered those who had rallied behind him, and in secret, they devised a plan to change fate. Knowing what they did of Rangvald's plans, they concluded that the Time Keeper either didn't see...or didn't care. They convinced themselves that only they could prevent this evil.

"One Seer in particular was of Kamon's mind. Word had it that his own village had been quietly taken by Rangvald, and neighboring towns were secretly being claimed by the first prince as well. He was so utterly persuaded of Rangvald's intentions and ability to fulfill his plans that he and his friends didn't stop to consider the audacity of the plan they'd conceived."

As Eirin spoke, she tried to address each of Rangvald's soldiers with her eyes, willing them to hear what she was saying. Hoping they would see the truth about the master they served.

"After much deliberation, Kamon convinced this Seer to carve a stone like those in the circle. Over it, they uttered the fate they hoped for. They declared it and sought the end they envisioned. And then, when the Stones began to move as they always did to make way for new stones, the Seer plunged this stone into the circle where a new stone should have had its place."

Eirin could see the doubt beginning to creep into the soldiers' eyes. She was losing them. They were again seeing Kamon as the enemy. So as she spoke, Eirin closed her eyes.

Let them See, she prayed. And she was rewarded by a chorus of gasps and even a few shrieks.

A new sensation filled her chest, and she couldn't help wondering if it was anything akin to what Drystan felt every day. When she opened her eyes, she knew they could see what she had witnessed in the tower. Her visions now surrounded them all as if they had gone back one hundred years together. Buoyed by this, she continued.

"The curse began when the foreign stone was forced into the circle. But," she looked at Rangvald again, "it was cemented when the sons of Faradoon refused to act. You let your people face the curse without a king, because you would were afraid it wouldn't be you."

Around them, the people beheld the horrifying scenes Eirin had been subjected to only hours before. The black mist flowing from every palace window and door, darkness overtaking the world. People running, screaming as they fell.

"So you see," she continued. "The evil of Kamon was in thinking he could do what the Time Keeper had not. But the evil was not his alone to bear. The Seer who helped him was guilty as well. And you, Rangvald, are at the curse's very heart. For you were the first to rebel against the ordinances of the Time Keeper, abandoning the duty and privilege that were your birthright from Solevar's birth. Unwilling to accept another as king and covetous of life without death, you had already begun your rebellion, quietly taking over the land that should have been given to the prince who won the rite. It was not the curse but your aggression that drove both your brothers to abandon Iilaedin without fulfilling the sacred duty that came with the privilege of being a son of Oreck. The curse was both the wrath and the saving hand of the Time Keeper, brought down to stop every one of you from further subverting His ways."

Those in the crowd began to whisper amongst themselves as heads turned toward Rangvald. Eirin allowed herself one glance at her husband. She wanted to faint from relief that he was still alive, though the blood running down his forearm was concerning. He met her eyes but seemed nearly as awestruck as everyone else.

Unfortunately, not all were shocked into immobility. Rangvald, his tail flicking this way and that, seemed to grow more and more agitated as his own people began slowly backing away from him. Eirin knew his submission to her orders wouldn't last much longer.

"What about the sun?"

Everyone turned to look at Qeb, who was looking straight at Eirin.

"How was it that Kamon's heir freed us from the poison of the sun?"

Eirin resisted the urge to run over and hug him. As always, Qeb seemed to know just what Drystan needed. And this time,

Eirin couldn't help smiling at Drystan as the vision she had conjured around them disappeared.

"We assumed," she said, "that the poison was in the sun itself. But it was we who had changed. The darkness that fell upon Solevar when the curse fell permeated our very beings. And before we could live free of it once more, that darkness within us had to die."

"But what does that have to do with the sun?" someone else called out. "Or with Kamon's descendent?"

Eirin turned to face them. "Everything. The sun was trying to do what we could not. Its rays were attempting to burn the poison out of our blood. But none of us were strong enough to withstand its rays. None of us," she smiled once more at Drystan, "except one of Oreck's sons. The magic within the hearts of the Dragon kings is the only magic strong enough to withstand that kind of purging."

"So," someone said, "any of the princes could have done it?"

"Yes," Eirin said. "But none did. None except Kamon's heir. When he sacrificed himself for one who had sworn fealty to him as I had, he once again took up the mantle of the kings. A mantle that had been abandoned when the three princes refused to take part in the Rite of the Blood Fire Throne, abandoning their duty and their people."

She took a deep breath. Her time was running short. She had to convince them soon. She doubted Rangvald would give her much more time.

"When he threw himself over me and remained there, the fire within and the fire without worked in tandem to burn away the poison within his blood. None but a son of Oreck could have withstood such cleansing. And because of his birthright, the poison of all who have vowed to follow him has been burned out as well."

"Perhaps," said Rangvald's captain, looking around him

uncertainly, "we ought to hold the rite." He nodded at Eirin. "To keep the Time Keeper's ordinances and all. Seems to me nought's been wrought of breaking them but death."

Eirin smiled. "I thought no one would ask."

The Griffin turned to Rangvald. Eirin could see the strain in his face, and her heart went out to him. She knew from speaking to Qeb that for a Griffin, trying to separate from the one to whom the Griffin had tied himself to was unspeakably painful.

"Your Highness," he said, his voice somewhat unsteady. "I have pledged my loyalty to you. I have served you faithfully for all my life." He looked back up at Eirin and then at Drystan, who was watching the scene with a look of wary insecurity. "And if you would indeed take your part in the rite, we will follow you to the end." He swept his hand behind him, as though speaking for Rangvald's entire army. As none objected, perhaps he was. "But *only* then."

Drystan, who had been standing not far from the dais, lumbered over to stand beside Eirin. Once there, he shifted into his Human form. Eirin did her best not to exclaim over his many wounds.

"I am ready to end this if you are," he rumbled in his Dragon voice. "One or the other, the rite will decide."

Rangvald sneered at him, but after looking around, seemed to realize that objecting would be unless he wished to alienate his entire army. He had little choice. So after another pause, he shifted back into Human form as well and made his way up to the dais to join them.

He paused before the throne upon which the great Dragon tooth was upturned and looked at Eirin.

"There are only the two of us, yes? You know of no more rivals?"

Eirin's stomach turned uneasily. What was he alluding to? It was an odd question, and considering his vast knowledge of Solevarian history and law, she didn't like it. She also got the distinct feeling that he meant not to accept the outcome of the rite if he lost. The desperation in his eyes was thinly veiled. And in her visions, she had seen how much he feared death. It was the reason he had never given away a single scale. It was this fear that had driven him to such great lengths to begin with.

"Who else would there be?" she asked carefully. "Demetrius and all his sons are dead. And Drystan's father is as well."

Rangvald studied her for a moment before grunting and turning back to the tooth.

The stone throne, which sat at the back of the dais facing out from the palace, was a sight more terrifying in real life than it had been in Eirin's visions. The single Dragon tooth that stuck up from the throne's left arm was at least the length of Eirin's hand. And Eirin had to keep herself from wincing when Rangvald lifted his hand and brought it down upon the tooth. The tooth cut in through the palm and out through the back of his hand, and immediately, blood began to floow.

As soon as Rangvald's blood began to flow down the front of the throne, the sky went black as night. People screamed, and only the little fires which had been started during the battle lit the dais.

Blood gushed from Rangvald's hand down the back of the chair and then onto the dais, where it began to fill the channels carved within the mosaic. And to Eirin's chagrin, the blood began to dance with flames.

Eirin didn't like how brightly it glowed. Some in the crowd cheered, and others began to talk amongst themselves. Rangvald didn't utter a word. Instead, he simply stared over the flames at Eirin and Drystan, his mouth curving up into a leering smile. Then he turned to the crowd.

"Lest anyone be tempted to doubt," he called, raising his voice so it echoed over the square, "I am the first son of King Faradoon, son of Oreck. And my magic was made for this day." He returned his gaze to Drystan.

Drystan moved toward the throne, but before he could pierce his own hand, there was a bang from behind Eirin as the palace doors flew open again. Mannish, covered in blood and ghostly white, appeared on the threshold. He was breathing heavily as he pointed at Eirin.

"Rangvald!" he gasped. "Don't listen to her! There is another...another heir!"

The roar of voices erupted from the crowd as Eirin's heart fell into her stomach.

"There is...another heir!" he cried again as he began to limp toward them. Drystan moved in front of Eirin, his eyes flaming amber. But Mannish continued until he was at Rangvald's side.

"She's carrying his child!" he cried. "A boy! That vixen is carrying another heir!"

Chapter Forty

Drystan froze for the longest second of his life.

How...But that wasn't even possible. They had only been married for one night.

Drystan was the first to admit that he knew very little about pregnancy and childbirth. But even he knew this wasn't possible. And yet...

He looked back at Eirin. The color had drained from her face, and her left hand was pressed against her belly. And then Drystan understood.

His scale.

Her wish.

The Time Keeper had granted Eirin her wish.

And as soon as Drystan understood this, he also realized with horror that Eirin was in mortal danger.

The Time Stones had been fixed, and with Mannish still alive, Rangvald no longer needed her.

Though Eirin was only inches away, Drystan shifted, master of his magic more than he ever had been before.

And his shift was none too soon. Rangvald, who had shifted as well, launched himself straight at Eirin.

Drystan threw himself between them and knocked the other Dragon away. They rolled several times from the impact, but as soon as each had stopped, he was on his feet once again.

Their first fight had been child's play compared to their clashes now. Rangvald was by far more experienced than Drystan. He was larger and had been trained in combat for over a century longer than Drystan had been alive. But he was unable to reach Eirin. For this time, a new kind of rage burned inside Drystan.

That his uncle would try to kill Eirin—and their child—brought forth wrath with a potency Drystan had never known before. And it fueled him. His body no longer felt corporeal, but instead as though he were made purely of flame. He moved faster and faster, biting and scratching and flaming each time Rangvald tried to reach Eirin.

Everyone watched as the two Dragons danced their deadly dance. Rangvald could not reach Eirin, but neither could Drystan make any true progress. He was at a disadvantage, and he knew it. All he could hope for was to run Rangvald ragged before he could truly hurt Eirin.

Could Drystan hold out that long?

And then, Rangvald made a misstep.

He had gone after Eirin again, who was now being secreted away by Qeb, Thane, Nuru, and a number of other creatures who were trying to hide her. Rangvald saw this and let out a roar of rage as he dove down at them from above.

Trusting his best friend as he never had in his life, Drystan waited until Qeb had yanked Eirin out of the way at the last moment. Then Drystan bore down upon Rangvald from behind, smashing him into the ground. Remembering how Rangvald had killed Karolus, Drystan attempted to bite down on the back of Rangvald's neck.

But Rangvald was too fast. He rolled over onto his back. Drystan somehow managed to stay on top of him, but because he was facing Rangvald's head, he didn't see his tail until it was wrapped around Drystan's neck.

Nothing but another son of Oreck could have choked Drystan through his scales. Rangvald was a son of Oreck, however, and he smiled as he yanked Drystan by the neck down onto the dais. Then he pinned Drystan to the ground as Drystan had done to him seconds before.

Drystan tried to use his tail as his uncle had done, but Rangvald had expertly positioned himself higher up on Drystan's chest and was out of reach. Drystan strained every muscle in his body, fighting to get free before he ran out of air.

Rangvald bent so his snout was to the side of Drystan's head. "I've wanted to do this," he hissed, "for the last hundred years." Then, in a move so fast Drystan didn't realize what he was doing, he bit down on Drystan's neck with his teeth.

"No!" a familiar voice screamed.

Drystan felt something warm and wet run down the sides of his neck. He had the vague impression of a Griffin with a war hammer and a another man with a sword running at Rangvald from different angles. Rangvald swatted both away like rag dolls. Drystan continued to fight, but he could feel the strength draining out of him with his blood. He was losing too much too fast.

He managed to turn his head to where Eirin was fighting to run to him. Nuru and Thane were holding her back, but only just.

How he wished he could tell her how sorry he was. He had failed her. She had given him everything, and he wasn't strong enough to protect it. He couldn't protect her or the new life that was so precious within her.

But even as he watched her, she stopped struggling, and her mouth fell open. Her face changed to a strange orange hue, as did the faces of those around her. Then he couldn't see her anymore as flames leaped up between them, lapping greedily at the air.

Rangvald, whose deep violet scales reflected the flames, let go and nearly tripped over himself as he scrambled backward, the clumsiest Drystan had ever seen him. And as he did, Drystan began to feel something new.

His limbs suddenly regained the sensation of strength. The blood, which had continued to pour out of him, was stopped, and he felt a new fire ignite within him. Getting to his feet, he looked at Eirin once more. Her eyes were round, and her hand was over her mouth. Nuru and Thane looked just as shocked. Qeb, looking a little worse for the wear, put his arm around her as though afraid she would run to Drystan. The flames that now surrounded Drystan reflected in their eyes, and Drystan finally had the sense to look down to see that the dais, which he still lay upon, was on fire.

Where Rangvald's blood had flickered here and there by comparison, the entire mosaic was now ablaze, flames leaping as high as Thane was tall. The blood which Rangvald had drawn from Drystan's neck now filled the trenches of the mosaic stones. And as they continued to glow brighter and blaze hotter, understanding finally donned on him.

The Time Keeper had chosen *him*.

Drystan allowed himself a small smile. Then he launched himself at Rangvald. And in one swift bite, Drystan extinguished his uncle's heart fire forever.

When Rangvald's lifeless body hit the ground, there seemed to be an eternal moment where the world was silent and still. Then Qeb, blood still trickling down his temple, lifted his war hammer above his head.

"Long live King Drystan!" he shouted.

In response, the people fell to their knees.

"Look!" Thane shouted. As he spoke, the sky began to

brighten again. And with the return of the day came new reason for awe. Where blood had stained the cobblestones before, flowers began to sprout. And not a single person screamed or ran for cover as the sun's rays covered them. The air was fresher and cleaner than Drystan had known possible, and in his heart, Drystan knew the curse had been broken.

Drystan turned, and shifting as he ran, sprinted back to Eirin. Catching her up in his arms, he lifted her into the air and twirled her around before pulling her in for a kiss. That seemed to break the spell of silence that had hung over the people, for the crowd burst forth into a cacophony of cheers, wails, and exclamations. Drystan chose to ignore them, though, as he pulled back from Eirin, tracing her face with his hands before pulling her back in for another kiss. Then his memory caught up to him, and he pulled away again.

"You...you wished for a son?" he asked breathlessly.

Eirin smiled, her eyes shining with unshed tears. Only when she wiped his cheeks with her own hands did Drystan realize he was crying.

"If I was going to lose you," she whispered. "I wanted to keep a piece of you for my own."

"Why didn't you tell me?" Laughing felt strange as the tears continued to fall.

Eirin shrugged. "You didn't need anything else to distract you. And it seemed like such an impossible wish." She placed his hand on her belly. "Can you feel him?"

Drystan blinked. "What am I feeling?"

Eirin laughed. "He's warm. His fire is already strong." As she said the words, Drystan realized she was right. A familiar heat warmed his fingertips.

"You're...you're not upset, are you?" Eirin asked, her brown eyes wide. Unable to restrain himself any longer, Drystan pulled Eirin in for another kiss.

"I told you," Drystan said, his heart about to beat out of his chest. "This is everything I thought I could never have." He placed his forehead against hers and cupped her face in his hand. "And I have it all because of you."

"I'm sure your room from last night is still open," someone behind them said. Drystan growled at Nuru, which made Thane and Qeb laugh. Alys appeared at the edge of the circle as well, and Eirin let out a scream of joy before pulling herself from Drystan's arms to embrace each of their friends. Qeb and Thane put strong hands on Drystan's shoulders. Drystan pulled them both in for an embrace as well. Together, Drystan, Eirin, and their friends basked in the light.

They weren't alone in their jubilation, for around them cries of celebration rose into the sky. And with them, tears in his eyes once more, Drystan sent up an eternal prayer of thanks.

They were whole.

They were together.

They were free.

CHAPTER 41

Epilogue

Eirin wanted nothing more than to catch up with her friends while simultaneously collapsing in relief. She was more exhausted than she could ever remember being. But Drystan was alive, as were her friends. Everything they had dreaded and hoped and dreamed for had come to pass in some form.

And more.

Unfortunately, there was no time to relax. Even as both armies exulted, turning the city from a battlefield to a place of celebration, there was work to be done. Bodies needed proper burials. Homes were in disrepair. Food had to be found, and for these and every other problem in Iilaedin, the king was needed for answers.

To Eirin's great relief, Drystan seemed to know exactly what to do. He immediately fell into talks with the committee, Lady Phaidra, and his grandmother, Lady Luna, who had accompanied Alys to the city. Even Rangvald's captain was included in the decisions that had to be made before nightfall. Drystan had exchanged one set of burdens for another.

But then again, Eirin reminded herself, he had been raised to be a king. His knowledge of what was needed from him seemed innate. Still, Eirin found herself in awe as she watched him, wondering how he had ever doubted himself. Leading came as naturally to him as his Dragon form. But maybe...maybe that was why. Drystan had been born to be king. Royalty quite literally flowed through his blood.

Eirin smiled to herself. She would have to find time later to remind him that she'd been right all along.

Drystan, seeming to feel her eyes on him, turned and gave her a brilliant smile.

Even as he turned away, however, Eirin felt her grin fade. Drystan might have been born to be a king, but Eirin was now queen by default. And she had never in any way exercised any sort of official authority, aside from bullying everyone to travel to Iilaedin. Most of her life had been spent just barely managing to hang on. A new icy fear hit her as she looked around, wondering what in the world she could do to help these people. They didn't need anyone to read the Time Stones right now. They needed food and shelter and clothing and direction, and she had not the first idea of how to give that to them.

"You'll be fine."

Eirin looked over to see Alys at her side. Eirin threw herself into her friend's arms once again, and they both cried a little. Eventually, they would speak of all that had happened since they'd been separated, but for now, tears and embraces would do.

When Eirin looked up, she saw Nuru standing nearby, too.

"Oh, no," Nuru said, taking a step back. "We did this already. You're on your own for now. I'm going to find something to eat."

Alys stared at her, mouth hanging open as Nuru walked away. "I meant to ask you...the hug earlier." She shook her head. "That was...different." She turned back to Eirin, her blue eyes wide. "She hasn't tried to kill you again?"

Eirin laughed. "You wouldn't believe it, but she's rather

mother-hennish. I'm not allowed to do anything without asking her permission."

Alys shook her head. "You're right. I don't believe it. But we can talk about that later." She stepped back and shook her head. "Eirin, you're a wife! And a mother! And a queen!"

"And you're here!" Eirin exclaimed. "How are you here?"

Insisting that Eirin should probably sit down after the excitement of the morning, Alys led Eirin to a small stone fountain, which was now flowing with water, and made her sit down on the little stone ledge. Then she proceeded to tell Eirin how, after her father hadn't come back, Drystan's grandmother had helped her shift for the first time, as she had done with Alys's older brother in secret. Together, they had taken Torbaine back from the Elders.

"What did the people think?" Eirin asked. "And my mother and father?"

Alys smiled. "They're just fine. Your sister arrived just a month ago, so they couldn't come with us. That, and your brothers would have pranked everyone to death before we got here. But your father wanted to come. He wanted to so badly. Once he learned the truth about everything, he nearly went mad trying to learn what had become of you. He tracked me down every day to ask if I'd learned anything new."

Eirin's chest ached with a familiar hollowness, one she had tried to beat down when it got too strong.

"What about the bruthsi root?" she asked in an attempt to redirect her thoughts.

"Oh, that was the hardest part. We couldn't wean everyone all at the same time. We took volunteers at first, then slowly, the rest of the city one neighborhood at a time. And then, of course, everyone had to get used to what they really were, and *that* was interesting."

"But why did you come here? How did you know where or when to go?" Eirin asked.

"Well, as soon as some of our flyers were strong enough, we sent them out as messengers to well-known locations throughout Solevar to see what had become of you. Your dad helped with that. He made us lots of maps because only a few of the Elders remembered the old world. I knew you were going to Mhaedin of course, but we didn't know if you had gotten there or if you had been taken or..." Alys stopped and ran a hand through Eirin's now messy hair. "I just hoped I hadn't sent you to your death," she whispered.

Eirin took her friend's hand and squeezed it. "But what about the battle? You arrived just in time!"

"Right. That began with the messengers. We eventually heard that you had been to Mhaedin, but there had been a battle, and you had escaped and were thought to be going to Iilaedin. We were told about Rangvald as well, so a group of us decided to go to Iilaedin to help you if we could. Some of those from Mhaedin joined us along the way." Alys paused and shivered delicately. "We were almost too late. But yesterday, we were found by a Phoenix."

"Callispa," Eirin said.

Alys nodded. "She had come looking for aid, and when we learned that the battle was imminent, those of us who could travel fast immediately set out. We were close enough that we were able to make it just in time. The others are still following behind."

"What about the sun?" Eirin asked. How did you travel during the day?

"That was strange. When the Phoenix showed up, she claimed that if we swore allegiance to Drystan immediately, we would be free to travel in the sun as we wished. Of course, no one believed her. Except for Elder Luna. She said it made perfect sense, and that she would leave any of us behind who became hung up on such stupidity." Alys laughed. "You know Drystan's grandmother. We knew better than to question her, so we did as she said, and sure enough, the next day, we were in the sun. And we ran and flew faster than we ever had." She shivered again. Then she looked down at Eirin's belly. "But enough of my story. *You* have some explaining to do."

Eirin laughed. "That's an even longer story." She glanced around. "And probably for another time." A flash of red caught Eirin's eye, and she stood. "Callispa!"

The Phoenix girl froze and then turned slowly to look at Eirin. Eirin beckoned her to come.

Callispa obeyed. As soon as she reached Eirin's side, she knelt and bowed her head. "My queen."

"Join us," Eirin said, patting the spot beside hers on the stone bench. "I hear you're to thank for finding my friends."

Callispa raised her head but kept her eyes downcast. "It was my honor to help my king and queen." She paused. "Do I have leave to continue?"

Eirin sighed but nodded. "Thank you again, Callispa." It was going to take some time getting used to being addressed as royalty.

A lot of time.

"What's wrong with her?" Alys whispered as the Phoenix walked away.

"I'm afraid some wounds take longer to heal than others," Eirin said quietly.

A ruckus at the other end of the square made Eirin and Alys look up. Two Griffins were dragging a man backward by the arms. When they got to the dais where Drystan was speaking with Aodhan, they threw him at Drystan's feet. It was Mannish.

"We found him trying to sneak away," one of the Griffins growled. "What do you wish for us to do with him, Your Highness?"

Drystan sent Eirin a look, and Eirin stood. Coming to stand at Drystan's side, she addressed Mannish coldly.

"Why did you help Rangvald?"

"You chose the Dragon," Mannish spat out, though his face

was pale, and he shook slightly. He faced Eirin directly. "Why? Why did you choose him? I offered you everything you ever could have wanted, and you threw it in my face! And I have a right to know why!"

Eirin met his gaze evenly. He didn't really have that right, but Eirin was perfectly content to answer. "Because you weren't him."

Drystan's eyes were a bright mixture of azure and liquid amber, but Eirin put a hand on his arm.

"As much as I would love to see him brought to justice, we are unfortunately rather short on Humans. It might be prudent not to kill him immediately."

"Very well," Drystan said, nodding at the Griffins. "Lock him in one of the dungeons until we decide what to do with him." He paused, then added, "And don't make him too comfortable."

* * *

For the next few days, people continued pouring into the city. Drystan and his newly appointed advisers were kept busy directing the reconstruction of homes quickly enough to house everyone while trying to rightly restore property to its original owners. The palace itself needed a great deal of work as well, and as it was housing many of the weary travelers, the work couldn't long be delayed.

Unfortunately, most of those who had worked on it in days of old were now dead, so Drystan and his helpers sent out word asking any skilled builders to return to the palace in exchange for food and shelter.

To their relief, their calls were answered. Giants began to appear in the days following, and the work, once begun, went quickly.

Aside from food and wood, some of the materials needed most for the rebuilding were metals. The Dwarves in the mountains, having suffered less than any of the others, were only too happy to sell their vast stores of precious metals and rock in exchange for food and other supplies from Solevar that the people could provide. They were, it seemed, vastly tired of roots and fish.

Food, not surprisingly, was Solevar's most pressing need. But, it seemed, the Time Keeper had anticipated this as well. For when the farmers cautiously returned to their fields, they found that new crops were already well on their way to being harvested, despite the farmers never having planted them. And as soon as the ports were fixed, many having caved in due to rot of age, fish became once again a bountiful food source.

Drystan also concerned Eirin. He flew in and out of the palace daily and generally stayed out until after dark. He never complained of fatigue. But Eirin could see it in the dark rings beneath his eyes and the way he fell into bed each night, unable to do much more than to put his arm around her before beginning to snore.

This would have been even more terrifying, considering Eirin's new status as queen, except for Alys. Alys, with her father's status as Elder, had been raised almost as royalty in Torbaine, and she set forth immediately to helping Eirin accustom herself to her new place in life. Nuru continued on as Eirin's bodyguard and was just as bossy and short-tempered as ever. But in a way, this was a comfort to Eirin, knowing that not everything had changed.

Qeb was generally at Drystan's side, and Thane, who continued sending Nuru long looks over the table in the dining hall, joined Marcus in the task of rebuilding Solevar's army.

Callispa seemed the least sure of what to do with herself. After locating her family in Mhaedin, she became one of the royal messengers, flying in and out constantly to deliver messages. Eirin wished she knew how to help the girl heal, but, as Alys pointed out, that was something the Time Keeper would be better suited for than anyone, not the girl who married the man Callispa had fancied herself in love with.

Unfortunately, Alys, though she would have preferred that Eirin not see it, was struggling herself. For it had soon been discovered after the collapse of the curse that Benjamin had been injured badly during the final battle, and by no other than Rangvald himself. Alys had been called to his side as soon as he discovered she had come, and there she had stayed for nearly three days.

"A Faerie," Benjamin whispered. "I should have known." He looked as though he wanted to say more, but a fit of coughing overtook his injured lungs. When Eirin had inquired as to what his injury was, she was horrified to learn that he had been hit by Rangvald's tail. He, along with Qeb, had tried to free Drystan from Rangvald's grasp. Unfortunately, Merfolk were not as large nor as sturdy as Griffins, and Benjamin had suffered for it.

Eirin, who came to visit him every day, tried to act cheerful and hopeful of his recovery. But her ability to see his magic, which was fading, made that difficult. She didn't broach the subject, however, until one day, when Alys had stepped out of the healing room, Benjamin had motioned for Eirin to join him.

"Can I get you anything?" Eirin asked, trying to summon a smile. He gave her a sad one in return.

"Your Highness, we both know I'm dying," he whispered, as he always had since the injury.

Eirin swallowed hard. "Alys–"

"Alys is the embodiment of everything good and beautiful," he whispered back. "And she will be fine."

"She cares for you," Eirin said.

"She thinks she loves me." Benjamin let out a raspy chuckle. "But when I'm gone, I want you to remind her that we barely knew each other." He swallowed and paused for breath. "And a few weeks of infatuation is hardly worth throwing her life away." He grabbed Eirin's hand suddenly and gripped it hard. "Tell her," he whispered fiercely, "to find someone who makes her happy. And don't let her settle for anything less!"

Alys returned then, preventing Eirin from replying. But perhaps it was just as well since Eirin had no idea what to say. It had occurred to her more than once that, while Alys had most definitely been infatuated with the Merman, it was unlikely to be love. At least, not yet. Still, when Benjamin did succumb to his injuries, despite the scale gifted by Drystan, Eirin held her tongue. One day she would tell Alys what Benjamin had said. But for now, she would let her mourn. And she would hold her hand the whole way.

Eirin's happiest moments, aside from the few she spent with Drystan, were those she spent with the Time Stones. As often as she could escape from the constant questions and requests, Eirin would steal away to the Time Stones, where she relished Seeing the visions and writing them down. Though she had recorded enough events from the time of the curse to break its hold, there were countless memories she now needed to See and record in the great book as well.

As she worked, however, a new sort of worry niggled in the back of her head. She couldn't possibly See or record all doings from the Time Stones by herself on this circle, let alone the stones that had reportedly been restored in all their original places around the kingdom.

What am I supposed to do? she asked the Time Keeper one evening. A week had passed since the curse had been broken, and though she loved her work more every day, a fear of failure loomed above her. She couldn't do it all. She simply couldn't. Even before the curse, in her visions, she'd Seen Seers going in and out of the sacred room constantly. There were rarely fewer than three in there at a time. Even if she had a daughter or several daughters after their son was born, the child wouldn't come into her gift for over a decade. And

Eirin knew she wouldn't be able to bear all that work on her own.

As if she'd shouted her prayer out the window, a knock sounded at the wooden door. Eirin stood and answered it to find one of the palace attendants standing outside.

"Your Majesty," he said with a bow. "I apologize most sincerely for disturbing you."

Eirin forced a tired smile. "How can I help?"

He gave her a funny look. "Sir Qeb says that you will want to see this." He indicated down the hallway.

Curiosity aroused, Eirin locked the door behind her and followed him out onto the dais, where she nearly fainted.

Standing before her were not one or five or ten but eighteen Humans. Men and women, young and old, they knelt when she entered and watched her apprehensively.

Qeb appeared on the dais beside Eirin.

Eirin turned to him, gaping. "But where–"

"Compliments of Lady Luna," Qeb said with a grin. "She would have stayed, but she thinks she knows where there might be more."

Eirin turned back to stare at the group before her. Humans. She and Mannish weren't the last Humans after all. A strange laugh bubbled from her before she could help herself.

A man, tall and thin with wrinkles thick on his face, stepped forward, crushing his worn hat in his hands as he bowed low to Eirin once more.

"Your Majesty," he said in a low, rough voice. "That Elf lady... Lady Luna has brought us to see if we might be of service to you."

"I'm most obliged," Eirin managed to say. "Um, if you'll come this way." She gestured for him to walk beside her into the palace. He, in turn, nodded to the others, who followed.

"I must admit," Eirin said as they walked. "You've taken me by shock. I...I thought I was one of the last in the kingdom."

"You probably think us cowards," the man said, still mashing his hat in his hands. "Us hiding and all."

"I would never assume cowardice," Eirin said carefully.

"You've a right to know," he continued on as if she hadn't spoken. "Most of our kin were taken until we were all that was left. And as most of us couldn't make the journey, we were trying to hide our few little ones left."

At the mention of littles, Eirin turned and looked again. Sure enough, four small children peeked out from behind their elders' legs, and two of the women held babies.

Eirin began to sob.

* * *

Two weeks after the curse fell, Eirin's greatest concern, other than making sure their people were fed and housed, was that she still hadn't seen her family. The gates she'd purposefully built up in her mind to keep her from despair without them had been broken down as she watched countless families reunite. Flying to see them was impossible. Their flyers were far too busy taking messages to and fro around the kingdom for Eirin to consider asking one to fly her home. And even if she had, neither Alys nor Nuru would have allowed it. And she didn't even dare suggest it to Drystan.

"You know I fought Mannish in hand-to-hand combat and won," Eirin grumbled at them. "I think I can walk on my own without tripping and dying for a few more months." She had presented her perfectly flat belly as if for proof. "I'm not even showing yet."

"That makes it worse," Nuru had said, narrowing her eyes. And to Eirin's great annoyance, Alys agreed.

So Eirin continued on, teaching the new Seers how to use the Time Stones, while Alys directed her in the ways of being queen. Drystan was always busy, but Eirin knew that couldn't be helped.

There was a constant stream of people returning to Iilaedin who needed to be housed and clothed, and decisions had to be made. Slowly, slowly, life began to take a new rhythm. Until three weeks after the curse broke when her new predictability was upended.

"Your Majesty!" one of Eirin's personal guards cried. "Take shelter!" Eirin, who was eating with several young Humans in the dining hall, immediately unsheathed her sword and fell into a crouch. Crashing and shouting came steadily closer.

Nuru tried to drag her away, but a flash of flying blue caught Eirin's eye. And she screamed for everyone to stop. And not a moment too soon, as Callispa, who was eating her midday meal as well, had lit and knocked a fiery arrow which was now aimed at the Will-o'-the-Wisp intruder.

Eirin sheathed her sword as she ran, and in a moment, she was in her father's arms. He crushed her against himself, kissing her face all over as he wept. Eirin wept in his arms as well, and once the confusion had been sorted out, he was given a bowl of food and seated beside her, keeping one arm over her shoulders the entire time.

"But where are Mother and the children?" Eirin asked. "I thought you had to stay behind!"

Her father grinned. She couldn't help noticing that the lines in the corners of his eyes had sharpened considerably since she'd left, and there were now gray hairs scattered all over his dark head. "They're on the way now, being pulled by a carthorse. I only came early to make sure you could be found..." He stopped and gazed at her, smoothing her hair affectionately. "Is it true? We heard you married the king, but..." His gaze dropped to her stomach, which was still perfectly flat. Eirin grinned and nodded.

"I am."

This made her father cry again.

Within the hour, Eirin was in the arms of her mother and brothers as well.

To her surprise, Drystan returned to the palace earlier than usual that night. Eirin was somewhat apprehensive about him meeting her family, but she realized soon after that such anxiety had been foolish. Her brothers, who sometimes bordered on insanity, decided they adored Drystan. To her relief, Drystan loved them as well. And as she held her baby sister and watched, she felt warm all over as Drystan wrestled with the twins, tickling and pouncing and making them laugh. All too soon, he and their son would be doing the same thing.

Eirin's parents agreed to stay, at least temporarily, in the palace, but Eirin told Drystan secretly that she was already considering reasons to get them to extend their stay, permanently if possible.

"We're preparing to take a new census," Drystan suggested. "Isn't he a mapmaker? He could spend over a year assisting with that alone."

Eirin threw her arms around her husband's neck. "Drystan, you are brilliant." Then she kissed him.

"I should tell you about my good ideas more often," he said, wrapping his arms around her and pulling her against him. Then he leaned his head against hers and sighed.

"You're exhausted," Eirin said softly. Keeping his head against hers, he just nodded. He didn't say it, but Eirin could sense, as she often did, that he was thinking of his parents as well, and what it would be like to have them suddenly appear too.

An idea struck Eirin. They were standing out on their bedroom balcony, and the late afternoon sun was washing over them, warm and golden. Despite the warmth, Eirin could feel autumn fast approaching, seemingly eager to make up for its lateness.

"Take me flying," she whispered.

He opened his eyes and leaned back to study her. "You mean it?" His voice sounded slightly less tired.

Eirin grinned and nodded. "Just...remember that I'm a little unsteady on my feet these days." It was true. Eirin didn't look like she was expecting at all. But for all her protests to Nuru and Alys, she sometimes felt as though she could barely walk in a straight line without tripping.

Drystan put his mouth beside her ear. "I'd never let you fall."

A delightful little shiver ran down Eirin's back.

Eirin hadn't been flying with Drystan often in the last few weeks, but she had done it enough to exult in the feeling of the chilly winds that cut past her face. Since the Time Keeper had chosen him, Drystan's Dragon form had grown significantly bigger than it had been, bigger even than Rangvald, which meant Eirin had more room to rest on his back.

It was always lovely to fly with Drystan. From above, Solevar looked serene and quiet, green crops growing and blue waters shimmering in the late afternoon light. As they flew north, Eirin could feel Drystan begin to relax.

They landed on an outcrop of one of the Northern Mountains. Not high enough to freeze, but high enough to make the ground below look dizzying. Drystan shifted back into his Human form, then he set to kissing her senseless. Then they contented themselves with holding one another as they looked out at their kingdom.

"When did you fall in love with me?"

Eirin looked up to see him gazing down at her. "Hmm." She stopped and pondered. "I suppose...I think it was the day I first saw fear in your eyes."

Drystan stared at her for a moment. Then he shook his head and ran a hand through his hair. "Well, that doesn't sound like one of my proudest moments," he laughed ruefully. "When was that?"

Eirin just snuggled deeper into his arms. "Rangvald's attack on the Citadel. You'd passed out, and I was dragging you back to your father's office."

"Well, it really wasn't my finest hour," Drystan rubbed the back of his neck with a grimace.

"Shush. I'm not done," Eirin slapped his arm playfully. Then she sighed. "For just a moment, you opened your eyes. And for the first time, I realized you were afraid."

"That doesn't necessarily scream romance."

"No," she continued, "but I saw how hard you fought anyway. And the fact that you were afraid, but you didn't give up... That gave me courage to fight too." She turned and looked up at him. "What about you? When did you first decide you could tolerate being stuck with me?"

He snorted then kissed the top of her head. "There wasn't really any one moment. Not that I could pick out, at least. But when you had to fight me during your Testing–a fight I hated myself for, by the way–I saw you in a different light. You knew it was hopeless, but you tried. And when you told me that you had been forced to train against your will..." He cleared his throat and blinked rapidly a few times. "I saw how strong you really are." He sat up and took her face in his hands. "The hard part isn't over, you know," he said softly. "You didn't marry into an easy life."

"I never asked for an easy life." Eirin kissed the palm of his hand. "And I wouldn't want it any other way."

Drystan's eyes took on a familiar amber glow, and he drew her close again, pulling her against him with his right hand while pressing his left against her belly.

"You know," Eirin said, "Nuru and Alys aren't here."

He laughed. "And?"

Eirin grinned up at him.

"Oh no. That look means trouble."

Eirin stood and walked backward toward the cliff, stopping just on the edge.

Drystan's wings appeared.

"Catch me?" she dared him.

Drystan's eyes brightened, and his Dragon voice seeped into his next word. "Always."

Eirin took a step back. Then she was falling, her body weightless as she sped toward the earth. But she feared for neither herself nor her child. For just as she knew he would, a second later, Drystan caught her safely in his arms and pressed her against his warm chest. And as they flew off into the sunset, Eirin knew she was right where she was supposed to be.

A mage who can't reveal her name...

...a fae prince who never had one.

A magical rose that will save or doom them all.

Experience the *Rose of Destiny Trilogy*
Coming 2023...

THE STORY CONTINUES...

King Drystan and Queen Eirin are piecing their kingdom back together, and after breaking a hundred year curse, they desire nothing but peace.

All too soon, however, trouble begins to descend from the Northern Mountains, and Eirin and Drystan's friends must answer their king and queen's call.

Return to Solevar and venture through its magic once more with Nuru, Thane, Callispa, Qeb, and Alys as a new evil rises, and heroes are needed once more...

Sign up for Brittany's newsletter to receive updates on future books:

Chronicles of the Time Stones

Return to Solevar when King Drystan and Queen Eirin must call on their friends to help save Solevar once more...

Stay tuned...

The Classical Kingdoms Collection

Full-length fairy tale retellings with clean, passionate romance, magical mystery, and heroic happily-ever-afters.

The Classical Kingdoms Novellas

Set in the same world as the Classical Kingdoms Collection, these slightly shorter fairy tale retellings feature the same romance, mystery, and happily-ever-afters as their longer counterparts.

The Forgotten Fairy Tales:

Wendy and Peter lived a fantastic fairy tale of their own. So when asked by the king and queen of Destin to contribute to the Fortress's great library, they're only too glad to add their own fantastical tales. Enjoy the same clean romance, magical mystery, and heroic happily-ever-afters in these lesser-known fairy tales as...novellas!

Legacy of the Time Stones Trilogy

A failing warrior.

A prince in pain.

A city in the mountain where they and their loved ones hide from Solevar's curse.

But this reality will soon shatter. For among the cursed ashes of Solevar, a Seer has been found.

The Autumn Fairy Trilogy

She's the most dangerous creature to live in a thousand years.

He'll embrace the power he despises to save her.

When evil threatens all they hold dear, can they save their isles together? Or will their combined strength tear the world apart?

The Rose of Destiny Trilogy

Coming soon!!!

My Air Force Fairy Tales

When these men in uniform meet their spunky ladies, their fairy tale-themed happily ever afters are sure to come true.

The Entwined Tales: Book #2

With more to come...

About the Author

Brittany lives with her Prince Charming, their little fairy, and their little prince in a ~~sparkling~~ (decently clean) castle in whatever kingdom the Air Force has most recently placed them. When she's not writing, Brittany can be found chasing her kids around with a DSLR and belting it in the church choir.

Subscribe: BrittanyFichterFiction.com
Email: BrittanyFichterFiction@gmail.com
Facebook: Facebook.com/BFichterFiction
Instagram: @BrittanyFichterFiction

www.ingramcontent.com/pod-product-compliance
Lightning Source LLC
Chambersburg PA
CBHW021230190726
48289CB00005B/1251